Fear of the Minister's Justice

Other Books Available from Geoff and Coy

Saul Imbierowicz Vampire Trilogy
Unremarkable
Untouchable
Unavailable

Unbelievable (novelette)

Constable Inspector Lunaria Adventures
Wrath of the Fury Blade
Joy of the Widow's Tears
Fear of the Minister's Justice

Myth of the Tenz River Troll (novelette)

Fear of the Minister's Justice

A Constable Inspector Lunaria Adventure

Geoff Habiger
&
Coy Kissee

ISBN: 978-1-951122-42-3 (paperback)
ISBN: 978-1-951122-48-5 (ebook)
LCCN: 2022933263
Copyright © 2022 by Geoff Habiger & Coy Kissee
Cover Art: © Mike Wagner
Cover Design: Geoff Habiger

Printed in the United States of America.

Shadow Dragon Press
9 Mockingbird Hill Rd
Tijeras, New Mexico 87059
www.shadowdragonpress.com
info@shadowdragonpress.com

Content Notice:
This book contains scenes of torture that some readers may find disturbing and traumatic.

Prologue

The feeling of being watched danced across the nape of Carum's neck, so he stopped and glanced around. A chill breeze from the bay carried in a fog that haloed the light from the lanterns that lined the road. Carum tried to make out the shapes that were barely visible through the diaphanous curtain of fog. Was it the grocer, sweeping up at the end of the day, who was watching him? Could it be the cat that was lazily cleaning its paws? Or maybe it was the elf walking on the opposite side of the road, the one with his dark cloak drawn tightly around his body? Carum shook his head. It could have been any of them, or even none of them.

He hurried on, but the feeling just wouldn't go away. He turned down a side street, his feet splashing through a puddle as he glanced over his shoulder. He sucked in his breath as the elf with the cloak came into view, and then let it out slowly as the elf greeted a friend and the pair entered a tavern. Carum's knees wavered, and he stuck a hand into the pocket of his cloak. The edge of the card that he felt there quelled his fear and spurred his feet back into motion. He had to tell them. He had to share with the constables the information he had only just remembered today. It wouldn't bring Hoehnea back, but it might calm her spirit and, hopefully, his own.

It had been three days since Hoehnea's death. Three

nightmarish days since he had discovered her naked body, staked to the ground outside of where she had worked. Three sleepless nights since Carum had seen the symbol that had been seared into her chest, a sickening brand that seemed to mark her like some sort of harlot or adulteress. Only Carum knew that it was much, much worse than either of those. The brand had marked her as being a sorcerer.

His finger traced the edge of the card in his pocket, and then over the surface, outlining the symbol that Carum couldn't quite feel but knew was there. A wave of guilt washed over him, and he jerked his hand out of his pocket as quickly as if he had been stung by a wasp. He crossed the street, glancing to both his left and right, avoiding the shadows.

The Narris constables had questioned him, of course, but he'd been an absolute mess. Hoehnea had been more than just a friend. They had been confidants, sharing each other's fears and deepest secrets. Her death had left a bottomless hole in his soul. The Constable Inspector had tried to question him, but Carum had been a gibbering idiot. Finally, the inspector had thrown up his hands and told his partner to try to get something of value out of him.

"I'm Seeker Cas Rubus," she had said, putting a hand on his arm. "I know this is hard, but I need you to tell me about Hoehnea."

"Why did this happen?" Carum asked, tears streaming down his cheeks. "Why is she gone?"

"That's what we intend to find out," the Seeker said, "but it will be easier with your help. I can tell that you cared for her, so please help us." She lifted the edge of her cloak and blotted a tear from his eye. "You may have been the person to know Hoehnea the best, so your help will be crucial in finding out who did this to her."

Her voice had soothed his shock, her gesture a balm for the trauma. "Anything," Carum had sniffed, wiping away more tears with the palm of his hand. "What do you want to know?"

The Seeker's questions from that horrible day now echoed in his head with each step that he took toward the constabulary. *Where did you and Hoehnea spend time together? Where did she live? Did she have any family? Where do they live? Did she have any enemies? How did she get along with her co-workers? When did she tell them that she was a sorcerer? How did they react to the news? Were any of them angered by this? Have you seen the symbol that was branded on Hoehnea before?*

He'd left the Seeker feeling like he'd helped and that, by answering her questions, he'd honored Hoehnea and their friendship. But he hadn't helped, or told the constables anything that was actually useful. The card that he fingered in the pocket of his cloak spoke the lie.

Hoehnea's death had hit him like a punch to the gut, and it knocked any rational thought from his mind. He told himself that was why he'd missed it. Why he'd forgotten about the card and the symbol that blotted its surface.

He *had* seen the mark before, as had Hoehnea. The card had been on her table at work, an omen of her impending death that they had both ignored. *Why? Why didn't we do anything about it then?* Carum stopped and looked up into the foggy night, fighting back the tears. He thought he heard a noise to his left, so he ducked his head and took the next right.

Hoehnea had found the card a week after she'd told her co-workers that she was a sorcerer. Being a sorcerer wasn't a crime, at least not anymore, but there was still so much stigma, so much misunderstanding and prejudice, that openly being a sorcerer was a risk that few were willing to take. Her co-workers were all wizards and, for years, she had pretended to be one, as had Carum and most of their other sorcerer friends. It was just safer that way. But Hoehnea felt that she was living a lie with all of the pretending, and that she was perpetuating the myths and intolerance. She wanted to live openly as a sorcerer, to be who she really was.

So, she'd trimmed the branches, gauging each of her

co-workers on their thoughts and beliefs. She'd been un-surprised by the outdated ideas, preconceptions, and subtle bias about sorcerers that her co-workers seemed to hold. As she slowly and subtly educated them, she was surprised to find them receptive to the idea of working with a sorcerer. She wanted to come clean to them.

She agonized over the decision for nearly a month, and then finally steeled her resolve and told one of her co-work-ers; one who she thought would be the most tolerant of the idea. To Hoehnea's relief, he had embraced her for who she was and had supported her in telling the others. Everyone seemed to be accepting, or at least unconcerned. She'd been ecstatic, relieved to finally be able to live her true life. Then she got the card.

Carum hesitantly put his hand back into his pocket and pulled out the card. The same symbol that had been burned into Hoehnea's skin seemed to mock him, so he quickly turned the card over. There, in a neat hand, written in dark blue ink, was: "You are an abomination. You will be cleansed."

Footsteps echoed through the fog and Carum turned away from them. He stuffed the card back into his pocket and picked up his pace. He had to give the card to Seeker Rubus. He had to make up for his mistake.

Hoehnea had shown the card to Carum that night at her apartment. She'd been so angry, so full of fury that she want-ed to tear up the card, but Carum had stopped her. Instead, she had tossed it to the floor, determined that no one was going to intimidate her. She had lived in fear her entire life, and she wasn't going to turn back now that she was finally free. Two days later she was dead.

Carum had forgotten the card until today, when he'd finally drawn up enough courage to go to Hoehnea's apart-ment and collect her things before her landlord threw them out onto the street. He'd found it on the floor where she'd thrown it, and the sudden shock at seeing the symbol again had caused Carum to recoil in horror. When he saw the sym-bol, his thoughts flashed back to Hoehnea's battered body, the same symbol burned into her skin. It was then that he realized his mistake. The constables didn't know about the card, about the threat. They thought that she'd been killed by a new thieves' guild, that she was just in the wrong place at the wrong time, her death merely a warning to others that there was a new guild in town. The card in Carum's pocket proved otherwise.

Carum again heard footsteps, this time growing louder in the foggy night. He looked around and found that he'd somehow turned away from the constabulary and was instead somewhere near the docks. The footsteps sounded closer. Carum's throat tightened with the sudden realization that he was being followed. The elf responsible for killing Hoehnea was after him now. He knew too much. Carum's hand again went into his pocket, touching the edge of the card. *Her killer doesn't want the constables to know about this.*

Carum took off at a run, heading away from the bay and trying to get to the constabulary. The fog thickened around him, and the sounds increased. *Was there more than one murderer? Is it a new gang?* He turned in a panic and headed down an alley that ended in a dead end.

Shit. He scanned the area, his mind racing, trying to find a way out.

"Nowhere left to run, demon."

Carum spun around at the voice, deep and threatening, yet calm and collected. The fog had thickened even more, an impenetrable mist that concealed everything. Finally, his own mental fog cleared. He reacted instinctively, waving his hands and saying, "*Beni korumak!*" The shield spell shimmered in a ripple of rose-colored light in the air just as a dart appeared out of the mist and glanced off, hitting the wall and clattering to the ground.

"You bargained away your eternal soul, and in return you got nothing but parlor tricks," the voice mocked from the fog.

Carum swallowed, his throat suddenly going dry.

"*Sürüklemek!*" he cried, thrusting his hands forward. A gust of air seemed to billow around him, gathering speed as leaves and litter swirled against the wall and then rushed forward, blowing the thick fog away.

The night became surprisingly clear as Carum now realized that the fog had been magically created. Before him stood a tall male elf wearing deep blue robes that had words embroidered in silver thread along the hem and cuffs. In his left hand, he gripped a staff with sigils burned into the polished redwood. The bottom of the staff was capped in copper, and a gemstone in a setting at the top reflected the newly revealed moonlight. His right hand held a small crossbow, with another dart already loaded. The wizard's face was a weathered birch color, lined with wrinkles showing age and hard labor. Long silver hair with moss-green highlights flowed from beneath a broad-brimmed blue hat that looked like it would be more appropriate on the head of a country priest than a wizard. He stared at Carum, his eyes filled with hatred and loathing.

"Ah, you choose to face your fate head on. Excellent! Perhaps I will spare you a coward's death as I send you to meet your demonic master."

"What?" Carum had no idea what the wizard meant, beyond plain bigotry, but the vehemence of his words and the hatred in his eyes caused Carum's legs to shake. He took a tentative step backward and bumped into the wall. He licked his lips. He was not an adventurer or a constable. He had magic, yes, but he'd only ever created a few offensive spells—stuff to keep away thieves or drunks at the pub. He was a translator, a scribe of ancient magic, not a fighter, but he was desperate. The only way to save himself and get revenge for Hoehnea's death was to take the fight to this bastard.

"You'll pay for what you did to Hoehnea!" he yelled.

The wizard laughed, "I hope you'll provide more of a challenge than she did. Maybe you'll give me what I seek."

Carum had stopped listening. He gathered his magic and said, "*havanın oku,*" as he swung his arm as though he was throwing something. The air hardened and flew at the wizard, striking him in the shoulder. The wizard grimaced in pain, a cruel smile curling his lips.

"Know that I will take great pleasure in what comes next, abomination." He tapped his staff on the ground. A mist of red light flowed from the gemstone and struck at Carum's shield, which quickly dissolved as the magic was countered.

Before he could do anything else, a dart seemingly appeared from nowhere, burrowing into Carum's chest. He pulled it out but, as it fell to the ground, the alley was already starting to sway. Blackness edged in at the corner of his vision. The image of the wizard blurred and became two, then combined back into a single person as he advanced toward Carum. Feebly, Carum tried to move, but a dark feeling of fatigue pressed down on his mind and he collapsed to the ground, asleep.

† † †

Carum regained consciousness with a start. He was bound to a chair and had been stripped naked. He blinked several times and shook his head to clear it. The space he was in slowly came into focus. He blinked again in amazement as he realized that he was in his own apartment! He looked around, twisting his head. He was in the middle of the small living space, and his few pieces of furniture had been shoved into a corner. He noticed that he had been placed in the center of a magic circle that had been drawn—carved?—into the floor. He'd never used magic circles himself, but his work as a magical translator had exposed him to several magical scripts. He recognized the ones that were scribed into his floor now. He was in a magic circle that protected against evil and demonic possession.

He heard a noise from his kitchen and turned to see the wizard sitting in a chair, his back to Carum, eating one of Carum's apples. The wizard had hung up his robe, leaned his staff against the wall, and removed his hat so that his long hair formed a curtain down his back. He wore simple breeches of a dark blue color and a pale green linen shirt.

"Wh... what do you want? If this is about the card, I won't go to the constables. You can take it or destroy it, or whatever you want. I won't say anything."

The wizard didn't respond, but gave a curt nod and took a final bite of the apple. He stood up, put on his robe, and pulled out a wand. He grabbed his staff and turned around, staring at Carum with a mixture of hatred and... sadness? No, maybe it was weariness. Carum couldn't be sure, although at this distance he could see that the wizard's eyes were deep pools of dark blue, almost black. His stomach churned under that gaze, and he struggled against his bonds. With his hands tied, he couldn't cast any of his spells. "Who are you? What are you going to do to me?"

"I ask the questions, abomination!" The wizard thrust his wand forward and jammed it into Carum's shoulder. Pain shot through Carum's arm, and his body jerked as electricity surged through him. The wizard pulled the wand back and the shock ended, though the pain lingered. Carum was panting, tears already streaming down his face.

The wizard straightened up. "I am The Minister," he said, "and you will answer all of my questions, demon spawn, or you will suffer the consequences."

"Wha...?" Carum was confused and scared. "Consequences?"

"I seek information," The Minister said, ignoring Carum's blathering. "Answer my questions truthfully and you will be freed."

Carum was smart enough to see through the lie. He was convinced that he was looking at Hoehnea's murderer. The thought seemed to give Carum some peace as he was sure that he was experiencing exactly the same thing that Hoehnea had endured. But he would be strong—for Hoehnea. He wasn't going to tell this wizard anything. Carum gave a bitter laugh, "You'll set me free in the same way that you freed Hoehnea? You may as well kill me now as I won't tell—" He couldn't complete his sentence as The Minister jabbed the wand into his other shoulder and pain exploded across his body.

"Tell me his name! You know of whom I speak. Tell me his name!"

Carum managed to gather enough saliva to spit at the wizard, but it just dribbled down Carum's chin. The action was enough to warrant another shock. Carum cried out, a loud, anguished yell. *Somebody will hear me. My neighbors always complain about the least bit of noise. Surely they will hear my screams and call for the constables.*

"Tell me! Who allowed you to steal Qurna's gift?" Another shock was delivered as Carum refused to answer.

"Which demon gave you this power?" Carum didn't have time to respond, or even to think, as The Minister jabbed the wand into his knee, causing more pain and more screams. Carum was panting again, trying to catch his breath. Saliva dripped from his mouth and sweat ran in rivulets down his body. His mind picked out a single word from the wizard's question. *Demon. He thinks I got my magic from a demon. Oh gods, I'm going to be killed by this bigot. I'm sorry, Hoehnea. I'm sorry you had to suffer this idiot in your final moments.*

The Minister took a step back, crossing his arms and pulling himself up to his full height. "You will tell me the name of the demon who has allowed you to steal Qurna's gift. Tell me, and I will end your suffering."

Why has nobody come? Have they not heard my cries? Carum's chest felt like it was going to explode. Pain stabbed throughout his entire body. He couldn't take it anymore. He knew that he was going to die. This "Minister" hated what Carum was. He hated sorcerers. And like many people who hate, he also feared Carum and what sorcerers could do. There was no way that he was going to let Carum live. *And I can't take any more pain.*

"Agna—," he tried to say. The word cracked as he spoke. He swallowed once and said again, "Agnatha." The word was something he'd heard before, an Arisportian term for a lamprey, if he remembered correctly, but it sounded good. By

The Minister's reaction, he had never heard the word before.

"Interesting." The Minister's eyes sparkled with pleasure and anticipation. "You've spoken a name I have not heard before. Perhaps this is the knowledge I need in order to finally rid Ados of you abominations." He then looked directly into Carum's eyes.

"Thank you. You will meet your end knowing that you have helped to bring an end to the rest of your infernal brethren. Rejoice, as I reclaim your ill-gotten magic and return it to Qurna!" The Minister whispered something as the wand stabbed again, straight at Carum's heart. The pain quickly drowned out Carum's fear, and then there was nothing.

†††

The Minster shook his head in disgust at the body slumped in the chair. He felt no pity, no sympathy for this devil. Why would one pity evil? He also held no illusions that the name he'd been given would be the one that he'd been searching for his whole career. He'd collected hundreds of demon names, and not one had ever been summoned in the ritual. This Agnatha was new for him, though. With the newness came a glimmer of truth and hope. He would again perform the ritual with the other members of the Qurundora and try the name. Even if it proved as false as all the others, at least he had removed one more stain from the world. Jansure's work was exhausting, but The Minister only felt excitement and elation at the completion of his latest task.

No, it's not completed yet, The Minister chided himself. He needed to prepare the body so that it could be left for other sorcerers to witness; a message to let them know that their taint upon this world was coming to an end. The Minister cut the ropes holding the body and let it fall to the floor. He then made the sacred gestures, spoke Qurna's blessed words, and cast his spell, burning the symbol of the Qurundora into the fiend's chest.

Chapter 1

Constable Inspector Reva Lunaria gave a distasteful glance at the crowd of gawkers who were being kept at bay by a group of Birches. The Betula Division constables had their hands full as patrons from several pubs had spilled onto the street to see what was going on. She hated being in West Gate Grove on a good day. Today was not a good day.

The grove was full of stinking pubs, decrepit taverns, shabby inns, illicit brothels, and shops selling everything that travelers and adventurers thought they might need. It was also crawling with adventurers, as this latest murder was like kicking open an ant hill; they all came out to stare and think that they could help. They were all itching to find the killer themselves so that they could be the one to stop him. Amateurs. It made her sick to her stomach.

She turned her back on the gawkers, her silver-red hair seeming to give the crowd a dismissive wave as she took in the murder scene. The victim lay in a crumpled pile of arms and legs at the intersection of two roads. One of the shop keepers had found the body and sent for a constable. The crime scene had been contaminated. So many people had tried to get a look at the victim that Reva was sure that there was no useful evidence around the body. She sighed, barely controlling her urge to go smack the people who'd messed up her crime scene.

The incessant chattering of the crowd was also starting to grate on her nerves. She looked up at the crowd again, contemplating if she should have the Birches move them all back. She shook her head and turned to find Senior Constable Ghrellstone, but she didn't see where Willem had gone, so she returned to looking at the murder victim. She had other cases that she was working on, and the more time they spent here was less time she'd have dealing with them. Ever since the fight at the port a month ago, she'd thrown herself into her work. It was her way to forget about everything that had happened. To forget about how Aavril had run away from her. He hadn't been able to decide that she was worth fighting for, or to admit his mistakes, so he'd given up. She knew he was at sea now, still running further away.

Despite the heavy workload, Reva wouldn't acknowledge that she was being stretched thin. That would be admitting defeat. Instead, she pulled out a small tin from a pocket, opened it with a practiced flick of her thumb, and then took out a pinch of red-orange powder and lifted it to her nose. The Wake had taken immediate effect. She felt as if a cleansing breeze had blown away the clutter of leaves from her head.

"Already?" Seeker Ansee Carya asked, with a condescending shake of his head. He should have been examining the body, but he had apparently been watching her instead of doing his job. "It's barely mid-morning."

"Mind your own business, Seeker, and do your damn job. You're not my mother."

She could see that Ansee wanted to say something back, but Constable Kai Gania chose that moment to step up to her. He handed her a card made from rough, heavy paper. "This was found on the body. One of the shopkeepers had it."

"Gods damn them, interfering with my case," Reva swore. She turned to look at the shops. "Which one of these *upstanding* businesselves did it? I'm going to rip them—"

"Ma'am," Constable Gania interrupted her. She turned to glare at him. "He took it to make sure that none of the others would take it. He was afraid someone would want it as a memento of the murder. He held onto it, and then gave it to Senior Constable Ghrellstone once we started interviewing people."

Reva gave a nod, her cheeks flushing a bit. "Thank you," she told Kai, and then as an afterthought said, "And give my thanks to the shopkeeper."

Constable Gania nodded and headed over to the shops where she could now see Willem conducting more interviews. With a look over her shoulder to see that Ansee was actually doing his job—she could see the golden glow around his eyes now—she examined the card that Kai had given her. A glance was enough for Reva to confirm that it was identical to the cards they'd found at two other murders in the past month. That in itself was significant, since it confirmed her suspicion that they were dealing with a serial killer. The card was made from rough paper, which was unusual, since parchment and vellum were cheaper, but their efforts to trace the maker had been fruitless.

Reva flipped the card over to look at the strange symbol there. It had been applied to the card using a deep black ink. It looked like a misshapen square, with the sides squished in, while a squiggle of ink—it looked like a lightning bolt—ran across the square from left to right. It didn't match any symbol she, or anybody else she'd asked, had seen before. She figured it was something the killer made up, as a sick kind of way to sign his "work" and, as such, it wouldn't lead them to their killer.

She pulled out her notebook, her hand caressing the leather surface and the caricature of an elephant that was embossed on the cover. The leather was worn, and the paint faded, the spine well creased from use. She ran her fingers over the fading words painted on the cover, "Remember, if you didn't write it down, it didn't happen!" She gave a small smile as she remembered better days with her father, before his untimely death. He'd given Reva the notebook as a gift when she'd been promoted to Inspector, and the memory tugged at thoughts that she didn't have time for. She opened the notebook to a blank page—the enchantment on the notebook guaranteed there was always a blank page, no matter how much she wrote in it—to make a new entry. She started to jot down the important details: the location of the crime, the date (3 Lyzar), and the details about the victim, but her eye caught the same symbol that she'd copied into the notebook from the other crime scenes, and found herself copying the symbol again. She drew it with hard, sharp strokes of her pencil, then drew it again, and again. Soon the page was filled with the symbol, in different sizes, and she started tracing over them again.

"Reva?"

She continued to trace, to darken the symbols that she'd drawn, pressing down hard on the page. The murders, her current cases, and other thoughts jumbled together and fought for attention in her mind. *Nobody gives up on me.*

"Reva?" A hand and red-colored bracer with a maple leaf worked into the leather gave a wave, but Reva's eyes were focused on the symbols. *I am worth fighting for.*

"Reva?" Ansee called a third time, louder. Fingers snapped under her nose, and she glanced up at him, glaring.

"Are you finally done, Seeker?" she snapped.

"Who pushed you out of the tree this morning? Or maybe you've hit the wall with your Wake use."

"I don't need you lecturing me. Did you find anything useful?" Reva closed the notebook and tucked it into a large pocket.

Ansee stared at her for a moment, and then said, "It's nearly identical to our other murder victims. There's evidence that he was casting magic, defensive spells from the look of things, but there are also traces of magic that affected him as well. They're from the murderer, just as in the other cases. There's evidence that he was struck with at least one, or possibly more, force missiles."

Reva slowly nodded her head. This matched with the other two murder victims. "Does our victim have anything on him to suggest that he's a wizard? We might be able to get somebody from Auros to identify him."

Ansee shook his head. "No spellbook. Not that I'd expect a wizard to just be carrying one around, but there's nothing that might be considered a magical focus either. No staff, no wand. I'm pretty sure that our victim is a sorcerer. Again."

Reva nodded. She'd hoped that it would have been different, but it was probably too much to hope that a serial killer would change his choice of victims. "Anything else?" she asked.

"Again, there were odd traces that he was affected by some kind of teleportation spell," Ansee added. "I still can't tell if it was cast by our victim or by his killer."

"You forgot the best part," Senior Constable Ghrellstone said, as he walked up to them. "His legs are broken in about fifty different places, along with his arms and probably the rest of the bones in his body. I'm sure the Alkies will be able to tell us for sure when they count up the number of pieces."

"Well, it's clear that this is our third victim," Reva said. "Please tell me that somebody saw something this time."

Willem shook his head. "Sorry, Inspector. As usual, nobody saw or heard anything. The elf that found the body," he jerked a thumb over his shoulder to a candle shop on the corner, "said that he found the body just before sunrise as he was getting ready to open his shop. He lives above his shop and he didn't hear or see anything last night."

Reva looked around at the buildings. Most of them had apartments built into the second or third story, either for the shop owner to live in or to rent out to others. "And nobody heard anything? There's a mage duel going on in the street and nobody knows anything?"

"Not that anyone will admit to," Willem said. "There are at least three pubs within sight of this spot, and you know how rowdy those places can get."

Reva shook her head in frustration, "Adventurers."

"And depending on the spells, the sound of casting might have been covered up by other noise. It's not like they were throwing fireballs at each other."

Reva had to nod in agreement. She knew that magic, despite all its flash and sparkles, could often be quiet. Unless they were hurling fireballs or lightning bolts at each other.

"Well, expand the interviews to other shops and homes. Maybe we'll get lucky."

Willem nodded, and then pointed toward the crowd. "Looks like the Alkies have arrived." Reva turned to see Thea Bromide and her staff working their way through the throng.

"Body's all yours," Reva said, by way of greeting.

Thea took a look at the body. "Another jigsaw puzzle?"

"Only on the inside. I think his skin kept most of the bones in there."

Thea gave a snort. "Any chance we know this victim's name? With this being the third victim, I'm sure that Aescel would authorize the expense for a Speaking ritual."

Reva turned to look at Willem and Ansee, who both shook their heads. Constable Gania approached them at that time and also shook his head. *Figures.* "Fresh out of true names today. We might be able to find out."

Thea waved the thought away. "By the time you do, it will be too late to perform the ritual anyway." She sighed and turned to her work.

Ansee gave a polite cough.

"What?" Reva said, then saw the look in his eyes. "No, not this again."

"Come on, I've not heard any brilliant ideas from you on how to solve this."

His tone was light and reminded her a bit of how her former partner, Cas, might have spoken, but Reva found herself gritting her teeth and clenching her fists.

"What idea?" asked Willem, clearly trying to distract Reva from Ansee's comment.

"I think our murderer works, or spends most of his time, at the Violet Clover Tavern."

"You mean the *violent* clover. That place is a wretched hive of scum and villainy."

"I thought the Violet Clover was an adventurer's tavern?" Kai asked.

"That's what he just said," Reva replied. She turned to Ansee and placed her hands on her hips. "We don't have any proof that our murderer works there. We've interviewed the staff and the regulars."

"And every other tavern and pub in the Grove," grumbled Willem.

"Nobody knows anything—"

"That they'll admit," interrupted Ansee.

Reva ignored him. "And everybody conveniently has an alibi for the times of the murders."

"But it's the only tavern in the Grove that all of our victims are connected to."

Reva glared at him. "And how do you know that?"

"We've already connected the previous two victims to the Tavern, and I saw our latest victim there when I was interviewing the staff. Our victims were adventurers, all sorcerers, and were either part of established groups, or looking for one. I didn't catch this one's name, but I know he was there looking for work, and trying to join a group."

"So, what's your idea?" asked Kai.

"We should disguise ourselves as adventurers and go undercover at the Violet Clover. That will allow us to lure out our killer and then arrest him."

Reva made a cutting motion with one arm. "No. And not just no, hells no. This is, by far, the dumbest idea anybody has ever come up with in the history of dumb ideas."

"So, when I think of going undercover it's the dumbest idea ever, but when you play dress up to infiltrate a deranged cultist and his merry band of Disciples, it's okay?" Ansee said, sarcasm coating his words.

"That was different," Reva retorted.

"Yeah, because *you* thought of it," Ansee snapped back.

"Look," Willem said, interjecting himself between Reva and Ansee. "It's not the craziest idea we've ever come up with." Reva glared at him, but the look just rolled off Willem's back. He turned to Ansee, "But it's also a long shot if I ever heard one." Ansee acknowledged that with a nod. "Maybe we should propose it to the First Constable and see what he thinks?"

Reva and Ansee each gave a reluctant nod. "Fine," she said, "but I am not going to dress up as an adventurer."

Chapter 2

Constable Acanta Sulwynd's boot connected with the loose stone, and it skipped along the broken cobbles and nearly struck the halpbloed that was trying to wash clothes in a barrel. The halpbloed turned to say something, probably thinking that it was unruly kids, and then quickly turned back to her work as Sulwynd leered at her. Beside him, Constable Senecio Gallwynn guffawed at her reaction.

The pair continued down the broken road. Once, when this had been called South Bank Grove, it had been neatly paved with smooth cobblestones. But ever since the passage of the third Purity Law, and the halpbloed had been shoved into the renamed Nul Pfeta Grove, they had pried up loose stones to build walls in order to add on to the existing buildings. It made the buildings look decrepit and dangerous, while the roads became pockmarked with deep holes and ruts as the rains washed the soil into the river.

"As I was saying," Gallwynn said, "she has the most beautiful ass you'd ever seen—for a halpbloed, that is. And she knows how to behave, if you know what I mean."

Sulwynd knew exactly what he meant, and he did his best to hide his revulsion. The thought of having sex with any halpbloed made his skin crawl. They were lower than vermin, and he did his best to avoid touching them in normal circumstances, let alone have sex with one. But he knew that

Gallwynn didn't care. He'd bed any female and, from some of his stories, Sulwynd thought he probably had. Young or old, pretty or ugly, it didn't matter to Gallwynn. "And what sort of favor did she ask for in return for her services?"

Gallwynn laughed, "It wasn't even for her. She wanted a pass for her brother to be out past curfew. He has to work late, and she was afraid that we'd throw him in the cells if he was caught."

Sulwynd joined in with his own laugh at that. "Are they really getting that dumb? She just had to show proof of employment to the Senior Constable or the Inspector, and they'd have written her a pass."

Gallwynn made to shush him. "Keep your trap shut, I don't want that getting around. I've convinced her she has to put out every week if she wants to keep her brother out of the cells."

"Well, just make sure she doesn't give you rootrot. It'd be a shame if your elfhood were to fall off." Sulwynd had to jump aside to avoid the kick that Gallwynn had aimed at him. It also meant that he avoided the splash of waste that fell right where he'd been walking. He quickly looked up to the building. It was four stories tall, and the upper floors leaned out over the road. There was an open window on the third floor, but he couldn't see anybody there. It might have been intentional, or just a careless halpbloed. He wanted to be angry, to charge into the building to scare the hells out of whoever had done it, but Gallwynn had broken into hysterical laughter at the near miss, pointing and saying, "Oh, you almost bought it that time."

Sulwynd gave a half-hearted laugh and walked on, doing his best to remember the building. He might still make a return visit to teach whoever lived there a lesson in respect.

They walked on, glaring at any halpbloed that dared to look at them, shoving those that couldn't—or wouldn't—get out of their way. They took a couple of loaves of fresh baked bread, even though it had a few weevils, along with grit from the millstone, in it. Then Sulwynd spotted someone up the road, carrying sticks and twigs in a wicker basket. He leaned over to Gallwynn and shoved his bread into Gallwynn's hands. "Hold this. There's a troublemaker up there that I need to deal with."

A gleam came to Gallwynn's eyes. He enjoyed putting troublemakers into place. "Need any help?"

"Nah," Sulwynd said. "He's a runt, like all the others, but he needs to learn his place. Just make sure none of the others start any trouble." He pointed a finger at his partner. "And don't eat my bread."

He turned and took off at a jog. Soon enough, the halpbloed looked over his shoulder at the sound of quickly approaching feet and noticed him. The halpbloed dropped his basket of kindling and took off at a run. Sulwynd smiled and gave chase. He liked it when they ran.

† † †

Inquisitor Rhus Amalaki pulled his cloak tightly around him as he watched the two constables from the shadows of a building. Space was so tight in Nul Pfeta that there were hardly any alleys between buildings, but the haphazard upward construction turned the roads into canyons that created deep shadows in the morning light. His dark green cloak did the rest, making him nearly invisible among the buildings.

His target was too absorbed in what he and his partner were discussing to have noticed Amalaki anyway. He watched as Constable Sulwynd kicked a loose stone, nearly hitting a washerwoman with it. The pair laughed and continued along their patrol. Amalaki didn't give the woman a second thought as he slipped between the shadows to keep his target in sight.

His investigation into Constable Sulwynd wasn't bearing fruit, and his superiors at the Red Keep were demanding that he either make an arrest or drop the issue. He was stretched thin, working too many cases, and the lack of progress was turning this lead into a thin branch. He'd asked for some

Novices to assist him, but Senior Inquisitor Heimia had refused to authorize any help. Amalaki had tried to explain that he was gathering evidence, when the Senior Inquisitor had interrupted him. "We're not the damn constabulary, Inquisitor Amalaki. If this Sulwynd is a threat to the King, then haul his ass into the Red Keep. We will pull the information out of him. We don't need evidence. You've been on this case for over a month now, and you haven't made any progress. Either bring in your target for questioning, or drop it."

Amalaki should have done that. He should have gathered a group of Novices and pulled Sulwynd from his home and taken him to the Red Keep. But here he was, sneaking around the stinking underbelly of Nul Pfeta, trying to find evidence that Constable Sulwynd was up to something. *Why in the hells am I torturing myself over this?* One thought immediately came to mind: Constable Inspector Reva Lunaria.

He didn't know why he was trying to please her. She'd wanted evidence that Sulwynd—a fellow constable—was up to no good before she'd agree to help him. It didn't make sense that he'd try to please her. He was a member of the Sucra, the King's secret police, charged with protecting the King and the Kingdom from all threats. His superiors were right, he didn't need evidence. He didn't have to prove that the threat existed. The mere possibility that there was a threat was sufficient. And if someone who was pulled in actually turned out to be innocent (it sometimes happened) then their experience became a warning to the others to never step out of line. Not even a little bit.

Instead of doing his job, he was risking his own career and position within the Sucra to try to please Reva. *Hells, Reva hasn't even shown up the last three times that I'd requested we meet.*

He watched Sulwynd and his partner dodge the night soil dropped from a chamber pot, then laugh and continue their patrol. Despite the laughter and the bravado between the two constables, Amalaki could tell that Sulwynd was bored. He was just going through the motions. It was clear that his mind was on other things.

A familiar feeling began to twist in Amalaki's gut. He knew that Sulwynd was up to something, but there was no way that idiot was the mastermind. If there really was a threat to the King, then Sulwynd was just a small cog in the plan. Bringing him in wouldn't give them the information they needed to stop the threat. Those behind it would just find another Sulwynd, another lackey who would take orders and carry out the plan. It would also prove to Reva that he did things differently—that he wasn't just another Malvaceä.

Amalaki watched as the pair of constables took loaves of bread from a baker's stall and continued their meandering patrol. He had to slow down when the pair stopped. Then he noticed a change in Sulwynd. The constable was now alert, excited, bouncing up slightly on the balls of his feet. He handed his bread to his partner, and then took off, quickly breaking into a run as a halpbloed saw him and fled.

Shit.

† † †

Halpbloeden and humans jerked away from Constable Sulwynd as he ran and yelled for his target to stop. The halpbloed kept running, naturally, and pulled away from Sulwynd, using the crowded street to his advantage. Sulwynd dodged around a cart pulled by a decrepit old donkey, and then had to jump over a stack of firewood. He spat a curse as the halpbloed made a quick turn to his right and headed down a narrow alley. Sulwynd shoved somebody to the ground, and then ran down the alley after his quarry.

The halpbloed turned to look behind him, and then tripped over his own feet and staggered, nearly falling, before regaining his footing. Sulwynd gained several paces on the halpbloed, but still wasn't close enough.

His target exited the alley into a cloistered close set between several buildings. At one time, there had been a tree growing in the middle of the small space, when sunlight gave life to it. But the buildings surrounding the close had grown taller and blocked out all but only the most daring noon-day light, so now only a dead trunk and bare branches remained. At this time of day, the close was cloaked in thick shadows and was quiet—save for the halpbloed's hurried steps—as nobody else was in the space. The halpbloed ran around the dead tree and then tripped over a fallen branch. This time he fell and slid across the dirt. Sulwynd gave a feral grin as he slowed up, approaching the halpbloed. The halpbloed was trying to get to his feet, but Sulwynd gave a swift kick to his stomach. There was a satisfying sound of air being expelled, and the halpbloed rolled toward a door.

Sulwynd gave another swift kick, "That's for making me run. I hate running."

The halpbloed moaned and tried to roll away, but was stopped by the closed door. Sulwynd bent down and grabbed the halpbloed, hauling him to his feet. He leaned into the halpbloed's face, wrinkling his nose at the stench. "I'm gonna make you pay for making me run."

He shoved the halpbloed back into the door, which opened upon the impact, and the halpbloed fell into the dark space. Sulwynd followed, kicking the halpbloed further inside and closing the door behind them.

†††

Nul Pfeta's horrible street layout and haphazard planning made following Constable Sulwynd relatively easy for Amalaki—at least, for the first hundred paces or so. The constable's path through the crowded street was easy to track, as he left a trail of fallen market goods, sprawled bodies, and flying curses. It was a risk for Amalaki to be following so closely, but he stayed in the shadows, and most of the halpbloeden were too preoccupied with the constable and his prey to notice Amalaki. But he couldn't risk getting any closer, as that would be noticed, by the halpbloeden and by Sulwynd.

He saw Sulwynd dodge around a cart and then jump

a pile of firewood. Sulwynd's attention was entirely on his target, and his partner—Amalaki took a quick look behind him—hadn't given chase and was continuing his leisurely pace. *Why is that?* If this was a criminal being chased, both constables should have been in pursuit. *So why is his partner acting like he doesn't care what happens?*

Amalaki moved around the same cart and saw the halpbloed make a sharp turn into a hidden alley. Constable Sulwynd was maybe twenty paces behind and made the same turn. Amalaki had to slow down as he approached the corner, and then he stopped in a shadow and looked down the dark alley. It was more like a tunnel than an alley, as the upper stories of the buildings on either side covered the space. It was dank, and smelled of urine and rotting cabbage. He heard someone stumble, and then heard the sound of running feet. Amalaki slid from his shadow into the darker depths of the alley.

The space magnified the sounds as they echoed off of the walls. Ahead, he could see a lightening of the blackness that filled the alley, as well as the sound of someone falling. More running feet, then a clear sound of someone being kicked. *The halpbloed made a critical error and is going to pay for that.*

Amalaki held back, finding a spot—an old bricked up doorway—where he could fade into the background. Once Constable Sulwynd had caught his quarry, Amalaki was certain that he'd lead the halpbloed back this way and rejoin his partner. He heard more grunts, and Sulwynd complaining about having to run. Then, after a few more breaths, there was no more noise.

Amalaki instinctively pulled his green cloak around him tighter, even though he was already a dark shadow in a black well. He started counting slowly, waiting for Constable Sulwynd and his prisoner to pass by. When he got to thirty, he strained to listen, to determine if the constable was still there, maybe talking quietly. He heard nothing.

When he got to sixty, panic started to creep into

Amalaki's thoughts. *Could there be another exit that Sulwynd used? Why chase this halpbloed if he wasn't in trouble for something?* Constables in Nul Pfeta were petty, vindictive bullies, but they were also lazy and didn't just chase halpbloeden for the fun of it. If they gave chase, and the halpbloed was stupid enough to run, it was because they wanted to make an arrest.

After reaching one hundred, Amalaki slipped from his hiding spot and crept slowly toward the back of the alley. It opened upon a small square, a close surrounded by buildings on all sides. He could see the sorry remains of a tree that once had grown in the center of the close, but it was apparently too pitiful now to even be used as firewood. He saw a couple of other alleys heading off in different directions, and four or five doors that opened onto the close, but he didn't see Constable Sulwynd or his quarry.

"Shit."

† † †

When the door closed, Constable Sulwynd leaned down and offered his hand to the halpbloed laying on the dirt floor. For the briefest of moments, he saw anger and hatred flicker in the halpbloed's eyes, but then he grabbed Sulwynd's hand. Sulwynd pulled him up.

"You didn't have to make it so real," the halpbloed complained, as he rubbed his stomach.

"Well maybe next time, Cedres, you won't make me run so hard. I hate running."

"I was only making it look convincing for the others."

"Convincing is me giving you a shiner to show to your worthless friends, not me hurling up my breakfast from chasing you."

Cedres gave a small shrug, and Sulwynd could tell that he was proud of himself for this tiny victory. He wanted to give Cedres another kick for that, but he had other things to discuss, and little time to do it. Spending too much time here would make even Gallwynn suspicious of what really happened.

"Have you completed your task?" Sulwynd asked.

Cedres Vanda took a step back, and then held up his hands in a placating gesture. "I'm trying, but it's hard to find others."

Sulwynd snorted, *how typical*, he thought. *Halpbloeden are the laziest creatures on Ados. You can only motivate them with money or force.* Aloud, he said, "Why are they so reluctant when they are treated like this?" He made a sweep of his arm that took in all of Nul Pfeta and the halpbloed's situation. "They are treated as though they are less than elven because of a few indiscretions made by a long-dead ancestor. Doesn't that make them angry?"

"They *are* angry," Cedres spat, and Sulwynd knew that what Cedres really meant was that *he* was angry. "But they are also afraid." Sulwynd could tell from his tone that Cedres didn't include himself that time.

"Why are they afraid?"

"Why?" Cedres gave a bitter laugh. "We've been thrown out of our homes and lost our jobs. Many of us have lost wives or husbands, all because you fear us." He pointed a finger at Sulwynd. "You mark us as being different because you need someone to blame for all that goes wrong in the land. The King and his lackeys declared halpbloeden to be their scapegoat, and then he needed more, so he changed the rules to make more of us. He rules because he can distract his people with fear and scare them with the halpbloed 'threat.'"

Sulwynd kept his face impassive; he'd heard this rant from Cedres before, though he wasn't too far off the mark. Of course, Cedres didn't know the whole truth, but that didn't matter. "So, you'd rather cower than do something about it? To right these wrongs?"

Cedres jerked and stood up a bit. "I am not a coward, and I am not like these other halpbloed. I am an elf, despite these stupid laws. The King is wrong. He's been misled, and he needs to be shown the truth."

"And what is the truth?"

"That I'm just as elven as you are. That's not determined by some stupid law, or by who my great-grandfather slept with. I've done more to prove my elvenness than half the elves living outside these walls." Cedres made a slashing gesture with one arm. He then pointed at Sulwynd. "I stood up to the traitor that killed Lady Ochroma. I protected her. I am owed something for that. No other *elves* did that. That was *me*. I nearly gave my life for a noble, and I got *nothing*!"

Sulwynd couldn't keep the surprise from his face. He had heard about Lady Ochroma's death—everyone in the city had—and he'd known that Constable Inspector Lunaria had a witness to Ochroma's murder, but he'd never been able to find out who that witness was. It was all just leaves on the wind now. He said, "Then you know why it is important to do this. You've already proven that you are an elf, despite the stupid law. Aren't there others like you? *Elves*," he purposely used the term, "like you willing to fight for who they are?"

"There are a few of us," Cedres admitted. "And they may be afraid, but that's bred from an abundance of caution. There is great risk to join a group to fight for our rights when we risk everything and don't know what the fight is about, or what the outcome will be. You constables or the Green Cloaks will happily stretch our necks if we are caught. If you tell me what we will do, I will find you elves that will support you."

Sulwynd couldn't tell Cedres that, since he himself didn't know. It had taken him time to feel out potential halpbloed for this mission. Too many of them had accepted their fate, and they had no interest in fighting back. Others were too dwarf-headed, and were itching for a fight, which was just as dangerous. He knew that the timing for this mission, no matter what the actual target was, was critical. Patience was needed, in addition to passion. He'd come across Cedres Vanda about a month ago, and he had been taking his time recruiting Cedres for this mission. Cedres was filled with anger, but he wasn't a raving lunatic. He was convinced that he was in the right and had been falsely lumped in with the other halpbloeden. But only one halpbloed wouldn't work for this plan, Sulwynd knew that much.

"I can't tell you what is being planned," Sulwynd said, drawing a frown from Cedres. Sulwynd bristled at that; no matter what Cedres believed, he was still a damn halpbloed. He pointed a finger at Cedres. "That's for everyone's protection. I've been asked to find *elves* willing to fight for their rights. My patron needs to know of your commitment before risking his own position by giving you any information about what will happen."

"I am committed," Cedres said, and Sulwynd could see the fire of burning desire in his eyes. "I am owed my life back for what I have done for the King. I am due recognition. I was promised that after protecting Lady Ochroma."

Maybe you'd have gotten the recognition you seek if you'd kept her alive, you idiot, Sulwynd thought. "We need more than just you. We need others who are as committed as you are. There are other elves like my patron. They think the King has gone too far with the Purity Laws. They've lost friends, employees, and other good elves who didn't deserve to be punished. But you need to understand their position. If they move too quickly, the damn Green Cloaks will sniff them out, and then *you*," he pointed at Cedres, "won't have any chance to get your old life back. They need to know that there are elves *here*," he pointed to the ground, "ready to act. Show us that you can recruit others, and my patron will be willing to give you more."

Cedres was slowly nodding his head, and Sulwynd knew that he'd sunk the hook firmly. Cedres would bring others in on this mission. "Be sure to let them know that what they do will change everything in Tenyl. Those who wronged them will be punished, and they will reap the rewards."

"I will find others and have them ready."

"Good," Sulwynd nodded. "But I can't be running all of your asses down to give you the information. We will meet in three days at your apartment."

Cedres paled a bit. "Is that safe?"

"I'll make it safe. We'll meet before sundown. That way there will be no other constables around to spy on us."

Cedres nodded. "Three days. I will be ready." He slipped past Sulwynd and headed out the door into the close. Sulwynd waited until he counted to sixty, and then he left as well.

† † †

Amalaki had retreated from the alley, mad at himself for losing contact with Sulwynd. It was a novice mistake, and he considered waiting at the alley entrance for the constable to reappear, but there was no guarantee that Sulwynd would return to this road. Amalaki had waited for five minutes, but there was also no guarantee that Sulwynd was even still in the area. He might have hauled the halpbloed down one of the other alleys and taken him to the Victory Bridge gatehouse and tossed him in a cell there. Just doing his job.

Unlike me, he bitterly said to himself. He'd finally given up, and headed back toward what he thought was the way to the bridge.

But while he'd waited, he became sure that Sulwynd was up to something. The whole scenario felt contrived to make people think that a constable was chasing down another criminal. But Sulwynd's partner hadn't given chase. Amalaki had seen the constable waddle past the alley carrying two loaves of bread, completely unconcerned about what Sulwynd was doing. That meant that this chase had been a performance, as if this street in Nul Pfeta was the stage at Pfenestra's Playhouse. So why the act? Why put on a show for others? Amalaki supposed that the halpbloed could be an informant that Sulwynd used to learn about other criminal activity. He'd want to keep such a person safe from retribution. That was a possibility. But there were other reasons, too. It could have been a chance at payback for a previous slight or insult, although in that case, the other constable would have wanted to get in on the action. It could have been a shakedown for pfen or other goods, and it would make sense that

Sulwynd would want to keep any treasure for himself.

But as he walked, Amalaki kept coming back to the nagging suspicion that there was more to this encounter. *Why the secluded location?* If it was for payback or to collect money, any place would do, and no halpbloeden would have lifted a finger against the constable. Not in broad daylight, anyway. Amalaki supposed that it could have been a sexual tryst, which would certainly explain the desire for a quiet spot, but Amalaki didn't think that was the case. It was a possibility that he had to consider, but it just didn't feel right. That only left one possibility; that Sulwynd and the halpbloed needed to meet where others wouldn't know what they'd discussed, or that they'd even met at all. Again, that could just be Sulwynd meeting an informant, but there were also other reasons to meet in secret. Those reasons were usually to plot something illegal.

He could just arrest Sulwynd now, and bring him into the Red Keep. It would make his superiors happy, and he'd be able to find out why the meeting happened. If it was for sex, they'd let him go. If he was meeting an informant, there could be pushback from the constabulary, but that was nothing that couldn't be explained and washed over. But if it was for some other reason, then Amalaki would have done his duty to his King.

And what about those that ordered Sulwynd to turn traitor? A nagging voice said in his head. To his surprise, it sounded a lot like Reva. *This isn't just about evidence now; it's about seeing how deep these roots go and who else is involved.*

Amalaki shook his head, trying to get Reva out of his thoughts. He stopped in the shadow of an herbalist's shop and tried to get his bearings. Nul Pfeta was a maze in the best of times, and Amalaki realized that he'd gotten turned around as he'd been thinking. As he looked around, trying to find a landmark that would point him in the right direction, he spotted Constable Sulwynd. The constable was walking along, with a bit of a jaunty spring in his step, and he was whistling. This was clearly a change in his demeanor from earlier. But he was walking alone, with no sign of the halpbloed that he'd been chasing. Something good had happened, but what, exactly?

Amalaki had collected too many other small coincidences around Constable Sulwynd in the past month. He was sure that the constable was up to something. This latest event was yet another bud on the flower and, taken as a whole, it suggested that Sulwynd was up to no good.

He let the constable pass, staying hidden in the shadows. Sulwynd's plan, whatever it was, had taken a step forward, but if Amalaki brought him in now, he'd lose any others who were involved. There had to be elves who were giving Sulwynd his orders. Amalaki wanted them, too.

Chapter 3

The bell above the door gave a cheerful jingle, and Yasmine looked up from her work to see who had entered her shop. She gave a smile to Constable Inspector Reva Lunaria, and said, "Just a moment, Constable, while I finish with Mr. Peulldove here."

Mr. Peulldove turned around to see who had entered, and then gave a bow. "The beautiful Lady Lunaria; it's such a pleasure for you to grace me with your presence."

Yasmine saw Reva roll her eyes. "I've told you many times before, Mr. Peulldove, to call me by my real title. I am certainly no lady."

"Your modesty outshines your beauty, Constable Inspector," Mr. Peulldove said, as he attempted to straighten up. Reva had to step up and help keep him from falling over. Yasmine knew that Mr. Peulldove was more fit and spry than many other elves at his age, which was at least 230 years. He gave Yasmine a lecherous wink as Reva put her hands on his arm and back and asked if he was okay.

"With your gentle touch, I am more than fine."

Yasmine suppressed a smile, and tried to focus on completing Mr. Peulldove's order. She finished measuring out the herbs and put them into a large stone mortar. Picking up a pestle, she began to grind the herbs into a fine powder. They gave off an earthy, pungent odor that was quickly lost among the many other aromas that filled the apothecary shop. After a few practiced twists of the pestle, she transferred the powdered herb into a small clay pot.

"Why does your beautiful parrot no longer call you sexy?" Mr. Peulldove asked Reva. Yasmine couldn't help raising her eyebrows.

"Gabii was distracting Mother's customers. Some of them were complaining."

"Who are these uncouth degenerates? The truth should not be hidden away behind prudish sensitivities. It should be shouted to the world."

Yasmine saw Mr. Peulldove take a breath, and Reva's mouth forming words that couldn't get out fast enough, as Mr. Peulldove yelled, at the top of his voice, "Reva is sexy!"

Reva's face immediately took on a crimson color that ran all the way to her ears. She put a hand to her forehead and shook her head.

"Mr. Peulldove," Yasmine said loudly, getting his attention, "I'm finished with your order."

The elderly elf turned and smiled at Yasmine. "And this one will last longer?" he asked, as she handed him the clay pot.

"It will last for at least two hours, maybe longer if you pace yourself. Just mix it with your tea or wine at least half an hour before."

Mr. Peulldove smiled. "Thank you, my dear Yasmine. You are the most gifted of your profession." He gave a small bow, and then easily stood up. He turned to Reva and held up the pot toward her, "Care to help me try out Yasmine's latest creation?"

Reva was clearly confused and held up a hand, "Not today, Mr. Peulldove, I have a lot of work to do." She tapped one of her bracers.

"Well, let me know if you change your mind." He waved and walked out of the shop, the bell giving another cheerful jingle.

Reva stepped up to the counter and plucked a cherry

drop from the dish that Yasmine kept there. "And just what did you create for Mr. Peulldove?"

Yasmine smiled and put a hand to her mouth, trying to keep from laughing. "An aphrodisiac," she managed to say, "it will help him remain sturdy for at least a couple of hours."

The Constable Inspector's eyes widened, and she nearly choked on the cherry drop. Yasmine started to laugh, unable to contain it any longer, and Reva joined her.

"You mean, Mr. Peulldove is…" Reva managed to get out between laughs.

"Yes," Yasmine said, trying to catch a breath. "Apparently he's quite the lady's elf. He befriends older women—widows mostly—and he showers them with love and attention. According to him, they are so enamored that they beg for him to sleep with them."

Reva shook her head and got her laughter under control. "Really? OK, that's it; I'm not letting him back into Mother's shop alone ever again."

Yasmine gave a wave and said, "Oh, Constable, Mr. Peulldove is perfectly harmless."

"You're just saying that so I won't arrest him, and he can keep buying his 'love powders' from you."

"A woman has to earn a living." She put her hands on her hips, but also smiled to ease the defiant gesture. "And to get her entertainment from somewhere. Now, what can I do for you today, Constable Inspector? I've heard that you have been working some long days lately. Has the Wake been working?"

Reva sighed, and pulled out the small tin from one of the pockets on her uniform. "It's working, but it seems to be losing its effectiveness. I'm nearly empty again."

Yasmine picked up the tin and opened the lid. There was barely a pinch of the red-orange powder remaining. "You have been working a lot," she said. "You were just in not even a week ago."

Reva nodded. "I know. I have been working a lot lately, but is there any way that the Wake could be, I don't know, not working?"

"Wake is not magic, Inspector. It comes from a plant, and plants can be finicky. Some are strong and some are weak. You know how some fruits taste better when they are at their ripest, but lack flavor if picked too early or too late?" Reva nodded. "Wake is just like that. We do our best, but sometimes the roots we get may have sat around for too long on a ship, affecting how potent they are."

"That makes sense," Reva admitted.

"Have you had any other problems lately?" Yasmine asked. She bit her lip as Reva seemed to pause at the question. *I'm pushing too much.*

"Only that my partner can't keep his damn opinion to himself."

Yasmine let out a breath. "What opinion is that?"

"Ansee hates Wake, and he hates that I take it. And he isn't subtle about letting me know about it, either. He's always making snide remarks and comments or giving me a disapproving glare when he sees me using it. I hate it when people shove their own morals on others. It's my own damn life, and I can do whatever I want with it."

"It sounds like your partner had a bad experience with Wake. I know some users who were given a bad batch, either from disreputable apothecaries or elves trying to grind the stuff in their kitchens. I only use the best roots."

"I don't think Ansee has ever used Wake," Reva said. "Though I do know that he blames Wake for his sister's death."

"Wake doesn't kill," Yasmine said, a bit too defensively. She ran a hand through her auburn hair to calm her nerves. "Every person that uses Wake reacts a little differently," she explained, "but for most users, it is a wonderful stimulant that has no side effects. And I use only the best roots and prepare everything myself. You know the quality of my work." Reva nodded her agreement.

"People have been taking Wake for at least a century now, and nobody has died from it that I know of. If it was dangerous, I wouldn't prepare it or sell it."

"Well, Ansee has this stupid idea that Wake is deadly." She looked Yasmine in the eyes. "Do you know that he took my Wake away, right after he became my partner, and had the alchemists at New Port test it?"

"Test it? *My* Wake?" Yasmine felt her own anger rising, mixed with a slight twinge in the pit of her stomach. "Why would he do that?"

"He told me that it was affecting my personality. That I was too aggressive and short-tempered."

"And were you?" Yasmine's mind was racing, wondering if she should press Reva on what the alchemists at New Port had found out when they'd tested the Wake.

"Of course not," Reva said. *A bit too aggressively*, Yasmine thought. "Ansee had only been my partner for a couple of days at the time. He didn't understand me or know anything about me then. Hells, he barely knows me now. There was nothing wrong with me then, and there isn't now."

Yasmine hesitated, but then licked her lips and asked, "The alchemists at New Port, did they find anything wrong with the Wake?"

"Hmm? No. Once I found out what Ansee had done, I told Thea not to bother. She's so overworked that she hadn't gotten around to even looking at it."

A wave of relief flooded through Yasmine. "Well, we both know that Wake is perfectly safe. Maybe you should bring your partner here so that I can talk some sense into him." Reva's shrug seemed to say that was a hopeless task. Yasmine picked up the tin and said, "Well, let me go fill your order. I'll be back in a minute."

She walked through the beaded curtain to the back of her shop. A couple of oil lamps cast a warm glow in the space, but over her workbench, she had a light crystal that she now activated so that she could see clearly. She reached for a clay jar with a distinctive yellow and red glaze—it was actually one of Aeollas Lunaria's pots—that was unlabeled, but Yasmine knew what it contained. As she pulled the jar down, a voice whispered, "No, don't give the Constable any of the new Wake this time."

Yasmine started, and turned toward the voice. The person was standing in the corner of the room, out of the light, but able to see the front of the shop through the beaded curtain. "I didn't know that you'd arrived," Yasmine said.

"I got here as you were helping Mr. Peulldove. The new shipment is on the shelf."

Yasmine glanced over to one of the storage shelves and could see the burlap bag filled with roots. "Why don't you want me giving Reva this?" she asked, her hand pointing to the unlabeled jar. "We've given it to her before."

"And apparently it almost got into the hands of their alchemists," the voice hissed.

Yasmine bristled. "That wasn't my fault."

"I know. That was antsy."

Yasmine didn't understand what that meant. She mentally shrugged, and asked, "Are you sure you aren't getting cold feet?" She glanced out toward the front of the shop. "Maybe because of a certain Constable Inspector?"

"No," the voice said. "I don't care about Reva Lunaria and her antsy Seeker. Plans are changing, that's all. The formula continues to be refined, and we need to conduct more experiments, on a larger group. It's too risky at this point to continue to experiment on the good Constable, especially if Antsy is going to stick his branches in where they don't belong. We don't need the constabulary alerted to what we are doing. Not at this point."

Yasmine paused to consider this. It was clear that there was something else going on here, but it really wasn't her place to shake the branches. Not now. "Very well," she said, returning the unlabeled pot to its place. She pulled out another pot, which had a paper label glued to it that had "Wake" printed on it in Yasmine's neat hand. She quickly filled Reva's tin and deactivated the light, and then returned to the front of the shop through the beaded curtain.

† † †

Reva arrived home, and the smell of dinner assaulted Reva's senses as she rushed up the stairs. Her mother was sitting patiently at the table, the evening meal laid out neatly. Gabii squawked from her perch as she let a walnut shell fall to the floor. Reva ignored the meal, her mother, and Gabii, headed to her room, and shut the door.

"Reva," her mother called. "Reva, your dinner will get cold."

Reva rolled her eyes as she quickly pulled off her armor to change her shirt. She quickly filled the basin on her dresser with water and scrubbed some of the day's stink away, then pulled on another shirt. She then pulled on her armor and bracers again before running a brush quickly through her hair. Satisfied that she wouldn't scare the criminals away, she opened the door to find her mother standing there, her arms folded, her foot tapping.

"You're going back to work." It wasn't a question, and her tone made Reva's mind fly to all the times when she'd done something wrong growing up. It had always been Reva that got in trouble. Gale never seemed to receive any punishment for his many transgressions.

"I have work to do," Reva said, squeezing past her mother. She paused at the table to grab one of the rolls, and then headed toward the stairs.

"Reva, stop!"

Reva stopped at the top of the stairs and threw her head back, rolling her eyes at the ceiling. "I don't have time for this, Mother."

"Oh, so now you don't have time for me, is that it?"

"That's not what I meant."

"Yes, it is. All of this, everything I do, is just an imposition to you, isn't it? We haven't had a proper meal in a month."

"That's because I'm busy catching criminals," Reva retorted.

Gabii repeated Reva's mother, "Proper meal."

Reva pointed at the bird, "Don't you start, too."

"Reva," her mother said, stepping up to the table, "you've been working yourself to the roots. Your father said—"

Reva made an exasperated groan and clenched her fists, crushing the roll. "It's always Dad this, Dad that. I'm my own person. I'm not Dad."

"Don't speak ill of your father, young lady. He'd tell you to sit down and eat, and to stop being so dwarf-headed. You broke up with Aavril a month ago."

"What the hells does my job have to do with him?"

"Don't you swear at me! And you know very well that this is about Aavril. Ever since that incident at the port last month, you've been mad with him."

"I'm not mad at Aavril. I barely even think about the asshole."

"Yes, you are," her mother corrected, "and you can't lie to me. I know you, and I know how you get. Anytime someone shakes your branches you get like this."

"Like *what*?" Reva took a step forward, and Gabii flapped her wings.

"Like a *dwarf*," her mother said, her greatest insult, not counting what she called Ansee, and Reva didn't think that was said in anger anymore. "Anytime something doesn't go your way, you get all stubborn and work yourself to the roots."

"I do not!"

"When Gale said he was joining the rangers, you got so mad at him for leaving that you worked without a break for days, and you collapsed on one of your patrols."

Reva opened her mouth to tell her mother how that wasn't what happened, but she kept going. "When your father died, you worked extra shifts, without your boss's permission, trying to find out who killed him. You got so distracted that you couldn't keep any of your cases straight, and you nearly lost your job."

"That was completely different," Reva managed to say. "Nobody wanted to do anything to solve his case."

"I seem to remember that First Constable Aescel personally headed up the investigation and spent nearly a month tracking down leads. That seems like someone doing something to me."

"And we never did find out what happened," Reva said, trying to regain control of the situation. She had things to do, other cases to investigate, and this was not how she wanted to spend her time.

Her mom didn't care, and she continued to twist the knife that she'd jabbed into Reva. "And when Cas told you that she was leaving to help her mother, you got so dwarf-headed that you wouldn't talk to her for a week. If you had to tell her something, it was always told to a third person first. You wouldn't even let her do her job, though she hadn't even left yet. You tried to do everything yourself on that case until Cas finally knocked some sense into your knotty head."

Reva tossed the crumpled roll onto the table. "None of those things are related to this thing with Aavril."

"Ha!" her mother said, sounding triumphant. "So, you *are* still mad at him."

"I'm *not* still mad at him. He gave up on me, and I got over it right after it happened."

Her mother crossed her arms and started tapping her foot again. "And why are you working double- even triple-shifts? It seems to me that you are throwing yourself at your work again, because you don't want to face the problems in front of you."

"There are no problems." Reva pointed toward the front door. "If you haven't noticed, crime didn't stop in this city just because I broke up with my boyfriend."

"And I suppose you're the only constable in the entire city, then, is that it?"

"Only constable," chirped Gabii.

"I'm the only *good* constable," Reva snapped.

"Only *good* constable," Gabii repeated.

"Shut up!" Reva and her mother both yelled at Gabii. Gabii flew from her perch toward Reva's room.

"And your partners, Ansee, Willem, and Kai, what are they? Kobold spoor?"

"No," Reva spat. She gripped the chair in front of her so tightly that her knuckles turned white. "You don't understand what I have to do."

"I knew your father long enough," her mother said, glancing down at the spot where Reva's father had usually sat at the table, her voice soft. "I think I understand what it means to be a constable." She looked up. "And I know that he'd tell you to stop being such a dwarf and take it easy. If you continue to use your job as a crutch for the problems in your personal life that you won't face, then you are going to get hurt. Or worse, get someone close to you hurt."

"If I do my job, then nobody will get hurt at all!" Reva grabbed another roll from the table and stormed down the stairs, ignoring her mother's pleas to stay.

Chapter 4

Lord Constable Inspector Nyssa Betulla gave a polite laugh at the comment just made by Luminary Elmere Sorellen, the head of the Merchant's Guild. It was the first time that the Luminary had ventured out of his home since the dreadful attack by Roya Locera at Pfeta fey Orung, and he was starved for attention. He had monopolized most of the conversation at dinner, and now Betulla was just being polite when she responded to one of his stories. As Sorellen refilled his wine glass and started in on a new tale that was sure to bore the other guests, Betulla was thinking that it was too bad that Locera hadn't managed to kill the buffoon at that tragic dinner.

She refilled her own wine glass from the carafe on the table, as the servants hovered about and replaced the plates with the dessert course. A small bowl sat before her with a light brown cake filled with gooey-looking brown splotches. The whole concoction was sitting in a thick cream. Betulla looked up from the strange dish and turned to their host, Grand Inquisitor Lahar Agera. Agera was wearing a high-collared dark green coat with gold buttons and piping over a silken shirt that was the color of new grass. He sat at the head of the table with Luminary Laural Calastii, head of the Builder's Guild, on his left, and *Shádpfed* Jorus Asclepias, some sort of magic professor from Auros Academy, on his right. Several of the other guests were also looking at the strange dish in front of them.

"By Basvu, what is this strange dish, Grand Inquisitor?" asked Margrave Breanna fey Pavesa, with a subtle laugh that Betulla was sure was meant to sound light and humorous, but came off as sounding churlish. She was also glad that the Margrave had been the one to ask the question and not her. Betulla kept her face impassive, like she already knew the answer.

The Grand Inquisitor picked up a spoon, and cut into the dessert as the bowl was placed in front of him. "An excellent question, Margrave," he said with a smile, and Betulla could hear sighs and muttered comments from the other dinner guests. "This is a recipe that a merchant shared with me from the United Shires of Albion."

Betulla had to wrack her brain to recall where that tiny country was located, and finally gave up. It wasn't important.

"They call it a 'brownie' which is like a spice cake but, instead of fruit, they include a special cacao in it."

Betulla picked up her spoon at that. She had a fondness for cacao drink, so she was curious to see what this tasted like.

"It seems," Agera continued, "that the Albionians have a method of collecting a butter from the cacao seed, and they mix this with sugar and other ingredients to create a block of cacao. It has a sweet cacao flavor." The Grand Inquisitor lifted a spoonful of his brownie and took a bite. All the other guests did the same, and a collection of 'oohs' and 'aahs' filled the dining room. Betulla closed her eyes, letting the cream and spice from the cake flow over her tongue, and then she tasted the cacao. It was a divine taste, and she let out a small moan of pleasure at the mix of flavors.

The Margrave turned to Agera after a few bites and said, "You must provide me with this recipe so that my cooks can prepare it back in Pavesa."

The Grand Inquisitor picked up his napkin and dabbed some cream from his lips. "I believe the merchant who gave it to me is planning on opening a new bakery here in Tenyl to start offering this dish. I promised him that I would share his dish with my guests, knowing that it would boost his business." Betulla could see the pout that was starting to form on the Margrave's pretty face. "But in your case, madam," Agera continued, "I'm sure that we can make an arrangement with the merchant so that you don't have to always travel all the way to Tenyl just to indulge in your newest cacao habit."

There were titters of laughter around the table, and the guests greedily devoured the brownies. Betulla was not too worried about requesting a second serving from one of the halpbloeden servers after seeing a few of the other guests, including Margrave fey Pavesa, also requesting a second helping.

The dinner continued with more conversation—gossip mostly—that the Grand Inquisitor did his best to encourage. Betulla knew that Agera was playing his little game, gathering useful information while being the gracious host. She didn't like most of Agera's games, and she didn't trust him, especially in a supposedly informal setting like this dinner. He was still the head of the Sucra, as well as another, more secret, order, and he collected information the way that dwarves collected gold. Betulla had no desire to add to his wealth of knowledge, otherwise, she wouldn't have anything to use in her own consolidation of power. She and the Grand Inquisitor may share similar agendas, but she hated being under his canopy.

The dinner eventually broke up, several of the guests tipsily rising from their chairs and having to be helped by the servants to their carriages and litters. Betulla walked out with the Margrave fey Pavesa, who was also walking a bit unsteadily. She'd apparently had several glasses of the apple brandy that Agera had served after dinner. A pair of servants approached, carrying the women's cloaks. At the same time, Grand Inquisitor Agera walked up. He smiled politely to the Margrave, taking her hand and giving it a kiss. "Do stop by tomorrow, Margrave, and we'll arrange for you to have that brownie recipe."

The Margrave smiled, "My pleasure, Grand Inquisitor." She turned, and one of the servants escorted her to her carriage.

Betulla was pulling her cloak on over her red and black satin dress when Agera said, "Would you have a drink with me?"

Betulla was tired, and she wanted nothing more than to get to her litter and go home but, while it was a polite question, she could hear the subtle command behind Agera's words. She put on a smile and said, "Of course, but some hot cacao if you please. I'd rather not stumble out of here like your other guests."

Agera smiled, gave an order to one of the servants, and then led Betulla away from the dining room and down the hall to a small study. Despite the many dinners and meetings she'd had over the years with Agera in his home, she didn't think that she had ever been in this room. Agera pointed to a plush armchair covered in a green and gold brocade, "Please, have a seat." He took off his coat and hung it from a stand by the door, and then turned to a sideboard and began to pour himself a drink as she sat down. As he took his seat, the door opened, and a servant came in with a tray and set it down on the small table in front of Betulla. The servant bowed and left.

Betulla picked up the small pot and began to pour the hot cacao into her cup.

"What is bothering you this evening, Nyssa?"

Betulla paused briefly before saying, "Nothing is bothering me. It was a wonderful dinner." She sat up and held her cup, letting the heat fill her hands. That hadn't been the full truth but, as with information, she wanted to keep her troubles from Agera as well.

"Come now, Nyssa," Agera chided her. He swirled his drink as he spoke. "You were clearly not yourself at dinner. At least not until the dessert course was served. I can tell that something is bothering you."

Betulla blew on the hot cacao and took a slow sip as she collected her thoughts. She dreaded giving Agera anything that he might use as leverage against her. She had her troubles, yes, but she didn't want to share them with the Grand Inquisitor. Finally, she responded, evading his question with one of her own. "I've noticed that Senior Inquisitor Malvaceä has not yet returned from his banishment. How long will he be punished?"

Agera's glass stopped moving and he narrowed his eyes, ever so slightly. He took a drink, clearly buying time in the same way that Betulla had done. He set his glass down on the table. "Our Underforest emissary was very upset with Malvaceä about the loss of the Fury Blade. Duchess Tubaria wanted me to execute him for letting her cousin's troops recover the weapon."

"Why isn't he dead, then?" Betulla hadn't heard that the dark elf Duchess, who was plotting along with Agera's group to overthrow both kingdoms, had wanted Malvaceä dead.

"Because I was able to convince the Duchess that the Senior Inquisitor could still have a purpose in the larger plan. I told her that, while the loss of the Fury Blade was a setback," Betulla couldn't help but chuckle at that understatement, "our plans were not ruined. She finally agreed, and she allowed me to banish Malvaceä rather than kill him outright."

"That seems quite generous of the Duchess. I'm surprised that she hasn't tried to assassinate Malvaceä, even after agreeing with you. She's been waiting a lot longer for everything to happen than we have."

"The Senior Inquisitor had the same concern when I sent him away, but he can look out for himself. As to Duchess Tubaria, she's never had the patience needed to play the long game, despite being involved in this for longer than you and I. She approaches obstacles like the loss of the Fury Blade like a dwarf pounding out gold from a vein."

Betulla smiled at the analogy as she took another drink. Tubaria was bull-headed and full of anger, which was not always the best combination when plotting to overthrow two kingdoms. "So, is the Senior Inquisitor banished forever? Will he ever be allowed to return to Tenyl?"

"Malvaceä is being kept in the brambles on the exact nature of his current assignment, but it is critical to my overall plan. Should he do well on this assignment, then he will be welcomed back into the fold."

"And are we any closer to initiating the plan?"

Agera picked up his glass. "No." He took a drink and held the glass, looking at the liquid. "There are still many pieces in motion, many details that need to be worked out. I will need everything, and everyone, to be in place and ready to act when the time is right." He lifted his gaze from the glass to Betulla. "And that includes my head of the RTC."

His head? I am not one of his pawns that he can manipulate and order about. The Constabulary is my domain, not his.

"It hasn't just been the dinner tonight," Agera said, catching Betulla by surprise at the change in topic. "Ever since the incident with those strange Disciples of Dreen, you've been distracted. What is bothering you?"

Betulla knew that she couldn't tell him the truth; that she was trying to consolidate her own power base so that she could stand up to Agera. He'd been making a lot of mistakes lately in the plan, and maybe, just maybe, it was time for the Emissary to make a change in leadership. The Duchess might approve of someone who took a more direct approach to things instead of this slow plodding that Agera seemed to favor. Betulla had her own ambitions after the coup; she wasn't going to be Agera's lackey forever. But her own plotting was putting a lot of stress on her, since she couldn't let Agera know even the barest of hints about what she was doing.

She realized that Agera was staring at her, waiting for an answer. She took a quick drink of the cacao, scalding her tongue, and said, "It's Constable Inspector Lunaria. She has continued to be a thorn in my side ever since I took over the Constabulary."

"I thought Constable Inspector Lunaria has been very productive in the past few weeks. My information is that she's made several high-profile arrests and broken open at least two cold cases."

"That's true," Betulla admitted, grudgingly.

"And I believe that Mayor Sovien has even mentioned her work several times to the Alders and to the Guild heads. I even heard that Magistrate Syllaph was speaking highly about her work."

That toad, Betulla fumed to herself. "So, you can see why I can't do anything about Lunaria."

The Grand Inquisitor raised one eyebrow as he slowly swirled his drink. "Why would you want to do anything about one of your best constables?"

"Why?" Betulla asked, not bothering to hide the bitterness. "Because she mocks me."

Agera paused his swirling and actually stared, wide-eyed, at her statement.

"In the way she acts, in the tone of her voice, she mocks me. She flaunts my orders."

"Openly?"

"Unfortunately, no. Otherwise, I would take action. And First Constable Aescel won't control her."

Agera finished off his drink. "Are you sure that you have your facts straight? I admit that Constable Inspector Lunaria can be infuriating, at times." Betulla rolled her eyes at the understatement, but Agera seemed to ignore her. "But despite her unorthodox methods, she has been getting results. Results that are winning her friends among elves of power in the city. If you make any move against Lunaria, even the merest implication of an action against her, it will be met with condemnation by the city leaders."

Agera leaned forward in his chair, his voice dropping to a menacing tone, "And I can't have that. There are too many leaves in the wind right now with my plans. I won't have you disrupting them because of some petty notion that you think a lowly Inspector is out to get you."

Betulla's face reddened at the rebuke but, inside, she was relieved. *If Agera thinks that I'm more concerned about Reva Lunaria, then he won't be looking for me to gather my own forces and demand a change in leadership from the Emissary.*

Chapter 5

The candles gave off a warm, sensual glow as their light reflected off the red silk that was hanging over the bed. Olwyn stood naked, holding two glasses of wine, while he watched Norah get undressed. The light danced across her back as she pulled her shirt up and off, her hair cascading down like a red wave. Olwyn walked over and set the glasses down on the side table, picked up a hairbrush, and then crawled onto the bed. He knelt next to Norah and began to brush her hair. The brush made long, smooth strokes through her silken locks.

He paused and leaned over, kissing the nape of her neck. "Why aren't you counting?" Their usual game was to see how many brush strokes Norah could go before she'd turn around and kiss him. She rarely got past twelve.

"Hmm? Oh, sorry," Norah said, her voice a bit distant. She arched her back and leaned into him. "Start over, please."

Olwyn smiled, and started to brush again.

"One," Norah counted. "Two. Three." Then she stopped again, as he made the fourth and fifth strokes. Olwyn held up the brush and looked at it for a moment, then set it down.

"What's bothering you, love?" he asked, planting a soft kiss on her shoulder.

Norah sighed, blowing a strand of hair out of her eyes. "I'm sorry, I'm just not in the mood tonight." She sat up and hunched her shoulders.

Olwyn looked up at the ceiling for a moment, and then lay on his side, propped up on his elbow. "That's pretty clear. Do you want to tell me why?"

"Like you care." There was bitterness and hurt in those words. Olwyn had to suppress the exasperated sigh that wanted to escape his lips.

"You know that I care about you," he said, as he traced a finger up and down her arm.

Norah's only reaction was a muffled "humph" as she pulled away from him. "If you really cared about me, you wouldn't let them keep doing things to me." The pain and anger she felt came through loud and clear.

Olwyn reached out to touch her again, but then stopped, and let his hand rest on the blanket. "Do you want to tell me what happened?"

Norah sighed, and shook her head. "Why should I tell you? Are you actually going to do anything about it this time?"

Olwyn couldn't suppress his sigh this time, which earned him an angry glare as Norah scooted away from him on the bed. This had been going on at least once a week since they had finished the Dreen cult case, when Norah's life had been saved by the actions of Seeker Carya. Actions that had shown that Seeker Carya was a sorcerer and not a wizard, something that Norah had long suspected. But the problem was that nobody at New Port seemed to care about this fact, save for Norah. When she'd brought it up with Aescel, he'd brushed it off without a second though. "He does his job. That's all I care about," Aescel had said.

Norah kept trying to make it an issue, but first the Senior Constables, and then the other Seekers, had made it a point of slapping her down. The Senior Constables, all of them still stung by Shanna's death, saw Norah as too self-centered in her own crusade to acknowledge the death of one of their own, and they took out their frustration at Norah's expense. Olwyn knew that Senior Constable Ghrellstone had threatened to dunk Norah in the horse trough if she kept making accusations. It never happened, but the Senior Constables constantly reminded her of the threat every chance they got. There had been other, more petty incidents: broken quills, spilled ink, and other childish things.

The other group, the Seekers in Acer and Betula Division, were crueler. They were all wizards, like Norah, but none of them seemed to care that Seeker Carya was a sorcerer. They taunted Norah mercilessly, telling her that if it wasn't for the sorcerer, she'd be just as dead as Shanna. When Norah pushed back, accusing them of siding with a demon spawn, or whatever she referred to Seeker Carya as, they started doing things like using magic to pull her chair away, or causing her spellbook to disappear for a day. Again, they were all childish actions, and it had gotten to the point that Olwyn had wanted to complain to Aescel about it. He hadn't done anything because he thought that Norah was being just a bit too stubborn about the whole thing.

"Was it the Senior Constables or the Seekers this time?" Olwyn asked.

Norah didn't reply, just sat with her shoulders hunched and her arms crossed.

He stroked her hair. "How can I help you, if you won't tell me?"

"It was the Seekers," Norah said, reluctantly.

"What happened today?"

"Why does it matter what they did if nobody cares? They all keep picking on me, teasing me for my principles, for what I believe in, and nobody does a damn thing!" She was on the verge of tears. "Not the First Constable, not any of the other Constables, or any of the Inspectors. Certainly not Reva, and especially not *you*!" She turned and glared at him, her tears replaced by anger.

"Aren't you letting this get under your bark just a bit too much?"

"Ha, thank you for proving my point." Norah stood up and began to gather her clothes.

"Norah, darling, can't you see that's why they keep picking on you?"

Norah stopped and turned to look at him, her clothes held tightly in front of her. "Oh, so, you think that it's okay for them to pick on me?"

"I didn't say that," Olwyn backpedaled.

"It's not fair that I'm the one that is harassed and ridiculed for what I believe, and nobody will acknowledge that he's a real threat." She sat in a chair and started to put on her clothes.

Olwyn sat up on the edge of the bed. This was not how he had planned on spending his evening. It was certainly not how he expected Norah to be leaving. But Norah needed to understand that she was part of the problem; the harassment wouldn't go away unless *she* changed. "Look, nobody else seems to think that Seeker Carya is a threat. Just you. And nobody can understand why you keep hacking at this stump after he saved your life. That's why they keep picking on you. You're just entertainment to them, and as long as you keep feeding fuel to the fire, they will continue to do it."

"So, now you're defending them instead of me?" Norah stood up in a huff. She was clothed, but hadn't yet put on stockings or boots.

Olwyn stood up and spread his arms. "I'm not defending anybody."

Norah had moved toward the door and stopped. "And that's the problem," she said, not bothering to turn around.

She left his bedroom, and then he heard his apartment door open and close. He got up to call after her, pulling on his breeches as he headed toward the door. When he got there, he paused. He could hear crying coming from the other side of the door. After a couple of minutes, the crying ceased, and Olwyn opened the door. Norah was gone.

Chapter 6

Reva stepped up to the bar, set her mug down, and signaled to the barkeep that she wanted a refill. He grunted an acknowledgement and went to grab a pitcher of beer. It was Reva's third time getting a refill since they'd arrived at the Violet Clover Tavern, but the beer was so watered down that she wasn't even slightly buzzed.

The place was filled with so many adventurers that Reva's skin was crawling. There were at least two dozen people in the tavern, most of them in rowdy celebration, although a few seemed to just be drowning their sorrows. The place smelled of burnt meat, beer, sweat, and a few other odors that Reva couldn't, and didn't want, to place. She was just grateful that the place didn't smell of urine. The crowd was mostly elven, though she'd spotted a few humans, some obvious halpbloed, and even a halfling and a couple of other races. Most of them were armed to the teeth with weapons that would get them arrested in other parts of the city, and the place practically buzzed with magic.

"Remind me again why we're doing this?" she asked the elf standing next to her, who was waiting to fill his own drink.

"To draw out our murderer," Ansee murmured. He was disguised to look like a down-on-his-luck spellcaster, wearing a fraying robe and a threadbare cloak. He wore a set of bracers that were clearly intended to be his character's prized possession, and was armed with a pair of daggers.

"Yeah, it's going really well so far." Reva's own disguise consisted of a rusty chainmail shirt with leather pauldrons, a longsword and dagger, and a cloak that was worth more than Ansee's entire disguise all put together. She also wore a pair of bracers, but hers gave off a slight reddish glow.

"This will work," Ansee said, doing his best to keep his voice down. They weren't supposed to know each other. "Remember, I'm the bait."

"I still want to know what you did to get Aescel to agree to this stupid plan."

"I didn't do anything. He saw the merit in what I suggested."

Reva laughed, the sound harsh and bitter. "Tell me another one." The barkeep set her beer down, and she put a Pfen on the counter. "Just remember that you're the one taking the fall for this fiasco when nothing happens, and we have to explain to Aescel why it didn't work." She turned away from the bar, and went back to her table.

A filthy adventurer in an ugly cloak had dared to take her seat, and she stepped up to the table, pulling herself up to her full height, and loomed over the person. "You're in my spot," she growled. She didn't have to pretend to be angry and irritated. Being stuck in the tavern since mid-morning had already done that.

The adventurer turned, his cloak shifting to reveal a patchwork of materials and colors. A bright yellow vest practically glowed in the smoky light of the tavern, and gaudy yellow-and-green-striped leggings made Reva's eyes water. "Why Inspector, fancy meeting you here."

Reva's mouth didn't open in surprise, but only because she was too angry. She sat down opposite the halpbloed cleric. "Coleus Pfastbinder, what in the hells are you doing here?"

"I'm a leaf on the wind," he said, making a fluttering gesture with his hands. "Cleric of the god of chaos, remember. I go where my skills are most needed."

"You go where you can best fleece some hapless adventurer from their coins."

"Banok does move us in mysterious ways." Pfastbinder smiled and leaned back in his seat, spreading his arms across the back of the bench. "I know why I'm here, but what brings you to this glorious little slice of Tenyl?"

"None of your business."

"Ah, working, are we? Your secret is safe with me." He gave Reva an exaggerated wink. "Though you've had better disguises in the past. The one last month as the maid was much better."

Reva ignored him and drank her beer, letting her eyes scan the crowd. Ansee had gotten his drink and was making his rounds of the tavern again. He had been introducing himself to different groups, offering his services as a sorcerer, always being clear that he was not a wizard.

"So, if *you* are here," Pfastbinder tapped a finger to his chin, and glanced around the room. "Let's see. I can see Constable Gania," he pointed to a figure standing stiffly against one wall. "But he sticks out like a sunflower in a patch of creeper vines, so that really doesn't count."

Reva had to nod her head at that. Constable Gania looked like he was guarding something, and he kept glowering at everyone. He looked exactly like a Constable who was pretending to be an adventurer.

"And I suppose that means that the forlorn and bedraggled looking sorcerer who is trying to prostitute himself to every party in the place must be Ansee." Pfastbinder gave a finger wave toward Ansee as he moved from one table of adventurers to another. Ansee's eyes widened as he shot a questioning look at Reva. She just shrugged, rolled her eyes, and lifted her beer.

"And that means that the good Senior Constable should be..."

Reva kept her expression neutral as Willem stood behind Pfastbinder, about to grab his head in his large hand. Pfastbinder twisted away at the last moment and grabbed Willem's hand, giving it a playful kiss. Willem pulled his hand away and wiped it on the back of his dirty cloak. His other hand held a large mug of beer.

"What's this leech doing here?" Willem asked, as he leaned against the bench.

"Leaving," Reva stated.

Pfastbinder gave a laugh, light and lilting, "Oh, Reva, your mouth says leave, but your eyes are begging me to stay."

"I never beg for anything," Reva countered, staring hard at Pfastbinder.

"But if I go, how am I going to help you find your mysterious murderer?"

Reva set her beer down and leaned on the table. "I don't want to know how you figured that out, but I'm going to insist that you leave before you completely blow our cover and cause us to lose our suspect."

"Don't worry. Most of the dupes in this place will never figure out that you're undercover. Well, except Gania. Everybody in here knows that *he's* a Constable."

"He said he didn't know how an adventurer was supposed to act," Willem offered.

"It's easy," Reva said, continuing to look at Pfastbinder. "Just pretend that you don't have a brain and you'll fit right in."

Willem belched. Nobody would mistake him for anything but an adventurer. He adjusted his sword belt and finished his beer before wandering back toward the bar for another refill.

"Figuring out what you were up to was easy for someone with my skill," Pfastbinder continued. "You really should give me a set of bracers. I could be really useful in your plan to capture the killer."

"You'd fit right in," Reva admitted, "since there is no plan."

"Why, Reva," Pfastbinder gave her a sly grin. "You're becoming a true follower of Banok lately. You've always had flashes of chaotic inspiration, but usually you are so methodical and orderly." He gave a shudder.

"You can't pin this one on me," Reva said. "This was all our sorcerer's idea. I don't even want to be here."

"And miss out on all the wonderful characters here? And the atmosphere of this fine tavern?" Pfastbinder raised his hands in a gesture to take in the whole building. Reva gave a snort.

"What you need is someone with my charming personality and skill to flush out your quarry."

Reva gave another snort, "If he's even here."

"Oh, I'm sure he's here," Pfastbinder said, leaning forward conspiratorially. Reva raised her eyebrows. "Well, I mean," Pfastbinder added, "this is where I come for most of my marks. Why wouldn't our murderer be any different?"

"*My* murderer," Reva corrected. "You don't work for me."

"But I should. I fit in with this crowd. And I see what's not there," he tapped the side of his forehead by his eye. "Banok has blessed me with sight that lets me see through the ordinary. Maybe our killer is in here right now. Maybe it's him." Pfastbinder pointed to a human with bulging muscles and a large broadsword strapped to his bare back.

"I think that's a barbarian."

"They're all barbarians, aren't they, Reva?"

She acknowledged that with a nod. He wasn't wrong. "But I doubt that particular barbarian is a magic user, too."

"What about him, then?" Pfastbinder pointed again.

"Ranger."

"Him?"

"Fighter."

"Then what about him?" He pointed to a person at the corner of the bar.

"That's the waitress, and she's a she," Reva said, with a shake of her head.

"Actually, that's Eric, and he identifies as male," Pfastbinder corrected. He gave a little wave to Eric, who waved back. "but I meant the man that's hunched over his mead there at the bar."

Reva took a look at the human. He wore a large, broad-brimmed, pointed hat, and had a long grey beard that flowed down his chest. He wore a grey cloak over disheveled grey robes. A long-stemmed pipe was clutched between his lips, and a cloud of tabak smoke circled his head. A large staff—it looked like a tree branch—leaned against the bar at his side. He was mumbling around the pipe, the smoke leaking out of his lips.

"He's harmless," Reva said, and then added. "Well, he's not my murderer, at least. He keeps trying to dupe adventurers into some silly quest to throw a magic ring into a volcano. He claims it's the only way to stop some 'Dark One' from destroying the world. You and he would get along well, I think."

Pfastbinder bristled, "What?"

"Yeah, the last time we were here interviewing witnesses, he almost got a party of halflings to agree to undertake his quest. Luckily, their ranger friend convinced them that it was a stupid idea, especially when the ranger questioned him about how dangerous this ring could really be if he," Reva nodded to the human, "was holding on to it."

"Why, the nerve," Pfastbinder put a fist down onto the table. "This is *my* tavern. These are *my* marks. He needs to find his own place if he wants to dupe adventurers." He stood up, flung his cloak over his shoulder and strode to the bar.

Reva smiled to herself. That had been the best part of her day. Everything else had been a complete waste of time. Their killer wasn't going to attack here in the tavern, even if they *were* here, and Reva had her doubts on that. Not everyone was as easy to play as Pfastbinder had been.

Ansee finished his circuit of the room and approached her table, his shoulders slumped. He was clearly discouraged, and she started to sympathize with him, but then remembered that it had been his idea to waste the entire day here on this stupid plan. Having to tell FC Aescel that he'd been wrong, and that they hadn't been able to lure out their suspect, might do Ansee some good. She knew that letting Ansee take the heat for this debacle would at least be good for her.

"This isn't going to work," Ansee said, dejectedly, as he took a seat at the table.

"Wow, I would have never guessed," Reva said, letting the sarcasm fill her words.

Ansee squared his shoulders and glared at her. "It was a good idea. It was certainly no worse than pretending to join a cult."

"Yeah, at least I knew where my cult was."

"Because I told you where they were."

Reva shrugged. "Look, next time, don't waste my time on some gnome-brained idea. We have to work from evidence, not gut feelings."

"That seems like the lake calling the ocean wet," Ansee sulked.

Instead of smacking Ansee, Reva stood up. "Let's go. Maybe tomorrow another idea will hit you, and we can waste our day on that, instead." She started for the door, signaling Willem that they were done. Willem nodded, and he and Kai headed out of the tavern.

"I didn't think this would be a waste of time," Ansee said. "And neither did FC Aescel when he agreed to it this morning."

Reva knew that meant that Aescel was just as desperate as Ansee was, grasping at branches like this. Real detective work didn't involve wild shots in the dark. "Maybe you *should* think next time," she said, angrily, as she walked out of the tavern. "Then you won't waste my time."

"Maybe you should stop being such an asshole," Ansee said, acid lacing his words. "You're mad that you can't find this killer, and you're mad at *me* because *I* was the one to suggest something that could have worked."

Reva scoffed as they walked away from the tavern. "That's not why I'm mad at you. And your suggestion was—"

The words died on her lips as searing heat, flames, and a concussive blast filled the road.

Chapter 7

Ansee suddenly found himself flying through the air, super-heated air and flames licking his body. He landed hard on the ground, sliding and tumbling, his ears ringing. He was lucky that his shield spell had triggered at the moment of the explosion, protecting him from the worst of the blast, but he knew that he was going to have several bruises. He rolled to his side and propped himself up on one arm, looking around, trying to determine what had happened.

A circle of singed dirt and stone marked the spot where he and Reva had been walking just moments before. *Reva!* He started to stand up, but the ground spun wildly as his ears continued to ring. He could only manage to get to his knees, but he could see Reva laying on the ground several paces away, apparently blown in the opposite direction by the same blast. Then the realization of what happened hit him.

Fireball.

Ansee looked around for the attacker: the wizard that had just tried to immolate him in the fireball spell. The wizard that had killed three other sorcerers in the past month.

"That's right, whelp, kneel to my superior power!"

The voice sounded distant, due to the ringing in his ears, but Ansee turned to see someone coming around the corner of the Violet Clover Tavern. It was a male elf, with flowing crimson and black wizard's robes, and long golden hair that fell in an unkempt, chaotic mess, covering part of his face. A brown belt was cinched tight around his waist. From a thin sheath, he withdrew a wand.

Ansee gritted his teeth and stood up, doing his best to ignore the vertigo that tried to swallow him up. There were too many unknowns to just sit on the ground until he felt better. He didn't know if Reva had been injured—he refused to think that anything more serious had happened to the Constable Inspector—or how quickly she'd be able to join the fight. He also didn't know where Constables Ghrellstone and Gania were. He was sure that they had heard the explosion—the whole Grove had heard it—but how long would it be before they could return to investigate? While he had been lucky that his shield spell had activated, he knew that it would only last for maybe another thirty seconds, at most.

"I bow to nobody," Ansee said, "especially to elves who think they are superior to anybody else." He gripped the comforting handle of one of his daggers, and then pulled it out from its scabbard. He could see a few faces poking out of the Violet Clover's door, but none of the adventurers were venturing out. Ansee was beginning to see why Reva despised them so much.

The wizard's blue eyes gleamed, and he gave a harsh laugh. "You are a fool as well as an abomination unto Qurna, bringing a knife to a magic fight." With a flick of his wrist, the wand glowed briefly, and then three red balls of light, each about the size of a Skip, flew toward Ansee. They struck Ansee's shield, about a hand's width in front of him.

"I'm sorry, was that supposed to impress me?" Ansee taunted. "If you are having performance issues, we can do this later when you're better prepared." Ansee was trying to sound unconcerned, but he was shaking on the inside. His shield had stopped the force missiles from the wand, but for how much longer? How long had he been on the ground? Had he blacked out at all, and lost any time? He saw the wizard visibly shake at Ansee's casual remark. *It looks like someone has a bit of an ego.*

Ansee held out his hands in a placating gesture. "Look, I am clearly better than you, so you may as well give up now."

"I do not submit myself to your kind. No sorcerer is better than a wizard, despite your demon master's assistance."

Ansee made a show of sighing and rolling his eyes, which seemed to anger the wizard even more. Three more force missiles flew from the wand and harmlessly struck Ansee's shield. *That may not happen the next time*, Ansee realized. Since the wizard seemed to be more interested in talking, Ansee willed the magic for his shield to end, and then recast the spell with a simple word. That caused the wizard to flinch, at first, and then sneer when it seemed to him that nothing had happened. At least it bought Ansee a minute more of protection. But he needed to act now.

He took a step forward, "That's why you killed the other sorcerers, because of some myth that we get our magic from demons?"

"The truth is not myth, demon spawn! You defile Qurna by your very existence!" Spittle actually flew from his mouth as he yelled.

Out of the corner of his eye, Ansee saw Reva get to her feet. The magical parts of her disguise—the illusion that had hidden her constabulary bracers—had fallen away when she had lost consciousness. She turned around to face Ansee and the wizard, drawing her longsword. "You are under arrest," she called.

"You really aren't much of a wizard, are you?" Ansee taunted again. "You couldn't even stop two of us with a fireball." He let the illusion on his own bracers end, the red and black colors shining in the afternoon light. "You should give up now, since we have you surrounded."

"I think not, demon," He made a gesture with one hand and spoke a command, and then a wall of flames, at least five paces tall, erupted in a circle around Reva. She was trapped. Another wall of fire erupted in front of the entrance to the

Violet Clover, causing the few onlookers to fall back into the tavern. It wasn't like they had been much help, anyway, craning their necks to see what the commotion was, but certainly not sticking them out to offer any assistance.

The wizard sneered at Ansee. "No interference, Seeker. This will be even sweeter knowing that it's *you*. I saw you snooping around the tavern all week. Sticking your nose in places where it doesn't belong. I am on a holy mission, and only Jansure's will can stay my hand."

What is he talking about? Ansee wondered. *Who is Jansure?* Based on the wizard's fanaticism, it was clear that Jansure was some god, but Ansee had never heard of them before. *There are too many gods for me to keep track of them all.* "Your god won't help you now," he said.

The wizard flung three more missiles from the wand. Again, each of them struck harmlessly against Ansee's shield.

"I can do this all day. I think we both know who the better spellcaster is. You're just embarrassing yourself now. You're under arrest. Drop the wand before somebody really gets hurt."

"Never! No demon spawn commands me, and I will not let you continue your evil ways. You will soon surrender to me and tell me who your demon master is."

Ansee groaned. *Why can't that stupid theory just go away? It's bad enough that I hear this tripe from Norah at work.* He took a step forward, finding the balance for his dagger. "Sorcerers don't get their magic from a demon. I know *I* don't."

"More lies!"

Ansee continued to step toward the wizard, getting within ideal throwing distance for his dagger. "But you admit you did kill those sorcerers?"

"I didn't kill *sorcerers*. I killed *demon spawn* infiltrating our world to spread their evil. I killed them because they refused to repent. They refused to give up the name of the demon that gave them their power!"

Ansee licked his lips. He was playing a risky game here.

As long as the wizard continued to talk, it meant that time was running out on his shield spell. But it also meant that Willem and Kai would have time to arrive, and for the wall of fire surrounding Reva to dissipate. That would easily swing the odds into his favor. He didn't know what other surprises this wizard may have, but the teleportation magic that was found on the bodies of the other victims tickled his memory. *What had he done to them?*

"Did you ever stop to consider that they couldn't tell you because there is no demon?"

The wizard laughed, "Nice try, demon spawn. I see the lies come easily to you, but you will soon repent!"

"Drop the wand!"

Ansee looked behind the wizard, and saw Willem and Kai running up the road, their swords drawn.

The wizard turned his head and frowned as he spotted the two constables. "It seems that fate will not let me question you." He turned and pointed the wand at Willem and Kai as three force missiles flew toward the pair. They struck Willem, who flinched and stumbled, clearly in pain.

Ansee hesitated, watching the attack on Willem play out before he even thought of reacting. The wizard's attention had been on Willem, which left him open to an attack from Ansee, but by the time Ansee uprooted himself, the wizard had turned back to face him. Ansee still let his dagger fly, aiming for the wand arm to try to disarm the wizard.

It seemed that the wizard had been ready for this tactic. He made a quick gesture with his hands and spoke a single word. Yellow light flashed around the dagger, and it disappeared. Ansee looked around, and then realization literally hit him as he felt a jabbing pain in his lower back, and his dagger struck home.

Ansee's eyes watered as he reached behind him and gripped his dagger, pulling it out of his back. At the same moment, he saw the walls of flame that were surrounding Reva and blocking the entrance to the tavern fizzle out. Reva seemed to be covered in sweat, and she gestured to someone exiting the tavern, pointing toward Willem. Ansee had to ignore them and focus on the wizard. He mentally cursed himself for making such a dumb mistake.

The wizard swore. "I won't have the time to do an interrogation, but I will be satisfied with knowing that I rid the constabulary of your evil." The wizard made another gesture, fingers held just so, hands dancing. Ansee couldn't hear his words, and then felt a tingling sensation cover every surface of his body. It was a familiar sensation—he'd done this himself many times—and Ansee tried to resist, to will himself to stay where he was, but the pain in his back made it difficult to concentrate. There was a flash of brilliant yellow, and a loud POP, and Ansee was suddenly looking down on the street from high in the air. The puzzle pieces, the teleportation aura, and multiple broken bones from the victim's bodies, suddenly fell into place.

"Shit," Ansee exclaimed, as he began to fall with them.

Chapter 8

Reva was angry at herself for being caught in the blast of what had clearly been a fireball—a fireball that could only have come from their suspect. She remembered the searing heat and flame, and then nothing until she regained consciousness. It had taken her a moment to understand what had happened, then she spit out dust and a bit of blood from a split lip. When she glanced up, she saw that Ansee was facing down someone who appeared to be a wizard, at least from the black and red robes he was wearing, and the wand he was holding, which the wizard flicked toward Ansee. Three red embers of light flew straight toward Ansee. She was relieved to see them impact harmlessly against his shield spell. *That must be why he's still standing and why my ass is on the ground.*

Ansee made a gesture. From her angle, Reva saw the air in front of Ansee seem to clear up, but then shimmer as if heat was rising around him. Ansee stepped toward the wizard. "That's why you killed the other sorcerers," he said, "because of some myth that we get our magic from demons?"

Is that what this is about? Reva thought, her anger growing. People had been murdered for stupider reasons, but she hated people who forced their beliefs onto others, especially in such a violent way.

"The truth is not myth, demon spawn!" The wizard

yelled. "You defile Qurna by your very existence!" Reva could see spittle fly from his mouth.

Reva got to her feet, ignoring the bruises that throbbed on her shoulders and back. She noticed that the illusion that was covering her bracers was gone, confirming that she'd lost consciousness for at least a few seconds. Out of the corner of her eye, she could see several people standing in the doorway of the Violet Clover Tavern, craning their necks like spectators of a *hoaralle* game. It looked like only one of them, Pfastbinder, was trying to make his way through the crowd to get out the door. All the other *mighty adventurers* seemed to be content to watch from a safe distance.

Reva drew her longsword, "You are under arrest!"

"You really aren't much of a wizard, are you," Ansee said. "You couldn't even stop two of us with a fireball." Reva saw the illusion on his own bracers end, revealing the Acer Division colors. "You should give up now, since we have you surrounded," he said.

"I think not, demon," the wizard said. She saw him make a gesture with one hand and, before she could react, a wall of flames erupted in a circle around her. She was trapped, and mad at herself, again, for getting trapped like *this*.

"Shit," she spat, the spittle sizzling as it hit the flames. Sweat started to run down her face, across her neck, and under her armor. The flames were eerily quiet, adding to the surrealism since they gave off plenty of heat. It was tempting to try to jump through them, but she had no desire to test just how well her armor might protect her.

Reva was fuming. Actually, she was baking. The wall of flames that surrounded her was barely two paces away, and the heat was enough to make her feel like one of Mother's pots in her kiln. But while the heat was unbearable, what made her blood boil had nothing to do with the stupid spell.

She could follow what Ansee and the wizard were saying to each other, and that had only added to her growing anger. She hated being useless. She hated not being in control. And she hated that Ansee seemed to be *playing* with the wizard.

69

Why isn't he engaging him? He'll blast me with a lightning bolt for taking Wake, but then he takes the time to have a nice chat over a cup of cacao with a serial killer? She spat again, the saliva evaporating before it reached the flames this time.

After several seconds, Reva heard a shout from Willem—she'd recognize his voice anywhere—"Drop the wand!"

Then there were several sounds that seemed to jumble together. Cries of pain and alarm, curses, and then the wall of flames disappeared. The heat was suddenly gone, and Reva stared, open-mouthed, at the scene before her.

Ansee was reaching for something behind him, and she was shocked to see him pull a dagger—his dagger—from his back, the blade coated in his blood. At the same time, she saw Willem laying on the ground, and saw Pfastbinder finally breaking out of the door from the tavern. He gave Reva a questioning look. Reva gestured toward Willem, and Pfastbinder raced toward the Senior Constable.

The wizard swore. "I won't have the time to do an interrogation, but I will be satisfied with knowing that I rid the constabulary of your evil." Before Reva could react, she saw a yellow light surround Ansee, and then a loud POP as Ansee disappeared. She looked around to see where he might have gone, and heard the wizard laughing. He smiled and pointed up. Reva looked up to see Ansee falling from what seemed to be thirty paces in the air.

"Shit," Reva said. She saw the wizard running away and hesitated. Give chase after her suspect or... what? With Cas, this wouldn't be a problem. In the first place, Cas wouldn't have let herself get teleported like that. But she also had her feather fall spell. Cas had cast it on Reva enough times for her to know that. But Reva had no idea what sort of spells Ansee had. *Does he have something like a feather fall spell? What do I tell FC Aescel if I capture my murderer, but let one of his Seekers slam into the ground? How many of my own bones will get shattered if I try to catch him?*

As Reva hesitated, the wizard kept running, and Ansee continued to fall. "Damn it," Reva tossed her sword to the ground and ran toward the spot where it looked like Ansee was going to make a big dent in the ground. She had no idea what she could do other than share in his injury, but she had to try. Maybe Pfastbinder could put them both back together. That thought caused her to shudder.

As she ran forward, preparing to catch Ansee, a yellow light blossomed around him and there was a loud POP. He disappeared just as he was barely two paces above the ground. Reva looked around and spotted another flash of yellow that appeared directly in front of her fleeing suspect. The wizard yelled in surprise, and tried to jump out of the way, but Ansee had picked up considerable momentum from his fall. He had teleported himself, and he had somehow changed his orientation, so that he flew toward the wizard as if he had been shot from a ballista. Ansee collided with the wizard, and the pair hit the ground, rolling and tumbling before coming to rest just three paces from where Reva stood.

Reva strode forward, as Ansee roll off of the wizard. He gave a cry of pain and brought his right arm up to cradle his left shoulder. Reva heard the sound of running feet, and saw Pfastbinder, Willem, and Kai, all racing toward them.

Ansee forced himself to his feet, and Reva pointed at him. "I think he broke something," Reva said to the cleric.

Pfastbinder nodded, but Ansee shook his head, and then grimaced and said, "No, check him." He nodded his head toward the wizard.

Pfastbinder shrugged, and knelt down next to the wizard's body. The wizard hadn't moved since Ansee had rolled off him. Pfastbinder confirmed that he was dead with a shake of his head. "Sorry," Pfastbinder said, "It looks like you broke his neck. There's nothing I can do. Hells, there's nothing anyone can do unless the Constabulary is willing to spend the coin to resurrect him."

"For a murderer?" Willem asked. "Not a chance."

Reva saw Ansee start to shake, his face suddenly going pale. "Shit, shit, shit. I didn't mean to kill him. I just wanted to stop him."

Pfastbinder stepped over to Ansee and had him sit down so that he could tend to his injuries. Now that the action was over, people had spilled out of the tavern and the other shops, and they were gathering around to try to get a look at the body. Reva picked up her sword and swung it around, pointing it at an adventurer who'd gotten too close for her comfort. "Everybody back," she commanded, her glare freezing the gawkers in place. "Just give me an excuse to arrest all of you for interfering in constabulary business."

The crowd took several steps back, and Reva turned back to the body.

"It's hard to mean to do anything when you are trying to save your own life," Willem consoled Ansee.

"But now we won't know if he was working alone," Ansee started, as Pfastbinder placed his hands on Ansee's shoulder. A golden glow radiated from the spot. "Or if he killed anyone else," Ansee finished.

"Those are the breaks," Willem said, apparently unconcerned by the morbid pun that he'd just made.

Kai searched the wizard's body. "Find anything?" Reva asked.

Kai opened a pouch, and withdrew several items. He turned to show them to Reva. She could see the strange symbol that they had found on the cards from the other victims. "At least we can prove that this was our serial killer," Kai said.

Finally, some of Reva's anger started to flow away. The case was as good as closed. She took the cards from Kai and turned to Ansee. Pfastbinder was still casting his spell to heal Ansee's injury. "Don't be too worried about this murderer's death," she told Ansee. "I'm pretty sure FC Aescel will understand. You did a good job, given the situation."

Ansee gave her a quizzical look. "You're taking this rather well for having a dead suspect on your hands."

"Dead *murderer*," Reva corrected. "Besides, for once, it wasn't me who killed him."

Chapter 9

It was getting close to sunset when Reva and the others, including Alchemist Bromide and her team riding in the wagon that was carrying the wizard's body, arrived at New Port. Reva was hot and tired, her body sore from the earlier fireball, as she walked alongside. She reached into her pocket, pulled out her tin of Wake, and took a quick sniff.

"I hope you don't need this one fast," Alchemist Bromide said. "I wasn't planning to start looking at him tonight."

"No bark off my tree," Reva said. "I know what killed this one." She nodded her head to Ansee, who was walking behind her. "I just need a basic inspection from you to see if we can identify this murderer before we let him become mulch."

"Good," Thea nodded. "I will have my report ready tomorrow afternoon." She flicked the reins and guided the mules pulling the wagon toward the Feedshed.

Reva and Ansee headed into the main building, and she gave a nod to Constables Whitlocke and Solanum who were making their shift change. "The First Constable has been asking when you'd get here," Constable Whitlocke remarked.

"Apparently, it's now," Reva said with a smile. She didn't bother to hurry up the stairs. Ansee remained quiet, as he had ever since they'd begun their trek from West Gate Grove with their dead murderer.

As they entered the Acer Division Stable, First Constable

Aescel stuck his head out of his office. "Reva! Ansee! Get your asses in here!"

Reva tossed her cloak onto her table as she walked to Aescel's office.

"He sounds mad," Ansee said.

"He sounds grumpy," Reva countered. "I guess he expected to be home by now."

Aescel's door was open, and they entered the cramped space. His office had always been full of parchmentwork, but it seemed that more than the usual parchment, papers, and other detritus had taken up residence on Aescel's desk. There was no place for anyone other than Aescel to sit down, so Reva leaned against the wall.

"What in the hells happened out there?" Aescel waved an arm vaguely toward the window that looked out onto the Stable. "You were supposed to arrest your suspect, not have a magic duel with him in the middle of the damn street." He shot a glance at Ansee. "This isn't Arisport. I expect you to do your job without causing a lot of property damage or risking citizen's lives."

Reva knew that Aescel was just rustling his leaves, since he didn't like having to deal with what was naturally a messy situation. Aescel understood that messy situations happened, but they made more parchmentwork to clutter up his desk.

"What property damage?" Ansee asked, confused. Reva sighed, lowered her head, and put a hand to her forehead. "The only damage that happened was what happened to me."

"Don't argue with me, Seeker Carya," Aescel griped. "I don't like being corrected."

Ansee wisely kept his mouth shut after the rebuke. The First Constable returned his glare to Reva. "At least tell me you'll be able to get a confession from this one so that we can learn if he's working alone or with a group."

"Well... that will be a little hard to do," Reva replied, averting her eyes.

"Damn it, Reva!" Aescel smacked his hand down on his

desk. The loud SMACK caused Ansee to jump. "I can't have you conveniently killing your suspects all the time."

Reva stood up from the wall, shaking her head and pointing a finger at herself. "It wasn't me this time." She turned the finger to Ansee. "Constable Carya killed him."

Aescel turned his glare on Ansee. "Really? It seems that you're spending too much time with Reva. You're starting to pick up her bad habits."

"It was an accident. I didn't mean to kill him. His neck broke when I ran into him."

Aescel leaned back and was about to say something when Reva interrupted, "You *ran into him* from fifty paces in the air."

"What?" Aescel asked.

Ansee countered, "It was forty paces."

"Oh, so you had enough time to measure it?" Reva asked.

"I think I was in a better position to be able to tell how far I fell."

"Will someone tell me how in the hells you got fifty paces into the air?" Aescel demanded.

"It was only forty," Ansee corrected, and in return, he received a glare from Aescel that could have wilted plants. Ansee shuffled his feet before explaining what had happened after they left the Violet Clover.

Aescel remained quiet, listening to the explanation for a few minutes, before asking, "So how *did* you get into the air?"

"Well, as I said, we had him surrounded, once the wall of fire that had kept Reva bottled up had expired. He knew he couldn't fight us all, but he was determined to kill *me*." Ansee's voice was eerily calm, considering that he was talking about events that could have ended in his death.

"He did the same thing to me that he did to his other victims. We could never explain how our victims had auras for teleportation magic, and so many broken bones, like they had fallen from a tall tree or something." Aescel gave Ansee a look that told him to get to the point.

"He teleported me straight up into the air."

"Forty paces?" Aescel asked, his eyes widening.

Ansee nodded. "As I started to fall, I realized there was only one thing that I could do to save myself and try to stop our suspect, so I cast my own teleportation spell. I had to adjust the spell so that I wouldn't just appear above the wizard. You see, I needed to change the orientation of the end point of the spell so that I arrived ninety degrees off of my starting orientation. That's not as easy as it seems, since it involves a change in how the spell is cast, requiring a different set of commands for the magic."

"I don't need a damn magic lesson, Seeker. Just tell me what happened."

"I teleported so that I appeared right in front of the wizard as he was making his escape. That's when I collided with him and we both fell to the ground."

"So how did he die?"

"It seems that Ansee hit him so hard that his neck broke from the whiplash," Reva said.

"I didn't expect that I would be going that fast."

"Well, you had been falling for almost fifty paces," Reva said, with a sly smile.

"Forty," Ansee corrected again.

"Shut up, both of you," Aescel grumbled. He pointed a finger at Ansee. "That's the most absurd explanation for a suspect's death that I've ever heard, and with her," he pointed to Reva, "I've heard a lot. But if that's what happened, then I had damn well better see that explained, in full detail, in your report."

"Yes, sir," Ansee said, looking relieved.

"And I want it on my desk before you leave tonight," Aescel added. "I need to be able to explain what happened at my meeting with the LCI tomorrow."

"Yes, sir," Ansee responded, dejectedly.

"Go," Aescel commanded, and Ansee and Reva started out of the office. "Not you, Reva."

Reva stopped and crossed her arms, unaware of how defensive the gesture looked. Once Ansee had left the office,

Aescel motioned for Reva to shut the door. Reva complied, thinking that this was never a good sign.

"I'm hearing complaints from the Sucra that you are ignoring your meetings with Inquisitor Amalaki," Aescel stated.

"I'm not ignoring them. I know all about the meetings. I'm just not attending them." Reva had found the first couple of meetings to be pointless, even though they had been less aggressive than her similar meetings with Senior Inquisitor Malvaceä. But they were certainly a waste of her time when she had so much else to do.

"Damn it, Reva. Our relationship with the Sucra is strenuous at the best of times. I can't have you making it worse because you don't like them."

"That's the reason that I didn't meet with them when Malvaceä was here, but the reason that I don't meet with Inquisitor Amalaki is because he's *wasting my time*. He always wants to go over everything that we've already covered, rehashing the same thing again and again. I have more important things to do with my time." She made a gesture to the Stable. "I have plenty of cases to keep me busy without having to spend so much useless time with the Sucra."

Aescel leaned back in his chair and sighed. "Maybe that's my fault. You've been working too much lately."

"Just doing my job," Reva countered.

"You look tired, Reva."

"I'm fine."

"You're not fine." He shook a finger at her. "I'm not stupid, Reva. I know you've been working double shifts, sometimes even working days straight without a break. It's going to affect your work."

Reva crossed her arms again. "*Has it* affected my work?" She glared at the First Constable, knowing full well that it hadn't.

"No," Aescel sighed, and he picked up a quill from his desk. "But that's not an excuse," he shook the quill at her. "I need *all* of my constables to be at their peak. If you keep this up, you're going to make a mistake that could get yourself, or one of your team, hurt."

"I'm fine," Reva repeated, not realizing that she had clenched her jaw. "I don't make mistakes."

Aescel tossed the quill down on his desk. "Damn it, Reva, you're more stubborn than a tick on a warhawk." He pointed a finger at her. "I need you at your best, because we're stretched thinner than I would like right now. I'm ordering you to take the night off. Go home."

"But... what about my report for the sorcerer case?" Reva's stomach was in knots. She didn't need to go home. She wasn't going to make any mistakes. Aescel shouldn't be ordering her around like this.

"I don't care about *your* report," he gave her a small smile. "*You* didn't kill anyone, for once. You can turn it in tomorrow. Go have a night to yourself. I know it's been a while since you went to a play. Go see one. Or go take your mother to dinner."

Reva couldn't suppress the grimace that last suggestion caused. After her mother's recent attitude about how Reva was living her life, she had absolutely no desire to spend more time with her mother. She supposed she could always take some parchment and head to a secluded spot in New Port to write up her report, or at least work on another case.

"And if I catch wind that you've stayed here to work or that you've come back here before tomorrow morning, I will bust you down to night watch on the South Gate. I need you at your best. Go. Home."

Reva shrugged as she headed out of Aescel's office. He didn't have the right to tell Reva what she could or couldn't do. She was doing the best work that she'd done in months, and she certainly wasn't tired. She didn't need to take a night off. She pulled out her tin of Wake and stuck a pinch to her nose, inhaling deeply. *Aescel can order me out of New Port, but I can do other things.*

"Be sure to turn that in to Aescel tonight," Reva reminded Ansee, as she picked her cloak up off of her table.

"I know," Ansee sniped, annoyance coating his words.

"Don't snap at me. Just make sure you do *something* right today."

She swung the cloak over her shoulders and headed toward the stairs.

Chapter 10

Ansee stared at the parchment, watching the ink dry on the few lines that he had written. As he tried to organize his thoughts on the events from earlier in the day, all he could see was a flash of yellow light, the wizard appearing directly in his path, their collision, the pair of them tumbling and rolling along the road, and then coming to rest. As Ansee pulled himself off the wizard, he had known, deep in the pit of his stomach, that the wizard was dead. Seeing the wizard's body lying in the road, his neck askew at an unnatural angle, merely confirmed what he hadn't intended.

He wrote a few more words, and then stopped and re-read the few sentences that he'd managed to put onto the parchment. The wizard's final moments replayed again in his mind. He was having a hard time dealing with the elf's death and, try as he might, the image of the dead wizard just wouldn't go away.

As with the aftermath of Roya Locera's ambush, Ansee kept reliving the events, running through every step, every action, every word spoken, and every gesture made. How could he have done things differently in order to get a different outcome? What if he'd moved faster instead of keeping the wizard talking? Maybe he could have disarmed him sooner. What if he'd tried to incapacitate the wizard with his shock spell? That would have kept the wizard alive. What if he'd used a different spell to stop his fall? What spell? In the panic of the moment, he'd done something that was natural for him—he always used a teleportation spell when in danger. But what if he'd cast something else? What spell could he have cast? He had learned many different spells, most of them not in the standard RTC spellbook for use by Seekers, but he couldn't create spells on the fly. (Ansee grimaced at the unintended pun.) It took time for him to learn exactly how the magic was supposed to work before he could master any new spell.

He closed his eyes and took a deep breath, forcing his mind to go to a place of solace. It took him a few minutes, as the wizard's face refused to go away, but finally Ansee was able to picture the scene in his mind. It was a secluded spot along the north bank of the river, near the fort in Old Grove. Ansee had found the place many years ago, when he'd first moved into his apartment. He could sit there and watch the sky change colors as the sun set, the Tenz River placidly burbling along. It was a place where he could take refuge from a hectic day, and Ansee had enjoyed ending many of his evenings there when he had worked in Nul Pfeta Division, although it seemed that, ever since he had been transferred to Acer Division, he had been there only a few times. But the point was to picture a place that was calm, relaxing. It was an exercise that he had started doing to calm himself after waking from his Locera nightmares, and he'd continued to do it when those had been supplanted by nightmares about the Disciples of Dreen. Sometimes the nightmares alternated nights, giving him no reprieve from the traumatic events that had seemed to plague his life ever since he'd joined Acer Division. He'd had less excitement when he'd been stationed in Nul Pfeta Division. *Maybe I should request a transfer back,* Ansee thought. *At least I might get some sleep.*

Ansee watched the river in his mind, letting the stress of the day's events bleed off. After a couple of minutes, Ansee opened his eyes and continued his report. The image of the dead wizard didn't completely go away, but it was enough so that he could ignore it and focus on the parchmentwork.

His stomach gave a loud rumble, causing Constable Brillow to look up from his own work several tables away. He hadn't had anything to eat since breakfast, and that had only been a quick bite of bread and some tea here in the Stable as they had waited for First Constable Aescel to arrive, so that Ansee could pitch his idea about the undercover mission. He'd been so nervous that he had barely kept the bread down as he spoke. (Reva made him do all the talking. Since it was his idea, she'd wanted nothing to do with it.) He hadn't had anything to eat or drink at the Violet Clover either, unlike Reva and Willem. That had been because of nerves, as well as the fact that most of the food served at the tavern had looked decidedly unappetizing.

He thought about rushing through and turning in something that just glossed over the details and covered the highlights. Something like the constables in Nul Pfeta might turn in, or even a few of the constables here at New Port, but Ansee couldn't bring himself to do that. He was hungry, but he wasn't going to turn in a sloppy report just so he could go to dinner.

He lit an oil lamp as the daylight faded, and he finally got into a rhythm as he wrote the report, leaving no detail out. He found that, as he wrote and replayed the events, there was very little that he could have done differently that might have resulted in a better outcome. Their mystery wizard had been determined to kill Ansee—being a target was something else that had plagued Ansee's life since joining Acer Division—and Ansee realized that the ultimate outcome would have probably been the same, no matter what he had done.

He was almost done with the report when loud voices came from the stairs. "Why are you hiding up here?"

Ansee turned to see Seekers Alchemilla Kupferhedge and Ardea Hedera standing at the top of the stairs. Both were still in their uniforms, Alchemilla wearing the blue and red birch bracers of Betula Division, while Hedera was the third Seeker in Acer Division. When Ansee first joined Acer Division, Kupferhedge and Hedera had completely ignored him. Ever since the fight with the Disciples at the port last month, the two of them had started inviting Ansee out for drinks and the occasional dinner. They weren't quite friends, but they were certainly acting a lot nicer than Norah had been. They had even sided with Ansee on more than one occasion, telling Norah that she was wrong about him.

"I'm finishing up my report for the First Constable," Ansee said.

The pair walked across the Stable to hover over Ansee at his table. Alchemilla released the braid that had held her straw brown hair in place for her shift. It fell loose around her shoulders. "Come on, Ansee," she said, running her hand through her hair. "We've had the most horrible day, and we want to go blow a few leaves."

"And I know you spent all day up in West Gate Grove, so you clearly didn't eat anything while you were there," added Hedera, as he leaned his arms on Reva's table. "There's not a decent place to eat anywhere in that Grove."

"Let's go," Alchemilla prompted. "You can finish your parchmentwork in the morning."

Before Ansee could answer, there was a commotion at the top of the stairs as Constable Inspector Pflamtael and Seeker Pfinzloab entered the Stable. They'd been talking loudly, clearly in disagreement about something, but Norah quickly shut her mouth as she saw the three Seekers. The Constable Inspector turned to see why she had stopped talking, and then gave a sigh that was audible from clear across the Stable. He walked toward his table and Norah followed, glaring at their group as she stalked across the room. Pflamtael gave them a cursory nod of greeting, and continued his conversation with Norah, although in a more hushed tone. Ansee could tell that there was some tension between the two. He couldn't be sure exactly what was wrong, but the way that Norah seemed to be glaring daggers at Alchemilla and Hedera gave him a hint.

"She doesn't look very happy with the two of you," Ansee commented, keeping his voice low.

"She just can't take a joke," Hedera whispered, as he cleaned dirt from under his fingernails with a small knife.

Ansee shook his head. "What did you do this time?"

Alchemilla put a hand to her mouth in an effort to suppress a laugh, though she couldn't hide her grin. "It was nothing. Much. It was just a prank." She leaned down and whispered, "She thinks that she's better than the rest of us."

"Well, I know why she hates *my* guts," Ansee said, "but why does she hate the two of you, besides the currently obvious reason?"

"Oh, I don't know if I'd say it's strong enough to qualify as hatred," Hedera began, putting his knife away. "She just can't stand that we're breathing the same air as her. She thinks that because she graduated at the top of her class at Auros, and because she has some *very important* ancestor, that she's better than us. But, rest assured, she does hate you more since you are the *evil sorcerer*." He gave Ansee a conspiratorial wink.

Ansee sighed. "So, what did you do?"

"It was nothing really, just a prank," Alchemilla said, twirling her hair around her finger. "We just put a wizard lock on her spellbook so that she couldn't open it." Ansee stared at her, wide-eyed. "It wore off," she stated, somewhat defensively. "Eventually."

"That could be why the fair Constable Inspector is miffed at our high-and-mighty Seeker," Hedera proposed. "Since they got a pretty late start this morning."

"Well, to be fair, it took her a while to get the ink stains off her tongue, too," Alchemilla added. "You know that black tongue is a symptom of kissing a Pflamtael." She grinned, her smile wide and bright.

Ansee covered his mouth, and did his best to keep from laughing out loud. "Ink stains?"

"Ink in her tea," Hedera explained.

Ansee shook his head, "What are we, in primary school

again? I appreciate the support, but I really don't need you two defending me. I can take care of myself."

"That's not why we do these little pranks," Alchemilla countered.

"Well, it's not the *only* reason," added Hedera. Alchemilla nodded agreement. "Norah needs to understand that we, all of us Seekers, are a team," Hedera said. "We're all overworked here, and she needs to remember that. She is always using the fair Constable Inspector as an excuse—"

"Or a threat," interrupted Alchemilla. Hedera nodded and pointed a finger at her.

"To get out of all of the shit work around here," Hedera continued.

"Well, every time you two do something to her, she gets even more upset with *me*."

Hedera blew a raspberry. "Pish. It builds character."

Alchemilla pointed over toward Norah and Pflamtael. "Looks like there might be storms brewing in paradise." All three of them turned to look over at the pair. They were having an intense, albeit quiet, discussion. It appeared that Pflamtael was doing most of the talking—pleading?—while Norah just sat with her arms crossed. Finally, the Constable Inspector grabbed his cloak. With a glare at the three of them, he stalked out of the Stable. Norah continued to sit and pout.

"If she's not careful, she won't be able to stand behind her boyfriend to get out of the hard work anymore," Hedera said.

Despite the threats, accusations, and multiple attempts to get him fired, Ansee felt sorry for Norah right at that moment. "And maybe if you two eased up on her, she wouldn't continue to hold a grudge. You could take the high branches, you know."

"Where's the fun in that?" Alchemilla asked.

"Besides, she started it," Hedera said. Ansee wasn't sure if that was true or not, but he decided to not make anything about it. He didn't want to risk the new friendship that he felt he'd made with Hedera and Alchemilla.

"Now come on, set that parchmentwork aside and let's go to dinner," Hedera demanded.

"I can't," Ansee replied. "I need to finish this and turn it in to Aescel tonight or he'll have my ass."

Alchemilla looked around, "I don't see First Constable Aescel around. Just turn it in first thing in the morning, before he gets in. He'll never know."

"He'll know," Ansee and Hedera said, at the same time.

Hedera reached out and picked up the report, "Let me see, maybe I can offer you some advice, since you are still a sapling here in Acer Division. I know what Aescel wants to see in his reports."

"Give me that back," Ansee said, as he tried to grab the parchment. "I'm almost done."

"Oh, my gods!" Hedera exclaimed in a loud voice, his eyebrows raised and eyes wide. "You killed the sorcerer serial killer?" Everybody that was in the Stable at that moment, including Norah, turned their heads towards Ansee. He could feel his ears growing hot.

"I didn't mean to do it," he said, again trying to grab the report back, but Alchemilla snatched it instead and started reading.

"Oh, you *must* tell us about this over dinner. I want to know *all* the details."

"It's not finished," Ansee repeated, finally snatching the report back.

"Oh, yes, it is," Hedera said. "You write too much, and Aescel doesn't care. He gets eyestrain from reading your reports."

"No, he doesn't," Ansee replied.

"Well, he will if he reads *this* one. How do you write in such a tiny script anyway?" Hedera asked.

"Come on, I'm hungry," Alchemilla said. "I'll buy the first round if you promise to tell us what happened."

Ansee sighed. His report was done enough, and he really liked the idea of going out with his new friends. "Fine," he said, "But I get to pick the restaurant this time." He stood up to walk the report over to Aescel's office, but Hedera grabbed it from his hand.

"Allow me," he said and, with a gesture, the parchment was carried by an unseen force across the room and slid into the box that hung on the First Constable's door. "Now we can go," he nodded, tossing Ansee his cloak.

The three of them walked out of the Stable, Alchemilla already trying to pry the details out of Ansee. Norah glared at them from under a furrowed brow as they sauntered across the room. It was time to get some payback for all their childish pranks. As they descended the stairs, she stood up and walked over to Aescel's office.

Chapter 11

The evening air was crisp, and the smells from fireplaces, vendors roasting chestnuts, and the river, all blended together to fill Reva with a sense of nostalgia. She recalled nights as a child, walking with her father along the riverbank. A slight smile touched Reva's lips as she walked up the street. As she came close to Pfenestra's Playhouse, she noticed that the lamps that usually glowed brightly outside on nights of a performance were dark. There were no crowds milling outside the theater, and the small café that sat across from Pfenestra's only had a couple of patrons enjoying their meal in the cool evening air. Reva continued past Pfenestra's and walked into The Beehive. Pfletcher had a fire going in the massive fireplace in the front room in order to hold the creeping autumn chill at bay. The bar was subdued this evening, with only a dozen people in the place: mostly regulars, instead of the usual theater crowd. That suited Reva, and she walked across the room to a small table on the other side of the fireplace; close enough for a bit of warmth, but not so close that she'd melt.

She noticed that the back room, where Pfletcher would let musicians, bards, and others entertain his guests, was mostly empty, with several benches stacked on the small stage. She sneered at the sight of a small group of adventurers that had holed up at a corner table. They were huddled together, whispering quietly among themselves, a halfling giving her a curious look as she took in their group, his eyes drawn to the sword at her hip and the Acer Division bracers on her arms. Reva rolled her eyes and took a seat, purposely turning her back on the adventurers. She'd had quite enough of adventurers today.

She'd barely settled into the chair before Pfletcher appeared in front of her. It was as if he'd teleported from his usual place behind the bar, with a goblet in one hand and a bottle in the other. "It's been a while, Constable Inspector," he remarked, as he set the goblet down and poured the wine. He kept pouring, only stopping when the wine overflowed the goblet. "Oh, how careless of me," he said.

Reva let a rare smile touch her lips. "I've been busy," she said, carefully picking up the goblet and bringing it to her lips. She managed to lift it without spilling a drop.

"I think the last time I saw you was the night *Talia* opened next door. I hope you got a chance to see the play before it ended its run?"

Reva set the goblet down, a considerable amount of the wine already gone. "I did," she replied, as the goblet seemed to magically fill with more wine.

"That's good," Pfletcher nodded, as he finished refilling the goblet. "It was a good play, and I was worried that you might have missed it. I thought you might have been ill or something."

"I haven't been sick," Reva said. Pfletcher leaned back and tilted his head just a bit, giving her a critical appraisal. "What?" Reva grumbled.

"Well, if you'll forgive me, Reva, you *are* looking pretty haggard. And I usually see you at least once a week, so I figured you might have been ill, since you haven't been here in over a month."

"Nope, I'm just working a lot."

"Well, you need to tell your boss to give you some time off, or at least a night off here and there, because all this work doesn't look like it's doing you any good." He gestured around The Beehive. "It's a good thing it's quiet tonight. *Talia* ended yesterday, and Pfenestra's new play won't start for a couple of days."

Reva gave a little frown and turned her head a bit in thought, but she couldn't remember hearing what the next play was going to be at Pfenestra's. She usually knew everything about a new play before it started: who the playwright was, the actors, what sort of costumes Amaryllis had designed. It bothered her a little that she had no idea about the new play. *Have I really been working that much?*

Pfletcher seemed to sense her discomfort and said, "The new play is called *Faerie Rising* by another new playwright, A.E. Lowan, although I've heard that's just a pen name and that it was written by three women from over in Mipfae. Danitha Moraea is playing the lead character, a witch named Winter, who must use her magic to keep dark elves from infiltrating her home village. And Orem Lissanthe is playing the romantic lead, an elven knight who is protecting a dark elf princeling."

Reva raised her eyebrows at that. "Protecting a dark elf? How did they get *that* past the censors?"

"Well, I would tell you, but that would ruin the play for you. You know my policy."

Reva shook her head in amusement. Pfletcher had a close relationship with Pfenestra, and he got to see their new plays, even while they were working on them, before they opened. Pfletcher was a good critic, and praise from him had been known to turn a seemingly mediocre tale into a crowd-pleasing (and profit-making) production. He also would never spoil the play for people, insisting that, if they wanted to know what happened, they needed to go next door and pay for a ticket. Most people did.

"Let's just say that it did get by the censors and leave it at that." He crossed his arms. "And I think this one may do better than *Talia*."

Reva picked up her goblet and pointed a finger at Pfletcher. "You say that about every play, that it will do better than the one before it."

"And have I ever been wrong?"

"There was—" Reva started to say, but he cut her off.

"You know the rule, Reva. We never speak that play's name in my bar." Reva took a drink and smiled, holding out the goblet. Pfletcher obligingly refilled it.

"Well, I'll just have to see if I can get some time off, so I can go to this new one."

"Good, because you look like you could use a little relaxation." He gave her another appraisal, moving his head up and down slowly as if she was a rare jewel, or maybe a sick patient who was seeing a healer. "Make that a *lot* of relaxation."

"If I wanted this kind of criticism, I would have gone home," Reva stated, trying to sound unconcerned, but realizing that it had come out strained. "Can I get some food to go with the wine?"

Pfletcher pursed his lips, then nodded. "The usual?" he asked.

Reva nodded in reply, and he left to get her food. She took another drink of the wine, letting the woody flavors tease her tongue. A loud laugh came from behind her, and she automatically turned and glared at the table of adventurers. The halfling noticed her and gave a shrug, pointing to his companions, and then spoke to his friends. A human turned to glare at her, looking like he wanted to say something that she was sure would piss her off, so she held up her hand to flash her bracer at him and the human thought better of it. They continued their conversation, but in a more subdued mood.

She turned back to look at the bar, watching Pfletcher talk with his guests and pour drinks—none as plentiful as he gave her. But she wasn't focused on his generous portions, but on his earlier comments on how she looked, that she needed time off. *Why does everyone have to comment on how I look? Or tell me that I'm working too much? They don't know me. They don't know what I'm doing. It's none of their busi-*

ness. Everyone seemed to think they knew what was best for her. They kept butting in, trying to tell her what she should or shouldn't do, but she didn't need *anything* from them. She took another drink of the wine. This time, she barely tasted it.

A plate of food—grilled portabella mushrooms drizzled with cheese and spices, some roasted red potatoes, and butternut squash covered with a glaze of honey and cinnamon—materialized in front of her, but Reva didn't see it, or even notice Pfletcher as he stood there for a moment before he shrugged and returned to the bar.

I'm doing everything *that I want to do. I'm doing what* needs *to be done,* she told herself. *Nobody gets that. But Aavril would've understood. He* knew *me.* Reva sat back in her chair, surprised by the stray thought about Aavril. She frowned, *No, he* wouldn't *understand. He didn't know me at all!* Her hand reflexively moved to her pocket and withdrew the tin of Wake. She opened it and pulled out a pinch, lifting it to her nose. *If he really understood me, if he really knew who I was and what I wanted, then he wouldn't have lied.* She inhaled the fine powder with a sharp snort. *He'd have kept his promise, instead of abandoning me. He ran away.*

"Mind if I join you?"

Reva looked up to see someone standing in front of her table, holding a mug in their hands. She found herself frowning at the interruption, the Wake still tingling her nose. She blinked, and the person came into focus, his brown hair in a simple braid, his acorn brown eyes looking at her with concern and anticipation.

"Amalaki," Reva said, distracted by his sudden appearance and her lingering thoughts about Aavril. She gave a nod.

Amalaki pulled out a chair and sat down, setting his mug down. "You haven't touched your food," he observed. "Are you feeling alright?"

"Why does everyone have to act like my mother? Yes, gods damn it, I'm alright!" She picked up her fork, jabbed it into one of the potatoes, and shoved it into her mouth, chewing it in an exaggerated manner. She swallowed. "Happy, *Mother*?"

"Don't forget your vegetables," Amalaki replied.

Reva held her fork in a threatening manner, but that just caused him to smile, so she instead scooped up some of the squash. Despite herself, she enjoyed the flavor and realized that she was hungry. She also knew that she was being rude. While Green Cloaks, in general, probably deserved that attitude, Amalaki, at this moment, didn't. She relaxed a bit, and tried to put a smile on things.

"Sorry," she said, "I spent all day surrounded by adventurers. I guess their manners rubbed off on me."

"Well, I can certainly see how that would push anyone over the edge." Amalaki lifted his mug in salute before taking a drink.

"So, why are you interrupting my dinner?" Reva asked, as she cut into the mushroom and took a bite. It had cooled a bit, but still tasted great.

"I was passing by and noticed you here. Since you've been avoiding me at work, I thought I'd try a more direct approach."

Reva's gaze flicked to the perpetually smoky windows that lined the front of The Beehive and knew that Amalaki was lying. *I hate liars.* She pointed her fork at Amalaki. "Look, you live in Bay Grove and I know that the only reason you usually come this way is to attend a play next door." She pointed the fork at the wall that The Beehive shared with Pfenestra's. "And Pfenestra's is closed for a couple of days until her new play opens." She stared into Amalaki's eyes. "So, why are you following me?"

"I wasn't following you," Amalaki put on an air of innocence.

Reva narrowed her eyes. "Don't lie to me."

She was happy to see him lift his mug and take a drink. It was an obvious cover to show that she had struck a nerve. "I wasn't following you," he repeated, but then quickly added, "But I had asked a few of our Novices to keep an eye out and to let me know when you popped up."

"Oh, so you were *spying* on me. That's *so* much better." Reva rolled her eyes and took another bite of her dinner.

"If you hadn't kept ditching our meetings, I wouldn't have to resort to these tactics."

Reva noticed that he hadn't denied spying on her. While she should have been upset, she knew that the Sucra spied on everyone; it was in their nature. Instead, she decided to tweak Amalaki in a different way. "How sweet," she said, lifting her goblet. "You've had your underlings stalking me. I didn't know you cared so much."

The blush seemed to envelop his ears immediately. "I... wouldn't call it... *stalking*," he stammered out. He quickly took another drink. "You know," he said, regaining his composure, "with as much as you've been working, I didn't think I would need to ambush you like this."

"So, you aren't just here to see me? I'm hurt." That caused another blush.

"Would that be so bad?"

This time Reva felt her own ears start to redden. She quickly took a drink, draining the goblet in a long gulp to hide her blush. She hadn't expected that, and apparently neither had Amalaki, as he had quickly licked his lips.

"So, what do you want?" Reva asked, trying to get back onto the path. She took another bite of her meal, trying her best to show that she hadn't thought anything of his previous comment.

"Constable Acantha Sulwynd."

Reva couldn't help but roll her eyes, but she was relieved that he really *was* here to talk business. "What about him?"

"He's up to something."

"You've said that before. And like I've said before, what evidence do you have? The fact that he's still working in Nul Pfeta tells me that you have nothing, otherwise you and your fellow Green Cloaks would have whisked him off the street in the middle of the night to *chat* with him in the bowels of the Red Keep."

She saw him briefly clench his jaw. "I don't work that way."

Reva picked up her goblet, but then frowned as she realized that it was empty. She held it up to signal Pfletcher as she said, "You'll never get promoted to Senior Inquisitor with that work ethic."

"And you've never gone with your gut when you've worked a case?"

Reva stared at him, knowing that she couldn't tell him no. She went with her instincts so many times that Aescel didn't bother to call her on it when she didn't follow procedure anymore. She got results, which is what mattered. Amalaki also knew that.

Pfletcher arrived and refilled Reva's goblet. "Let me know if he's bothering you," he said, jerking his head toward Amalaki.

"Oh, *Inquisitor* Amalaki is not bothering me. He's just being a pain in the ass right now." She smiled and noticed Pfletcher's eyes going wide a bit, and a frown from Amalaki. Now Pfletcher knew that Amalaki was a Green Cloak, something that Amalaki had managed to keep a secret. Now Pfletcher would spread the word with his regulars, and they would all be more careful with what they said around Amalaki.

"Would you like a refill, *sir*," Pfletcher asked, a bit stiffly.

Amalaki nodded, keeping his eyes on Reva. "Yes, please."

Pfletcher took the mug and retreated to the bar. Reva and Amalaki continued to stare at each other, Reva with a small grin as she carefully sipped her overly full wine goblet. They remained quiet for the minute or so that it took Pfletcher to refill Amalaki's drink. The barkeep returned and set the mug down, saying, "Well, enjoy the rest of your dinner," as if he thought it would be impossible for her to enjoy anything with the Green Cloak at her table.

"That was uncalled for," Amalaki complained, taking a drink.

Reva taunted him, "Are you going to pout now? Or are

we going to talk about Constable Sulwynd?"

Amalaki looked like he wanted to chew her out for outing him to Pfletcher, but instead, he said, "There is more going on with Sulwynd. He's been meeting with others—halpblooed. If I pull him in now, it won't get us anywhere, and the rest of his network will dry up and blow away."

Reva paused with her fork halfway to her mouth. She found herself intrigued by this new information. It wasn't the evidence that she'd been insisting upon, but part of that had just been her tweaking the Green Cloaks. More specifically, Amalaki. But now she saw an opportunity. Aescel had practically told her to stop working extra shifts, so she was effectively cut off from doing extra work at New Port. (Not that that would have stopped her.) But here was a chance to do some extra work with Amalaki. Aescel wouldn't have to know, so he'd be kept happy. Plus, she wouldn't run the risk that her idle thoughts might return to Aavril.

"What do you have on Sulwynd?" she asked.

Amalaki grimaced a bit. "Not much, I'm afraid."

If this had been Senior Inquisitor Malvaceä, she would have made a snarky comment about Sucra intelligence, but she actually wanted to work with Amalaki on this. "Sometimes we start with even less," she said, smiling, but then her tone hardened. "But if you are going to work with me, then you can't keep your Sucra secrets. I get to know what you know."

"*I'm* working with *you*?" Amalaki asked, with a shake of his head. "Get this right, Reva. *You* are working with *me*," he pointed his thumb at his chest. "This is *my* case, and *I'm* in charge."

"Tell yourself whatever you want, if it makes you feel better," Reva said, patronizingly. Amalaki just snorted and rolled his eyes. "So, tell me what you have," she said.

Amalaki spent several minutes outlining what he knew and what he suspected. Reva listened, finishing both her meal and her wine. When he finished, she said, "Yeah, that is a pretty thin branch you have there, but I agree that it sounds like Sulwynd is acting suspicious. Now I understand why you've decided to not follow the normal Sucra tactics and haul him to the Red Keep. If you're right, and there *are* people controlling Sulwynd, then doing that will spook them, as well as anyone he's trying to recruit."

Amalaki smiled and held up his drink. "Now you can see my dilemma. My superiors are insisting that I do just that."

Reva smiled. "Superiors don't bother me. Mine or yours."

"I know." Amalaki smiled in return.

Chapter 12

The Red Rock Tavern was one of the few privately owned stone buildings in the city. Tenyl was known for the creative way its architects made use of trees in construction, whether it was the newer *Na Pfeta* style that was popular with many of the nobles, the more traditional Wood Elf style that was primarily found in Old Grove, or the neo-classical style that incorporated living trees along with cut lumber which was found throughout much of the city. Cut stone was typically reserved for Royal or government buildings. But Red Rock Tavern was built overlooking the deep quarry that supplied nearly all of the red-colored limestone that was used in the Royal buildings, and the original owner had merely collected the scrap stone and cast offs from the quarry to build the tavern.

It was a sturdy building, with three large rooms where patrons could mingle and drink. There was a large flagstone patio that overlooked the quarry. During the summer, it would be full of guests enjoying a late meal and some drinks, but there was a definite nip in the air tonight, and the patio was empty, as all of the patrons were inside being warmed by the roaring fires in the half dozen fireplaces. And the alcohol.

Constable Sulwynd had grabbed a corner chair at one of the two bars when he'd arrived, giving him a good view of the largest of the three rooms. A pair of musicians were playing lively tunes and telling bawdy jokes between songs, entertaining the large crowd. A group of patrons was playing stars in one corner, throwing the sharpened star-shaped weapons at a wooden target. They were so drunk that most of the stars merely bounced off the wood and landed on the floor, which prompted much laughter from all of the players. In the corner of the room, Sulwynd glowered at a bulky human who was challenging anyone who wanted to try their luck at arm wrestling. This was supposed to be an elven bar, but nobody else seemed to be upset by the human's presence.

Sulwynd drained the last of his plum brandy and set his glass down. The barkeep, a young elf with skin art of trees and dragons on his arms, wasn't too busy and would have gladly refilled his drink, but Sulwynd turned to the young, and quite attractive, waitress standing to his left. He reached down and gave her behind a squeeze, laughing as she squeaked in surprise. "Get me a refill, love."

She leaned into his hand, encouraging him to give her another squeeze, which he did. She smiled, and then turned to the barkeep. "Allyn," she called above the din. When Allyn turned to her, she pointed to Sulwynd's empty glass. Allyn nodded, and she then patted Sulwynd's leg. "Happy now?"

"I'm always happy when you're working, Sylvie," he said.

Sylvie smiled, tossing her blond braid over her right shoulder. She pushed a slim finger into his chest, "Then you better leave a good tip this time. I don't care if Allyn gives you your drinks for free. I have bills to pay. And if you want to keep squeezing this," she tapped her rear, "then I need to see some Skips."

Sulwynd pulled a couple of silver coins from his pouch and held them up. Sylvie smiled and held out her hand, but he reached over and dropped them into the top of her blouse, letting his hand rub against her breast as he did so.

Sylvie scowled as she reached in and withdrew the coins. "You cheeky bastard," she said, but she smiled as she put the coins into a pocket on her breeches. She turned and picked up a couple of drinks from the bar, and then headed into the crowd.

Sulwynd picked up his refilled drink, saluted her re-treating form, and then took a drink. He couldn't understand why Gallwynn wanted to chase halpbloeds when there were plenty of pure elven beauties that could be had. And he'd had Sylvie, though he'd only slept with her the one time. He had to see what he could do to convince her to do it again.

Thinking of Gallwynn brought back the memory from his interaction with Cedres from that morning. He wondered when he would be given more information on what his mission with the halpbloed was supposed to be. He understood the necessity for secrecy, but he was getting tired of dealing with the damn halpbloeden. He'd been promised that he would be moved from Nul Pfeta once the mission was finished. He knew the mission, whatever it was, was important, but he was getting sick and tired of Nul Pfeta, and especially dealing with Cedres.

He took a drink, finishing off the brandy, and scanned the crowd. Cedres was such an idiot, thinking that he was anything like Sulwynd or other elves. The moron just couldn't understand that he would never be accepted as a real elf. He had been marked by royal decree, and that mark would stick with him for his entire life, no matter how hard he tried to convince himself, or others, otherwise. As far as Sulwynd was concerned, Cedres deserved what he got. He was so full of himself, thinking that he was better than the rest of the filth that was crammed inside Nul Pfeta's borders. Again, he wished his orders would come soon so that he could complete the mission. Despite not knowing what he was supposed to do, he had no concerns about his ability to complete the mission. He'd get it done. His only concern was that Cedres might survive whatever was being planned. Sulwynd really hoped that, whatever the mission was, Cedres would get what he deserved.

The musicians finished their latest song and started telling another one of their jokes. The crowd grew quiet as they described the woman and the man in the joke, each musician interrupting the other with some detail or tidbit. When they finished, Sulwynd laughed along with the rest of the crowd, doing his best to picture the scene, and wondering if he could convince Sylvie to try that. He turned around to face the bar, about to ask for another refill, when he noticed that a full glass of brandy had been placed in front of him, a green ribbon tied around the glass.

"About time," Sulwynd said to himself. He removed the ribbon and dropped it to the floor, where it would get lost among the other trash. He picked up the glass and downed the brandy, the liquid burning the back of his throat. He set the glass down and stood up, looking toward the back of the tavern where a door led to the outhouses. He slipped his way through the crowd, spotting Sylvie and blowing her a kiss. She laughed and rubbed her fingers together, signaling that she wanted more coin. He considered it for a moment. If things went well, he might consider it as a way to celebrate.

He continued to make his way to the back but, just before he reached the hallway that would take him to the outhouses, he slid into a booth. The candles that were normally lit had been blown out, casting the booth in shadow, but Sulwynd knew who had summoned him.

"She seems like an attractive woman," Grand Inquisitor Agera stated. He was wearing an undyed shirt of simple cotton and a dark brown cloak with the hood pulled up so that his face was in shadow. He looked like anyone but who he really was, which was the point, after all.

"She is," Sulwynd said, before realizing his mistake. *Shit.* Never give the Grand Inquisitor information that he could use against you. He knew that even a simple slip up, like admitting that he found a woman attractive, was enough for Agera to store the information away to be able to use it as leverage against him should the need arise. Sulwynd tried to calm himself with the knowledge that he would never give Agera any reason to use that sort of leverage.

"And you seem to be enjoying your evening," Agera continued, as if he'd not really heard what Sulwynd had said. But the Grand Inquisitor pulled in information and knowledge like a spider pulled in flies to its web. Agera *had* heard him and *had* stored the tidbit away to recall it whenever the need arrived.

"It's the only way that I can get the stench of Nul Pfeta out of my nose," Sulwynd groused.

"Yes, I can see how the smell of piss and stale alcohol would wipe the smell of the halpbloeden away."

Sulwynd smiled, but then wondered if the Grand Inquisitor was making fun of him. He probably was, but he dared not say anything. He valued his life too much for that.

"Have you a group ready for me?" Agera asked.

Sulwynd paused for the briefest of moments, and then said, "No. Not yet." Agera didn't move, and Sulwynd couldn't see the Grand Inquisitor's eyes, but he could feel the glare of disapproval crawling on his skin. "I do have one halpbloed," Sulwynd added quickly. "He's ready to play *hoaralle*, but he's having difficulty getting others to join him."

"What seems to be their problem?" Agera asked, in a calm voice. There was no anger, no disappointment in the words, but Sulwynd was even more nervous because of that.

He licked his lips, having found that they had suddenly gone dry. "They, uh, they seem to be afraid to join a group without knowing what the reward will be," he said, anger now giving him a bit of confidence. He leaned forward and whispered, "They're typical halpbloeden. They refuse to do anything unless you kick 'em or pay 'em, and even then, they'll complain and whine the whole time they do the work."

"You know," Agera began; Sulwynd could almost hear the smile in the words. "According to the Purity Laws, *you* are just as much a halpbloed as those that are scraping out an existence in Nul Pfeta."

Sulwynd could feel his blood boil as he hissed out in a loud whisper, "*I am not*! I am *nothing* like that *filth*!" He leaned back and looked around to make sure that his little outburst, as quiet as it had been, hadn't drawn any unwanted attention.

"I'm a *pure* elf," he said, with pride. "I have the blood of the elves and the Underforest running through me. I am more elven than even these idiots in this tavern." He leaned forward again, placing one arm on the table. "Those halpbloed in Nul Pfeta have been tainted by human blood. They are mongrels; they're no better than sheep."

Agera also leaned forward. Sulwynd could now see his pale green eyes as they bored into him. "Then why haven't you gotten them corralled?" he asked in a low, menacing tone that caused a shiver to run up Sulwynd's spine. "Why haven't you gotten them ready to execute my plan?"

Sulwynd swallowed, finding that now his mouth had gone dry. He wished that he had a drink in front of him, and he clenched his hands together to grasp for something that was not there.

"Need I remind you," the Grand Inquisitor said, somehow putting even more menace into his words, "of what happened the last time that someone messed up my plans?"

Sulwynd's stomach twisted into a tight knot of acid, and his blood seemed to stop moving. He remembered what had happened. He didn't know what Senior Inquisitor Malvaceä had been working on, but he knew that Malvaceä had failed Agera. Malvaceä had been exiled from Tenyl for his failure and, if the rumors Sulwynd had heard from the others were true, Malvaceä was lucky that had been the only thing that had happened. After that, their meetings had been moved, no longer held in the secret chamber beneath Pfeta fey Orung. Now their meeting places constantly moved, never being held in the same place twice, and nobody seemed to know if Malvaceä would ever be allowed to return to the fold.

"No, sir," Sulwynd responded, the words sounding raspy in his dry throat.

Agera gave a nod and leaned back, the cowl on his cloak again hiding his features. He reached a hand into the folds of the cloak and withdrew a small black felt pouch and a folded sheet of parchment. He placed them both on the table. "This is the basics of the plan that I need you to set up. Timing is important for us to pull this off, and I need you to make sure that the halpbloed will play their part. Their involvement is critical to the overall success of my plan." He slid the pouch and parchment across the table. "I am counting on you to make sure that they do not fail."

"Yes, sir," Sulwynd replied. His fear had been replaced with anticipation and excitement. Finally, things were moving forward. He was closer to getting his reward, closer to watching Cedres and the other halpbloed get what was coming to them. He still didn't know what Agera's plan was, but he was sure the halpbloed would suffer. He would make sure that happened, no matter what.

He reached out to grab the pouch and paused, as Agera asked, "When are you meeting with the halpbloed next?"

"The day after tomorrow. My contact has promised to get a small group of halpbloed together by then." Sulwynd knew enough to not share names with Agera. The Grand Inquisitor kept everything compartmentalized in order to reduce the risk of information getting out. That included himself. He had no need to know who Sulwynd was going to use, he only needed to know that they would do what needed to be done.

"Good. Make sure you hold them to their promise. I will not accept failure."

"Yes, sir."

"Make sure they understand what must be done. I don't care what you tell them, but they must be ready to act when I give the word."

Sulwynd wanted to know when that would happen. How much time did he have to get this set up? But he also knew that Agera wouldn't tell him. Not yet. He didn't need to know that information yet, and sharing it now would be a risk that Agera wouldn't want to take.

"We'll be ready," Sulwynd promised. He still didn't know what the plan was, but he couldn't say anything else.

"Good. *Reis naeht*, Constable." The Grand Inquisitor

slipped out of the booth and headed toward the back door.

Sulwynd picked up the pouch, feeling some coins within. He set it aside and picked up the parchment, unfolding it. He squinted in the dim light of the booth and read the plan, his eyes widening, and a smile forming on his lips. It was time to spend a few Skips to get Sylvie to leave with him for the night.

Chapter 13

First Constable Malys Aescel waved a greeting at Constable Whitlocke as he pulled open the door to New Port. A gust of cold morning air came in with him, blowing his hair into his face. "*Reis hoestii*, Constable," he said, pulling the hair back.

"Good morning, First Constable," Whitlocke replied. She gave a noticeable shiver. "Seems like the summer heat has finally left us for good."

The First Constable nodded. "I noticed several trees starting to turn this morning. We should have some wonderful autumn colors here soon. A nice change from this summer."

Malys headed up the stairs, his thoughts returning to what needed to be done today, instead of the city taking on the red and golden hues of autumn. Today was the weekly meeting with the other First Constables and Lord Constable Inspector Betulla, and he had several cases to review before the meeting. Reva's sorcerer serial killer case was closed now, but she had a burglary and another unnatural death that she was investigating, plus the old gingerbread murder investigation that had resurfaced after having gone quiet for a month. Olwyn had a pair of burglaries, an assault, and a sexual assault. Shawna had a break in with assault, her own burglary case, a floater, and an apparent kidnapping. None of that included what might have happened overnight.

He walked across the Stable, nodding greetings to the constables. He noticed that Constable Inspector Kiliaopii— Shawna—was already here, along with Seeker Hedera, but his other Inspectors and their respective Seekers seemed to be absent. Not an unusual occurrence, especially with their caseloads, but it was still frustrating. He liked to give his constables the freedom to go wherever the cases took them; the work that Acer Division did was not as repetitive or mo- notonous as what happened in Betula or Nul Pfeta Divisions, but that didn't keep LCI Betulla from accusing him of letting his constables run amok, as if he had no control over them. But his constables got results, and it was hard for the LCI to argue with that.

Aescel opened his office door and pulled out the stack of reports from the box that hung next to it. He tossed the pile of parchment onto his desk, and then hung up his cloak before sitting down. He started going through the reports, looking for the neat, exceedingly small handwriting that belonged to Seeker Carya. He didn't see it, so he flipped through the reports again, thinking that he had missed it. No, it wasn't there.

He leaned back in his chair and looked out the window that was set in the top half of the Stable door. He saw that Olwyn and Seeker Pfinzloab had arrived, though apparently still in the peak of whatever lover's quarrel they were having. He sighed, wondering, not for the first time, if he shouldn't have put a stop to that relationship sooner. They'd kept it discreet, though that also meant that everyone in the divi- sion knew they had been seeing each other. It was not neces- sarily a bad thing, and it certainly was not against the rules for constables to date each other, but deep down, Aescel felt sorry for Seeker Pfinzloab's husband.

He sat up and went through the other reports, review- ing them to see what progress was being made on some of the cases. Not a lot, though it looked like Shawna and Hedera had managed to close their floater case. They hadn't found out who the victim had been, or any evidence that might have said that it had been anything other than another tragic suicide. Still, it was a closed case. Sometimes, that's all that mattered.

He looked up and saw that Seeker Carya had shown up. He was hanging up his cloak and heading over to the tea nook where Senior Constables Ghrellstone and Abasata were already hanging out.

Malys stood up and prepared himself. He had an image to keep up. He stepped out of his door. "Seeker Carya!" He yelled across the Stable. "Get your ass over here!"

Ansee jumped, and everyone in the Stable stared at him as he turned and walked toward Malys's office. Malys didn't wait, but returned to sit down at his desk. It didn't take long before Seeker Carya stood in the doorway and gave a salute.

"You wanted to see me, sir?"

"You know, Seeker Carya, I sort of expect this kind of thing from Constable Inspector Lunaria, but I thought you knew better."

Seeker Carya looked confused. "Excuse me, sir?"

"Do you want to explain why you didn't complete your report for the sorcerer killer," Malys leaned forward in his chair and raised his voice just a bit, "like I explicitly told you to do?"

"But... but, I *did* complete it," Seeker Carya said. "I was here late finishing it up." He gestured toward the Stable, "Hedera and Kupferhedge can confirm it. They saw me put it into your box."

Malys narrowed his eyes. He had learned over the years to read his constables, to know when they were being straight with him, and when they were lying. Seeker Carya had only been here for a couple of months, but he was easier to read than some of the others. He was lying about something, but he didn't think that it was about the report. Or at least about completing it.

Malys pointed to the stack of parchment on his desk. "Well, it wasn't in my box this morning. Everyone else seems to be able to follow my instructions. Why can't you?"

"But I... it was *there*. It was in your box before I left last night. I *swear*."

"Swearing is CI Lunaria's thing, not yours." He paused and gave Seeker Carya what he considered to be his fatherly look. "Look, Ansee, I know that this is the first time you've messed up like this."

"But I *didn't* mess up," Ansee pleaded. "My report *has* to be there. Maybe it fell out of the box and got kicked someplace." He started to turn around, looking at the floor. "Did you look?"

"Seeker Carya," Malys ordered, "Stop acting like an idiot. Your report is not here, like I instructed you to do. Like I said, this is the first time that this has happened, so I'm willing to let this pass, as long as you can have the report to me this morning."

Ansee looked like he was about to hyperventilate, but then his shoulders sagged when Malys gave him the reprieve. "Fine, I'll have it to you before lunch."

Malys shook his head. He was willing to give his constables a second chance, but he did have a reputation to uphold. "No, I need it in my hands by the time I get back from my meeting with the LCI." Ansee's eyes widened. "If you can't do that, then I will be forced to dock your pay."

Seeker Carya stood still for a moment, stunned. "Do you understand?" Malys asked.

Ansee nodded his head. "Yes, sir."

"Good," he made a shooing motion with his hand. "Then get out and start writing."

Seeker Carya's shoulders slumped as he headed out of the office, clearly angry at the situation. Malys didn't give it any more thought. Ansee would complete the task, or he wouldn't, Malys wouldn't hold his hand, and he wouldn't give him any leeway that he wouldn't give the rest of his staff.

Malys went through the other reports from his box, making a few notes in a bound notebook. One of the constables brought in a mug of tea that Malys ignored for several minutes as he finished reviewing the morning parchmentwork, and then started in on the other reports that were stacked on his desk. He lifted his head at a knock on his door, and saw Constable Whitlocke standing there.

"She's ready now, First Constable," she said. She didn't wait for a response, and just returned to her duties.

Malys stood up and picked up his tea. It had grown cold, but that allowed him to down half of the mug in a single gulp. He set the mug down, picked up his notebook and a pencil, and then took the back stairs up to the second floor. He headed to Betulla's office, and nodded to Senior Constable Calendula, Betulla's aide, before walking into the LCI's office.

The Lord Constable Inspector was already seated at the table that sat next to a large window that was set within a dormer that looked out onto the New Port courtyard and the rest of the city beyond. Next to the LCI sat First Constable Marissa Pueraria. The LCI had hand-picked Marissa to take over her position at Nul Pfeta Division, and it hadn't been for Marissa's talent as a constable. Marissa had been the inspector in Nul Pfeta working under Betulla, and had long ago succumbed to Betulla's charm and influence. It was only natural that Betulla would reward Marissa for her unwavering support, and Marissa continued to support everything that the LCI suggested or did.

Marissa wore a constabulary uniform with orange bracers trimmed in blue, the Nul Pfeta pinecone embossed in the center, while the Lord Constable Inspector wore a dark green jacket with gold braid embroidered on the sleeves over a pale green blouse. The LCI had her Pfeta fey Orung badge pinned to the lapel of her jacket. The pair had been talking as Malys had walked in, but they quickly grew quiet. "*Reis hoestii*, Lord Constable," he greeted Betulla. She gave a smile and returned the greeting as he sat down. "Good morning, Marissa," he said. The smile she gave him was pinched. Malys wondered what had rustled her leaves, but then decided that he really didn't care. He had no time for the petty politics that Marissa and Betulla seemed to enjoy so much. An uneasy silence hung over the room as they waited for First Constable Churlsleaf to arrive.

"*Reis hoestii*," boomed First Constable Churlsleaf, as he finally sauntered in and closed the door to Betulla's office. He carried a mug of tea and a notebook, and he took the last seat at the table. A small frown crossed the LCI's face. When Gania had been the Lord Constable Inspector, prior to her murder, she had tried to keep these meetings casual and informal. Gania felt that familiarity and friendliness built a rapport among her constables. She didn't stress about when the meetings started, or how long they went, and there were no formal topics. Most of the meetings would start haphazardly, with a lot of small talk being made before discussing the important business of running the constabulary. Betulla had always bristled at the informality of those meetings, and had insisted on keeping her meetings formal affairs, starting with her meetings beginning on time.

"Let's get started," Betulla said, with a trace of annoyance in her voice, but not bothering to point out Lhoren's transgression. That immediately put Malys on alert, as Betulla always enjoyed focusing on the petty transgressions of those around her. She turned to First Constable Pueraria and nodded to her, "Please get us started, Marissa."

"Inspector Touradoor is making progress on the counterfeiting ring. We hope to make arrests on that in the next week." The LCI nodded her head at that. Counterfeit potions had been flowing into circulation, creating resentment among the city's wizards, and resulting in loud, and progressively more vehement, calls from Auros Academy for something to be done.

"We are starting to see evidence that goods are being smuggled into the Grove through Salicae Woods, bypassing the tax collectors on the bridge." Marissa turned to look at Churlsleaf. "And I'm not seeing any support from your constables, Lhoren," she said, her bitterness clear.

"My constables have been over every square hand in that area, and they've seen no evidence of smuggling."

"Then they must be blind," Marissa spat. Malys saw Churlsleaf bristle at the accusation.

"Do you have any concept for how big of an area the woods take up? Maybe if your constables could find where these goods are appearing in Nul Pfeta then we might have more luck."

"We've given you everything we have on these smugglers. You just need to throw more constables at this."

Lhoren laughed. "And where shall I pull them from, Marissa? Shall we let the pickpockets ravage the nobles at Ilvalé Arena? Or let the thieves' guilds have their way in the port?"

Marissa's lips formed into a pout, and she turned to Betulla for support. "Unfortunately, First Constable Churlsleaf is correct here," the Lord Constable said. "We have been asked to provide an extra presence around the arena with the start of the *hoaralle* season. He will already be spread thin to provide extra constables for the games."

Marissa looked like she had just drunk a cup of buttermilk. "We will see what we can do to narrow down where the smugglers are coming from in Salicae Wood, then," she said, clearly unhappy with the way things had gone. Malys couldn't tell if she was mad at Churlsleaf for not being able to give assistance, or mad at Betulla for not supporting her.

They spent the next half hour going over everything else that was going on in each of the divisions. They covered ongoing cases being investigated, what the Betula Division constables had been seeing and hearing on their patrols, what requests the Sucra had been making (Malys had to continue to dance around this issue, since Reva hadn't been meeting with Inquisitor Amalaki), and how the magistrates had been ruling on cases that had been brought before them. Betulla normally interjected her opinions and criticism during this review, but today she was subdued and seemed distracted.

When they finished and Churlsleaf started to discuss the budget, the LCI interrupted. "I want to discuss another issue before we talk about the budget."

Malys and Churlsleaf exchanged a glance, while Marissa perked up, clasping her hands in front of her in eager anticipation.

"I've been reviewing our arrest reports and cases, as well as talking with several members of our community. I think that our Inspectors are starting to stagnate, and are not getting enough valuable experience. They are promoted within a division and never move from that position; they never get any experience beyond that limited exposure. And what they do learn is often tainted by a closed culture that is unwilling to learn from new experiences. The same goes for the Seekers."

Malys felt his stomach do a bit of a flop. He didn't like where this was going. He was open to change, to seeing how things could be done better, especially if it could help catch more criminals. That didn't sound like what Betulla was talking about.

"I am also concerned about a growing familiarity between Inspectors and Seekers."

What does she mean by that? Malys asked himself. *Is she referring to Olwynn and Norah?*

"I am hearing rumors that cliques are forming among the Inspectors and Seekers, keeping other Constables from gaining valuable experience because they are pushed away. All of this is leading to a breakdown in morale."

It was clear to Malys what the LCI was after now, and what surprised him wasn't that Betulla was attempting to split up Inspectors and Seekers—specifically Reva and Ansee—but that she would be willing to take such a drastic action that would disrupt how the constabulary operated on a day-to-day basis.

"I think," Betulla said, her gaze touching on each of them, "that we need to split up the partnerships between the Inspectors and Seekers and reassign them to different divisions, so that we can remove these dangerous cliques, allowing them to gain new experiences and learning to work with others."

"That's a great idea," Marissa said. "We need new opportunities for our Constables."

"Are you crazy?" asked Lhoren, earning him a sharp glare from both Betulla and Marissa. He didn't care. "The Inspectors won't like it. You will end up with a revolt on your hands."

"They don't have to like it," Betulla said. "They just need to do their damn jobs and what they are told to do."

"It's not just that the Inspectors and Seekers won't stand for such a move," Malys said. "It takes time for the partnerships between Inspectors and Seekers to really coalesce, to build trust. Splitting them up will break that trust."

Churlsleaf nodded his head, grasping what Malys was saying. He picked up the thread. "Breaking up these partnerships will cause problems, as the Inspectors and Seekers try to adjust to each other. You can't expect them to start working together and have that bond just *be* there."

"It will also lead to a decrease in arrests," Malys continued. "And that is something that the mayor will notice." He caught a glare from Marissa as he invoked the office of the mayor, but Malys didn't care. It was the truth, and he wouldn't let the LCI ruin the efficiency of his division just because she had a petty grudge against Reva. Because that was what this entire mess was all about, after all.

"Don't exaggerate, Malys," Marissa said. "We've always had Inspectors and Seekers being split up and reassigned."

"Then why do we need this crazy plan to shake all of our branches, then?" Churlsleaf asked. That earned Marissa a glare from Betulla. The LCI leaned back in her chair and brought a finger up to her chin. Malys could see the gears turning behind her green eyes. A thin smile crept across her lips.

"Certainly, we don't want to do anything that would interfere with our mission to keep this city safe." She got nods from Malys and Churlsleaf.

"But there is merit in giving more experience to our Constables," said Marissa. She'd said it so smoothly, and quickly, that Malys wondered if this is what they had been discussing before he'd arrived at the meeting. Had Betulla anticipated how this meeting would go? It seemed like an unusual amount of foresight for the LCI, who was usually more concerned with forcing her will upon others.

"What do you suggest?" Betulla asked. Malys now was certain that they had rehearsed this, and he wondered if he and Churlsleaf had just jumped into the pit trap that had been prepared for them by Betulla.

"Well, what about the other Constables?" Marissa asked. "I've spoken to many Constables who feel they are not getting opportunities for advancement. They are assigned to one division and resent that they are not afforded the chance to move to a different division in order to gain new experiences. It makes it hard to get noticed, and even harder to advance to become an Inspector."

"So, instead of splitting up the Inspectors and Seekers, we should move around the Senior Constables and Constables?" Betulla asked, a little too innocently.

"Exactly," Marissa said. "This will be valuable experience, so that they are ready for promotions when they become available. It also has the added advantage of allowing the Inspectors and Seekers to work with different Constables. They will benefit from new perspectives by working with different people."

"I think this is an excellent idea," the LCI said. "It will give necessary experience to our Constables, making them more ready for promotions," she said, with a nod. "And it has the added benefit of having the Inspectors work with new Constables."

Malys didn't like what he was hearing, but he couldn't understand exactly what Betulla was after. He could understand why the LCI would want to break up the Inspectors and Seekers, as that was a petty move to get back at Reva, and to keep any single Inspector from becoming too popular and gaining too much influence. He could see the merit to what they were suggesting, even though the way that

Betulla had maneuvered everything suggested that this had been her ultimate goal. On its own merit, it was a reasonable suggestion, but the way that it had come about gave off a bad smell to Malys. So why had she made such an elaborate effort? *What is Betulla really after?*

"This sounds like a reasonable idea," Churlsleaf said, a note of caution in his voice. "I think we can put a small team together from each division to make suggestions on who to reassign."

A small kernel of doubt still nagged at Malys, like a bit of food stuck between his teeth, but he couldn't put his finger on what was bothering him. With Churlsleaf coming out in favor of this plan, he also had to support it, if he wanted to avoid getting on Betulla's bad side. If he knew what the problem with this idea was, he might be willing to walk out onto that branch, but doing it now, without justification, would only put his position at risk. He had never had any desire to sit in the LCI's chair, but he saw it as his duty to make sure that his Constables succeeded. That was the sign of a great leader, to develop the people that worked under them so that they could succeed and advance beyond their leader. It was something he had seen LCI Gania do to develop the Constables under her. Betulla had never shown that kind of leadership. She was petty and vindictive, and if he pushed too much here, she might retaliate against him. That would put his Constables at risk.

"I think we can get this enacted in the next few weeks," Malys said, adding his support to the idea.

Betulla shook her head. "This needs to happen sooner. We take too long to change things around here, and I don't want to delay on this. It will be a waste of time to get people from each of the divisions together, and there's no guarantee that they will make a decision at all. That's the problem around here." She poked the table with one finger. "I want the reassignments made by the end of today, so that the Constables can start in their new positions tomorrow."

"But that's impossible," said Churlsleaf. "You can't

change up the Constables and Senior Constables on that short a notice. It will be chaos."

"Nonsense," Betulla scoffed.

"We'll start small," Marissa said, and again, Malys thought that this had been set up for her to sound reasonable. "We can just move a couple of Constables from each division to start with. That way we can see how everything will work before rolling it out to the entire constabulary."

Betulla was nodding her head. "See, we don't need to spend weeks figuring this out. Marissa and I will put some names together to get this started. We can make the announcement this afternoon. We can then get your group together," she gave a glance at Churlsleaf, "and start deciding who else we should move as we evaluate these first reassignments."

Malys found himself reluctantly nodding his head along with Churlsleaf. Betulla had outmaneuvered them, and he knew that he'd lost any chance to sway the decision. Her mind was made up, and he was sure that she and Marissa already had a list of names. He could push back, to argue about which names would be chosen, but it wasn't worth the energy to fight that battle. Lhoren must have felt the same way, since he also kept quiet.

"Now that that's settled, let's see what Pfen are left in our coffers this month," Betulla said, with a smile. She'd gotten exactly what she had wanted, though Malys still didn't know exactly what it was.

Chapter 14

Reva walked across the Acer Division Stable, her boots squelching and leaving wet footprints behind on the floor. She hefted a sack that she was carrying and tossed it onto her table, followed by a dagger. It landed with a dull thud, with bits of mud and grass falling off. Ansee looked up from what he had been working on, and he waved his hand in front of his nose, disgustedly.

"What did you get into?"

"Nymph Creek," she said, taking off her cloak. "Near the bridge along Tolan Highway. That's where I found *that*." She pointed to the dagger.

"Our murder weapon?" Ansee asked.

"I sincerely hope so. Otherwise, I got soaked for nothing." Reva sat down, moved the dagger aside, and opened the sack. She had spent the morning going back over the crime scene for a possible homicide of a shopkeeper in Forest Grove. It had been an unnatural death, something that had merited at least a cursory investigation by the constabulary. Two days ago, when they had first been called to the shop to investigate the death, Reva hadn't been sure if it was a murder or not. It had looked like an accident; the body of the weaver's assistant had been found under a heavy bookcase that had fallen, cracking the woman's skull. The weaver had been distraught, and had called the constables right away, showing concern, lamenting the tragedy that such a thing could happen.

But Reva had her doubts—she always did—and had insisted that Thea take the body to confirm the cause of death. The Alchemist had checked the body, which was when she had found a stab wound, right in the victim's back. The injury had been covered up by the damage from the falling bookcase, but it was clear that the bookcase had not been the cause of death.

"What about the weaver?" Ansee asked.

"He wasn't there."

"Did he flee?"

"I hope not," Reva replied, starting to sort through the items in the sack; it was the evidence that she had collected at the weaver's shop that morning. "But the place hadn't been cleaned up since we were there the other day. I gave a description to the Birches working in Forest Grove so they can keep an eye on the place."

"Any idea why he might have killed his assistant?" Ansee asked.

"We don't know if it was him, or if it was someone else. I do know that our victim was pregnant," Reva stated. "Thea confirmed that she was with child yesterday. My guess is that it was the weaver's child."

"So maybe it was the weaver's wife? Killing her husband's lover?"

Reva nodded, "That's one possibility," she agreed, as she pulled out a parchment from the sack. She held it up for Ansee. "But our victim was also blackmailing someone."

"Oh, what a tangled web," Ansee commented, earning a snort from Reva.

"What are you working on?" she asked.

"My case notes from our gingerbread killer."

Reva felt her hands clench, and she furrowed her brow as she glared at Ansee. "Just now? You were supposed to do that this morning so that you could interview the witness today."

"I can still get the interview done," Ansee snapped.

"You were supposed to do it this morning! That way we could go over what they saw before we went back to question Zingiber this afternoon. I needed you to do one simple thing, and now our whole afternoon will be wasted. What in the hells were you doing instead?"

"I was rewriting my case notes from the wizard fight."

Reva stared at him, "Why did you have to rewrite them?" Ansee still wasn't up to the same standard that Cas had been, but in the brief time she had been partnered with him, Reva knew that he was meticulous about his reports. Sometimes too meticulous; she got eyestrain trying to read his tiny script.

"Aescel never got them. I wrote them up yesterday and turned them in before I left, just like he asked me to do, but he never got them. He said they weren't in his box this morning. He gave me until he was done with his meeting with the LCI this morning to get them done."

"And did you?"

Ansee hung his head. "No. And he docked me a day's pay because of it."

Reva was angry, but she didn't know who to be angry at. Ansee for messing up and having to redo his work? Aescel for insisting on a report that wasn't that urgent, just to make one of his points? Or whoever took Ansee's report, because Reva knew Ansee well enough to know that if he said that he turned it in last night, he did. The whole thing was a mess, and it would now cause a delay in her investigation just when she was hoping they might be able to make a breakthrough. Since she couldn't focus her anger on any one person, she pulled out her tin of Wake and took out a pinch.

"Well, hurry up so we can get that witness interviewed today," she grumbled, dusting the few specks of Wake that remained on her fingers onto her breeches. "I want to be able to talk with Zingiber tomorrow."

She stared at the sack of evidence and the dagger, but she couldn't focus on that right now. Her mind was racing through the gingerbread case, as well as whatever events that had conspired to make her lose a day on that investigation. She had closed it a month ago, without finding out who their killer was, but also thinking that it was an isolated incident. But the body they had found three days ago, his stomach filled with raw gingerbread dough, had forced Aescel to order her to reopen the case.

Willem walked up to her table, holding out a mug of something to her. "You look like you could use something to drink."

"Does it have alcohol in it?" she asked.

"Nope. Only the finest tea that was brewed two days ago and left to sit in the kettle," Willem replied.

Reva shook her head and held up a hand. "No thanks."

Willem shrugged as Kai walked up, sipping from his own mug and making a face in the process. "Anyone know what this meeting is about?" Willem asked.

"What meeting?" Reva and Ansee asked simultaneously.

"The one that's about to start in a few minutes out in the courtyard. Everyone here is expected to attend," Constable Gania said, setting his mug down and pushing it away.

"Damn it," Reva complained, "I don't have time for this. Some of us have *real* work to do."

Just then, First Constable Aescel walked out of his office. "Let's go, people," he said, his voice raised in order to be heard over the din of the Stable. "The LCI is going to speak to everyone in a few minutes."

He headed across the Stable, ignoring the questions being thrown his way. Reva sighed and stood up, leaving her cloak in place, as the day had grown warm. She, Ansee, Willem, and Kai joined the rest of Acer Division as they all shuffled out of the Stable and down the stairs to head out into the courtyard. It was the only place in New Port that was large enough for all the constables that were on duty to congregate.

The courtyard was nearly full of constables from different divisions, clustered together in their own groups. Reva was surprised to see members of Nul Pfeta Division standing in a group near the entrance to New Port. Most meetings like this only affected Acer and Betula Divisions. Nul Pfeta was practically their own constabulary most of the time, generally ignored by folks here at New Port. Reva moved away from the entrance and found a spot along the edge of the crowd, where she could hear, but not be in the direct line of sight to LCI Betulla. A feeling of dread was slowly building in her stomach; the last large meeting had resulted in her suspension for a week.

Nobody seemed to know why this meeting had been called, though there was a lot of speculation that Reva did her best to ignore. It wasn't worth the trouble to guess what was going to happen when they would find out momentarily. Sure enough, a couple of minutes later, Lord Constable Inspector Betulla walked out of the front doors, followed by each of the First Constables. She looked smug, but that didn't give Reva any insight; that was how Betulla always looked.

The crowd noise subsided as everyone focused their attention on the LCI. "My fellow constables," she said, her voice carrying clearly across the courtyard. "I have made a decision, after consulting with the First Constables," Reva saw FC Pueraria give a broad, sycophantic smile, while FCs Aescel and Churlsleaf gave embarrassed, half-hearted smiles. That was the first clue that this was not going to be good, despite how Betulla would spin it.

"That," she continued, "in the interest of increasing advancement opportunities for all constables in the RTC, and also to foster improved communication and synergy between the divisions, effective tomorrow, we will be instituting a trial program to rotate constables across the divisions."

A murmur rose from the assembled constables.

"No longer will constables be constantly stuck in less prestigious posts," Betulla continued, raising her voice in order to be heard over the crowd, "without the opportunity to be recognized for their efforts and contributions to the constabulary. This trial program will rotate six constables, two from each division, and reassign them to a different division. In a few weeks, we will rotate other constables until we have reassigned at least half of the constables to new positions. We will then rotate constables twice a year, so that no one is left to stagnate in their post."

The crowd continued to grumble, clearly not seeing the same wonderful vision that the LCI was preaching. Reva didn't blame them. There was a lot of stubborn tradition within the constabulary, and many constables, especially the senior constables, enjoyed the positions they had, and hated the very idea of change. Reva hated the idea, too. Not because she hated change so much (even though she did) but that she hated having to work with people she didn't know and hadn't yet built any trust with. Reva also knew that this would impact her directly, even if it was only the constables that would be transferred. She knew that whatever this plan of Betulla's was, at the heart of it was a way to get back at Reva, to make her suffer just a bit more.

She leaned over to Willem, who stood grim-faced as he stared up at the LCI. "You know you are going to be one of these that will be reassigned."

Willem nodded, but remained silent.

"I have come up with a list of six constables," Betulla said, "with the assistance of the First Constables." A smirking smile of defiance from FC Pueraria this time. Churlsleaf just frowned, while Aescel seemed to shake his head, ever so slightly. "These constables will begin working in their new postings starting tomorrow. Senior Constable Hollbrush and Constable Lynnus will be transferred from Betula Division to Acer Division."

The crowd noise rose a bit at the two names. Reva wasn't surprised, as she considered Senior Constable Hollbrush and Constable Lynnus to be two of the constables who were the least prepared to make the transition to Acer Division.

"Constable Sulwynd and Senior Constable Slywynd will transfer from Nul Pfeta Division to Betula Division."

Reva considered that move, keeping her conversation

with Inquisitor Amalaki last night in mind. She wondered if Betulla was aware that Sulwynd was being watched by the Sucra. There were implications either way that Amalaki would have to consider. Not to mention the fact that his main suspect was now going to be reassigned out of Nul Pfeta. Would that put Sulwynd in the clear, or would it just make it that much harder for Amalaki to conduct his investigation?

"And finally—"

"Here it comes," Reva whispered to Willem, who merely grunted his acknowledgement.

"Senior Constable Ghrellstone and Constable Gania will be moved from Acer Division to Nul Pfeta Division."

The grumbling from the crowd grew in volume even more at the last two names. Willem was one of the most senior constables in the constabulary, and was respected by many within the force, while Gania had a lot of sympathy going for him after the murder of his parents, including the former Lord Constable Inspector. It was hard to not see these last two names as being anything other than a petty move by Betulla.

As the hubbub around her continued and Betulla tried to regain control of the crowd, a loud voice called out, easily heard above the din, "You take away useful constables in our division, but you'll let a dangerous *sorcerer* remain?"

Everyone in the courtyard turned to Seeker Pfinzloab, who stood with her hands planted on her hips. She began to wither under the stares, and eventually slinked away from the crowd. This allowed Betulla to regain control of the meeting.

"There will not be any changes in these assignments," she said, defiantly, "and I expect to see these orders carried out. This is a new opportunity to better the whole constabulary." She gave a curt nod, and then walked back inside New Port, followed by Pueraria.

Reva headed directly toward the doors, pushing her way through the milling constables to try to reach Aescel before he slipped into the building, but he seemed to have anticipated that Reva, at least, would come looking for an explanation. He stood there, arms crossed, jaw set, as she reached the door.

"Don't even start, Reva," he chided.

Reva ignored the order. "This is a mess... sir," she added, hastily, at the end, as she caught the look in Aescel's eyes. She made a sweep of her hand to take in the courtyard. "Most of them would agree with me on that point. How could you let her do something like this?"

"Would you prefer the alternative, Reva?"

"And what was that?" she sniped. "Actually cutting off our arms instead of metaphorically doing it?"

"She originally wanted to split up all of the Inspectors and Seekers. Would you have preferred that, Reva? Do you enjoy breaking in new Seekers so much that you'd like to do that again? Or maybe you were itching to be reassigned to Nul Pfeta Division yourself?"

"You know why she's doing this. She hasn't had any success in attacking me directly, so she's doing this to punish me indirectly."

Aescel gave a derisive snort. "You are *not* that important, Reva. You may be a good Inspector—"

"I'm a *damn* good Inspector," Reva interrupted.

Aescel conceded the point with a nod. "But the constabulary doesn't revolve around you. There are other constables that work for me, and they all think that their shit doesn't stink like everyone else's." He sighed and shook his head, before looking at Reva and meeting her eyes. "Do you know how hard it is to keep all of you happy? Do you have any idea how exhausting that is? Every single one of you has their own issues, their own problems, and all of you bother me with them. Between your griping about everything under Lyzar, Norah's constant complaints of harassment and demands that I get rid of Ansee, and Olwynn acting like he's going to be the next Lord Constable, it's enough to make me want to chuck all of you into the river." He swept his hand to take in the courtyard. "Honestly, I'm starting to like the Lord

Constable's idea of splitting you all up, just so I can get some peace and quiet."

Aescel turned and opened the door, stalking back into the building. The heavy wooden door slammed home with a note of finality.

Chapter 15

"Daddy! Daddy!" The cries came just before the mattress bounced, as a small body landed between Willem and his wife, Hosta. Willem's hands darted out from under the covers, and his fingers danced over his daughter's body. Premna erupted in laughter from the tickling assault.

"Daddy, stop!" she squealed through laughs, as she squirmed and twisted on the bed.

"Stop what?" Willem asked, as he continued to tickle Premna. Hosta pulled the blanket back and sat up in bed.

Premna continued to giggle and Willem picked her up, swinging her high as he sat up. He put her down on the floor and gave her a playful pat on her rump. "Go wake your brother up." She ran off with a playful gleam in her eyes.

Willem leaned back on the bed with a sigh. "Reis hoestii, love," he said.

Hosta leaned down and gave him a kiss. Willem brought a hand up and ran it through her silky brown hair, trying to make the kiss linger. All too quickly, Hosta broke the kiss as a squeal came from the other bedroom, indicating that Premna had woken up her brother. She gave Willem a pat on his shoulder, and then stood up and put on a dressing gown.

Willem pulled himself up and completed his morning routine, which was made considerably more difficult than normal as Premna came back in and insisted on "helping" him with his puttee. Once they were on, he spent a few minutes braiding her hair, the simple repetitive motion allowing him to collect his thoughts. He did this every morning, but today the ritual didn't seem to have the desired effect.

"Can't stop the wind from blowing," he muttered.

"What, Daddy?" Premna asked.

"Nothing, sunshine," he replied, as he tied a bright red ribbon to hold her braid. She ran off before he could give her a kiss; she was a bundle of energy that never seemed to stop. Willem finished putting on his uniform, hesitating for a moment as he picked up his Acer Division bracers, before finally tying them on.

I shouldn't be this upset about a stupid transfer, he told himself. He'd worked in each division during his time in the constabulary, though he had spent most of his time in Acer Division. Despite the perception that the Lord Constable Inspector had about the permanence of constables in the divisions, Willem knew that there was always a chance of being transferred. He'd seen it enough over the years. But LCI Betulla wasn't making this change for any other reason than to prove who had the power at the RTC.

He left the bedroom and entered the small kitchen. His home was a simple one-story building in the south of Alnua Grove. There wasn't much space, something that was becoming more apparent as his children were growing up, but at least it wasn't an apartment with neighbors to complain about the ruckus his children made.

Premna and Kalmia—Kal—were eating their breakfast of bread, cheese, and some dried fruit when Willem walked in. Kal set down his glass of milk and asked, "Where are your new bracers?" He was too interested in what was new and different to notice the frown that his mother made.

"I won't get them until I get to work this morning," Willem answered. He picked up a glass and poured himself some water from the pitcher.

"Cool," Kal nodded. "Are you going to beat up some halp-bloeden today?"

"Kal!" Hosta exclaimed, the disapproval clear in her voice.

"That's what Malen said that constables do in Nul Pfeta, to keep those dirty halpbloeden in line."

Willem shook his head. "No, Kal, I don't plan on beating anyone up. I'm there to keep the peace, the same as I did when I worked in Acer."

Kal looked confused. "But I thought that halpbloeden weren't people. That's what Malen and his parents say. And it's what Ms. Hollybrook said in school."

Willem sat down and grabbed a piece of dried apple from Kal's plate. "Halpbloeden are still people, even if the King has said they are not elves. And as long as any person— elven, halpbloeden, human, or halfling—follows the King's laws, then I won't have to do anything." He gave a look at Hosta that she acknowledged with a nod. They were going to have to sit down with Kal, and probably Premna, too, and explain things to them about the Purity Laws and halpbloeden. He'd been hoping to put it off for another year or more at least, but clearly that talk needed to happen sooner rather than later before Kal's friends—and teachers—filled him with all sorts of rot. The law said that halpbloeden were not elves, and therefore not citizens, but that didn't mean that they should be treated like animals. Too many elves held that opinion, and Willem was not going to teach that to his children.

"So, you don't get to beat them up?" Kal asked, sounding disappointed.

"No, son, I don't. As long as they obey the law, which most of them do. They're just like you and me, trying to earn a living and provide for their families."

Kal scrunched up his face as he tried to understand how any halpbloed could be just like him. *We definitely need to have that talk soon.*

Willem stood up and patted his son on his head. Kal squirmed and tried to pull his head away, afraid that his father would mess up his hair. Willem knew that it was enough of a distraction that it would get Kal to stop thinking about beating up halpbloeden, at least for a while.

"I gotta run," Willem stated.

"Aren't you going to walk me to school?" asked Kal. On most mornings, Willem walked Kal to the small school on his way to work. "Sorry, son, I need to leave earlier today. It's a longer walk to Nul Pfeta, and I don't want to be late on my first day." He gave Kal a hug, and then turned to Premna. She'd been quiet while eating her breakfast, primarily just nibbling at it, as most of her food was still on her plate.

Willem snagged a piece of cheese from her plate, eliciting a squeal of protest.

"That's mine, Daddy!"

"Well, you weren't eating it." He popped the cheese into his mouth. "I'll see you tonight, sunshine," he said, giving her a hug.

She hugged him back, "Bye, Daddy." She then picked up a stuffed cat and held it out to Willem. He dutifully took the cat and gave it a kiss on the head. "And I'll see you tonight too, Wiggles." With a smile, Premna returned to her breakfast, holding up one hand to protect it from her father, and she glared at him as he pretended to steal more food. Hosta grabbed a piece of dried apple from the other side as Premna was distracted.

Willem patted Premna on her head and gave her a kiss, and then patted Kal on his shoulder as he headed to the front door. Hosta met Willem there as he pulled down his sword and dagger from the high shelf next to the door, away from where Kal or Premna might try to grab them.

"Be safe," she commanded, crossing her arms.

Willem buckled on his sword belt. "I'm always safe," he reassured her.

"But you don't always work in," she paused, and then glanced around to make sure that the children weren't in earshot, then lowered her voice and continued, "that hells hole."

"I'll be perfectly safe," Willem said, resting his hands on

her shoulders. "I'm a good constable, and what I told Kal is right. Most halpbloed only want to live their lives. They don't want to cause trouble."

"I'm more worried about your fellow constables," Hosta said. "You know who I mean."

Willem nodded. "Can't be helped," he said. "But I can handle him, too. And the others. I'm a big elf. I can take care of myself." He leaned in and gave her a kiss, savoring the feel of her lips, when the clatter of a fallen plate and a high pitched "Hey" coming from the kitchen broke the moment.

"I think you have the harder job, dear," he said with a smile, "keeping the peace here."

She returned the smile while also rolling her eyes. The sounds of the quarrel rose in pitch, and she gave a wave and turned back to the kitchen as he stepped out the door.

† † †

Willem crossed the second span of Victory Bridge and walked into the stone gatehouse that overlooked the river and Mill Island. Traffic was already flowing as halpbloeden heading to work showed their passes to the two constables guarding the bridge, making sure that only those authorized to leave the Grove were doing so. Considering how many halpbloed were employed in the rest of the city, it was generally a perfunctory check, otherwise there would be a queue stretching back into the Grove, and nobody would be happy—neither the halpbloeden trying to earn the meager living they could scrape together, nor the employers who depended on the cheap labor in order to earn their profits.

The inside of the gatehouse, the official home of Nul Pfeta Division, was stuffy and hot from a large fire blazing in the fireplace. It was cooling down with the onset of autumn, but Willem felt that the fire was a bit of overkill. Several constables were sitting around, doing their best to do as little as possible. It was a big change from the more productive bustle that Willem was used to at New Port.

He saw that Constable Gania was already here, speaking with a female constable at one of the few tables that had been crowded into the room. Kai gave a nod in greeting, and Willem turned to join him, when another constable blocked his path. The constable's armor was stained and nicked, and his brown hair hung in thin, greasy strands across his shoulders.

"Who'd you piss off to get sent here, Ghrellstone?" Constable Gallwynn asked. His breath stank of onions. Willem had never had the pleasure of working with Gallwynn, thankfully, but he knew enough about him through reputation and the general gossip that seemed to travel through the roots of the constabulary faster than anything. He was a slob, a womanizer, and probably a thief as well. He belonged in one of the thieves' guilds, not the constabulary.

"Me?" Willem feigned shock. "Oh, I didn't piss anyone off. Didn't you hear? They sent me here to teach you lot how a *real* constable is supposed to act."

It wasn't much of an insult, but it apparently struck a nerve with Gallwynn, as he clenched his jaw tight. Two more constables walked up behind Gallwynn: Senior Constable Allen Eleapflam and Willem's cousin, Constable Lhoren Ghrellstone. Each had smirks plastered on their faces.

"You won't be teachin' nobody nothin'," Eleapflam said, "except how to follow orders. All your work in Acer don't mean shit here. Your rank don't matter, as *I'm* the Senior Constable here." He crossed his arms, trying to convey... something. Willem wasn't sure exactly what. Bravado? Control? Power? Whatever it was, it didn't matter; he'd dealt with this shit from better constables than Eleapflam for years. Next to Eleapflam, Willem's cousin mimicked the move and continued to smirk.

"Well, if I need advice on how to watch over a pigsty, I'll know where to come," Willem smiled. "Until then, just remember that I got my rank without having to stick my nose up other people's asses." He pushed through the small knot of constables and headed over to Kai.

"Winning friends already, I see," Kai said, handing him a

pair of bracers. They were painted a bright orange with blue trim outlining the pinecone worked into the leather. With a sigh, Willem pulled off his old bracers.

"Who? That lot?" He gave a derisive snort. "They're just dogs pissing to mark their territory."

"Dogs tend to bite," a female constable retorted.

"Who are you?" Willem asked as he pulled on the Nul Pfeta bracers.

"Constable Rhianna Bourreria," she replied, with a smile. "You can call me Rhi."

"Well, Rhi," Willem said, finished putting on the new bracers, "I've worked with my share of dogs over the years, and they always back down when faced with someone who isn't afraid of them." He jerked a thumb toward the other constables. "That group is just pissed they didn't get picked to leave this wonderful paradise, and they're trying to intimidate us acorns." He gestured at Kai and himself. "We don't intimidate easily."

Rhi nodded, and was about to say something when a call to attention came from the other side of the room. All of the constables stood up, and Willem noticed that only a few were standing at proper attention; most were slouched against tables or stood with sullen expressions.

First Constable Pueraria walked down the stairs and entered the room, her long, blond hair pulled into a tight bun that circled the back of her head. Her boots were polished, her puttee looked to have been freshly made, and her armor gleamed in the firelight. She took in the scene, ignoring the sloppiness of most of her division and giving a hard glare at Willem and Kai. It was pretty much as Willem had anticipated.

She turned to Senior Constable Eleapflam. "Are our acorns ready to do real constable work?"

Eleapflam nodded. "I was just about to give them their *orders*," he smirked and looked at Willem. "Constable Gania will work with me today, while Lhoren and Gallwynn will show the sights to our *esteemed* Senior Constable."

Willem had expected nothing less. Splitting them up would give the Nul Pfeta constables an opportunity to haze the newcomers, maybe even leading them into a part of the Grove where some of the locals might be able to give them a "proper" welcome, in exchange for some small gift from the constables.

"I don't have time to coddle these acorns," Pueraria shook her head, and Willem saw Eleapflam's shoulders sag at the declaration. "And I don't want to spare my experienced constables to babysit these two." She turned to look at Willem and Kai. "You'll patrol on your own. I expect my constables to know every square hand of this Grove like it is your lover. Supposedly you two are the best constables in the whole constabulary," she sneered. "So you should be able to handle this without us having to hold your hands."

Willem just nodded, which seemed to satisfy the First Constable. She made a few more announcements, and then the meeting broke up, with Rhi and the other night shift constables leaving, and the rest set to begin their patrols. Willem noticed that the others were not in a hurry to begin their patrols, and he wasn't sure if they were waiting so that they could follow him and Kai and possibly try something, or if they were just lazy. He finally settled on the latter.

"Let's get going, Kai," Willem stated. Together, they walked out to start their first patrol in Nul Pfeta.

Chapter 16

Constable Sulwynd stood at the top of the stairs looking into the Betula Division Stable. The place was full of constables. Some sat at the tables and appeared to be writing reports, while most of the others stood around and chatted in small groups. As Sulwynd walked in, his shoulder was bumped a few times by hurrying constables, always with a polite "ghelred." In passing, he overheard some of the conversations, and it sounded to him like the night patrol constables were passing on information to their daytime counterparts. He shook his head in disbelief; it was very different from what he was used to in Nul Pfeta.

He saw that a long table was set out with several urns of tea and what appeared to be a selection of baked goods. He even saw small bowls filled with honey and other accessories. He headed over to the table, picked up a chipped ceramic cup, and poured himself a cup of tea. He grabbed a slice of sweet bread and turned to take in the scene. It was chaotic, but also orderly in the way that things moved and were handled. He spotted Senior Constable Slywynd standing in a corner, his eyes slightly wide at the scene.

"A bit different than what we're used to, ain't it?" Sulwynd asked.

"Just a bit," the Senior Constable replied. "Just proves that Nul Pfeta is the ass end of the constabulary." There was a bit of pride in his voice.

"So, you want to go back?"

"Not on your life." He grinned at Sulwynd. "They'll have to pry my cold dead hands away from this place to get me to go back to Nul Pfeta. It's about time that we were given an opportunity to do something productive for a change."

"Instead of watchin' the menagerie and makin' sure the animals don't get out," Sulwynd commented. The Senior Constable nodded.

"Go see Inspector Thallmus," Slywynd pointed to an elf who was seated at a table. "She'll have your new bracers." He held up his own arm to show off the blue and red-trimmed bracer he wore with the birch leaf tooled into the leather. He then turned to refill his own tea cup.

Sulwynd worked his way through the crowd to stand before the Inspector's table. She looked up and said, "You must be Constable Sulwynd. Welcome to Betula Division." She picked up a pair of bracers and handed them to him. He'd expected some kind of comment about Nul Pfeta, or at least a sneer or glare, but the Inspector seemed to be sincere in her greeting.

"When will I be given my duty assignment?" he asked.

"The First Constable will announce that in the morning meeting in a few minutes."

Sulwynd left and headed to a quiet part of the room to change his bracers. As he did so, he reflected on the sudden transfer and, for the hundredth time since yesterday afternoon, asked himself if he'd maybe upset Grand Inquisitor Agera. He was overjoyed at being pulled out of the hellhole of Nul Pfeta, but he was also wondering why he had been pulled out when he was so close to bringing Agera's plan to fruition. Had he done something the other night at the bar that had made the Grand Inquisitor doubt his loyalty to the cause? Had Agera changed his mind about allowing him to carry out the plan, and ordered LCI Betulla to transfer him? The Lord Constable Inspector was a member of the order, but Sulwynd was sure that she had no knowledge of Sulwynd's part in Agera's plans.

He finished changing his bracers and tossed his old ones into a trash bin. He had no desire to put them on ever again. As he waited for the morning meeting, he wondered if he should go talk to LCI Betulla? Had Agera brought her into the plan? Does she know what's going on? As he watched the room, he realized that he couldn't go to Betulla. Even if she was involved and aware of Agera's plan, there was no way that she would know of Sulwynd's part in it. Agera kept everything compartmentalized for security reasons, so alerting the LCI to his role would be violating Agera's rules and his trust. The Grand Inquisitor would not be happy, and Sulwynd could easily find himself exiled from Tenyl just like Senior Inquisitor Malvaceä.

Then, another thought occurred to Sulwynd. What if this move was not part of Agera's plan? If Agera still expected him to meet with the halpbloed in Nul Pfeta to carry out the plan, how would he do that when he was stuck somewhere else?

As these thoughts ran through his mind, the door to the First Constable's office opened, and First Constable Churlsleaf stepped out. The chatter among the assembled constables died down, and Churlsleaf began to speak.

"Reis hoestii," he greeted, and there were replies and nods from most of the group. "We have another busy day ahead of us, but before I get to the particulars, I want to extend a welcome to our two transfers. Senior Constable Slywynd and Constable Sulwynd. They've earned their bark in Nul Pfeta, and now we will put their expertise to use here in Betula Division."

Sulwynd nearly gagged on the sweet introduction. *Our expertise?* He saw polite looks from many of the constables, but also a fair share of hard glares.

"I've made some changes to the patrols to accommodate our new arrivals," the First Constable continued. Sulwynd found that he was gritting his teeth. *I don't need any accommodations,* he told himself. He was sure that was some sort of code from the First Constable for the others to hold his hand and make sure that he could do the job.

He realized that he had not heard part of the First Constable's message when he suddenly heard his name being called. "Constable Sulwynd will be taking the day patrol in Bay Grove."

Sulwynd felt a heavy weight fall in his stomach. Bay Grove was about as far as you could get from Nul Pfeta without being in Castle Tenz. How would he be able to perform the duties that Agera needed him to do if he was all the way down there? He again wondered if maybe he had been pulled from Agera's plan, and this was some kind of punishment. *But the First Constable is not part of the order, so how would he know to put me in Bay Grove? Unless Agera told the Lord Constable Inspector and she told Churlsleaf where to assign me.*

Sulwynd shook the thoughts away. He needed to overcome this challenge. He was sure that this was not a punishment, and Agera would have told him if there had been a change in plans. *Wouldn't he?* Sulwynd needed to continue to assume that he was still necessary for the plan, so he needed to figure out how to make everything work while being pulled from Nul Pfeta. The Grand Inquisitor would expect nothing less. He'd pull his patrol today in Bay Grove and still have time to return to Nul Pfeta to meet with Cedres and the other halpbloed.

"The second *hoaralle* match is being held this afternoon at Ilvalé Arena," the First Constable said, "and the LCI needs us to put in a show of force. There were too many pickpockets working in the area during the first match, and we need to show people that it is safe to attend the games. I have personally told the LCI and the Mayor that we will be there to ensure that those attending are safe. So, there are special assignments posted for duty at the Arena this afternoon. Those selected will be pulled from their normal patrol, and will work the area around the arena beginning at least an hour before the match, throughout the game, and for an hour after the match is over. We will have a phalanx of constables there that will deter any pickpockets and show our fellow citizens that they are well protected." Churlsleaf puffed out his chest a bit, as if he was a general giving orders to his troops.

There were a few more mundane items that were discussed, and then the meeting broke up. Sulwynd headed to look at the special duty list, expecting to find his name there. He pushed through the crowd and found his name listed, along with around two dozen other constables. It made sense, as he was new to the division, but at the same time, his stomach churned at the realization that he was probably going to miss his meeting with the halpbloeden.

† † †

Constable Gania shifted his hand to the hilt of his sword as he and Senior Constable Ghrellstone passed a group of six halpbloed loitering outside a small tea shop. At least, that's what he assumed it was. The building had a cracked window and falling plaster, with a wooden plank set across stacked boxes of tea to make a makeshift table. The tea boxes had markings indicating they had come from a plantation in the southern part of the Kingdom. He didn't see a tax stamp on the boxes, implying that they had probably been smuggled in.

The six halpbloed all held tightly onto their tea mugs, and glared at Kai and Willem as they walked by. From the bottle that was surreptitiously being nudged out of the way by one of the men, Kai was sure that their mugs contained more than just hot water poured over tea leaves, if they even contained any tea at all.

Kai gave them a nervous smile as they walked by, which was ignored by the halpbloed, though the feeling of being watched didn't go away until he and Willem turned a corner.

"Stop being so obviously nervous," Willem chastised. "You're attracting more attention than if you were just walking along casually, like taking a stroll through Nuphar Woods."

"If you didn't notice, this is not Nuphar Woods."

"It's not about the place, but your attitude. The reason that you keep getting all these looks is because you're making the locals nervous. They're afraid you'll be just like the other constables here. If you act confident, and stroll along like you're just taking a walk in the woods, then you won't be nervous, and the locals won't be expecting you to do what they expect you to do."

"What they expect me to do?"

"To be an asshole, and to make their lives even harder than it already is."

They walked along and took another turn, wandering further into the winding maze that made up Nul Pfeta. Kai was thoroughly confused by where they were, but Willem seemed to be totally at ease and unconcerned as they walked around. Everywhere that Kai looked was another reminder of just how different Nul Pfeta was from the rest of Tenyl. He vaguely remembered how the Grove had looked before it had become this random mess.

"Do you remember what this place was like before?" Kai asked.

"You mean before Nul Pfeta became Nul Pfeta?" Willem asked. Kai nodded. "Yeah, but a lot has changed since those days."

"I was twenty-eight when the Third Purity Law was passed," Kai stated.

Willem nodded. "I remember that time." They passed a vegetable stall filled with small, shriveled carrots, turnips, and potatoes. Kai tried to adjust his attitude, and the way that he walked, as he passed the vendor. He gave a smile that was ignored by the old woman.

"I remember when the King's Guard, the Sucra, and the RTC started forcing all the newly declared halpbloed to move here." He gave a half-hearted wave at the surrounding buildings. "My mom was the FC for Betula Division at that time, and a lot of her constables were involved in the roundup."

"That must have been a hectic time," Willem commented, turning down what had to be an alley, since the buildings were so close together.

"I'm not sure about the details, but I know that Mom wasn't around a lot during that time. She was always at work. She had to support the law, of course, but on the few times that she was home when I wasn't asleep in bed or at school, she would tell Dad how much she was against the law."

"She thought our King made a mistake?" They passed through a small courtyard surrounded by tall buildings, with a single dead tree standing in the center of the space.

"No," Kai quickly replied, his voice echoing off the walls. "She thought it would breed resentment and prejudice, not only among the halpbloed, but also among the elves that would have to give up their homes here in South Bank Grove." They turned onto another road. Kai had long past given up on trying to tell where they were. "She also thought that moving the halpbloed here would create a stigma for them. She didn't understand why the forced relocation was necessary, and she thought that it would create its own problems."

Willem nodded, "That was prophetic by your mother."

"The riots."

Willem nodded again. "Yep. That first winter after the halpbloed were moved here was hard. The elves put a pinch on the halpbloed for gathering firewood. People froze, and then food supplies ran low. I was in the army then, and my unit was called in to break up the rioters. It was not pretty."

"I remember my mother's reaction. She was really mad at the stupidity that had led to the riots." They passed several children who were playing a street-level version of *hoaralle*. Several of the kids could have passed for elves in their appearance.

"And things only got worse ten years ago," Kai said.

"The Fourth Purity Law."

"The law added so many new halpbloed, and they all had to be stuffed into here."

"Which created a lot of resentment," Willem added.

"New halpbloed thrown in with old halpbloed. This

place is a simmering pot ready to boil over."

"Which is why we patrol and keep the peace."

"How can you be taking this so well?"

"Taking what so well? The sorry history of the Purity Laws, or us getting stuck with this wonderful new assignment?"

"Either. Both."

"Well, I have my reasons. And who's to say I'm taking this well? Just because I show one face to the public doesn't mean that I like what happened." Willem turned to Kai. "Just like your mother. But for now, we have a job to do."

Willem made a seemingly random turn and headed down another road that seemed to Kai to be just like all the others. "Getting lost is our job now?" Kai asked.

"Who said I was lost?"

Chapter 17

Seeker Norah Pfinzloab let out a curse that caused a few heads to turn in her direction as the nib on the goose feather quill she was using snapped. She flung it down onto the table with another curse, as she wondered if the mistake could be corrected or if she'd have to scrape the ink off and start again.

"Why don't you use the pen I bought you for your birthday?" asked Olwyn. "The fine gnomish crafting would keep you from breaking your quills."

Norah looked at the fancy pheasant feather quill with the bright brass nib, its surface barely stained with ink. She'd been pleased with the present at the time, but she couldn't remember the last time that she had used it. She picked it up now, running a finger along the soft vane of the feather, and then set it back down and picked up another ordinary quill.

"I am starting to feel unappreciated," Olwyn stated. "You have barely spoken to me, you haven't been over to my home for days, and now you are rejecting my presents. If I didn't know better, I would say that your husband was back in town."

"Why does everything have to be about *you*?" Norah asked. "*Your* needs. *Your* feelings." She tossed the quill down and picked up the fancy one, stabbing it into the inkwell. "Are you happy now?"

"I'm only happy when you are."

"Then why are you not doing anything about it?"

"Am I supposed to fight your battles for you?" Olwyn asked, leaning back and crossing his arms.

"I never asked you to defend me," Norah retorted. "But would it kill you to at least support me?"

"I've always supported you."

"When?" Norah snorted, her voice rising. "I haven't seen any evidence of support from you in the past month. You're always supportive when there is something in it for you, but when it's my feelings you couldn't care less!"

Norah froze, realizing that the entire Stable had grown quiet, with all of the constables staring at her. She felt heat rising along her cheeks and ears. She tossed the quill to the table and stormed out of the Stable, ignoring the calls from Olwyn and the stares of the other constables. She headed down the stairs and nearly ran into Constable Whitlocke, who was coming up the stairs.

"Oh, Seeker," Whitlocke said, "I was just coming to find you."

Norah stopped, her embarrassment still burning on her face. "What?"

Constable Whitlocke's face took on a pinched expression as she said, "The Lord Constable Inspector has asked to speak with you." She turned around and went back down the stairs.

Norah ran a hand through her hair, and then turned around and headed up to the second floor. She approached the LCI's office, and stopped before her aide's desk. "Seeker Pfinzloab to see the Lord Constable."

Senior Constable Calendula said, "One moment, Seeker," and stood up, knocked on the door, and then stepped into the LCI's office, closing the door behind him. A moment later, the door opened, and Calendula said, "The LCI will see you now," holding the door open for her.

Norah walked in, taking in the large office and the furniture, including a large, imposing desk that the LCI sat behind. Norah had never been in the office before, and she was struck by how intimidating it felt. She walked up to the desk and saluted. "Seeker Pfinzloab reporting, ma'am."

LCI Betulla gave a perfunctory smile and gestured to one of the chairs sitting in front of her desk. "Have a seat, Seeker."

Norah sat down, perched on the edge of the chair. Betulla leaned forward, resting her arms on the desk. Norah couldn't help but notice how clean it was; everything looked like it had been placed there for decoration rather than usability.

"What did you mean by your outburst yesterday, Seeker?"

"Ma'am?" Norah asked, wondering what Betulla meant.

"You said something at the end of my meeting yesterday," Betulla prompted, "something about a dangerous spellcaster working in the RTC?"

Norah relaxed, sliding back into the chair. Now she might actually get someone to finally do something about Ansee. "Did you know that you have a *sorcerer* working in the constabulary?"

Betulla stiffened, although Norah thought it was from responding to the LCI's question with one of her own, rather than on the threat that Ansee represented.

"Why should it matter if there is a sorcerer working here? There is no regulation against it."

"There should be," Norah stated, emphatically. "They are dangerous."

"Dangerous?" The LCI's tone clearly indicated that she thought that Norah was being dramatic. Now was Norah's chance to educate the LCI, and maybe get her to act on removing Ansee.

"*Very* dangerous," Norah said. "They have cheated the natural order of things to be able to cast magic, signing a pact with a demon to do so. They are in thrall to their demon masters, and this makes them dangerous because you never know when they will turn on us, attacking anyone to do their master's bidding."

"Certainly, that's not true. Otherwise, people would be

hunting down sorcerers in the streets."

Norah couldn't help but smile, "They have been."

"Excuse me?"

"The recent serial killer that CI Lunaria and Seeker Carya were investigating. He was a wizard who was attacking sorcerers who had sold their souls to their demon master so that they could cast magic."

"What serial killer? Why is this the first time I am hearing of this?"

"I don't know, ma'am," Norah replied, "I know that FC Aescel was aware of the case."

The LCI's face took on a pinched expression; clearly Norah had struck a nerve. Maybe this was the chance she needed to push her case. "The serial killer and Seeker Carya had a duel in the streets. While I would never condone an attack on a constable, had the wizard managed to seriously injure Seeker Carya, or even killed him, gods forbid, then your sorcerer problem would have been solved."

"*My* sorcerer problem?" Betulla asked. Norah held her breath, wondering if she had pushed it too far. "How would Seeker Carya's death have solved anything?"

"Because Seeker Carya *is a sorcerer*," Norah said triumphantly, as if she was unmasking the villain on Pfenestra's stage.

"Seeker Carya? A sorcerer? But..." Betulla looked away for a moment, as if remembering something. "He always studied his spellbook every morning when he worked in Nul Pfeta. What proof do you have that he's a sorcerer?"

"He's been pretending to study his spellbook here, too," Norah frowned. "But that's all he's doing, pretending. As for proof, the attack at the port last month is all the proof I need."

"That incident with the undead that nearly destroyed the port?"

Norah knew that was an exaggeration, but she wasn't going to correct the LCI now, not when she could see her salvation in reach. So, instead, she nodded. "Yes, ma'am. While we were dealing with the cultist, Seeker Carya cast several spells that are not part of the standard RTC spellbook."

The LCI leaned back in her chair, steepling her fingers. "Well, maybe Seeker Carya studied at a different wizard school. There is no regulation requiring our Seekers to stick to our standard spellbook. That sort of versatility keeps us a step ahead of the criminals."

"Not possible," Norah retorted. "I was there at the port, on the ship. There is no way any wizard could have anticipated the kind of spells that would be needed on that raid. I went in as prepared as any Seeker could have been, but I was caught by surprise by what we faced. Not Ansee. He cast any spell that he needed, on the fly, without knowing what was coming. Only a sorcerer could do that. Only someone in thrall to a demon could have done that."

Betulla tapped a finger against her chin. "But he saved your life, didn't he?"

Norah's lips formed a thin line, recalling all the taunts from the other Seekers and Senior Constables. Was the Lord Constable Inspector aware of everything? Was she just allowing Norah to climb to higher and higher branches?

"The report that I read said that Seeker Carya saved your life with a shield spell. Isn't that correct?"

"Yes," Norah admitted, the word coming out in a single, sulky breath.

"So, how does all of this relate to your outburst at my meeting yesterday?" The LCI asked.

"Yes, Ansee may have saved my life, but that doesn't eliminate the risk that he poses. He is still in the control of his demon master. He is still a danger to us. He is still a threat lurking in the underbrush. We don't know when he might strike. The serial killer knew this, which is why he was murdering sorcerers."

"Are you condoning the murder of a fellow constable?"

"No," Norah said quickly. "But the murderer proves my point. He knows that sorcerers are a threat. I don't condone his actions," though she was pleased with the results, if she had to admit it to herself, "but I think that's proof that Seeker

Carya is a threat. Whether he turns on us or not, his mere existence in the constabulary is a threat."

"I can't just fire a constable," Betulla said, "at least without cause. And what seems to me to be a personal grudge by you against Seeker Carya isn't enough of a cause."

"And if you had confirmation? Proof that Ansee is a threat?"

"What sort of proof can you give me that would change my mind?"

"Not me, ma'am," Norah said, thinking. If she wanted Ansee kicked out of the constabulary, she was going to need to push this into a different direction. Reva and Ansee had stopped the serial killer, but they didn't know the whole story. They hadn't dug deeper into who the serial killer was, or why they had been attacking sorcerers. But Norah thought that she knew, and had kept that information to herself.

She'd heard rumors about an orthodox group of wizards—even more orthodox in their beliefs than she was—who wanted nothing more than to kill sorcerers. She wanted Ansee gone, but she didn't know if she wanted him dead. Sure, if it happened in the course of his work, she wouldn't mourn his loss, even though he *had* saved her life. She'd even gone so far as to check to see if Ansee was evil, looking for some kind of justification for her feelings, but her spell had indicated otherwise. Betulla wasn't going to act without some additional information, something that would nudge her into taking action. Giving the LCI this information would certainly give Betulla the cause she would need, but it might also put Ansee's life at risk.

Betulla was staring at Norah, clearly getting impatient with her. *Hells, Ansee climbed his own tree when he made the pact with the demon to get his magic.*

"There is a professor at Auros Academy who will confirm what I am saying. He knows the threat that sorcerers pose to all of Tenyl. He will explain to you what sort of stain Ansee is having on what we do. What sort of a risk he really is."

"And who is this professor?" Betulla asked.

"Jorus Asclepias. He teaches magic history and magic theory. He will confirm what I have been saying."

"Áeorias, Seeker Pfinzloab, I will take what you said into consideration." She leaned forward in her chair. "But I don't want you interrupting my speeches like that again. I expect a high level of decorum and professionalism from my constables." She made a dismissive wave as she leaned back in her chair.

Norah nodded and stood up, confident that she had made the right decision. *In a few days, Ansee will finally be out of my hair.*

Chapter 18

Aslight breeze blew across the plaza outside Ilvalé Arena, carrying the smell of roasting chestnuts and fried meats to Constable Sulwynd. His mouth watered at the scent, and he made a mental note to stop at one of the vendor carts on his next circuit around the plaza. The plaza was filled with hundreds of elves heading into the arena for the upcoming *hoaralle* match. Most of the elves were wearing red and black striped cloaks, the colors of the local team, though he could see a few who were wearing the green and blue colors of the team from Eoelle. It wouldn't be much of a match. The team from Eoelle was not very good, but Sulwynd would have preferred being in the arena to watch the match rather than being on patrol outside.

Hells, he thought, *I'd rather be in Nul Pfeta than here.* The thought initially made him chuckle, as no elf in their right mind would ever wish that, but it was true, and that made him tighten his jaw muscles.

He would have been in Nul Pfeta, except for the timely intercession of the Lord Constable Inspector. He still wasn't sure if that had been a good thing or not. He'd spent his day on patrol in Bay Grove pondering that question, and he still hadn't come up with an answer. After wandering around the plaza for the past hour looking for pickpockets, he was pretty sure that it was not a good thing.

Instead of preparing to meet Cedres and the halpbloeden that he was supposed to recruit and get the Grand Inquisitor's plan underway, he was here looking for pickpockets that would be nearly impossible to find in this crowd. One of the thieves would have to be stupid enough to try to steal someone's coin purse right in front of him in order for Sulwynd to see it. Unfortunately, most thieves were not that stupid.

Sulwynd rubbed his hands together to keep off the chill that was starting to creep into the evenings. He spotted a couple of halpbloed carrying burlap sacks and picking up discarded food wrappings, and he wondered if he could slip away from here and make it to Nul Pfeta in time to meet Cedres. He spotted Senior Constables Jurasee and Agathistle moving through the crowd, clearly looking for anyone who was breaking the law, but he was sure that they were also looking for constables who were shirking their duty as well. Senior Constable Agathistle met Sulwynd's eyes and gave a nod, simultaneously acknowledging his presence and telling Sulwynd that he was being watched.

Of course, I'm being watched, Sulwynd groused to himself. *I'm from Nul Pfeta, so obviously I don't know what I'm doing.* He spotted another Betula Division constable, walking through the crowd, who was also watching him just as much as the crowd.

Hells, I'm not going to be able to get away until this thing is over. That would be well after the match was over, as they would need to be just as vigilant when all of the elves left the arena and went either to celebrate the win, or to drown their sorrows at a loss. He probably wouldn't get finished until well after dark, which was way too late to meet Cedres. He could try to slip away anyway and risk his absence being noticed, but he was sure that if he were discovered, it would result in him being immediately returned to Nul Pfeta. Despite the irritation of being unable to complete this simple task for Agera, he was happy to no longer be assigned to that hells hole.

Sulwynd reached the end of the plaza, and then turned back to begin a new circuit. He was near the entrance that was reserved for nobles, rich merchants, and other elves of influence. Despite his anger over the stupidity of this assignment, he made sure to be alert in this area; it wouldn't do to let one of these people get attacked.

As he scanned the area, watching the crowd for trouble, he spotted Grand Inquisitor Agera walking toward the entrance. The head of the Sucra wore black jodhpurs, black riding boots, a red and black striped shirt, as well as a red and black striped cloak. *So, the Grand Inquisitor is a supporter of Tenyl's* hoaralle *team.*

Sulwynd almost let the Grand Inquisitor and his party go by without saying anything, when he realized that he had an opportunity to find out if his transfer from Nul Pfeta had been done with Agera's approval or not. If the Grand Inquisitor knew about the move, then he'd probably approved it, and that might have implications for Sulwynd's mission. *Though why not tell me about it?* Sulwynd wondered. *Why meet me the other night with the mission notes if he knew about my transfer?*

The implication, then, was that the Grand Inquisitor was not aware of Sulwynd's transfer, and therefore did not know that the mission might be at risk because of it. Agera would expect for Sulwynd to adapt to the situation no matter what, but he should at least alert the Grand Inquisitor to the wrinkle in the mission.

Constable Sulwynd stepped up to the Grand Inquisitor and gave a salute. Agera came to an abrupt stop, his eyes widening in surprise. "Constable... Sulwynd, I believe."

"Grand Inquisitor," Sulwynd replied.

Agera nodded and turned his head to his companions. "I believe that I know the constable's father from Pfeta fey Orung." He turned back to Sulwynd, his eyes narrowed. "I was not aware that your duties in Nul Pfeta extended all the way to the Ilvalé Arena."

"I hope there's no halpbloed issues with the match," one

of the Grand Inquisitor's companions commented.

Sulwynd ignored the elf. He held up an arm, waggling his blue and red bracer. "I was transferred from Nul Pfeta this morning, sir."

"Well, congratulations," Agera said. "Why we spend the resources on any officers in Nul Pfeta is beyond me." His friends laughed.

"So, you weren't aware of my transfer?"

The Grand Inquisitor laughed, though his eyes showed no mirth. "I have enough trouble keeping the Sucra in order. Why would I bother myself with what LCI Betulla does?" Agera gave a nod and started to move past Sulwynd. "I do hope your duties here won't keep you from anything else important."

Agera headed away, leaving Sulwynd still wondering if the Grand Inquisitor had known about his transfer or not. Sulwynd was about to turn away when he saw someone bump hard into the Grand Inquisitor, knocking him down. Sulwynd began to move to see if Agera needed assistance when he saw the elf that had knocked Agera to the ground pull a coin purse from one of the Grand Inquisitor's pockets. The thief leaped to his feet, and then took off into the crowd.

Sulwynd immediately gave chase, following the thief through the crowd. The thief was running erratically, bouncing off people like a *hoaralle* ball bouncing off branches. Sulwynd shoved people aside, the chaotic movements of the thief allowing him to gain ground. As they neared the food vendors, Sulwynd launched himself at the thief, tackling him.

The thief squealed like a halpbloed, turning and thrashing. As he struggled and rolled, trying to get away, two pouches fell out. The thief's eyes widened, and he immediately grabbed for one of the pouches. It wasn't the Grand Inquisitor's coin pouch.

Constable Sulwynd pulled on the thief's arm, dragging him closer. He put one arm around the thief's neck, pulling his arm tight, grabbing his wrist with his free hand, and quickly applying pressure. Sulwynd was distantly aware of a crowd of people watching him, but it didn't matter. They were not important. Stopping this thief was the only thing that mattered right now.

He continued to squeeze, tightening his grip. He could hear shouts and cries coming as if from far away.

"Stop!"

"You're killing him!"

Suddenly, he felt a pain on his head, and hands grabbed his wrists. He released his grip, letting the thief fall to the ground. He looked up to see Senior Constable Jurasee tending to the thief. Sulwynd could see that the thief was apparently unconscious, but still breathing.

Sulwynd picked up Agera's coin purse, as well as the other pouch the thief had dropped while Sulwynd restrained him. He stood up, ignoring the looks from the crowd that had gathered. The Grand Inquisitor walked through the gathered elves and gave a glance at the thief.

"Here's your coin purse, sir," Sulwynd said, handing the pouch to the Grand Inquisitor.

"Thank you, Constable," Agera said. "I will have to have a word with LCI Betulla to commend you for your action." He tucked his pouch into a pocket with a nod, then drifted back into the crowd.

Sulwynd snorted at the Grand Inquisitor's casual nature. He looked down at the other pouch, wondering what could be so important that the thief would grab it rather than the coins just stolen. He pulled it open, angling it to get some light, and saw a reddish-orange powder. He brought it up to his nose and caught the distinctive smell of Wake.

He didn't have time to ponder the incongruity of a thief grabbing Wake over coins, as Sulwynd saw a pair of constables pick up the thief, grasping him under his arms to help him to stand. He also saw Senior Constable Jurasee stalking toward him.

† † †

Pfastbinder stretched out his legs, lazily crossing one

over the other as he leaned back against the wall of his temple. The late afternoon sun was dipping below the city walls, casting this part of Nul Pfeta into a shadowy twilight. He packed his pipe with a special blend of canab he'd taken from two of the plants he grew. He watched the stream of halpbloed pass by as he applied an ember to the canab, enjoying the opportunity to commune with Banok while he watched the people. Few ever gave his small temple more than a second glance, if they even noticed it at all, and fewer still ever left an offering. Luckily, he earned better income by duping gullible adventurers than depending on the kindness of his fellow halpbloed.

He gave a contented sigh as the strong canab began to weave its magic. He would have to remember this blend. It might even be worth selling. There were always artists, and the occasional cleric or priest, who liked the mind-expanding properties of canab. He took another pull, enjoying the feeling, and thought he might just keep it all for himself, instead. He wasn't *that* desperate for coin at the moment.

He watched the halpbloed walk past his temple, recognizing several regulars who were returning to their homes or heading to one of the dozen tiny businesses that would exchange horrible alcohol for the few Pfen that the workers earned. Anything to escape their reality, Pfastbinder supposed, wondering if he might be able to gather more followers if he offered afternoon services where they could escape their reality through the teachings of Banok. He quickly gave up on that idea, as he realized that it would cut into his own afternoon escapes.

Through the crowd, he spotted the distinctive armor and step of a constable. He sat up as he recognized Senior Constable Ghrellstone and Constable Gania. *How curious*, he mused, already standing up and weaving his way through the crowd. He slid into step behind the pair.

"Are you sure we haven't been here before?" asked Constable Gania. "I swear that bakery looks familiar."

"Nope, this is our first time down this street," the Senior

Constable replied, "though that bakery does look like several others."

Pfastbinder stepped in between them and put his arms on their shoulders. Both constables jumped. "Fancy meeting you here, so far from home. Are you lost?"

Both constables pulled away and turned to face him. Gania was the first to speak. "Yes, we're lost."

"Speak for yourself, Constable," Ghrellstone said. "I ain't lost. Just figuring out the lay of the land on our first day."

"We've been figuring out everything since this morning, and I don't know which way is up right now, let alone where the bridge is."

"First day?" Pfastbinder looked down at their arms and noticed the distinctive orange and blue color of their bracers. "Have you decided to work in Nul Pfeta now?"

"No," Ghrellstone shook his head. "We were reassigned."

"Ah," Pfastbinder nodded sagely, and started to walk across the street back to his temple. He gestured to the pair of constables, and they followed him. "Banok does move in mysterious ways. It's why I must broaden my horizons to understand his motives." He took a puff on his pipe.

Constable Gania coughed as he walked through the plume of canab smoke, waving his hand to clear it away. "This wasn't Banok," he said.

"You didn't piss off Constable Inspector Lunaria, I hope?" Pfastbinder asked, as he resumed his seat.

"It wasn't that, either," replied Ghrellstone. "We just got caught up in RTC politics."

"Politics? Chaos?" Pfastbinder waved the air to blur the distinction between the two words. "Practically the same thing. How do you think Banok works?"

"Apparently through smoking large amounts of bog weed," Gania complained, trying to wave away more of the smoke.

"You should relax more, Constable," Pfastbinder said, offering his pipe to the young elf. Gania's ears reddened as he waved his hands to decline the offer.

"I'm good," he said, "and it won't help us get back to the bridge. We're still lost."

"We are *not* lost," Ghrellstone grumbled. The Senior Constable crossed his arms.

"Then it is a good thing your fellow constable is here to lend assistance," Pfastbinder said.

Ghrellstone turned a questioning look at him. "Fellow constable?"

"Of course! Constable Inspector Lunaria promised to make me one for helping you with your sorcerer killer. I'm just waiting for my bracers. I'd even accept to be stationed here in Nul Pfeta rather than Acer, just so I can work with the pair of you."

The Senior Constable rolled his eyes while Gania stammered out, "But... you're a doped up halpbloed—no offense."

Pfastbinder feigned shock. "I'm a cleric who is communing with my god. Do you chastise followers of Basvu for eating their special mushrooms, or followers of Brand for drinking the blood of their enemies?"

The young constable's entire face turned red. Ghrellstone said, "Reva would never make you a constable, bog weed nor your heritage withstanding."

"After all I have done to help the constabulary over the years?" Pfastbinder huffed. He stood up, poking his pipe at the Senior Constable. "Need I remind you of all the times I have given you my assistance? Maybe I should let you wander around like lost little lambs until it gets full dark and the wolves come out?"

The two constables again began to argue as to whether they were lost or not, but Pfastbinder ignored them, his attention drawn to the bakery. Several halpbloed had gathered at the base of the stairs.

"Well, Pfastbinder?" Gania asked.

"Huh?"

Ghrellstone turned. "What stole your attention?"

"It's nothing," Pfastbinder said. The gathered halpbloed were now starting to argue, a couple of them pointing at a third, who was trying to convince them to go up the stairs.

"That doesn't seem like nothing," Ghrellstone stated.

"Maybe we should see what the trouble is," offered Gania.

Pfastbinder stepped in front of them. "Nope, that is not a good idea. I'm sure they're just upset because the bakery is out of bread." The canab and Banok were telling him to get Ghrellstone and Gania away. Not for their safety—the halpbloed probably wouldn't put up a fight with the two constables—there was another reason. The halpbloed were all new, having arrived in Nul Pfeta since the last Purity Law had been passed. Pfastbinder also knew that the halpbloed who was trying to get them to stay was new, as well. He'd recently moved into the small room above the bakery, maybe just two months ago. Pfastbinder still didn't know why the halpbloed had taken the room, since the roof leaked and the floor was rotted through in places. It had also made it such a pain when he'd had to move his canab plants out of the space.

"Let me show you the way to the bridge," Pfastbinder prompted.

The argument was getting louder, and people were making a wide detour around the small group of halpbloed. Ghrellstone put a hand on the hilt of his sword. "I think we should see what the problem is."

Pfastbinder held up a hand. "It's not a big deal. This is your first day in the grove, and you really don't want to step out onto the branch. I'm sure they're just upset because the bakery is out of bread. They never make enough, and they always close early. And they never seem to have any left to make a donation to my temple. Can you believe the nerve of that baker?"

"Yes," Ghrellstone deadpanned.

"It looks closed," Gania added. "Most bakeries close by lunch, don't they?" At that moment, the young constable's stomach gave a loud and noticeable grumble.

"Food!" Pfastbinder practically yelled, pushing the two

constables away from the bakery. "Come, I will show you the best place for a constable to get a meal here in Nul Pfeta. Why, they hardly *ever* spit in your food." He grabbed his cloak off a hook and closed his door, urging Ghrellstone and Gania forward. "And then I can show you how to find your way back to the bridge."

Ghrellstone's eyes narrowed as he stared at the group, but he slowly turned and allowed Pfastbinder to usher him away. Pfastbinder glanced over his shoulder to see the group disperse, heading off in different directions; the only one remaining was the tenant of the small room. He looked upset, and a bit mad. At the other halpbloed? At something else? Both? Whatever it was, Banok was telling him that it was important, and that it was important for *him* to find out, not Ghrellstone and Gania. He didn't always understand Banok's motives or reasons. What mortal could? But he was sure there *was* a reason.

"We can find our own way back," Ghrellstone said. "Just point us in the right direction."

Gania gave a snort, as if this confirmed for him that the Senior Constable really was lost.

"Nonsense," Pfastbinder put his arm around Ghrellstone's shoulders. "We constables have to stick together."

Chapter 19

Lord Constable Inspector Betulla's boots clicked along the marble floor of the vast entry hall of Auros Academy. The white marble walls and the statues of famed wizards standing like silent sentinels gleamed a subtle pink from the setting sun that was shining through a tall window. Cupolas with brilliant stained-glass windows spaced along the roof cast rainbow patterns along the floor and caused the large, perpetually green oak tree that grew in the center of the hall to shimmer under a rainbow of light. It was a space that was designed to cause visitors to stop and marvel at the opulence and might of the wizards of Auros Academy. It was a space designed to impress.

Nyssa was not impressed.

She walked at a quick pace across the hall, ignoring the grandeur and weaving her way through the students who sat in small groups with the *Shádpfed* giving them instruction in the magical arts. The professors stood out in their fancy robes and peaked hats, and Betulla scoffed at how they looked down upon their students.

She reached a set of double doors, the wood polished to a brilliant gleam, and passed through into a smaller, though still ostentatious, hallway. There were more statues here, this time depicting magical creatures, sitting in small alcoves and niches along the walls. Doors were spaced at irregular intervals and had words like "Potions", "Wands", "Evocation", and "Abjuration" painted in golden letters upon them.

She took the wide stairs at the end of the hallway, the smell of the beeswax wood polish almost overwhelming, up two floors to a still smaller hallway. It was also seeping with grandeur and portent, with dark wooden walls, and a deep, plush, red and black carpet, the Auros Academy seal stitched in gold at regular intervals, which had to have cost a king's inheritance. There were no statues here, only bronze busts sitting on narrow wooden tables and giving off a metallic luster under the brilliant, magical illumination of light wands.

Here, Betulla's pace slowed a bit as she had to read the names on each of the doors, looking for the right one. She finally stopped in front of the door with "*Shádpfed* Jorus Asclepias" painted in red letters with gold highlights. She almost opened the door, but then paused and remembered to knock first. Most wizards were sticklers for protocol and rules, and she knew from Grand Inquisitor Agera's many dinners that Jorus was no exception.

"Enter," responded a quiet, but clear, voice.

Betulla turned the handle and walked through into the *Shádpfed's* office. The space was no less opulent than the rest of the Academy. His office was about the size of her own at New Port, though she could see another door set in the back wall that likely led to another room. A thick, green and black carpet covered the floor. The walls were lined with a pale wood that curved and flowed to make an irregular, natural shape. Small nooks and shelves were grown into the walls and displayed several books, tomes, crystals, small statues carved from rare minerals, and other assorted knick-knacks. More wealth on display in the classical Wood Elf design.

Shádpfed Jorus Asclepias sat behind a large, wooden desk with curves that matched the natural character of the rest of the room. Jorus had long hair that had been brown in his youth, but was now turning a respectable silver. Age lines framed his eyes, and Betulla knew that Jorus was at least 170 years old, although she wasn't sure about his exact age. He'd been in his current position at the Academy for at least 50 years.

His desk was practically empty, with only a fancy light wand lamp, an inkwell, and a couple of quills to fill the vast surface. Jorus had been reading from a book and making notes in a bound journal. He set the book down and frowned upon seeing Betulla. She ignored him, walked up to the desk, and took a seat in one of the two chairs.

"Good afternoon, Jorus," Betulla greeted, a practiced smile gracing her lips. She brushed a hand down her leg to smooth out a wrinkle in her dress.

"What do you want, Nyssa? I am very busy."

"I was hoping we could have a chat."

"I didn't want to talk with you the other night at Agera's. Why would I want to talk to you now?"

Betulla couldn't help the frown that broke up her carefully planned expression. *What an annoying piece of hawkshit*, she thought, remembering why she hadn't wanted to talk with him at the party, either. She swallowed her annoyance and replied, "I wanted to keep you apprised about the murder of several sorcerers in the city."

Jorus gave a snort. "This is a first, the constabulary giving information instead of always asking for it from the Academy." He leaned back in his chair. "And why would I care about the deaths of some sorcerers? Good riddance."

"You seem pretty pleased with their deaths."

"Pleased? I am ecstatic." The only change in Jorus's expression was a thin smile. "Sorcerers are a blight on my profession. I will not shed any tears at their deaths." He leaned forward and pointed a finger at Betulla. "Do you think I had anything to do with their deaths?"

"If we did, one of my inspectors would be here."

"So, why are you here bothering me?"

Betulla leaned back in her chair and crossed one leg over the other. "The murderer was stopped through the actions of one of my Seekers."

"Well, I am glad to hear that one of our graduates is having an impact on protecting our city."

"Yes, our Seekers are good at their job, but in this case, the Seeker is not one of your graduates." She watched his expression and body language carefully, taking a bit of pride in seeing him wilt a little.

"Well, the academy in Narris is okay, though not up to our standards."

"This Seeker has not trained at any academy," Betulla said, savoring what was coming. It was worth it to see Jorus trimmed back.

"You mean…"

"He is a sorcerer," Betulla confirmed, not bothering to hide her smile.

Jorus squirmed. "I heard some rumors, but I never thought such blasphemy would ever be allowed to happen."

Blasphemy? That is an interesting choice of words, Betulla thought. "Nothing prevents us from having a sorcerer as a Seeker. In fact, he's been one of my better Seekers."

Betulla thought that Seeker Carya was mediocre at best, and not an outstanding Seeker in any sense, but she was enjoying seeing Jorus twist and squirm at this bit of news. The more agitated he was, the more amenable he would be to her request. She had no real interest whether Seeker Carya was in the constabulary or not. But allowing Jorus to have a hand in removing the Seeker would mean that he would owe her a favor. And a favor from Jorus would come in handy, especially with her need to consolidate power.

"A sorcerer? It's bad enough that the King allows them in the Kingdom, but to allow them to serve in the constabulary? In a position to do such great harm? That is misguided." He pointed a finger at Betulla. "And dangerous. How can this be allowed to happen?"

"As I said, there is nothing that prevents a sorcerer from being a Seeker." She leaned forward and changed her tone of voice. "But it is becoming a problem for me. Seeker Carya's presence is becoming a disrupting influence, causing morale problems with my other Seekers."

"You're lucky that's the only problem you are facing."

Betulla gave a knowing nod. "Maybe there is something that you can do about that. You are clearly passionate about this issue. If you can get rid of Seeker Carya, then things will improve, and our city will be safer."

"Why me? Certainly, you can concoct some reason to fire this Seeker?"

"Of course, I can get him out of the constabulary easily enough, but he'd still be out there. A threat."

Jorus nodded slowly. "What's in it for me?"

This was what mattered. How much would she need to give to this pompous fool? She had an idea of what he would demand, and she knew she wasn't willing to give him that much power. How to find the right compromise?

"I'm willing to send more consultations to the Academy, to have you involved in more of our cases."

Jorus gave a snort. "Not good enough. I want oversight on the Seekers. Approvals on hiring. Overseeing the magic they learn and use, and how they are assigned to cases."

He'd grabbed for the higher branch, as Betulla had expected. Now to get him to climb down a bit to something reasonable, because she was never going to give him that much authority.

"I do think that Auros Academy should be more involved in our selection of Seekers, as you have more expertise in judging a candidate's magical abilities."

"But…" A frown creased Jorus's face.

"A hiring committee can be set up with three members, two from the Academy and one from the RTC. The committee would interview candidates and provide recommendations on whom to hire. I'm willing to overhaul the list of standard spells. We've had too many instances lately where the current spell repertoire has been insufficient. We could use some more offensive capabilities. I think having the Academy be part of those changes would be most useful. Case assignments will continue to reside with the First Constables. They would revolt if I took that authority away from them."

Jorus rubbed a hand across his chin and tapped a finger on his desk. Betulla waited. It was a reasonable compromise, and it gave him most of what he wanted. She hadn't told him that she would still retain the right to overturn any decision the hiring committee made. That would just confuse things.

"I believe I can assist you with your sorcerer problem."

† † †

Jorus feigned a smile as LCI Betulla got up and made her goodbye. She sashayed across his office and out the door, thinking that she had pulled one over on him. She had denied him exactly what he wanted, and she probably thought that she would retain control over things—probably a final approval on hiring decisions. If he had been negotiating from her position, that's the sort of thing he would have done and kept to himself. It wouldn't matter. If he could get a foot onto a branch he would have access and, with time, access would be all that he'd need.

He knew that Grand Inquisitor Agera had practically hand-picked Betulla for the position of Lord Constable Inspector when LCI Gania died. He suspected that meant that Agera was pulling her strings, as he liked to control as many things as possible. Betulla was certainly not smart enough to have gotten to her current position based on merit. Though, by the blessed aurora, he couldn't think why Agera would want to put her into that position. As head of the Sucra, Agera had access and control to many areas of the Kingdom, and he supposed that Agera would also want to have some control over the constabulary as well.

Agera loved his machinations and being the power behind everything, but Jorus couldn't be sure where Agera's loyalties lay. Jorus was sure that now was the time for the Qurundora to exert more influence over what was going on in the Kingdom. If Agera had his own plans, then it was important that Jorus and the Qurundora did as well.

Doing this little task for Betulla would allow him to move those plans forward. Jorus had never thought that the

Qurundora might do anything more than rid the world of sorcerers to find the demon that controlled them and gave them their powers. Now he realized that they had an opportunity to do even more, to become a bigger player. They should have been doing more all along. He realized now that their narrow focus on hunting the demon to the exclusion of everything else had been a mistake. With the Qurundora's power, they could do more to influence other events. But what events should they influence?

That would have to wait until he could meet with the other members of the Qurundora. This was not a decision that he could make on his own. It would take planning to decide what the right move would be.

However, there was one decision that he could make now, on his own, and it would be the one that he'd need to get onto that first branch.

Jorus stood up and walked to the door in the back of his office. He pulled out a key and unlocked it, letting the heavy wooden door sweep open. Inside was a small library, the shelves filled with his collection of historical texts, spellbooks, and ancestries. A table and chair sat in the middle of the room, an easel for holding large tomes taking center place on the table. He walked over to one of the shelves, and pulled down an object covered with a black silk cloth and set it on the table, sliding the easel out of the way.

He sat down in the chair and pulled away the cloth, revealing a large crystal ball. It sat inert for the moment, the crystal a deep, inviting pool. As he placed a hand on the top of the ball, he began to chant, his finger tracing a pattern on the crystal's surface. A blue-green light began to pulse within the crystal, getting brighter with each pulse until it resolved itself into a solid glow. Within a moment, an aged, birch-colored face appeared, long silver hair with moss green highlights framing eyes so blue they were almost black.

"I have need of your services here in Tenyl," Jorus said.

Chapter 20

Reva walked into the Acer Division Stable on time for a change. She was able to enjoy her usual hot cacao and sweet roll at Ilium's shop this morning, something that she hadn't been able to do much of lately with the extra work she had been taking on. It felt good to have a normal morning, and she started to wonder if she had been taking on too much work lately. Then she saw Senior Constable Hollbrush sitting at the table that, until yesterday, had belonged to Willem, and she frowned and realized that she would have to do even more now to keep on top of the cases.

Across the Stable, she saw that Olwyn and Norah seemed to be back to normal as well. At least they weren't arguing anymore. Reva wondered if that meant that they had sex last night, or if there was some other reason. By the way that Olwyn was gesturing and staring longingly at Norah, she guessed that the calm was not due to sex. Reva took off her cloak and saw Norah turn and give a look to Ansee, a small smile barely touching her lips. It was a small, coquettish smile that Reva would have associated between lovers, but as Ansee had his head down to concentrate on his writing, and Reva was sure that Norah would never want to have sex with Ansee, she knew there had to be another reason. Maybe it was just in response to something Olwyn had said. Whatever it was, it wasn't important.

"Morning, Inspector," Ansee greeted her, as he continued to write. "And before you ask, these are my notes from our interview with Zingiber yesterday." He looked up as she sat down, pointing the feathered end of his quill at her. "And I think I made a connection in the burglary case."

Before Reva could ask what the connection was, First Constable Aescel's voice came shattering across the Stable. "Reva! Ansee! Get your butts in here!"

"What did we do now?" Ansee asked, as they headed to Aescel's office.

"We're not in trouble," Reva replied.

"How do you know that?"

"He said 'butts' instead of 'asses'." She smiled and opened the door, not bothering to knock.

Aescel sat behind his desk, which looked even messier than usual, with parchment and paper scattered about. One stack was at least two hands tall, and it looked ready to topple over. Aescel himself looked just as bad, his hair starting to come loose from its braid, and he had bags under his red-rimmed eyes.

"Are you alright, sir?" Ansee asked, clearly not knowing when to keep his mouth shut.

"Do I look alright, Seeker?" Aescel growled. "We've got cases falling on us like autumn leaves in a stiff wind, and not enough constables to go around."

"Maybe if we hadn't just lost our best people," Reva prompted.

Aescel turned his gaze to her and jabbed the air with his finger. "Don't you start on me, Reva."

"What did you want?" Reva said, trying to sound contrite, but it came out sounding sullen, instead.

Aescel fixed her with a stare, and then turned and pulled off a stack of parchment from one of the piles on his desk. "As I was saying, we've got a lot of cases coming in, and I need to know how you're doing on your current workload."

Reva crossed her arms. "We're making progress."

"Any of them ready to close?"

She shook her head. "No, but if there's more work to be done, we can do it."

"Any progress in the gingerbread case?"

"Ansee and I interviewed Zingiber yesterday. We're still going over what he told us, seeing if we can corroborate any of it or if it's all just hawkshit."

"You think he's the murderer?"

Reva shrugged. "Not sure yet. He's not a spellcaster, so—"

"He's not an Academy-trained wizard," Ansee cut in. "But he knows magic."

"So, is he a cleric or something? A sorcerer, maybe?"

This time it was Ansee who shrugged. "It's not like we can detect each other, but I don't think so. And the magic that was used to get the gingerbread into the victims isn't divine in nature, so he's not a cleric."

"Then how is he doing it?"

"That's what we're trying to find out."

"Well, try harder." He turned to look at Reva. "If you don't have any evidence to bring him in, then set the case aside. I can't afford to let you focus too much on one case right now."

Reva felt herself stiffen at the comment. She was far from focused on only one case right now. "That's not fair, sir," she retorted. "We've also got the burglary in Merchant Grove, and the death at the weaver's shop in Forest Grove. In fact, I think my caseload is rather light right now." She waved a hand toward the window that looked out onto the Stable. "I know that Olwyn's got his burglaries, an assault case, and two rapes, after you gave him that new one yesterday. And I'm sure that you also gave him something juicy based on the way he's been acting this morning."

Aescel nodded. "A murder case just came in."

Reva rolled her eyes and continued her point. "And I know Shawna's got more on her plate, too. The break-in and assault, a burglary, two stabbings in the port, and the floater."

"She's welcome to the floater," Ansee added.

"She and Seeker Hedera closed the floater case yesterday," Aescel said. "But she's got two kidnappings now to deal with after I gave her a new case this morning."

"So why in the hells are you complaining about me focusing on one case ,now, when there's all this work to do? I'm starting to think you're keeping cases from me."

Aescel shifted in his seat.

"Damn it!" She flung up her hands. "You *are* keeping cases from me!"

"Reva, you've been doing good work in the past month, but if you keep taking on every case that comes in the door, you're going to burn yourself out."

"That's hawkshit," Reva snapped. "I don't burn out." Her hand headed to the pocket where she kept her tin of Wake. She let it rest there, leaving the Wake where it sat, and willed herself to ignore it. She wasn't in the mood for a lecture from Ansee right now, and it would just play into Aescel's argument that she was overworked.

"We can handle another case," Ansee said. "I made a connection in the burglary yesterday, so I think we will be able to make an arrest today."

Reva held out a hand to Ansee as if to say, "See, we have things under control." Aloud, she said, "What do you have for us?"

Aescel gave a long, hard look at both Reva and Ansee, his hand resting on the stack of parchments. Finally, he sighed, pulled out a few pages, and handed them over to Reva. "Fine, you can take a look at this break-in down in South Grove."

"Oh, come on. A break-in? That's it?" Reva pointed to the rest of the stack. "What else have you got?"

Aescel shook his head. "Nothing you need to worry about. I will give these to some of the senior constables."

Reva snorted. "Maybe if you hadn't just lost our most competent one."

"I don't need that from you," Aescel said, pointing his finger at her again. "Senior Constable Hollbrush is a competent constable."

"Competent?" she snorted again. "If you consider letting

two murder victims walk out of a murder scene competent."

"Damn it, Reva, I don't need that attitude coming from you. Hollbrush followed procedure last month. He did nothing wrong." He emphasized his point by stabbing his finger down on his desk. "And I expect you to not make a big deal about it, or to lord it over him."

Reva blew out a breath and rolled her eyes. This earned her another chastisement from Aescel. "Leave him alone, Reva."

"Why did we have to get stuck with *him*, though? Why couldn't Betulla have transferred Senior Constable Jurasee? At least she's as good as Willem."

"We had no control over who was selected," Aescel said, his voice suddenly muted.

"Did you even try?"

"Damn it, Reva! You can be so dwarf-headed at times, you know that? Just let it go. You know it could have been worse."

"Worse?" Ansee asked.

"The Lord Constable wanted to break *us* up," she gestured with her hand to include him and her. "But Aescel *spared* us from that fate."

"I don't need your sarcasm, Reva." He stared at her and she met his gaze, not backing down. She liked Aescel. He was easy to work for, at least, most of the time. But he knew that she was right in this case. Betulla had taken years of tradition and routine and tossed it into the river, causing more problems than she was supposedly trying to fix. Aescel knew that. Hells, Churlsleaf also knew it. They had bowed to Betulla's whim to appease her, and they knew that had been a mistake. She wasn't going to stop pointing that out.

Aescel finally broke his gaze and dug into the stack of cases. He handed one to Reva. "Here. You can go investigate this break-in over in Port Grove. Someone broke into a warehouse and knocked out a guard to steal something."

"What did they take?" Ansee asked.

Aescel smirked as he answered. "Honeycomb."

Hells, now Aescel was just playing with them. But she didn't care, it was another case, and she'd made her point. "Anything else in there you want to give us?" she asked sweetly, twisting the dagger now that it had been jabbed in.

"I think two new cases is enough," Aescel stated.

Reva gave a playful shrug and opened the door.

"One more thing," Aescel said. She and Ansee stopped and looked back at the First Constable.

He pointed at Ansee. "I expect *you* to do better, or I'll transfer you back to Nul Pfeta myself."

"Sir?" Ansee asked.

Aescel held up a parchment. Reva knew it was one of Ansee's reports from the tiny, cramped script, but it was also spotted with splotches of ink. "Had I known that your report looked like this when you turned it in, I would have docked you another day's pay. I expect my constables to do better."

Ansee stepped forward and took the parchment. "But it wasn't like this when I turned it in, sir. I swear."

"I don't care, Seeker. Get it fixed. And do better."

Ansee nodded and walked out of the office, his head down. Reva followed him, closing the door behind her. A laugh from across the Stable caught her attention. She saw Norah and Olwyn chatting about something, but Norah's eyes were fixed on Ansee as they walked back to their tables.

Chapter 21

Cedres walked up the road through Nul Pfeta, stepping around the muddy holes filled with water and urine in the broken cobblestones. He reeked of manure and sweat, and he didn't want to add another awful odor to the mix. Ever since he'd lost his job as a litter-bearer, after the death of Lady Ochroma, he had not been able to find steady work. He'd been forced to work odd jobs from day to day. One day, he might work at the docks as a laborer, unloading cargo from ships. Another day, he might work cleaning out the muck from a ditch, or hauling grain or lumber from an outlying farm. His best days were when he could get a job as an assistant to a blacksmith, where he could actually use his experience. Inevitably, he would make a comment, usually pointing out an error or mistake that the blacksmith made, and he'd be fired. Nobody wanted a halpbloed to tell them that they made a mistake. His second best days would be spent working at the mill, as he could often sneak out a bit of flour, which he could trade to the baker that lived below his room for a small loaf of bread.

Today had not been one of the good days. The only work that he'd been able to find had been to clean out the stalls for the warhawks at the Royal Barracks. He'd almost not taken the work; he had been anxious to find out why Constable Sulwynd had not shown up yesterday. But he needed the pitiful wage he would earn, and he had spent so much time loitering around the constabulary trying to spot Sulwynd that, by the time he gave up, cleaning out the stalls had been the only work available.

He spent the day fuming at Sulwynd, wondering why the constable had abandoned him. He'd been led along like a child, promised a reward if he'd do a simple task, and then forgotten. He didn't know why he should have expected anything more from the constable, as he was just like everyone else, treating Cedres no better than an animal.

No, Cedres told himself, *animals get treated better.*

That thought caused his blood to boil as he looked at the halpbloeden around him. *I am better than these people. I am not one of them. And I will prove it.*

Cedres didn't know what Sulwynd had planned, only that it would be something that would make the King take notice. It would be something that would cause everyone to give him the recognition that he needed to regain his status as a citizen, to rid him of the stink and shame of being thought of as a halpbloed. He would get his life back, and then he'd get his children back. He'd be able to show Rhea that he *is* an elf, and make her understand the mistake she had made by turning him in.

Cedres ducked around a knot of halpbloed that had gathered outside a grocer. They were well along the way to getting drunk on the cheap apple brandy that the owner made in the back. He snagged an apple from a basket while they drank, and then moved back into the evening crowd. As he approached the bakery, he could smell the sickly-sweet stench of the ditch weed being smoked by the halpbloed that lived across the road. Cedres wrinkled his nose and crossed the street to avoid the halpbloed. He glanced over his shoulder and spotted him, sitting in front of his "temple", blissfully smoking the stinking weed, as he usually did every day. He was typical of the halpbloed that Cedres saw around him, looking for any opportunity to escape the pitiful reality that had become their daily routine. It was just another reminder of why Cedres was different from them.

Cedres turned back to head up the stairs to his room above the bakery, but came to a sudden stop as a figure stepped out of the shadows on the stairs, blocking his way. He was about to bolt—it was never good to have people surprise you from the shadows; it usually ended with the few copper Pfen that he'd earned being stolen—when he recognized the armor and bracers of a constable. That didn't guarantee that he wouldn't be robbed or beaten up, but he gave a sigh of relief as he recognized Constable Sulwynd.

Cedres forgot his earlier anger at the constable; the excitement of seeing Sulwynd gave him renewed hope that his ordeal was soon to be over. "Where were you last night? Why didn't you come?"

Sulwynd didn't say anything, and pulled him closer to the stairs, away from the halpbloed on the road.

"Everybody was here," Cedres said, the irritation clear in his voice. "And they left when you didn't show up. I don't know if they'll come back."

Sulwynd gave him an apologetic smile and held up a bracer. "Sorry, I was reassigned."

Cedres looked at the bracer and saw the red and blue of Betula Division. "Reassigned? What does this mean? Are we still doing your plan?"

Sulwynd pulled him up the stairs, looking around with a quick, jerky movement of his eyes. "It means I was reassigned, and I couldn't get away. Now, let's get inside."

† † †

Pfastbinder tapped out the remains of his latest pipe of canab, and proceeded to clean the bowl with the nail of his pinkie. The sun was already setting, and it would soon be dark; already the shadows were long in the street. There was also a noticeable nip in the air, hinting that it would get cold tonight, maybe even cold enough for a frost. Pfastbinder had mixed feelings about the autumn. He enjoyed the fall colors, and it was a good time to enjoy staples like roasted chestnuts (when he could get them), but it also heralded winter, which was his least favorite season. Sure, there was less mud on the streets and the fetid odor that was common throughout the summer was gone, but it was nearly impossible for him to stay warm during the long, cold nights. Pfastbinder much preferred the long, warm days of high summer.

He sighed, knowing that he couldn't do anything to change the seasons. Not even the followers of Nera could manage that feat.

Pfastbinder pulled out a pouch, the leather soft and supple from repeated use, and examined the contents with another sigh. The pouch was nearly empty of the dried buds and leaves that he blended for his own personal use from the few plants that he grew. He might have to start seeking alternate sources if he hoped to maintain his prayer sessions.

He shrugged, knowing that it wasn't worth trying to plan for anything in the future. Banok would provide, as he always did. He pulled out some of the canab, though a bit less than he might normally have, packed his pipe, and lit it from a twig from the small fire burning at his feet. He gave a satisfied puff, and then leaned back in his chair to continue one of his favorite pastimes: people watching.

The people here were not as entertaining as the people outside of Nul Pfeta. Here, it was a regular stream of dreary halpbloed, struggling to earn a living and provide the bare minimum existence for themselves and their families. Outside the Grove, there was a flamboyance and sense of wonder by the many different people that he could see. But the problem was that, out there, if he spent too long watching people, he'd get rousted by a constable for loitering. Still, he often saw things outside his small temple that made up for the usual monotony.

Things like what he was seeing right now.

He spotted the halpbloed who lived above the bakery navigating through the crowd, having just pilfered an apple from the grocer's stall. He was not so subtly walking away from the temple, and Pfastbinder felt a bit of annoyance that this halpbloed apparently didn't like him. There was no reason not to like him. Pfastbinder got along with everyone.

The halpbloed was watching Pfastbinder over his shoulder as he approached the bakery. Satisfied that Pfastbinder wasn't going to—what? Pray for the salvation of his soul?—the halpbloed turned back around and nearly ran into someone who had stepped out of the shadow of the stairway.

"Constable Sulwynd," Pfastbinder murmured around the stem of his pipe. He recognized the constable, even though he was wearing the wrong bracers. He knew that Sulwynd had been transferred to Betula Division after Ghrellstone and Gania had filled him in on everything yesterday. So, he was now very curious why the constable was back here in Nul Pfeta. People only came to Nul Pfeta because they were ordered here—elves and halpbloed alike. Nobody chose to be here.

Sulwynd was known as an asshole throughout Nul Pfeta, one of many constables that the locals avoided when they could. Many of the locals were quite happy when they had learned that he was one of the constables that had been transferred. He was a bully, and he enjoyed causing pain for no other reason than he got pleasure from it. He wasn't into the whole sex for favor thing that some of the other constables seemed to enjoy, and Pfastbinder knew that nobody in Nul Pfeta was wealthy enough to shake down for protection money, although he supposed that wouldn't necessarily be a deterrent. In his experience, elves enjoyed kicking people when they were down, especially halpbloed.

Still, none of this explained why Sulwynd would be meeting with a halpbloed. He watched Sulwynd look up and down the street, and then guide his neighbor into the room above the bakery. Pfastbinder wondered if he should do something. He took a thoughtful pull on his pipe, enjoying the flavor of the canab. Maybe he should mention it to Ghrellstone or Gania if he saw them.

Then his eyes widened as Banok's inspiration struck him. *Why should I tell them? I'm practically a constable my-*

self! I should investigate this dastardly situation to give my fellow constables more insight into what is happening!

Taking a final pull on his pipe, Pfastbinder put it into a pocket and stood up. He adjusted his multi-colored cloak and strode confidently across the street.

† † †

Sulwynd closed the door, and the little bit of light from outside was cut off. Cedres walked across the room—mostly from memory, due to the sudden darkness—and picked up his fire striker and flint, striking it a few times to get an ember onto the torchwood. Sulwynd remained silent, and he stayed by the door while Cedres finished lighting the candle. It offered a weak light, but was enough so that they could see clearly.

"You were transferred?" Cedres asked, turning to look at Sulwynd. "What does this mean? Is the plan off? Will we still be able to be noticed? To be recognized for who we are?"

"Whoa, slow down," Sulwynd interrupted, holding up his hands. "Everything is still going to happen, but our time is short. Are you still committed?"

"Yes," Cedres immediately replied. He was fully committed if it would get him what he deserved.

"What about the others?" Sulwynd asked. "This plan can work, but only if you have people helping you. You can't do this alone, Cedres."

Cedres felt his ears flush at yet another example of someone underestimating him because he was supposedly a halpbloed. If Cedres was the only one capable of pulling this off, he would do it alone, if he had to, but he also knew that this was Sulwynd's plan, and it was the only chance that Cedres had at getting what he deserved. He looked down at the floor, "I don't know. They were pretty angry with me after being stood up last night. Some of them may not want to come back."

Sulwynd nodded his head. "I can understand that." He pointed at his chest. "How do you think I feel? I didn't expect to be transferred. I wanted to be here. This is as important to me as it is to you." He pulled a stool closer and took a seat. "Let me tell you what you will be doing, and then you tell me whether you think you can get the others back on board or not."

Cedres nodded his head and crossed his arms.

"The plan is quite simple, but it will be very difficult to pull it off. But when you do, you and the others will finally have the recognition you've been seeking." He paused for a moment, and Cedres sighed at the dramatics. This was real life, not some play.

"You will be kidnapping Prince Orlean," Sulwynd finally said.

"What? Kidnap the Prince?" Cedres felt his mouth suddenly go bone dry. "We want to be recognized as the elves we are, not executed as traitors to the Kingdom. How will putting a death sentence on our heads help us?"

"You are not thinking about this from the right perspective, Cedres," Sulwynd replied.

"The right perspective? What sort of perspective should I have that doesn't involve me starting up at a Sucra torturer?"

"The Sucra won't be involved. You are going to kidnap the Prince, but not hurt him. He will be the leverage that you need to finally get the King's attention." Sulwynd gestured to Cedres. "You've said before that doing good deeds hasn't gotten you the recognition you deserve."

Cedres found himself nodding, recalling how he'd stood up to the masked killer that had attacked the litter that was carrying Lady Ochroma. Ceres had been stabbed by the killer while attempting to protect the head of the treasury, and he had helped the constables by describing the killer's mask. He had been promised that he would be recognized for his help, promised to have his citizenship and his rights returned to him, but he'd been turned loose from the constabulary without a word, and without any help. He had lost the room he had shared with several others, and when he'd tried to get his old job back, Earldown Pflies, the owner of the litter company, had pretended to have never heard of Cedres, and said he wasn't hiring. No, Cedres hadn't gotten any recognition from doing the right thing.

"This needs to be a show of force," Sulwynd continued. "That is the only thing that the King will understand. With the heir to the throne in your control, the King will do anything to get him back alive. He will give you whatever you want to get the Prince back."

"What about the Sucra? What's to keep them from just charging in and taking the Prince from us?"

"They won't want to risk his life. That's the beauty of this plan. The Prince is both the leverage you need and the insurance that will keep the Sucra away."

Cedres lowered his head and put a hand to his chin. There were so many things to consider, so many questions. "How would we even kidnap the Prince in the first place? How will we convey our demands to the King?"

Sulwynd held up his hands and gave a smile. "Don't get ahead of yourself. We will work out the details on how everything will happen, but I can't do that until I know that we have the others with us."

"I think I can get most of them to come back."

"Good." Sulwynd nodded, pulled out a pouch, and handed it to Cedres.

"What is this? Money? I'm not a mercenary."

"It's money, but it's not what you think." He gestured for Cedres to open the pouch. "When we are all gathered together and ready to implement the plan, I will get you money to get the supplies we will need—weapons, armor, and anything else you'll need. That," he pointed at the pouch, "is to show you where your support is coming from—who I'm working for."

Cedres opened the pouch and pulled out a coin. It was a Skip, the lustrous silver glinting in the candlelight. "So? It's just a Skip."

"Look closer."

Cedres turned to have better light, flipping the coin over in his hands. It had been a while since he'd had a Skip to call his own, and it took him a moment to recognize the difference. "The King's image," he finally said, looking up at Sulwynd. "It's reversed."

"Exactly," Sulwynd said, standing up from the stool. He pulled out a coin and looked at the image of the King. "On a normal Mark, the King's profile looks to the right. On these, he looks to the left."

"So, these are fake coins?" Cedres asked, confused. "How does *that* help us?"

"I can assure you those are not fakes. They are *real* Skips," he paused for a moment. "And who do you think has the power to mint real coins with this change?"

Cedres's eyes went wide as he fingered the coin, rubbing his thumb over the glittering surface. "You mean—"

Sulwynd quickly held up a hand to quiet him, turning his head to look at the door. An audible creak had come from the other side.

† † †

Pfastbinder groaned inwardly as the board beneath him gave a loud creak. He had been listening at the door as Cedres—he'd managed to finally catch the halpbloed's name—and Sulwynd discussed their plans. And what bold plans they were! Kidnapping the Prince? He had been shifting his weight in order to get into a better position when Banok had caused the wood to creak. He could hear someone moving in the room, and he quickly stood up, raising his hands up in supplication.

The door opened, and Constable Sulwynd stood in the doorway, glaring at Pfastbinder, a hand on the hilt of his dagger.

"I beseech you, Lord Banok, to hear my prayer."

"What are you doing here, halpbloed?" Sulwynd growled. "Why were you listening at the door?"

"Hmm?" Pfastbinder turned to look at the constable,

being sure to not fix his gaze on anything, but letting his eyes wander and move, something that he knew most people found disconcerting. "Listen? The only one I listen to is Lord Banok, but lo, my prayer plant." He patted his cloak and pulled out his pipe from the pocket. "I am nearly out of my prayer plant," he opened his pouch and held it so that Sulwynd could see the nearly empty contents.

"Get that away from me," Sulwynd spat, pushing the pouch back.

Pfastbinder saw the candle burning in the room next to his neighbor, Cedres. He started to pack his pipe and tried to step past the constable. "May I trouble you for a light, friend? So I may commune with Lord Banok?"

Sulwynd stepped in front of him and pushed him back. "What are you doing here, halpbloed? What did you hear?"

"Hear? I hear Banok calling me to prayer, but this is the last of my prayer plant. I'm sure I left some here." Pfastbinder looked past Sulwynd to Cedres. "Maybe you've seen them, friend? I used to keep them here. I planted them in clay pots and kept them under the holes in the roof. You know how the roof leaks terribly when it rains? And the draft? I see you've had no better luck than I did in getting our baker friend to fix up this room. You know, with some whitewash and a bit of plaster here and there, I'm sure he could fix this place up. Maybe even rent it out to travelers from out of town, and bring in some needed tourist income to the old grove."

"Get back," Sulwynd gave Pfastbinder another shove. "You stink of that ditch weed."

"Do you think the baker is putting sawdust into his bread?" Pfastbinder asked, staring past the constable to Cedres. "I think it's been grittier than normal. Do you know anything about teeth?" He tried to take another step in, and was again shoved back by Sulwynd. "I think mine are starting to wear down." He opened his mouth wide, and he rubbed a finger across his teeth, making sure to exhale on Sulwynd.

The constable waved a hand in front of his face. "You stink, even worse than most damn halpbloeden. I should arrest you and have you rot in a cell." He took a step forward.

Pfastbinder jumped back, landing on the top step of the stairs. He fixed Sulwynd with his gaze and gave him a patronizing smile. "Why that sounds most hospitable, Constable Sulwynd, but I'm afraid that Lord Banok's prayers wait for no one." He took another hop down the stairs, then pirouetted on one foot, and skipped down the stairs with a wave of his hand. When he reached the road, he performed a smart turn that would have impressed any of the officers in the King's army, and then strutted down the road.

† † †

"Do you see why I am so committed to this mission?" Cedres said, gesturing to the door. Constable Sulwynd continued to stand in the doorway, watching the halpbloed walk away. "That halpbloed is crazy. He claims he's a cleric, of the god of chaos, no less, but all he does is spend his time smoking canab. No one ever comes to his "temple" that I have ever seen."

Sulwynd continued to stand there for a full minute after the halpbloed had left, and then finally stepped back inside and closed the door. "He is crazy," he said, as he turned to face Cedres. "But crazy doesn't mean that he isn't also dangerous. We don't know what he might have heard, or who he might tell."

"I can deal with him," Cedres offered. "He's not important."

"No, I'll deal with him. You need to focus on getting the others to help you."

Cedres shrugged and fingered the Skip in his hand. "I'll get the others to come back."

Chapter 22

Inquisitor Amalaki's breath trailed behind him in a visible cloud as he walked off the ferry and headed toward Poplar Hill. A smile crossed his face as he walked along the road, his thick, dark green Sucra cloak providing a welcome warmth from the cool night air. He exhaled a long cloud of breath, watching it billow out before him, and remembering how he'd pretend to be a dragon when he was a child, chasing his younger sister around as she squealed in fright before turning around to attack him with her own 'dragon' breath. Those had been better times, back before he had joined the Sucra and Calluna had joined the army. Certainly, he and Calluna had spoken more back then. He tried to remember the last time they had spoken, and he figured that it had to have been before the summer when she had been home briefly to meet with the marshals and other military commanders. They hadn't said more than maybe two dozen words to each other at that meeting.

He sighed, his breath framing his head in another cloud, and he kicked a stone that bounced off the cobbles in the road and into a bale of straw. Repairing the relationship with his sister would have to take an upper branch, as he needed to focus on his current case. A case that he thought had been completely cut down yesterday when he'd learned that Constable Sulwynd had been reassigned from Nul Pfeta. It had taken Amalaki most of the morning to find out where he had been reassigned, and he had then wasted most of the afternoon trying to find Sulwynd so that he could continue his surveillance, before finding out that the constable had been sent to Ilvalé Arena. Nearly the entire day had been wasted just walking around the city, time that Constable Sulwynd could have used to do anything. Maybe he had been working, doing his job as a constable, or maybe his transfer had been made so that he could advance his plot against the King.

That thought sent a shiver up Amalaki's spine that had nothing to do with the chill in the air. He unconsciously hurried his pace as he turned and headed up the hill.

Soon enough, he saw the hulking shape of New Port silhouetted against the night sky. The main gate was closed, and Amalaki slipped through the smaller door set into the wall. There was no guard, which was something that had always surprised him. He supposed that the constabulary thought that nobody would be stupid enough to attack them at their headquarters, but that hadn't stopped a crazy cultist from sending his zombies against New Port last month.

He pushed on the large doors and walked into the main building. He had just turned to the stairs when the watch constable called out, "Oy, you can't just go—" His voice cut off as he recognized the dark green cloak and black jodhpurs that were the Sucra's distinctive uniform. "Oh. Evening, Inquisitor," the constable said, with a nod, as he went back to whatever kept him distracted on his night shift.

Amalaki took the stairs and turned into the Acer Division stable. The room was mostly empty at this time of the day, with only a few constables working late. One of them had her head down as she concentrated on some parchmentwork on her table, her silver-red hair falling down to frame her face. Constable Inspector Lunaria looked up as Amalaki stopped at her table.

"Are you lost, Inquisitor?" she asked, a touch of humor in her voice.

"Not at all," he responded, with a shake of his head. "I

wanted to stop by and make sure that nothing untoward had happened to you."

"I'm sorry, I've been a bit busy with work." She gestured to the parchmentwork that covered her desk like a carpet of fallen leaves.

"I thought we'd agreed that we would work together on Const... on my case."

"I'm sorry if capturing a murderer is more important than your case."

Amalaki bit back his own reply; he hadn't come here to antagonize Reva. "Not at all. But there have been some developments that I would like to discuss with you. Is there someplace we can talk," he pointed around the Stable, "that isn't a closet next to the roof, or a cell?"

Reva leaned back and pulled a lock of her hair back over an ear. "Well, you haven't left me many options, Inquisitor." She tried to keep her face serious, but Amalaki heard a rumble emanating from her stomach, and Reva's face broke into a smile.

"It's easier to be intimidating when your stomach doesn't betray you," Amalaki smiled back.

"Very true. Look, I know a place we can talk if you'll buy me dinner."

"Why, Inspector, are you asking me on a date?" He gave her a playful smile. "What will your co-workers think?"

"I don't give a damn about my co-workers. They can think what they want because I'll knock any of them on their ass if they make this out into something more than what it really is." Reva turned and glared at a constable sitting at another table. The constable either had the will to ignore Reva's comment, or had weathered similar statements before, as he merely shrugged. Amalaki figured it had to have been the latter, since he had clearly been listening in on their conversation.

Reva stood up and put on a dark brown cloak with green trim. It was of a good quality, though it was showing its age. "That doesn't look like a Constabulary-issued cloak," he remarked, as they headed to the stairs.

Reva rubbed the cloak. "It's not. We only get issued one cloak, good for all seasons. It's too hot in the summer, and it's too cold in the winter. My mom knew that, with my father also being a constable, so she gave me this when I joined the RTC."

"That was thoughtful of her," he commented, as they walked down the stairs.

"It was, but she had an ulterior motive, as well."

"And what was that?" Amalaki asked, as he pulled open the door.

"She hoped that if I had a nice cloak, I would take it easy and not get into trouble, since she would harangue me if it got damaged."

"Did that work?"

Reva laughed, and turned to show him a large tear that had been sewn up. "I got that the first day I wore it."

Amalaki shook his head and they walked out of New Port. Reva turned to the right and headed down the road. She only went about fifty paces before she turned into a small restaurant, with three empty tables sitting outside. There was a small fire going in a fire pit, and Reva stepped up and stuck a new log onto the fire, sparks flying into the air. She brushed off a chair and took a seat.

Amalaki looked into the restaurant through the door, seeing the warm glow of a larger fire illuminating several people sitting at tables. "It would probably be warmer inside," he remarked.

"It probably is," Reva replied, "but there are also more ears to overhear us. But if it's too cold for your delicate nature, we can move inside."

Amalaki rolled his eyes, took a seat, and looked across at Reva, clasping his hands together.

"I said I was hungry," she stated, "and that you are buying." She pointed toward the door.

Amalaki sighed as he stood up and shook his head as he went inside. It was warmer inside, and the place was filled with savory odors and fresh bread. He noticed how the conversations at the tables all quieted or completely stopped as soon as people saw his cloak. He was used to that reaction, though he didn't understand why people did it. If the Sucra was interested in any of these people, they wouldn't know they were being watched.

Amalaki placed his order and waited while the drinks were filled. He found himself wondering what Reva might have done to have damaged her cloak the first time she'd worn it. It said a lot about her, how she approached life, and he wondered if it was a good thing or a bad thing. He figured if he could channel that attitude, then it would be a good thing.

The drinks arrived and he carried them back outside. The fire had died down a little, but he could feel the heat coming off the coals. He set a drink down in front of Reva and took his seat.

Reva grabbed the mug and inhaled deeply. "Hot cacao," she remarked, with a smile. "You sure know the way to a woman's heart."

Amalaki held up his own mug. "I aim to please."

"So why did you come all the way up to New Port this evening?"

"You heard that Constable Sulwynd was reassigned from Nul Pfeta to Betula Division?"

Reva nodded as she set her cacao down. "Me and everyone else in the constabulary. The LCI made a big deal out of the transfers." She put her hands on the mug to warm them. "Has that thrown wet leaves on your theory about him?"

"No, but it did make it harder for me to track him in order to see what happens."

"I know that he was assigned to patrol a grove, but I've been busy with my own work. I don't know which one, though I can probably find out."

"Not necessary," Amalaki shook his head, "I know he was assigned to Bay Grove."

"That's about as far from Nul Pfeta as you can get in the

city. Why would Betulla—" Reva stopped talking.

"What about the Lord Constable Inspector?" Amalaki asked, "Is she connected to this, other than reassigning her constables?"

Reva picked up her cacao and brought it to her lips, though she didn't take a drink.

Amalaki narrowed his eyes a bit, clearly picking up that Reva knew something that she wasn't telling him. A server came outside carrying their meal, so he decided to wait a moment before pressing her. He wasn't going to let this go.

Their meal was simple: a barley and mushroom soup, and thick slices of dark bread. Steam rose from the bowls, and Amalaki savored the smell. Reva picked up her spoon and dug into the soup.

Amalaki picked up his own spoon and held it over the bowl. "What does Betulla have to do with Constable Sulwynd?"

Reva lifted another spoonful of soup and took a loud slurp.

"Look, I know you are withholding something," he pointed at her with his spoon. "Something that I think that you think, or at least your subconscious thinks, is important. And I'm sure it doesn't have anything to do with whatever vendetta Betulla has with you."

Reva gave him a quizzical look, and then said, "Your soup is going to get cold."

Amalaki shook his head and took a bite of soup. "I keep reminding you that I am *not* Malvaceä. You don't have to keep secrets from me."

Reva dropped her spoon into the bowl. "And you aren't keeping any from me? I told you the other night that this partnership will only work if we're honest with each other."

"I've not been keeping any secrets from you."

"It may not be a secret, but you've been dancing around something ever since you sauntered into the Stable."

Sauntered? Amalaki wondered what he'd done to get Reva so upset. He ate some of his soup and realized that she was deflecting his push for information on Betulla. He picked up his bread and dunked it into the soup. "I haven't been keeping any secrets from you," he repeated, "and I wasn't dancing around anything either. I was building up to the important stuff."

Reva gave a snort and finished her soup. "So, what's so important, then?"

"What would you think if our prime suspect met with someone of importance?"

"Depends on who it was."

"Grand Inquisitor Agera."

Reva raised her eyebrows and picked up her bread. "Then I would say it depends on what the conditions were when they met. Was this out in the open or in secret?" She began to sop up the remains of her soup.

"It was in the open," Amalaki admitted, "but it was under unusual conditions. They met at Ilvalé Arena just as the Grand Inquisitor was accosted and robbed by a pickpocket."

"Was the would-be thief some kind of criminal mastermind, or just dumb?" Reva asked, with a chuckle.

"I'm pretty sure he was just dumb. Constable Sulwynd actually chased him and took him down with some aggressive moves."

"And are you going to tell me why you were spying on your boss?"

"I was watching Sulwynd. The Grand Inquisitor just happened to be there." Amalaki took a bite of bread. He pointed the bread at Reva. "But I think it is interesting that Sulwynd did meet with Agera before the incident with the pickpocket. They had a short conversation, and from what I could tell, the good Constable was upset about something."

"He was probably angry that he was having to work the arena to watch for pickpockets. It's not the most exciting thing a constable gets to do."

"Or he was upset that he wasn't where he wanted to be; in Nul Pfeta." Amalaki countered, dunking his bread into the soup and taking a triumphant bite.

"Don't start celebrating just yet. That's a really thin branch you're standing on."

"Maybe," Amalaki conceded. He finished off his bread. "Though if I knew how the Lord Constable Inspector was involved, then I might be able to build a stronger branch."

Reva picked up her spoon, and then realized that she had already finished all of her soup.

"Now who's not being honest?" Amalaki asked. He could see Reva stiffen, her shoulders going rigid as she looked toward the fire. He had struck a nerve, though he wasn't sure exactly what it was.

Reva looked back at Amalaki and he saw her chewing on her lip. Finally, she said, "I'm sure it's nothing. You know that Betulla was the First Constable for Nul Pfeta before becoming LCI?"

Amalaki nodded.

"Well, at that time, Sulwynd worked directly under Betulla. So, if he's plotting something in Nul Pfeta, then it's not with the LCI's knowledge. Otherwise, she wouldn't have transferred him out of the grove, or she would have just moved him to Marsh Grove where he could still get into Nul Pfeta fairly easily if he needed to."

"So, you think Betulla isn't involved?"

Reva played with a strand of her hair for a moment before saying, "I don't think so. She likes to have her hands on all the branches at all times. If she is working with Sulwynd on anything he might be planning, then she wouldn't have moved him."

Amalaki nodded. "Well, I guess we know a little bit more now."

"Yeah, but that still leaves us fumbling around in the bushes."

Chapter 23

Frost covered the railings on Victory Bridge as Constable Kai Gania walked across it and into Nul Pfeta. The sun was still below the horizon, and Kai knew that it was going to be another long day that would begin, and probably end, in darkness. He didn't mind the changing of the seasons so much, but why couldn't the amount of sunlight remain the same? He idly wondered that, if he began worshipping Lyzar, would the sun god answer his prayers and let the sun rise earlier? He doubted it, since he knew how fickle the gods were.

Kai sighed as he walked into the Nul Pfeta station. He was greeted by heat from the fire roaring in the fireplace, as well as the stench of unwashed bodies. He gave another sigh as he missed the smell of aged wood, hay, and horses that seemed to have been permanently imprinted on New Port, despite the long years that the constabulary had called it home.

Kai walked over to the table that was shared by most of the constables in Nul Pfeta, and said good morning to Constable Bourreria, who was sitting at the table. She gave a small laugh, and responded, "We've known each other most of our lives, Kai. I think it's okay if you call me Rhi."

"Sorry," Kai gave a timid smile. "I wasn't sure if you wanted to keep the fact that we grew up together a secret. I know how things would be at New Port if the other constables knew that. I can't imagine how things might be here."

"You don't have to worry about me. I can take care of myself. I've been a constable for longer than you, remember?"

"Only by six months," Kai countered. He pointed around the building. "Do you like it here?"

Rhi scrunched up her nose. "Nobody likes it here. This really wasn't what I had in mind when I joined the constabulary."

"Nul Pfeta's not anybody's idea of a picnic spot," added another voice. Kai turned to see Constable Gallwynn leaning against another table, chewing on something. He stood up and spit a stream of red-stained saliva onto the floor; Kai realized that he was chewing Wake root. *At least Constable Inspector Lunaria takes it as snuff,* he thought.

"But not all of us had their *mommy* get them a cushy position in Acer," Gallwynn continued, taking a step towards Kai.

Kai felt his ears redden and ignored the warning look that Rhi gave him. "My mother didn't open any clearings for me. I started where the first open position was available, in Betula."

"For two days, before your pretty little ass was plucked out and put into Acer. What did you do, sleep with Lunaria, or was it the First Constable?"

Kai felt his stomach begin to twist and do somersaults. He had never asked for favors—even if he had, his mother would have never granted them. She had been most insistent on that when he expressed his interest in joining the constabulary. He wanted to reply, but before he could, he felt a hand on his shoulder.

"That explains why you've been stuck here for so long, Senecio," said Senior Constable Ghrellstone. "You've got the ugliest ass in the entire constabulary. Nobody in their right mind would want to sleep with you."

Rhi gave a snort and quickly tried to cover it up, but still earned a sharp glare from Gallwynn.

"You think you two are so special coming from Acer?" Gallwynn asked. "Well, you're nothing but hawkshit here." He jabbed at the floor with a red-stained finger. "Got that?"

"As long as I'm not you, then I'll give praise to Basvu for that," Willem replied.

Constable Gallwynn glared at Kai and Willem, wiping at his mouth, and then stalked off.

"You always have to get the last word in, cousin?"

Kai turned to see Constable Lhoren Ghrellstone sitting at another table, his chair leaning back, and his muddy boots propped up on the table.

Willem turned to face his cousin. "With pompous asses like Gallwynn? Hells, yes."

Lhoren brought his feet down and stood up. "Well, he's right, you know. You don't work out of New Port anymore." He pointed toward the door. "Things are done differently here. The sooner you get that through your thick skull, the better."

"We're all constables," Kai blurted out. "No matter which division we work in, we all do the same thing."

Lhoren gave a derisive snort. "Heh, you're real funny." He stepped up quickly and pointed a finger in Kai's face. "You're wrong, momma's boy. We're not constables here. Here, in Nul Pfeta, we're the keepers of the menagerie. You should forget everything your mommy ever told you about being a constable, because none of it applies here. The halpbloed only respect us because they fear us."

Willem laughed, "Then you must get no respect around here."

This earned another laugh from Rhi, and a snarled glare from Lhoren. He turned on Rhi, "Watch it, Sap, you don't know what might happen in Nul Pfeta in the dark."

Kai took a step forward, forcing Lhoren to take a step back. "Don't threaten her."

"Or what?"

"Or I'll give my aunt something to be really upset about," Willem offered.

Kai could feel the tension growing as taut as a bowstring as Constables Gallwynn and Naraesh stepped up behind Lhoren.

"You'll all be upset when I dock you a day's pay for fighting," First Constable Pueraria's voice came from the stairs.

Lhoren sneered at Kai and Willem as he backed away and went back to his chair.

The First Constable stepped off the stairs, her eyes lingering longer on Kai and Willem, as if deciding if she should punish them anyway. "I am making a change to the shift schedules, effective today," she announced. She quickly looked at the group, her face stern, forestalling any complaints. She turned back to look at Kai and Willem, letting a thin smile show on her lips.

"Effective today, Senior Constable Ghrellstone and Constable Gania will move to the night shift. You will work your regular shift today, and then work the night shift tonight."

Kai felt himself slouching just a bit. Apparently, she *had* decided to punish him and Willem.

"Eleapflam and Naraesh will be coming to the day shift, starting tomorrow," the First Constable concluded.

Kai could see the two constables smiling. They were basically getting a paid day off. Standing next to him, Willem merely nodded his head to acknowledge the new orders. Kai knew it would be pointless to say anything, so he nodded as well. This was just another way for the members of Nul Pfeta to haze the two newcomers.

The First Constable went over a few more items on the morning agenda before sweeping back up the stairs. As the meeting broke up, Lhoren, Eleapflam, Gallwynn, and Naraesh all gathered around a table to congratulate themselves and have a laugh—probably at Kai and Willem's expense.

Kai felt a hand on his, and looked down at Rhi. "Well, look on the bright side," she smiled. "We'll have more time to catch up now."

Kai smiled back, "Always a silver lining."

"Let's go, Constable," Willem urged, tugging on Kai's cloak. "Nul Pfeta won't watch itself."

† † †

The day had warmed up enough to turn the Nul Pfeta roads and alleys into muddy trails. Kai's boots squelched, and he wondered where most of the mud came from, since there hadn't been any significant rain in the past few days. Then he saw a chamber pot being thrown out, and a thin, sway-backed mule let out a long stream of urine.

He and Willem walked around the thin yellow stream as they continued their morning patrol. They passed people carrying thin bundles of firewood, and others carrying flat loaves of bread or shriveled looking turnips and potatoes. Kai smiled at an older woman who was attempting to sweep mud out of her home. She spat on the ground and closed the door.

"There has to be a better way," he offered, stepping up to walk alongside Willem.

"Better way for what?"

"For this." Kai gestured to the grove around them. They had to walk around a spindly tree branch that was being used to support a building that threatened to topple into the road. A small group of children had been playing in an alley, and most of them shrank back as he and Willem drew near. Two of the older children stood defiantly, and Kai noticed that they held muddy stones in their hands. "They're afraid of us."

"What do you expect after thirty years of having people like Constable Gallwynn and my cousin patrolling Nul Pfeta? If you put bullies and thugs here all the time, you're not going to win any hearts and minds."

"It doesn't seem right."

Willem gave a snort. "Hells, Kai. It's not right." He turned to give Kai a sympathetic look. "But it is what it is. Your mother might have stopped all this. She could have made changes when she was LCI. Why didn't she?"

"My mother didn't cause any of this," Kai retorted, realizing how defensive he sounded.

"I didn't say she did," Willem replied. "But she also didn't make changes to how things were run here, did she?"

Kai took a few steps before saying, "No. And I don't know why."

"I know why."

"You do?" Kai asked, looking at Willem.

Willem nodded, ignoring the glares coming from the group of men sitting in front of what appeared to be a tea shop, though Kai was sure they weren't drinking tea. "As long as this place is out of sight, and nobody makes a big deal here, then everybody outside this grove will look the other way. They'll ignore anything that happens within this grove, by the halpbloed," he nodded toward the group of men, "or by the constables. As long as anything that happens here stays here, and doesn't affect the rest of the city, then nobody will care how that peace is maintained."

Kai watched a little girl struggling to carry a wooden pail of water up the street. The pail must have weighed at least half as much as she did. The girl gave him a defiant stare, and stuck her chin out as they walked past. "I just can't believe that my mother would ignore this."

"I don't think that she ignored it," Willem stated, "but I also think that she couldn't do anything about it, either. Do you know how many leaves would need to be blown away to reform things here? How much light that would shine on this cheery little grove in our city? Nobody wants that to happen. Certainly not the King, or the Mayor, or any of the Guild Luminaries or the nobles. Out of sight, out of mind."

They walked on a bit more, and then turned up one of the narrow roads that passed for a main thoroughfare. "Besides," Willem said, "where would the money come from? Our budget is thin enough as it is, and I know that Nul Pfeta is always sucking hind teat, even with a good LCI like your mother."

They continued on their patrol, and Kai did his best to

look past the stares and angry looks coming from the halp-bloed. He knew that he was just one constable, and that he likely would never make any impact on how the people here viewed the constabulary, but he vowed to himself that he would try to make a difference.

"Look on the bright side," Willem said.

"What's that?"

"Not *every* halpbloed here hates our guts." He pointed up the road, and Kai could see the flamboyant cloak that belonged to Pfastbinder sashaying toward them.

"Not exactly the kind of support I think we want," Kai stated.

Willem grunted as the cleric walked up to them.

"Reis hoestii," Pfastbinder greeted them. "Always a pleasure to meet my fellow constables."

"You're not a constable," growled Willem.

"Yet," Pfastbinder countered, holding up a finger, a manic smile gleaming on his face.

"Don't hold your breath," replied Willem.

Pfastbinder looked hurt, and then turned to Kai. "And I hope that you are less of a grumpy dwarf than your partner this morning."

"Hard to be cheerful after the morning we've had," Kai said.

"It cannot be that bad," Pfastbinder smiled, then gestured over his head. "The sun has risen, and the day is bright."

"Since when did you become a follower of Lyzar?" Willem asked, earning a reproachful glare from the cleric.

"It might be good for you," Kai grumbled, "but we just learned that we've been moved to the night shift, and that we have to work a double shift today."

"That is wonderful," Pfastbinder said, clapping his hands together. "About working the night shift, not about having to work two shifts. You really haven't lived until you've experienced the charm and beauty of Nul Pfeta after dark."

At that moment, a window opened two buildings down and a chamber pot was poured out into the street.

"Yeah, I'm sure it's way more charming than this," Willem deadpanned.

"But don't you see," Pfastbinder said, his eyes widening as if some inspiration had just struck him. "You can come by my temple tonight, and I can tell you my news."

"What news?" Willem asked.

"You can tell us now," Kai added. "We're already here."

"Nope. I must be off. Busy schedule. Lots to do."

"How can you have lots to do?" Kai asked.

"Being the only cleric in the service to Banok, my days are filled with excitement and wonder. No time to talk now. Stop by my temple tonight, and I'll tell you my news." With that, Pfastbinder flung his cloak over his shoulder and marched up the street.

"You know he's crazy, right?" Kai asked. "I don't know why Constable Inspector Lunaria trusts him."

"Crazy doesn't necessarily mean he's dangerous," Willem offered, as he continued on their patrol. "But I agree, I don't know why Reva has started to trust him, either."

"So, we're not going to meet him later tonight, are we?"

"Sure, we are," Willem grinned. "We've got to win the hearts and minds of the people. Might as well start somewhere."

"I was hoping for a mind that was a little more stable," Kai sighed, as they continued their patrol.

Chapter 24

A breeze blew out of the south, bringing warmer air with it, and hopefully heralding a break in the colder weather that had descended upon the region. The wind ruffled The Minister's robes as he stood on the deck of the small ship. He had boarded the ship yesterday morning after receiving *Shádpfed* Asclepias' missive to come to Tenyl, and the vessel, though cramped and full of an ill-smelling cargo of goats and poultry, had made good time.

The Minister could hear the crewelves prepare the ship to dock at the port while he stared ahead, seeing the city spread out before him. On his right, the tall red cliffs rose up from the bay, the red walls of Castle Tenz shimmering in the noonday sun atop the cliff. The large trees and congestion of Old Grove and the mouth of the Tenz River were directly ahead, and an unruly sprawl that seemed to grow like a cancer from off the port was on his left. The city had changed a lot in the five decades since he had last visited.

The Minister wrinkled his nose and narrowed his eyes as he took in the city. He was not happy to be back in Tenyl. Certainly not for the reason that he had been summoned. He despised the way that the city elders tolerated the presence of the sorcerous pestilence that had infected the city, and he felt that the wizards at Auros Academy did too little to root them out. He'd tried to make his case, to deal with the problem all those years ago, but he'd been overruled, the other members of the order bullied into rejecting The Minister's plan by one elf. They had been duped into thinking that taking necessary action in the capital would bring unwanted attention to their order. They were filled with trepidation and consternation about upsetting the ruling class, more concerned about keeping the new King and the nobles appeased after the coronation of King Aeonis, even though The Minister had shown them that the sorcerous scourge had penetrated even the highest ranks of the nobility. The Minister had left the city to bring justice to the rest of the Kingdom, without interference, and he hadn't returned until now.

He shook his head at the irony of being summoned to deal with a sorcerer threat by the very elf that had been so vociferous that the Qurundora should keep a low profile, to not shake the branches, all those years ago. Had he been allowed to deal with the threat then... The Minster chastised himself at the thought. The past was the past, and it couldn't be changed. He was here, now, and he had a mission to root out the evil that had infiltrated the world. Maybe this Seeker was the key to learning which demon was involved. It would make sense that the demon would have dug itself into the very city that The Minister had left. The few other members of the Qurundora that had worked in the city had been ineffective, at best; that much was clear. Even if this Seeker wasn't the key to the demon's power, it was probably time for The Minister to return from his self-imposed exile.

The ship was almost docked. The Minister returned to the small cabin that he'd been given for the trip and packed up the few items that he had removed from his satchel. He took his time, carefully folding up his prayer cloth and candles. He tucked away his spellbook, and then settled his dark blue cloak about his shoulders. He picked up his broad-brimmed hat and settled it on his head, careful to tuck his hair back. Finally, he picked up his staff, letting his hands caress the smooth, polished wooden surface. Satisfied. he left the cabin and walked back up to the main deck.

Once the ship docked, crewelves handled the lines to tie the ship to the dock. It took a few more minutes for the gangplank to be put in place, and The Minister then disembarked at a brisk pace. The docks were crowded with elves and halpbloed, and it took The Minister several minutes to make his way through the narrow and twisting roads to reach the main road. It took him another thirty minutes to reach Auros Academy.

He inquired with a *Shádpfed* who was teaching a class in the main hall, and received directions to Asclepias' office. The Minister ignored the ostentatious grandeur that was always on display at the Academy as he marched through the hall and up to the third floor. He opened the door to the professor's office without knocking.

Shádpfed Jorus Asclepias looked up from his desk, a spoon held halfway to his lips. "How dare you barge into my office?" he bellowed, his voice full of indignation.

The Minster stepped closer to the desk, and then stopped, leaning on his staff and glaring at Jorus from under the broad brim of his hat. "You summon me here, and then you have the audacity to be affronted by my presence?"

Jorus's eyes widened in recognition, and he set the spoon down in the bowl on his desk. "Pfe—"

"Minister," The Minister corrected, cutting him off.

"Minister," Jorus acknowledged, with a slight curl of his lip. "I wasn't expecting you until tomorrow."

"Your missive led me to believe that this was an urgent matter. Is that not the case?"

"Of course, of course. My apologies. Had I known you were arriving today, I would have sent one of our order to meet you."

"Then it is good that I arrived early. I do not need to be pampered, and I prefer anonymity."

"Of course," Jorus bobbed his head, sounding like one of those damned Cantullian parrots, repeating one phrase over and over again. "Would you like to rest and refresh yourself after your trip?" He pointed to his bowl. "Something to eat? I have arranged to have the best room at The Gilded Staff to be at your disposal while you are here."

The Minister let a frown crease his face. Did he not just tell this fool that he did not want to be pampered? The Gilded Staff was the inn directly next door to the Academy, a favorite of visiting wizards and a semi-permanent residence for many of the professors. It was as far from being anonymous as one could get in the city, at least among the wizard community. If he stepped one foot in there, his presence would be known to half the city before sunup.

"I have made my own arrangements," The Minister countered.

Jorus hesitated for a moment, and then nodded his head. "Of course. Is there anything that I can do for you to make your... task easier while you are here?"

"Yes. You can stay out of my way."

Jorus leaned back as if he had been slapped. Then he seemed to find his spine as he leaned forward and narrowed his eyes. "You still think you're better than everyone else, don't you, *Minister*? I remember how you used to think that *only you* had all the answers. How *only you* knew what needed to be done. The Qurundora is a group dedicated to a single goal, and we will only reach that goal by working together!"

"Which is why *you* summoned *me* to fix a problem that *you* haven't been able to fix in *fifty years.*"

"And in that same fifty years, you have discovered the name of the demon, then?"

The Minister leaned forward, menacingly. "I have been removing its infestation from the land, while you have allowed it to burrow in and fester."

"You *dare* accuse me of harboring the demon?"

"No," The Minister nearly spat. "I'm accusing you of ineptitude. Had you listened to me in the first place, we wouldn't have to root out a sorcerer from within the constabulary."

"You can't hang that failure in my branches," Jorus retorted. "I have no control over who the constabulary hires as their Seekers."

"You prove my point for me," The Minster smirked.

"I am getting that corrected."

"Conveniently *after* the warhawk has left the roost." He held up a hand to forestall the additional bluster that Jorus was about to spout. As much as The Minister would enjoy raking the *Shádpfed* over the coals, which he greatly deserved, doing that wouldn't solve the problem at hand. "I understand that our agent was having success at rooting out the demon before he was killed." Jorus nodded, clearly upset at the change in the conversation.

"We may not know how deep the demon's roots have been planted in Tenyl," The Minister continued, "but I am sure that the presence of a sorcerer within the constabulary is a symptom of that rot."

"He is clearly in league with the demon," Jorus said, stating the obvious. "To be able to have remained hidden from us for so long."

The Minister had his own thoughts about that, and it had nothing to do with how devious and creative the demon was at controlling its minions, but stating that fact wasn't productive. "I will deal with it. And then I will deal with the root of the problem here in Tenyl."

Jorus nodded his head, but The Minister could see the worry in his eyes. *He's thinking that I will be coming for him once I've dealt with the sorcerer. Maybe I will.*

The Minister turned to leave. "What are you going to do?" asked Jorus.

The Minister paused, and then glanced back at the professor. "What any good hunter would do. Flush out my quarry."

Chapter 25

The fire popped and crackled, sparks jumping as Willem tossed a log into the fireplace. It had warmed up during the day, and it looked like this night would be warmer than the night before, but the Nul Pfeta gatehouse was always damp—being right next to the river—and no amount of heat seemed to be able to chase the chill away. He turned back to the room and caught Kai stifling a yawn as he sat at the table doing some parchmentwork.

"Hey, no sleeping on the job." Willem chastised.

Kai pointed with his quill to the form of Constable Pfellcreek, who was slouched in a chair and snoring softly. "Tell that to him."

"He's not new to this division and under the scrutiny of the First Constable."

"Scrutiny?" Kai snorted. "I think the word you want is hazing. We shouldn't be forced to work a double shift."

"We work what we need to," Willem replied. "I've worked plenty of double shifts in my time, and we've had our share of long days working with Reva. We're here to do a job." He felt that he needed to remind Kai of what it meant to be a constable. "And we're better at it than the idiots that work here."

"Hey!"

Willem turned to see Constable Bourreria coming down

the stairs, and he felt his ears flush. "Sorry, present company excluded."

She smiled and gave a shrug, "I'll let it fall this time, but don't let Pfellcreek hear you say that. He'll be sure to rat you out to the First Constable."

"Good thing he's *asleep*," Kai offered.

Willem shrugged and poked at the fire. "I'm not concerned about Pfellcreek or Pueraria."

"Well, I just did our job for at least the next hour," Rhi said, as she took a seat. "I didn't see anything unusual going on from the roof. I'll check the gates in a bit, and then the roof again."

Willem nodded, but he heard a scoff come from Kai. "What's bothering you now?"

"That's not how things should be done!" He stood up and started to pace around.

"What do you mean?" asked Rhi. "Are you saying I'm doing my job wrong?"

Kai stopped his pacing and held up his hands. "No, that's not what I meant. You're doing great. But we shouldn't be hiding here like we're under siege."

"And just what are we supposed to be doing instead?" Rhi asked.

"What we do in every other grove in the city," Kai gestured with an arm toward the door. "We should be going on patrol, letting people know that we are there to protect them. That they can depend on us. That we are not a threat."

Rhi sat and stared at Kai, her mouth slightly open.

"Don't mind him," Willem smiled, "he's still got moss behind his ears."

Kai turned and pointed at Willem. "I do not. You know I'm right."

Willem shrugged, but continued to smile.

"But it's not safe to patrol here at night," Rhi countered. "We're only here to make sure that the place isn't burning down, and that nobody goes out after curfew. Senior Constable Eleapflam was very emphatic when he told me to never leave the area around the gate at night."

"That's absurd," Kai replied.

"Maybe, but he has a point," Willem added. "It's pretty clear that the halpbloed don't like us, and many of them would love to attack a constable. It's risky to do it during the day, but at night? I think there's more than a few that would love to take a shot at us, knowing that they could melt back into the darkness. And can you blame them?" He looked Kai in the eyes. "When we only put bullies and thugs here to watch over them?" He turned and smiled at Rhi. "Present company excluded, again."

Willem walked over toward the door. "You should only head into the heart of Nul Pfeta at night in force." He grabbed his sword belt and slung it around his waist, buckling it into place. He turned to look at Kai. "Let's go."

"Go?" Rhi asked, her expression full of concern. "Where? Out there?" She pointed toward the door.

Willem nodded, making sure that his dagger was in place. He picked up another dagger from the table and stuck it into his boot. "You and Pfellcreek," he pointed to the sleeping constable, "make sure the place is still standing when we get back. Kai and I are going on patrol."

"But..." Rhi stood up and put her hands on her hips. "It's not safe. You just said you shouldn't go out into Nul Pfeta without a large force."

Willem pulled on his cloak and gave her a wink. "I *am* a large force."

† † †

Willem set a fast pace as they headed into the heart of the grove. He agreed with Kai that the policies needed to change here, that some respect for the halpbloed might go a long way toward regaining their trust. Despite what he told Constable Bourreria, he didn't think that most of the halpbloed would try to attack them, although he still stayed as close to the center of the road as he could, away from the deeper shadows near the buildings.

Despite the late hour, he could see that there were many halpbloed out of their homes, gathered near burning braziers and fires. Many sat in front of their buildings, having conversations while their children ran about and played. Others stood at makeshift bars that had been set up outside of homes or other businesses. Most of the halpbloed glared at the pair of them as they passed, a few hands moved as if to reach for weapons, and more than a few spat in their general direction. But Willem also noticed a few nods coming from the older halpbloed.

"Do you blame them?" Willem asked, as they turned up another road.

"Who?"

"The halpbloeden. Do you blame them for being resentful of us? For hating our guts?"

"No," Kai shook his head. "But we're just doing our jobs. Why do they hate *us* so much?"

Willem hadn't realized how naïve the young constable really was. Despite his ideals and willingness to do things differently, he still didn't understand just how deep the resentment ran. Kai's heart was in the right place but, without understanding the deeper motives, he could end up making a mistake that could get him hurt or killed.

"Because we are the authority here," Willem answered. "We are the public face of the King's policies that put them here; almost all of them against their will. Sure, the Constabulary didn't pass the laws, but we are the ones tasked with keeping the peace. We are the ones they are more likely to encounter in their everyday lives. I think they have a right to be angry with us."

"Then why don't they do something?" Kai asked, as they passed yet another make-shift bar, the drinkers giving the two constables cold stares as they walked past. "Why aren't there *more* attacks on constables?"

"Because a lot of them, the older ones, remember the riots, too. That was an ugly mess." Willem shook his head. He had been in the King's army then, his unit called in to help quell the rioting. There were things he had seen during that horrible week that he had never spoken about with anyone, not even his wife, and they would haunt him until the day he died. "A lot of people died during the riots, elf and halpbloed alike. They remember how King Aeonis reacted then. He had only just been crowned, and he had to take a hard line to not only stop the riots, but to keep any other threats against the crown at bay. Would he react any differently today?"

"It's been thirty years. Things have changed."

Willem shook his head. "The more they change, the more things stay the same. Remember, King Aeonis enacted the latest Purity Law just ten years ago, stuffing more people into Nul Pfeta. The halpbloed know that nothing has really changed. Any outburst, any action here against the King's authority, would bring the Sucra and the army down on them like a felled tree."

"Then let's hope that nothing happens that will do that."

Willem nodded as they walked up the road, Pfastbinder's pitiful little temple finally coming into view. A flash of something in the darkness next to the temple caught his eye; sparks igniting, and then a flicker of flame. "What's that crazy cleric doing now?" Willem asked.

He brought a hand up, cupping his mouth and called out, "Hey, Pfastbinder, what are you doing?"

The flames were starting to grow, climbing rapidly up the side of the building. Willem suddenly realized that the fire wasn't in a firepit or brazier. The building was on fire! The figure that had been kneeling there stood up and turned around, his features silhouetted by the growing fire behind him. Willem caught the glint of metal as the person pointed a weapon their way.

"Weapon!" Willem yelled, shoving Kai out of the way. He then felt a sharp pain in his right shoulder, followed by intense burning. He took a step, trying to pull his sword, but his right arm was already useless. He looked up, and the road tilted and twisted as he watched Kai, sword drawn, running forward and calling out the alarm. Willem took another step and saw a person emerge from Pfastbinder's temple.

"Pfast—" Willem tried to call out, but then his vision went dark and he felt himself falling forward.

† † †

The first thing that Willem noticed was the skunky smell of canab. His eyes felt like they had been sewn shut, and he grunted with the effort that it took to open them. He blinked a few times, his vision coming back into focus. All he saw was the uneven and mismatched wood that made up the ceiling of the room, a flicker of light dancing across the surface.

He could now hear something, someone humming a simple tune; it took Willem a moment to realize that it was the tune to a children's nursery rhyme. He tried to sit up and grunted again with effort, his body refusing to move. His right arm began to tingle as if hundreds of needles were being stabbed into it.

Then a face came into view, a broad nose less than a hands-width from his own, green eyes full of concern. The smell of canab grew stronger, and Willem coughed and tried to push Pfastbinder away.

"Take it easy, Senior Constable."

Willem found his voice, though his tongue felt like it had never been used before. "Wha—What happened?"

Pfastbinder sat down and bent over to examine Willem's shoulder. "Let me check your injury," he said.

The events outside Pfastbinder's temple came back to him, a person standing up and shooting him. Kai running forward. "I was shot," Willem stated, again trying to sit up.

Pfastbinder helped him up, and Willem's head spun a bit. He realized that his armor and bracers had been removed. His arm was stiff, but the pins and needles were gone, and he could start to move it.

"Yes, you were," Pfastbinder replied. He picked up a small bolt. "With this. And it was poisoned with the same stuff that the Sucra love to smear over their own weapons. That's why you dropped like a dead tree in the forest."

Willem's head continued to clear. "There was a fire. The person who shot me was starting a fire." He looked up at Pfastbinder, meeting his eyes.

Pfastbinder shrugged. "The fire's out; Constable Gania made sure of that. It would have gotten out of control, but he got a few of my neighbors to help him."

"He did?" Willem looked around for his armor.

"Well, once I knew you weren't going to die on me, I helped convince them that he was on their side. But he did tell them that they'd all be homeless if the fire was allowed to get out of control."

Willem continued to look around, finally seeing his armor, but not seeing Kai. "Where is he now?"

Pfastbinder jerked a thumb over his shoulder. "Outside, chatting with them."

"Why was the Sucra trying to burn your place down—and all of Nul Pfeta with it?"

Pfastbinder looked at the crossbow bolt. It was small, clearly from a hand crossbow. "I don't think it was the Sucra," he offered. "It was the same poison, but this isn't a Sucra issued bolt. The fletching is wrong." Pfastbinder tossed the bolt into a wicker basket.

Willem nodded and tried to stand up. It took a moment for his legs to remember what they were for, but he managed to get to his feet.

"Careful," Pfastbinder prompted, though he made no effort to help Willem. "I healed your wound, but the poison has to work its way out of your system. You might feel a bit light-headed for a while."

"So, if it wasn't the Sucra trying to burn you out, who was it? Why would anybody be mad at you?" He took a tentative step over toward his armor. "Did you try to convert someone that didn't like it?"

"I would never do that," Pfastbinder huffed. "I offer the glory and majesty of Lord Banok to those who seek him. Forcing Banok on others is not his style, or mine. When people are ready to accept the chaos around them, I am here."

Willem snorted as he picked up his armor. "Does that chaos include mysterious strangers trying to burn down your home?"

"Occasionally," Pfastbinder laughed. "My faith in Banok allows me to adjust to any situation that may come my way. But I don't think this was a mysterious stranger. I'm pretty sure I know who our budding arsonist is."

Willem stopped putting on his armor. "You do?"

"It's related to what I wanted to talk to you about."

"I'll be back to buy you all drinks," Kai said to an unseen group as he pulled open the door. "Thank you for your assistance." He waved to them as he walked into the temple, and smiled when he saw that Willem was awake.

"I think I made some friends," he stated.

"I wouldn't get cocky, if I were you," Pfastbinder countered. "They may be friendly now because you offered them alcohol, but the next time they see one of you constables shove a woman to the ground and place their knee on her neck, they'll quickly remember that they hate your guts."

"Wait, that's actually happened?" Kai asked.

Pfastbinder nodded. "I saw it with my own eyes."

"Who tried to burn you out?" Willem asked, guiding them back to the path.

Pfastbinder turned and had an actual gleam in his eye. "Constable Sulwynd."

"Sulwynd?" Willem asked. "Are you sure?"

"Uh, he was transferred out of Nul Pfeta, remember?" Kai added. "We told you that the other day."

"He may have been, but he was here last night. I saw him here, across the street, in fact. He met with the halpbloed that lives there."

"Okay, you saw Sulwynd here," Kai shrugged. "So?"

Pfastbinder looked up to the ceiling in a gesture that seemed to beseech Banok for understanding. He returned his gaze to Kai. "Don't you think that's even a little bit unusual? He worked in Nul Pfeta every day for years. Why would any elf come here when they didn't have to? Alone? At night?"

Willem went back to putting on his armor. "Just how did Constable Sulwynd know that your temple was worth burning down? I agree that he's a son of a succubus and gets his kicks from being a bully, but that's a long way from being an arsonist."

Pfastbinder put his hands on his hips and stuck out his chin. "Because, like any good constable, I snuck across the road and listened at the door to hear what they were talking about. I heard quite a bit—some very juicy information—until Sulwynd opened the door and found me."

"Good constables don't sneak about like thieves and listen at doors," Kai grumbled.

"I think Constable Inspector Lunaria would approve. Especially when she finds out what I heard." He grinned.

Willem finished tying on his armor. "Spill it."

"I will, to the Constable Inspector." He took on a pious look, something that Willem had actually never seen from the cleric, and continued, "That's why I need your help. To let me out of Nul Pfeta tonight, after curfew, so I can go tell her."

"Uh uh," Willem shook his head and picked up his bracers. "I'm not playing games with you, and I'm not going to let you traipse around the city in order to bug the Constable Inspector this late at night." He took a step towards the door and motioned for Kai to lead the way. "Don't let your place burn down anymore."

"Wait," Pfastbinder groused. "Fine. We can tell Reva in the morning."

"In the morning? I plan on being asleep in my bed in the morning," Willem stated.

"Oh, you'll want to be up for this, my good Constable. Banok is weaving quite the plot under our noses. We'll need to see Reva as soon as we can in the morning."

"Why should I let you waste her time?" Willem asked. "Or mine?"

"Oh," Pfastbinder smiled. "It will definitely be worth her time."

Chapter 26

The Minister pulled his cloak tighter and smiled as he watched the pub from the dark shadows across the street from the building. A thin fog from the river helped to mask him, but it didn't keep him from seeing his quarry as she walked out of the pub. The pub was in the heart of Port Grove, a faded sign above the door proclaiming it to be the Full Sail, and it was frequented mostly by travelers passing through the city, either waiting for a ship or having just disembarked. A loyal friend in the Qurundora had confirmed that many adventuring parties used the pub, and that he was sure to find a sorcerer among them. The Minister was willing to take on an entire party of adventurers if he needed to, but luck had been on his side tonight.

Earlier in the evening, The Minister had been inside the pub, nursing a mediocre ale, while he searched for the right target. For that, he had designed a special spell that allowed him to detect sorcerers.

Clerics and priests had long used their magic to detect a person's alignment—whether the person was good or evil, lawful or chaotic—a boon given to them directly by their god. There was similar magic available to wizards, though it was cumbersome to use, as the initial spells created for this purpose had required specific material spell components and complex somatic gestures. These spells had been functional, but they were not as elegant as those created by divine magic. Over time, detection spells had been refined, requiring easier gestures and more common components. The Minister had used this magic, in his youth—before he knew better—to aid him in his search for sorcerers. It seemed logical that a sorcerer in the thrall of a demon that was bent on taking over the world would be an evil person, but over the years, The Minister had learned that "evil" was often a matter of perspective, and that many sorcerers actually believed they were doing good deeds despite their complicity in working with a demon. Their firm belief that they were not evil often made spells that could detect evil fail or give erroneous results.

There was also the most basic, simplest of magic, the first spell taught to all new wizards to allow them to detect magical auras; to see the glory of Qurna's aether. It had taken many years before The Minister had received divine inspiration from Jansure and made the connection that the basic detect magic spell was the key that he needed to complete his holy quest. If only he could make it work.

It had not been an easy task, but The Minister had been able to modify the basic detect magic spell and alter it so that he could detect arcane magic, as cast by wizards and sorcerers. It had taken even more time and refinement of the spell so that he could weed out the true wizards from the sorcerers. The spell was so similar to the plethora of divination and detection spells that had been created over the millennia that it had surprised The Minister that nobody before him had put the magic together in this way for this purpose. Since creating his spell to detect sorcerers, his holy mission for Jansure and Qurna had been so much easier, and more efficient. The time he had wasted before in surveillance and tracking potential sorcerers was now better spent in interrogating his targets in order to learn the name of the demon.

Tonight, he had cast his spell while he drank, and he had identified a couple of potential targets. One, a male elf, had been with a group of companions, and they looked like they would present a challenge if he tried to confront them as a group. He didn't fear them, and certainly all of the members of that party were complicit in harboring and protecting the demon sorcerer, so they deserved the penance that he would bring down on their sinful heads, but he did not want a long, drawn out fight that would attract unwanted attention.

His other potential target was a human female, who appeared to be alone. She had come in for a meal and a few drinks, chatting with the barkeep who seemed to be unconcerned by both her non-elvenness, as well as her taint of sorcerous evil. He would dispatch her quickly.

Satisfied that he had found his target, The Minister left the pub, heading across the road to take up his position across the street. Once she emerged from the pub, she headed up the road away from the port. The Minister let her take the lead, and then followed, far enough back that she wouldn't see him.

Tonight's mission was simpler than his usual duties. Tonight, he was only interested in a way to lure out his true target: the Seeker. He was not interested in what information this sorcerer might have about the demon that provided her magic. He didn't need to find a place where he could perform the long process of interrogation, or have to case her home for family or roommates that might raise an alarm. A small part of him would miss the chance to interrogate the sorcerer and learn her secrets, but there was little chance that she would tell him what he wanted to hear. No, she would serve an important service by becoming the bait to lure out the Seeker. Besides, one less sorcerer would be in the world, and that was consolation enough to not interrogate her.

The fog thinned as they walked away from the river. Despite the reputation for thieves and rogues in Port Grove, she walked along unconcerned. *Of course not*, he thought, *when she has the power of a demon at her beck and call.*

A cat ran past him, dodging in front of him and then jumping up to run along the edge of a fence. It gave a pitiful meow and then stuck out a leg and began to lick.

The Minister gave a hesitant glance at the cat, a burning ember of frustration taking root in his stomach. *The cat was her familiar!* He brought his staff up, but was too late as the woman whirled around, magic already shaped between her fingers. The spell she was released before he could dispel it, and the bolt of flame flew rapidly at The Minister.

He tried to move out of the way, but it still hit him in the shoulder, instead of his chest, where she had been aiming. The flame arrow washed over him, and he laughed as his own magic absorbed most of the magical flame. Her spell might have injured a would-be thief, or a rogue bent on assault, but his magic was superior to hers, and the fire barely singed him.

"Whoever you are," she called out, "I suggest that you leave me alone before I must do something that you will regret. You may have withstood my first spell, but my next one will not be so easy to shrug off."

The Minister caught the slight tremble in her voice; she knew that she was no threat to him. "You have courage," he replied, playing his own game, "but courage will not be enough to keep me from my holy mission. Unfortunately, you are just the bait; I would have enjoyed finding out just how deep the demon has burrowed into your soul."

"What are you babbling about, old man? I know of no demon, and I do not take kindly to threats." She began to move her hands, casting her next spell, but The Minister had been waiting for this. He gave a nudge of his staff, and a ray of red mist shot from the tourmaline gemstone and struck the sorcerer. She gave a cry of shock as her spell died before she could cast it.

Without pause, The Minister stepped toward her, holding his staff in one hand, his other hand outstretched, the palm facing her. He made the necessary gesture, a feeling of satisfaction and pleasure filling him as he spoke the required words, just as Qurna had taught the first wizards. Two searing rays of fire shot from his hand, striking the sorcerer in her stomach.

This time, the cry was full of pain as she collapsed to the ground like a rag doll that had been tossed casually to the floor. The Minister felt a moment of pride and satisfaction as he strolled forward. He rarely got to use his full repertoire of magic, due to the need to keep his targets alive for interrogation, and he enjoyed the feeling of tapping into a spell that he usually had to keep tucked into his spellbook for fear of his target dying before he could gather the information that he needed to banish the demon from the land. Which is exactly what happened.

He looked down at the body with neither wrath nor joy, only a grim satisfaction that the first part of his plan had been completed so easily. He still had work to do, but the riskiest part was done. He looked around, glad that the fog was getting thicker. Nobody seemed to have heard the brief fight, and there was nobody around at this late hour to cause a problem.

There was a hiss, and the cat jumped down from the fence, arching its back, and then it ran away into the night. The familiar's bond with its master was as broken as the bond between the dead sorcerer and her demon master. It was a shame that he would never learn the name of that demon from her lips, but he was satisfied by the role that she still had to play.

He prepared to cast his next spells. He knew exactly where he would leave his lure, and it wouldn't do to be seen along the way.

Chapter 27

The pounding on his door had awakened Ansee from a fitful sleep, interrupting his usual bad dream of Roya Locera attacking him with the Fury Blade while Ansee had to dodge around dozens of undead, their bodies alight with blue-green fire. This time, however, the wizard that had been killing sorcerers had looked on, cackling with laughter and calling Ansee names as Ansee's magic failed him. Ansee shook his head, wondering why his dreams enjoyed tormenting him so much. It had been bad enough when they had only included Roya Locera, but the addition of the wizard was disturbing.

The pounding came again and Ansee climbed out of bed, pulling on a robe to cover his nakedness. Ember, his pet fire salamander, had been curled up on the bed, but the noise caused her to scurry across the floor to the fireplace and bury herself in the dead coals from last night's fire. Ansee chuckled to himself, but then pulled a dagger from its scabbard and held it close to his side as he opened the door enough to see who had awakened him from his nightmare.

When he saw who was on the other side, Ansee relaxed, pulling the door wider. "Constable Brillow, come in."

Constable Brillow walked in, and Ansee could feel the night cold radiating from his body. He turned to the fireplace and called, "Ember!"

The fire salamander poked her head out from the coals. Ansee gestured and said, "Fire, Ember!"

The salamander's mouth widened in what Ansee always took for a smile, and then made a retching noise. Out came stomach contents that caught fire in the air, catching the coals, and soon a small fire was going. Ember gave a satisfied crackle and nestled into the flames.

"That's handy," commented Constable Brillow. "A bit gross, but handy."

"It is," Ansee admitted, "when she does it in the fire-place. It's a pain in the ass when she does it on the rug." He looked down at the rug, the constable following his gaze to see several scorched holes in the fabric.

"Yeah, I could see how that would be a problem."

"Why did you get me out of bed?" Ansee asked, having a decent idea what the reason might be. He'd only been work-ing in Acer Division for a couple of months now, but he knew that only murder created this kind of rousing early in the morning. Typically an unusual murder, or that of somebody important.

"We've got a bad one," Brillow grimaced, mimicking First Constable Aescel's usual phrase. "I'm supposed to bring you to the crime scene—immediately."

Ansee nodded, "Murder."

"Yes, sir. And it is just like that case you just closed."

Ansee shivered, which had nothing to do with the tem-perature in his apartment. "Let me get dressed," he sighed, turning to his wardrobe. He gathered his clothes and tossed them onto the bed, followed by his robe. He began to pull on his breeches.

"What do we know?" Ansee asked.

"That First Constable Aescel is mad as hell. He was awakened first, and he's already at the crime scene. I was happy to be the messenger to get away from his wrath."

If the First Constable was at the scene, that told Ansee that this was something more unusual than most murders. A copycat killer would certainly do that. He pulled on his shirt and then quickly rolled his puttee on his legs. They went on loose and sloppy, but time was more important than neatness right now.

"What about Constable Inspector Lunaria?" he asked, pulling on his boots.

"She's on her way. I went to her place first."

Ansee nodded as he pulled on his armor. Constable Brillow stepped over to help him tie the laces. "Where is the crime scene?" he asked.

"Practically outside your front door," Brillow replied. "It's in front of the Mayor's Oak."

Ansee paused, his eyes widening. "Seriously?"

"Yep. Now you know why the First Constable is so mad."

Ansee grabbed his bracers, his belt with its many leather pouches and scabbard, and his cloak. "Let's go. I can get this on as we walk there."

He closed the door behind him, and Ember gave a satisfied sigh as her tail swept more coals around her body.

† † †

Despite the early hour—the sun hadn't risen yet, although the distant horizon was beginning to lighten—a large crowd had gathered in the square that surrounded the Mayor's Oak. The Oak was said to have been the first tree planted here by King Arona when he founded the city. It was supposedly well over 6,000 years old, kept alive through a combination of tender, exquisite care and magic. It was also huge, well over thirty paces across at its base, and it rose over twice that in height. Its insides had been carved out and hollowed—again, primarily through magic—to house King Arona's court while the Red Keep had been built. When the King had moved into the keep, he had bequeathed the tree to the noble who he had selected to administer his city. It still held the Mayor's office, as well as the many offices for the administrators that ran the city. It was probably the third most important building in the city, after Castle Tenz and the Red Keep.

Ansee and Constable Brillow made their way through the crowd, and Ansee saw that most of them stood about, either in house robes that had been thrown hastily over sleeping clothes, or hurriedly thrown on garments. He did his best to ignore the chatter and speculation that was running through the crowd—he'd find out soon enough what had happened.

At the front of the crowd were about a dozen Betulla Division constables, who were working to keep the crowd back. As he and Constable Brillow walked past the Birches, one of them turned to Ansee and said, "Better you than me, Seeker. I wouldn't want to get within ten paces of the First Constable right now."

Ansee could now see the scene in front of him. In the background was the massive silhouette of The Mayor's Oak, its shape hinted at by the many flickering torches that had been brought in to light the scene. In front of the main entrance were several flower beds and small trees—redbuds and cherry—that in the spring and summer gave a colorful and festive feel to the square. Now the beds were fallow, the trees bare of all but just a few brown leaves. A cluster of people stood around the flower bed that faced the main entrance, and the body that was lying there.

Reva was a couple of paces away, speaking with another Birch. Ansee could overhear snippets of her conversation, asking the usual questions about who found the body and when.

Ansee had been preparing himself for something unusual as he approached the body. Constable Brillow had said that it was just like the case they'd just closed, but what he saw shocked him and made him stop.

The body was of a human woman. She had been laid branches wide—her arms and legs spread away from her body. Iron spikes had been pounded through her hands and into the soil of the flower bed. She was naked from the waist up, and the skin of her stomach was blistered and seared. Beneath her breasts was the same symbol that had been left at the scenes of the other sorcerer murders, but in those cases, the symbol had been left on calling cards. Here, the symbol appeared to have been burned into her skin.

Ansee's skin crawled, the hairs at the nape of his neck tingling, and he didn't think it had anything to do with the body, as horrible and grotesque as it was. He felt like he was being watched; that someone's eyes were boring into him. He looked up and around the square. Reva was still talking with the Birch, and he could see the other constables and the crowd. Everyone in the crowd was staring at him, but that was expected, and none of them seemed interested in him, only in the body that was before him. Ansee continued to look around, the feeling not going away, but he couldn't pinpoint the source.

He shook his head. *Focus*, he told himself. *Reva will expect answers as soon as she's done, and I better not be gawking at the crowd.*

He cast his detect magic spell and quickly went to work. The woman's body practically glowed from the magic that radiated off it. The first thing that Ansee noticed was that the symbol glowed with a bright blue energy. He'd expected that it had been branded upon her body, but now he knew that it had been applied magically. The blisters on her stomach glowed with a sickening orange light, while a faint aura of violet light dappled her back, the back of her arms, legs, and head.

Our killer had a partner, Ansee told himself, staring at the symbol as he pulled out quartz crystals. *He had a partner, and because I killed him in that stupid duel, we didn't know. I was careless, and I messed up. He died because of me, so we couldn't interrogate him, and now his partner has killed again. Her death is my fault.*

Ansee set his jaw, feeling his teeth grind together. *I won't let that happen again.*

He knelt and placed the first crystal on the victim's chest, casting his spell to collect the magical aura. *With this, I will find you*, he thought. The other auras were important, but this one, this mark, was personal for the killer.

"This one is a 'bad one'", he heard Reva say. He looked over his shoulder to see her standing at the victim's feet. Her clothes and armor looked to have been put on hastily, or maybe they had never been taken off in the first place. She pulled a tin from one of her pockets. Her hands moved of their own accord as she looked at the body, as if she wasn't even conscious of her actions. She lifted a pinch of the Wake and inhaled it, her eyes never leaving the body.

Ansee bit back the comment that he wanted to make. Her Wake use was becoming more problematic, more consuming, but this was not the time or place to bring it up. Reva would be just as on edge as the First Constable about this latest murder, maybe even more so, and he didn't need to push her over the edge with a comment about Wake.

"What do you know?" Reva asked, taking a step and kneeling down to look at the victim from a new angle.

"A lot of magic was involved, but the auras are very different from our previous victims. No teleportation was used and, from her condition, I don't see any broken bones."

Reva nodded as she grabbed a strand of hair and began to suck on the end of it.

"I should be able to identify the exact spells used, but I'm pretty sure that this," he pointed at the blister on her stomach, "evocation spell is what killed her. It's the only evocation aura I can see right now, but it is powerful. I would say it was the only blow she suffered."

"So, we're dealing with someone who's skilled and powerful. Great." She pointed to the symbol. "What about that?"

"An arcane mark," Ansee replied. "And most likely added post-mortem by the killer. I've already collected its aura."

Reva stood up, still sucking on the strand of hair. Finally, she let it drop from her mouth. "Make sure you check the area around here, but I doubt you'll find much. I don't think our victim was killed here."

"I agree," Ansee nodded. "There's magical evidence of a conjuration spell on her back. I will know more when I have examined the aura, but I would speculate that the killer conjured a floating disc to carry the victim here."

"And of course, nobody saw a wizard carting a body through the streets last night."

Ansee shrugged, used to Reva's sarcastic comments. They both turned at the sound of heavy, determined footsteps coming toward them from the main entrance to The Mayor's Oak.

"Gods damn it, Reva," First Constable Aescel bellowed, his birch-colored skin flush from anger. He glared at the two of them, and Ansee could see weariness mixed with wrath in his eyes. "You told me that you closed this case. That the murderer had been *dealt with*," his gaze bored a hole into Ansee. "So why is there a body staked outside the Mayor's residence?"

"It *was* closed, sir," Reva said. She had taken a step toward the First Constable and was doing her best to stare him down, despite being half a hand shorter than him.

"Then what in the hells is *this*?" He gestured to the victim. "It sure as hells looks like we have another victim. And the Mayor seems to think that, too, since he just spent the past few minutes chewing my ass off about it. Do you have any idea how bad this looks, Reva?"

"It's bad, sir," Reva admitted. Ansee could see that she had balled her hands into fists.

"The Mayor wants answers. Yesterday," Aescel demanded, looking between Reva and Ansee. He finally settled his gaze on Ansee. "He's not happy to have a dead body staked outside his front door. Especially from a killer that *you* said had been stopped."

"I'm not exactly thrilled by this, either," Reva said.

Aescel whipped around to glare at her. "Don't be flippant with me, Inspector!"

Ansee saw Reva flex her fists. "I'm not being flippant, sir. This victim means we that have *another* killer out there. I'm sure we will find out that this person was also a sorcerer, but we already know that the method of her death was different."

Ansee nodded. "The auras are different, sir." This earned him another glare from the First Constable, but it had softened, some of the fire going out as the facts were relayed. "This is somebody different."

"Maybe we are dealing with a group of assassins, or a new thieves' guild," Reva offered.

"Great," the First Constable sighed, rubbing his chin. "Just what we need."

"I'm just as mad as you and the Mayor are, sir," Reva said. "I don't like having to reopen a case that was closed."

"It's my fault, sir," Ansee added. "We might have been able to anticipate this, had we been able to interrogate our previous suspect."

"It's nobody's fault," Reva corrected him. "All of the evidence pointed to a solitary killer. Had you not done what you did, you'd have ended up splattered on the road. Don't ever take the blame for doing something to protect yourself."

"Look," Aescel said, meeting each of their eyes. "I will keep the Mayor and his friends off your bark as best as I can, but I need you to get this resolved, any way you can. And you need to do it fast." He held their gaze while they both nodded. "Good. Keep me informed."

The First Constable turned and walked back to The Mayor's Oak. Ansee turned back to the body and spotted the Alchemists making their way through the crowd. "Let me finish collecting the auras," he said.

"Will you be able to compare this evidence with our previous case?" Reva asked.

"I should," Ansee replied, pulling out another quartz crystal. "I haven't had a chance to clean out that evidence yet; too busy. Unless someone else got a burst of energy and decided to clean out the evidence room, I will be able to compare the auras." He gave a shrug, and Reva nodded. She understood.

"Well, since nobody is ever that energetic at New Port, you're in luck, then." She gave him a smile, which seemed to ease some of the tension.

"I still won't know who cast the spells, only whether it was the same person or a different one."

"I doubt it was the same person, unless he came back from the dead," Reva stated.

Ansee smiled. "After what happened last month, maybe we should also confirm that didn't happen."

"Gods," Reva said, with a laugh that was full of nervous anxiety, "don't even suggest something like that."

† † †

The Minister looked intently at the mirror he held in his hand. He did not see his own reflection, but instead viewed the crowded scene around The Mayor's Oak. He'd watched the scene intently from the moment that he had placed the woman's body there, pleased with himself at the reaction she had created, at the spectacle that had ensued. He had been most interested to watch the constables as they had arrived, first one, then more, until finally he had seen *him*. It was clear who the Seeker was once he had arrived and had begun casting his spells.

The Minister had been pleased to see the look on the Seeker's face when he had collected the aura from his arcane mark. The look of revulsion had brought a smile to The Minister's lips. He could feel the demon's aura radiating off the Seeker, and found it interesting that such evil did not repel everyone in the square. Clearly, it was the work of the demon's magic to keep the sheep from running in fear. But The Minister knew better.

He watched the Seeker perform the simple tasks of detecting the magical auras, then examining the area around the body while the Alchemists did their work. The Constable Inspector finally left the scene when the Alchemists took the body away, but the Seeker continued to look for clues that The Minister knew were not there. He continued to study the Seeker, though, knowing that his lure had caught its prey.

Chapter 28

The morning was damp as Norah stepped out of her home, and she pulled her cloak tightly around her to ward off the chill. She closed and locked the door behind her before heading up the street. The morning was overcast, and the low gray clouds fit her mood. Her husband was still away, and she had again spurned Olwyn last night, choosing to stay home alone rather than spending the evening with him. She had always found Olwyn to be a delightful diversion from the loneliness that she felt when her husband was on his trips. It wasn't just for the sex, either; Olwyn listened to her, and he cared about her in ways that her husband could never truly understand. She still loved her husband, and Olwyn knew that, which was part of the charm, but each of them gave her something different that made her life complete.

Or, at least, Olwyn had been doing that until he started to doubt her about Ansee. Olwyn hadn't understood the fear that she felt just by being around Ansee, and he had never understood the threat that the Seeker represented. None of them did. Even when she had tried to explain her feelings to Olwyn, he had only gotten to the bark of the matter, not the roots. He kept telling Norah to bend, to ignore the threat. That was what had bothered Norah the most. It wasn't that he didn't understand the threat. How could he when he was not a wizard? It was because he brushed off her fears and her concerns as if they were newly fallen leaves. He kept reminding her that Ansee had saved her life, and that the other Seekers were only picking on her because she was making an oak out of an acorn. He had been arrogant and condescending about it, too. And until Olwyn admitted that he had been an ass and apologized for doubting her, she was not going to give him what he wanted.

Norah headed up the short lane to the main road, still lost in her own thoughts, when a person stepped out from a narrow path that separated two of the homes. The figure was tall, nearly three hands taller than she was, and she had to look up to see his face, and to glare at him. She was a Constable, a Seeker, and she didn't enjoy being surprised like this. She was about to tell the stranger to get out of her way when he smiled, apologetically, lifting a blue, broad-brimmed hat just a bit from his head with an aged, calloused hand, a few strands of his long silver hair still clinging to the felt.

"My apologies for startling you," he said, returning the hat to his head. Norah now saw that the blue robes that he wore were covered with words of magic that had been sewn along the hem and the cuffs of his sleeves. In his other hand, he held a staff that was nearly as tall as she was.

"Well, I'm not used to strangers jumping out of the shadows at me, especially not the first thing in the morning."

The wizard—for there was nothing else he could be, dressed as he was—smiled again. It looked natural on his weathered face, but Norah could also tell that it was not a normal gesture for this person. "Please, allow me to rectify that. I'm afraid that I do have the advantage over you. A common friend at Auros told me where you lived, and I wanted a chance to meet you."

"You wanted to meet *me*?" she asked, doing her best to cover up her confusion. Her mind raced, trying to figure out what 'friend' the stranger was talking about. Despite being an alumnus of the Academy, she only knew a few people there, and she didn't consider any of them friends. "Why?"

"Because we share a..." he paused, and one corner of his mouth rose, indicating his pleasure at his words, and then continued, "...similar interest."

Norah couldn't help but look confused by the statement. The wizard leaned forward, his deep blue eyes sparkling. "We both know that there is an infestation within the constabulary that must be expunged."

Ah, Norah realized. *This has to do with Ansee.* She smiled. "Yes, we do share a similar interest. You must be here to remove Ansee."

"Ansee?" The wizard asked.

"Seeker Ansee Carya," Norah confirmed. "I learned that he was a sorcerer a month ago, but nobody else seems to care. They don't understand the sort of threat that he is to the constabulary, or to the city."

"Rest assured that *I* understand, all too well. That's why I was summoned here, to deal with this threat." He set his staff in front of him, grasping it with both hands. "I am The Minister. I am pleased to meet a wizard who understands the sorcerous threat as much as I do. For too long, we have allowed them to meddle in magic, to continue to infest the city. Their power is deep here, and we risk death and destruction, or worse, every time they cast a spell."

Norah found herself nodding. It was a relief to finally find someone who understood the threat that Ansee posed without her having to explain it. She had also heard the name before: The Minister. She didn't know much about the wizard himself. What she knew gave her hope that her problem would soon be resolved, as he was one of the most dedicated to their cause. "Yes," she agreed. "I've tried to explain how they are in thrall to their demon master, but nobody wants to listen to me. Ansee is a delayed fireball, just waiting to explode."

"Exactly," The Minister nodded. "I am glad that you fully understand the threat."

Norah smiled, her fear and anxiety beginning to blow away. "If you need my help to get Ansee out of the constabulary, let me know what I can do."

The Minister recoiled, and he glared at her from under the brim of his hat. "Clearly I was mistaken about your understanding if you think that getting him fired from his job is enough to remove the threat that he presents." He straightened to his full height, and Norah felt like he was looming over her. "My destiny is to rid Tenyl of every sorcerer, and to find out to which demon they have sold their souls. I am not simply pruning a hedge. I am ripping out a noxious weed by its very roots. The only way to make sure that happens is to eliminate every single one of them."

"You're... you're going to kill him?" She asked, the hesitation clear in her voice. Her previous excitement at finding someone who understood her fell into the pit of her stomach. She had told LCI Betulla that she wanted Ansee off the constabulary; she didn't want him dead. Yes, he was a threat, but he had also saved her life. That was a debt that needed to be repaid, demon spawn or not. She understood the danger that sorcerers represented, but she would be satisfied if she no longer had to work with Ansee ever again.

"Are you showing sympathy for this demon spawn?" The Minister asked, leaning forward to pierce Norah with his blue eyes. "Are you not committed to the cause? Are you not devoted to the faith? Have you been corrupted by this Ansee? Has he woven a spell to deceive you?"

Norah took an involuntary step back and licked her lips. She recalled something else that she had heard about The Minister. He was said to be the most ruthless member of the order. He never stopped, never gave up in his pursuit of sorcerers, and anyone who stood in his way was in as much danger as the sorcerer he was tracking. *If he thinks that I might care at all for Ansee, even in the slightest,* she told herself, *then he will consider me a threat, too.*

She straightened up and stuck out her chin. "I am devoted to the faith. I don't care what you do to Ansee, as long as he's gone. Just let me know if you need any help to get rid of him."

The Minister stared at her for a long moment, and Norah resisted the urge to fidget under his gaze. He finally gave a slight nod, grunted, and shifted his staff so that it rested in the crook of his right arm. "For now, I am merely toying with your Seeker, luring him out. I left him a present this morning to announce my arrival in town."

Norah groaned inwardly at The Minister referring to Ansee as *her* Seeker, but then realized that The Minister just admitted to her that he had murdered someone. A part of her was pleased that a sorcerer threat had been eliminated, but she had joined the constabulary because she believed in the rule of law. She had never believed in vigilante justice, even in the pursuit of saving the world from a demon. It made them no better than the demon that would enslave innocent people to further its own aims.

"I will string your Seeker along," The Minister smiled. "And let him know that I am coming for him. He will not be able to escape me." He tipped his hat. "It was a pleasure to meet you, Norah. If I do need any assistance to rid the world of this magical abomination, be sure that I will call upon you."

He turned around and headed up the lane, quickly disappearing into the crowd of people along the main road. Norah found that her mouth had gone dry. Another sorcerer was dead. They were a threat to the city, but the knowledge that she had been involved in the death of another person gave her pause. And knowing that she had just signed Ansee's death warrant left a sinking feeling in her stomach.

Chapter 29

The main doors to New Port felt heavier than normal as Reva pushed them open. It was only a few hours after sunrise, but Reva already felt like she had worked a full shift. Being awakened before sunrise for a murder was never a pleasant experience, but that was doubly true when the victim was left on display for the whole city to see. That the 'whole city' included the Mayor, only made things worse.

Reva nodded to Constable Whitlocke as she headed up the stairs. She hadn't had time for her usual stop at Iliam's House of Theobroma for her morning cup of cacao, and that put her into a foul mood.

She looked across the Stable and groaned as she saw Pfastbinder's multicolored cloak hovering next to her table. She thought about turning around and running back down the stairs, but the cleric had spotted her. "Hello, Inspector," he made a show of giving her an exaggerated wave. She trudged over and saw Willem sitting at her table.

"I hope this means that you arrested him for something," Reva said. "I'm not in the mood for his antics this morning."

"Antics?" Pfastbinder gave a huff, then changed his tone, "You say the sweetest things, Inspector."

"He's not under arrest," Willem stated.

"Well, I don't have time to chat." She folded her arms. "And aren't *you* supposed to be on duty right now?"

Willem stifled a yawn. "Got shifted to nights yesterday. I worked a double shift and I'd rather be tucked into my bed right now, but this idiot insisted that he had to see you." He cuffed Pfastbinder on the shoulder.

Reva pulled out the tin from her pocket. "Do you want some Wake?"

Willem waved it away, "Nah, I'm good."

Pfastbinder held out his hand.

"Not you," Reva said, pulling the tin back. Pfastbinder made a show of sulking.

"If this is just a social call, then hi, bye; I have work to do." Reva shooed Willem out of her chair.

"I think you'll want to hear what Pfastbinder has to say," Willem said, as he stood up.

Reva flipped open the lid on the tin and pulled out a pinch of Wake, lifting it to her nose. She turned to Pfastbinder and pointed at him. "This damn well better be worth pulling me away from a murder case."

"Ooo," Pfastbinder cooed. "Another murder? Maybe I can help you with this one, too." He held up a forearm and pointed to it. "By the way, I'm still waiting for my bracers."

Reva almost told him where he could shove his help, but she considered his offer as she put away the tin of Wake. She really wanted Willem's thoughts on the case. She missed his insight. "We found another murdered sorcerer this morning."

"A copycat?" Willem asked.

"I don't know yet. Ansee is checking the auras now, but it's not like our previous murderer has come back from the dead."

"Well, after last month..." Willem countered.

Reva couldn't help but smile. "Ansee said the same thing."

"Another dead sorcerer, but it's probably not your previous killer, unless you let some powerful cleric get his body in time to resurrect him. I doubt it would be a reincarnation, since those usually never bring the person back in their original form unless the cleric is really, really good—and the god is feeling generous. Now, with Banok, even a resurrection is never guaranteed to bring you back exactly as you were before. Banok loves to mix things up. Oh, and you can forget about being anything humanoid when you are reincarnated by Banok. Or even an animal, really. He tends to prefer something insect-like, to teach you humility. Though there was one person that I heard had been brought back—"

"Hey, squirrel-brain," Willem cuffed Pfastbinder across the back of his head. "This isn't why you're here."

Pfastbinder held up a finger, his mouth open, as if he wanted to say something, but then he craned his neck, looking around the room. He leaned forward and held up his cloak like he was trying to hide behind it, as if anyone could be hidden by its gaudy, clashing colors. "Is there someplace less crowded that we can talk?" he whispered.

Reva sighed, realizing that she would have to humor him if she wanted to get any real work done today. She walked to the back of the Stable and onto the landing of the back stairs, with Pfastbinder hot on her heels and Willem reluctantly in tow. "Well, spill it."

Pfastbinder made a show of looking up and down the stairwell, and then poked his head back into the Stable to make sure that nobody had followed them. He then turned to Reva and, still whispering, said, "I've uncovered a plot against the Prince."

"In Nul Pfeta?" Reva asked, not bothering to hide her incredulity.

Pfastbinder nodded. "And you'll never guess who's involved. Come on, guess." He turned to look at Willem. "She'll never guess it."

Despite the early start to the day, and the bizarre murder case that she had to deal with, the fog in her mind seemed to lift. The conversations with Inquisitor Amalaki seemed to jump up and down in her mind, waving at her in order to get her attention. "Constable Sulwynd," she replied.

Pfastbinder's mouth dropped open, and then he crossed his arms and pouted. "How did you know that? You spoiled my surprise."

Reva shrugged. "Just a lucky guess. What sort of plot is he involved in?"

"It seems that Constable Sulwynd is recruiting halpbloed to kidnap Prince Orlean. They want to use him to force the King to reinstate their citizenship and to declare them elves again."

"Idiots," Reva grumbled, but the pieces were starting to come together. Sulwynd was stoking resentment among the halpbloeden in order to incite an attack against the crown. That plan sounded much more nuanced than one that Sulwynd was capable of coming up with on his own. Now the innocuous meeting between Sulwynd and Grand Inquisitor Agera seemed considerably less innocuous. Had that been planned? Had the mugging been staged so that they could meet and talk without suspicion?

Reva unconsciously pulled a strand of her hair and stuck it between her lips as her mind returned to a dark room buried beneath Pfeta fey Orung. A secret room, hidden from all but a few: like Grand Inquisitor Agera, LCI Betulla, and Inquisitor Malvaceä. There had been many other names down there, displayed in family trees that proudly exclaimed their dark elf heritage. Had there been a family tree there for Sulwynd? She couldn't remember, but it was possible, as there had been dozens of family trees on display.

"There's more," Pfastbinder added, pulling Reva out of the memory. "Constable Sulwynd gave Cedres—"

"Who's Cedres?" Willem interrupted.

"The halpbloed that lives above the bakery. Cedres Vanda. I learned his name yesterday."

Willem turned to look at Reva. "Cedres Vanda."

Reva shook her head. "Shit."

"What?" asked Pfastbinder.

"You remember the murder of the Treasurer this summer, Lady Ochroma?" Willem asked. Pfastbinder nodded. "Cedres Vanda was a witness. We held him here to keep him safe, in case the murderer had wanted to keep Cedres quiet. He was let go right after LCI Gania was murdered."

"That is interesting," Pfastbinder said, tapping a finger against his cheek. "Since Sulwynd gave Cedres specially minted coins. I think it was so they could identify members of their little cabal."

Reva rubbed her chin, the cobwebs from the early start to the day now completely gone. The leaves were falling away, and she could glimpse what they had been hiding. After Lady Ochroma's death, a new Treasurer had been appointed by the King, but Ochroma had been part of Agera's little cabal. Her death must have left a hole in whatever plan he had been plotting. He had managed to put Betulla in charge at the constabulary, but what if he hadn't been able to control who the King had assigned to oversee the Treasury?

Reva looked at Pfastbinder. "Thank you. I'll take this information to the Sucra."

"The Sucra?" The outburst came from Willem. "They'll hit Nul Pfeta so hard that it will explode. It'll make the riots thirty years ago look like a tiff between *hoaralle* hooligans."

"I know, which is why I will take it to Amalaki. He's been sniffing after Sulwynd for a while now. He'll be able to take down Sulwynd and this group of plotters, but he'll do it *my* way."

She turned to Willem. "I need you to stay alert. I may need to coordinate things with you."

She then turned to Pfastbinder. "And I need you to keep an eye on Cedres. Find out where he goes, who he meets with. We'll need to know everything so that we can catch them all."

"What about my bracers?" Pfastbinder asked, crossing his arms and tapping one foot.

"They'd just clash with your cloak," Reva replied, pointing to the multi-colored garment. She turned to walk back into the Stable.

"But that's the point," Pfastbinder's words chased after her.

Chapter 30

Constable Sulwynd popped the rest of the sweet roll into his mouth as he walked out of the pastry shop. He licked the honey from his fingers as he looked up and down the street, trying to get his bearings. He was still getting used to patrolling in Bay Grove. The grove was as different from Nul Pfeta as night was to day and, he had to admit, the perks were way better.

He turned to his left and walked down the street, his eyes taking in the scene, which was different from Nul Pfeta as well. There, the halpbloed that couldn't get, or didn't want, jobs loitered about in front of their homes or the makeshift bars that marred every street. Here, almost nobody was loitering about. The elves that were out on the street were moving with purpose, coming from or going to somewhere. The shops and homes were neat and tidy and, while the road he was currently on was not cobbled, the packed dirt was covered with straw and woodchips to absorb the rain so that there were no deep ruts or holes. There was also the lack of the constant odor of piss and shit, since most of the homes in Bay Grove either had outhouses or a covered pit where chamber pots were emptied. He suspected that a few of them may even have had indoor water closets.

Sulwynd smiled as he continued his patrol. He hoped that, no matter what happened with Agera's plan, he would never have to set foot in Nul Pfeta again. As he wondered what other shops he should visit so that the locals would know that there was a new constable on patrol, and to remind them what might happen if he wasn't there, someone bumped into him, their shoulder driving into his own.

"Hey!" Sulwynd yelled, turning to give chase. He wasn't going to let anybody attack him, even if it may have been an accident. But as he turned, he felt something in his hand. Whoever had hit him had already disappeared—quite a feat, considering the lack of people on the road. He looked down and saw that he was holding a piece of parchment.

He opened it and saw a few words penned on the page. "Meet now. Knotty Pine Woodworking."

Sulwynd crumpled up the parchment and tossed it into a water trough as he walked up the road, looking for a cross street. He had walked past the carpentry shop on his patrol yesterday, and he thought that he remembered where it was. He hurried his pace, as he was sure that the message was from the Grand Inquisitor, and he didn't want to keep Agera waiting.

He spotted the shop and opened the door. The smell of freshly cut wood and varnish filled the building ,and there were several chairs, chests, and a large wardrobe in the front room. Before he could close the door, it was pushed shut, and a figure stepped forward. Sulwynd realized that this was probably the person that had passed him the note, and he recognized Inquisitor Aaroon, another member of their group. The creak of a floorboard alerted him, and Sulwynd turned around to see Grand Inquisitor Agera step out of the back room.

Agera stepped up to some of the chairs and looked them over, as if he was contemplating how good they might look in his dining room. He then stepped over to the wardrobe, opening the door and examining the drawers and detailed woodwork. Sulwynd found himself rocking from foot to foot, wondering why Agera had brought him here.

Agera shut the door on the wardrobe and turned to take

in a rocking chair. "I hope you are doing more than enjoying sweet pastries here in Bay Grove."

Even though Agera had his back to Sulwynd, he still brought up his hand and wiped it across his mouth. "I was sent here by the LCI's orders. I didn't ask to be pulled out of Nul Pfeta."

Agera gave the rocking chair a push and turned around, letting the chair squeak as it rocked back and forth. He fixed Sulwynd with his gaze. "I am aware of Betulla's orders." He paused, as the rocking chair slowly rocked. Sulwynd could tell that the Grand Inquisitor was not happy.

"What I want to know is what *you* are doing to ensure that *my* plan will be carried out. Without error."

The rocking noise was unnerving, and Sulwynd couldn't help but to think of Senior Inquisitor Malvaceä and his banishment after the incident two months ago. Sulwynd didn't know the details—he doubted that anybody other than Agera knew all the details, except maybe Malvaceä himself— but he knew that after whatever had happened, they had been forced to abandon the meeting place under Pfeta fey Orung. Agera had been very angry at that time, so he needed to make sure that the Grand Inquisitor didn't get that angry with him.

"I've met with the halpbloed and given him the instructions and the false coins."

"And this halpbloed is competent enough to carry out his instructions?"

"Yes," Sulwynd nodded. Cedres was a sorry excuse for a halpbloed, but he was determined to get back what he thought the King owed him. *Idiot.* "He's committed to the cause that I've given him."

"Then everything is going according to plan." Agera reached out a hand and stopped the rocking chair.

"Yes, everything is going according to plan," Sulwynd echoed. He watched Agera closely, hoping that he didn't pick up on the lie. There was still the cleric that had been snooping around Cedres' door that had to be dealt with. He didn't know what, if anything, the cleric had heard, or even understood, as high as he had been on that damn ditch weed. He would have been taken care of last night, if it hadn't been for the ill-timed interference from Willem and Gania. There was no reason that they should have been on patrol at night, away from the gate house, so Sulwynd had to assume that they were aware of what the damned cleric had overheard. At the very least, they were involved now. But Sulwynd wasn't going to tell any of this to the Grand Inquisitor. He couldn't let Agera know that anything had happened that might impact the plan, or that he couldn't handle it on his own, not if he wanted to keep his life. He would deal with everything on his own, and Agera would be none the wiser once the plan succeeded.

"When do you need me to execute the plan?" Sulwynd asked.

"I do not have the exact time yet, but I need your halp-bloeden to be ready in at least two days' time. That is the earliest that our opportunity to strike at the Prince will present itself." Agera nodded to Inquisitor Aaroon, who had been standing quietly in the corner. Aaroon pulled out a pouch and tossed it to the Grand Inquisitor, who caught it. Sulwynd could hear the clink of coins.

Agera handed the pouch to Sulwynd. "Take these and make sure that the halpbloeden use them to purchase their supplies. They can also be used as payment to them for the job. That should help motivate them."

Sulwynd took the pouch, feeling its weight. There was a small fortune here, at least to the halpbloed. He would have to make sure that they didn't just take the coins and run away. "I'll make sure that they are ready."

"Remember how pivotal your role is in this, Sulwynd."

Sulwynd nodded, as he tied the pouch to his belt where it would be hidden by his cloak. He caught Agera's double meaning. If he did what was needed and succeeded, then he would be rewarded. But if he failed, then he'd be lucky to be banished like Malvaceä.

Inquisitor Aaroon opened the door to the shop, and Sulwynd exited back onto the street.

† † †

Inquisitor Amalaki felt exposed as he watched the carpentry shop from across the street. He wasn't concerned about being seen—he was hidden behind a trellis that was filled with the stems of creeper vines that had lost most of their leaves. It gave him a great position from which to see the carpentry shop and still be hidden from view.

No, he felt exposed because it was just *him* watching Constable Sulwynd. A mission like this, trailing a suspect, should have involved at least two other Novices, maybe even a spellcaster, to keep an eye on the suspect. But it was just him to watch the Constable, and he felt that he was taking too many risks.

Amalaki had been following the Constable all morning. He had awakened early in order to get to Sulwynd's home in Quarry Grove, and then followed him across the city to the small building that the constables used as a meeting point in Bay Grove. It wasn't a formal watch house like the gate house in Nul Pfeta, just a small shack that could be used as a common place where the patrol constables could meet and exchange information between shifts. Sulwynd had met with his fellow constables, sharing a few laughs that Amalaki felt had been forced—playing the new constable from Nul Pfeta, just trying to fit in—and had then started his patrol.

All of the groves were too big for the constables to patrol them together, so Sulwynd had headed off on his own to begin his day, with Amalaki no more than twenty paces behind him. Amalaki was confident that Sulwynd was involved in something, and watching him on his patrol would let him recognize any patterns that might be changed later on. He hadn't expected for the change to come so quickly.

He had not been surprised to see Constable Sulwynd enter the pastry shop and emerge with a half-eaten honey bun. Amalaki had purchased sweet rolls from that shop many times, and he knew how good they were. He doubted that Constable Sulwynd had paid for his roll, though.

What had surprised him was the brush pass that he had witnessed outside the pastry shop. It had been done quickly and professionally, exactly as they taught Novices to do at the Red Keep. Amalaki had performed a similar pass many times on his own. The elf that had performed the pass had been very good, good enough that Amalaki had not gotten a look at him. Amalaki watched Sulwynd read the note, and then head off with a new purpose. His only mistake had been to toss the note into the water trough. That might have worked, had nobody been following him, but Amalaki retrieved the note and saved it before the water had completely ruined the ink. It was still legible, and it had ordered the Constable to a carpentry shop that Amalaki knew well.

Now Amalaki was in a quandary, and wished that he had more people. He knew that Sulwynd was meeting with someone; that was clear by the note. It was also a mistake on their part. Had Sulwynd been given the message verbally, he could have just visited the shop as part of his patrol, and Amalaki probably would have been none the wiser. But now, Amalaki had a chance to see who Sulwynd was meeting with. This might be just what he needed to break this case open.

The door to the shop opened, and Amalaki instinctively stepped further into the shadows. Sulwynd walked out and headed up the road, passing within a few paces of Amalaki's hiding place. He had to will himself to wait there, and to not follow the Constable. He needed to see who Sulwynd had been meeting with.

The carpentry shop remained quiet for several minutes. Nobody went in or out. Amalaki began to sweat. Had he made a mistake? Had the message been a lure to draw him out and allow Sulwynd to break his tail? Had the note implied a meeting, but instead was a dead drop for Sulwynd to pick up something?

More minutes went by, and Amalaki began to curse himself. He had messed up, and now Sulwynd had broken away from him. Who knew what he was doing now? Amalaki kicked the ground and was about to break cover, thinking that, if he hurried, hopefully he could catch up to Sulwynd, when the carpentry shop door opened. Amalaki backed into the shadows again as a head poked out and looked to the left and right. It was a dead giveaway that clearly marked the person as being up to something. (Amalaki realized that they should probably teach Novices to not do that, as it clearly draws attention.)

The person stepped out of the shop, and Amalaki had to suppress the gasp that tried to escape his lips. He recognized the person as Inquisitor Aaroon, even though he was out of uniform. Behind him, Grand Inquisitor Agera followed.

Did Sulwynd just meet with the Grand Inquisitor? Amalaki recalled the encounter between Constable Sulwynd and the Grand Inquisitor at Ilvalé Arena, but he had dismissed that as happenstance. *But this is clearly a planned event. Why? Could I be wrong about Sulwynd? I must be, because why would the head of the Sucra be meeting with him?*

Amalaki watched Aaroon and the Grand Inquisitor head up the road, wondering exactly what all of this meant.

Chapter 31

Cedres ducked through the curtain that served as a door for this tavern. Actually, tavern was too generous a name for this place. They did serve a kind of alcohol, and some weak beer, all brewed or distilled in the backs of people's homes, but even the worst dive in Port Grove was better than this place. A rotting wooden plank laid across two stumps served as the bar. The only seating in the place was also on stumps, or from a motley collection of stools and chairs that would have been better served as kindling.

The place was smoky from the fire burning in the corner, in an open fire pit rather than a fireplace, and the floor was a muddy morass of spilled alcohol, spit, urine, and other unknown liquids churned together with some straw to give it just enough consistency to stick to your boots. Tallow candles were scattered around the room, adding more smoke than light to the place. The only good thing about this place was that it was indoors, so it kept out the rain and wind.

Cedres spotted the person he had been looking for, sitting on a log that had been converted into a long, irregular bench. He walked across the room and sat down next to him. "Hello, Ronce. I'm glad I found you. I figured you'd be working."

Ronce grunted. "Only one ship needed unloading today, so I could only work half a day."

Cedres shrugged in sympathy. He was tired of being humiliated to earn a pittance. "That's why I need you," Cedres said, looking around and leaning closer. "That's what this plan will fix."

Ronce drained whatever drink was in his wooden cup, and then laughed. "What plan? Nobody showed up the other night. Why should I be bothered?"

Cedres gestured to the room. "Because *we* don't belong here."

Ronce snorted and started to get up. Cedres grabbed his arm. "Aren't you mad? Don't you want to do something about this? Are you satisfied having your home taken away—stolen right out from under you—because of the damn Purity Laws?"

"I am mad, but I ain't stupid."

"Come on, you used to be a woodworker. Like me, you had your own shop over in Bay Grove."

"*Had.*"

"*Exactly*," Cedres said, trying to sound sympathetic. "And what happened after the last Purity Law?"

Ronce sighed and leaned back against the wall. "You know what happened. My damn employee ratted me out to the Sucra. He stole my livelihood from me."

"And now you can only find work unloading ships for just Pfen a day. Don't you want your career back? Your home? Your life?"

"Sure, but you can't wave a magic wand to make that happen."

Cedres ignored the remark because he had the next best thing, and he knew he had Ronce's attention. "The King needs to know that he made a mistake with the last Purity Law. That he went too far."

"And what, are we just going to go begging to him? Get it through that dwarf skull of yours, Cedres, we're nothing but halpbloed now."

"Come on, Ronce," Cedres said, gesturing to the room again. "We're not like the others here. You and I have more pure blood in us than any of these halpbloeden."

Ronce snorted again, rolling the empty cup between his hands. "It doesn't matter. How can we convince anybody that we are really elves? How do we get the King to admit that he made a mistake? Sure, I want my old life back. I miss the smell of freshly cut wood. I miss taking something and shaping it under my hands into something new. But there's no chance in the many hells that will ever happen."

"It will," Cedres whispered. "With my plan."

"You can make the King forget he ever enacted the Purity Laws?"

"Maybe. At least for us."

Ronce narrowed his eyes. "How?"

Cedres looked around the room, and then leaned closer and cupped his hand next to his mouth as he whispered, "By kidnapping Prince Orlean."

Ronce's eyes grew wide. "How will—" he started to say, his voice carrying in the room.

Cedres quickly shushed him, and then looked around the room again. "Not so loud. I won't tell you anything where people might hear and snitch to the Sucra. But I do have a plan, and I have support from a noble."

"Support from a noble? Who'd be knotted enough to support a bunch of halpbloeden?"

Cedres smiled, and he held up a finger as he pulled out something from his pocket. He handed it to Ronce, who looked at the coin. "A Skip? What's this supposed to be?"

"Look closer."

Ronce started to lift the coin up to get it into better light, but Cedres pushed his arm down and hissed, "Don't let everyone see it!"

Ronce grunted, leaned over, and twisted to try to get a good look at the silver coin. After a moment, he said, "Wait, the head of the King is wrong. He's looking to the left."

Cedres beamed, as if his child had just answered a really hard school problem. "Exactly. And who has the power, the ability, to mint a coin that is different from all the others?"

Ronce's eyebrows shot up. "You mean... the Treasurer?"

"Of course. He controls the mint, so he's the only one with the ability to mint a coin like that."

"The Treasurer is behind this? Why would the Treasurer support us?"

"Of course he's behind this. I can only assume that he dislikes the Purity Laws as much as we do. And it doesn't matter *why* he's doing it."

"It doesn't?" Ronce asked, giving Cedres a dubious look.

"No. What matters is that he will come forward when we execute the plan. When we have kidnapped the Prince, he will back us. He will intercede on our behalf, and he will get us what we deserve."

Ronce squinted one eye at Cedres and leaned back. "Are you sure? More likely he'll denounce us to the Sucra at the first chance to save his own hide."

"This plan will work. We won't be just making noise, and the Sucra won't touch us because they'll be afraid that we'll harm the Prince. They'll have to take notice of us and listen to our demands, because they will want the Prince unharmed. And the Treasurer will be able to support us from behind the scenes, telling the King to listen to us, to make an exception to the Purity Laws. Nobody will know that he's on our side. We'll finally get our lives back."

"I don't know..."

"Are you scared? Afraid?"

Ronce leaned in close and whispered, "Hells, yes, I'm afraid! It sounds great now, but what about when the Sucra are kicking in our doors to drag us off to the Red Keep?"

"The Sucra can't take from us what is rightfully ours by birth."

"They seem to have done a damn fine job of that so far."

Cedres knocked Ronce's shoulder with the back of his hand. "They can only do that because we let them, because we believe them. We are *not* halpbloed. We are *elves*, and we will get the respect we deserve when we kidnap the Prince. Don't we deserve our lives back?"

"Maybe." Ronce sat up and fingered the coin. "Look, maybe if I heard it from your mysterious benefactor. From the Treasurer."

Cedres would have liked to have spoken with the Treasurer, too. In fact, he had asked Constable Sulwynd if they could meet. Sulwynd had said that wasn't going to happen, that the Treasurer was not going to risk getting caught conspiring with halpbloeden. Sulwynd had been patient in explaining it to him, but with Ronce, Cedres could be more blunt.

"You know that won't happen, Ronce. He can't show that he's connected to us. If he did, then he'd put himself at risk. Do you think the Sucra will pretend that he did nothing wrong if they find out?" Ronce shook his head. "Exactly. He can't help us if the King finds out that the Treasurer is helping us and the Sucra arrest him. That's why we're working with his representative."

"How do we know this representative is legitimate?"

"Because he gave us the coins, idiot."

Ronce nodded. "So, when can we meet with this representative?"

"He's going to meet with us, so I need you to be ready. He'll answer your questions, and he'll give us the final part of the plan, so we can succeed."

"*When* will we meet him?" Ronce asked again.

"Soon. Once I know when the next meeting will be held, I will leave a chalk mark above the rain barrel outside the bakery. When you see that, you will know to meet at my place that night."

"Do you think this will work?"

Cedres smiled. "Of course. This *will* work, if we do this together."

Ronce leaned forward and rested his arms on his knees as he looked at the room. He continued to finger the coin, flipping it over and over in his hand.

Cedres leaned forward as well, "Do you want to continue to be humiliated and denigrated for the rest of your life?

Or do you want to reverse the travesty that took your home, your job, the very essence of who you really are away from you?"

The coin continued to flip over and over in Ronce's calloused hand. After a moment, the movement stopped, and Ronce squeezed the coin tightly in his fist. "I'll be there."

Chapter 32

The sun had set two hours before and, normally, Ansee would have enjoyed a stroll through Old Grove, enjoying the crisp night air. But tonight, he was exhausted to the bone. He had lost track of how many hours he had worked today, but it had been too many. He wanted to get home and pour himself some *sloatii*, put his feet up, and let Ember crawl onto his shoulders.

It wasn't just the long hours that had him bothered; it was the lack of progress in the new murder investigation. Aescel had been hounding him all day long for answers, and had chewed him and Reva out at least twice for not anticipating that there would be another murder, and for not catching the culprit already. Their lack of progress hadn't been due to a lack of effort. Ansee had been able to compare the auras that he had taken at the crime scene with those from the previous victims (which had still been tucked inside their pouches inside the wooden box in the evidence room). None of the auras had matched, which was as Ansee had expected. That confirmed what he had known from the moment that he had examined the victim this morning: different spells had been used. The new murderer hadn't used any teleportation magic, which Ansee considered to be one of the calling cards for the previous wizard. That ruled out a copycat in Ansee's (and Reva's) opinion. A copycat would want to emulate the manner of death as well as the type of victim.

Though it wasn't a copycat, the cases *were* linked. The same symbol from the calling card had been burned into their current victim, which confirmed that. The symbol was too unique to be used randomly by two different people, and Ansee had spent part of his day looking through the few reference tomes that the constabulary had on magical markings and symbols. He had come up with nothing that matched it, but he still felt that the answer to who was doing the killing was related to that symbol.

Ansee finally arrived at his building, and he stopped before he went inside. He had gotten a feeling, like the one he had from this morning: like he was being watched. He looked around at the street that twisted in front of his door, seeing nothing but the trees of the other apartments and businesses that were his neighbors. A few elves were out for an evening stroll, or heading to dinner, or maybe heading home after a day of work, like him. Nobody was watching him; nobody seemed to even notice him.

The feeling wouldn't go away, so Ansee cast a spell, allowing him to see into the dark shadows that pooled around the many trees. Even with the enhanced vision, he didn't see anyone watching him. He shrugged, and he let the spell fall away from his eyes. "I've been working too much," he said, as he opened the door to his apartment building.

† † †

Reva stepped off King's Bridge and turned left to head for home. She had missed dinner (again) and was wondering if she had missed enough meals lately that maybe her mother wouldn't notice and make a big deal out of it (again). Even when she got home, she wouldn't have time to stay, which would be sure to make her mother even more upset. Reva had sent a message to Amalaki earlier in the day, saying that she would meet him at the Red Keep, but the time for that meeting had already come and gone as well. She could have gone directly to the Red Keep, but she wanted to freshen up and change out of her armor first, having been in it for over 14 hours already today.

She walked up Embankment Road, her feet carrying her along automatically as her mind wandered over the cases that were piling up around her. But even after taking on the extra cases, plus this mornings' murder, she was not going to ask for help. She would push on and get the job done. Somehow. That was what she did.

A shadow stepped out of the darkness next to her home and, while her mind had been wandering, she reacted swiftly, pulling out a dagger and sticking it to the neck of her would-be assailant.

"Whoa, Constable, it's just me, your friendly neighborhood Sucra officer," Inquisitor Amalaki said, his hands up deferentially. In his left hand, he held her note. "I thought we were going to meet, but not at the point of a dagger."

Reva relaxed and sheathed the dagger. "Sorry, I've had bad experiences with people waiting in shadows by my house, and it's been a really long day."

"No offense, but you're looking even worse than you did the other night at the Beehive."

"I'm fine," Reva groused, stepping over to the door.

"Since you seemed to be running late tonight," Amalaki said, "I thought I'd meet you here. Save you the time of having to walk all the way to the Red Keep." He gestured to her home. "Can we talk inside?"

Reva had been reaching for the door handle, but hesitated. "That's probably not a good idea. My mother is home."

"I'm sure your mother won't mind us talking."

"No, I mean it's not a good idea for you. Mom could give the Sucra lessons in interrogation techniques. And I don't need her thinking that I'm dating anybody."

"Are we dating?" Amalaki smirked.

"No, but that doesn't mean that my mother won't jump to that conclusion. Another trait that she shares with you Green Cloaks."

Amalaki chuckled. "I told you we don't do that. We collect evidence, just like you constables do."

"Whatever." Reva shrugged, but turned away from the door. She was still not going to introduce Amalaki to her mother. She started walking. "The King's Herald is just a block away. We can go there to talk."

Amalaki got into step with her. "Sure, but I think it's your turn to buy."

"After what I have for you, I think you'll be willing to buy."

"I doubt that. I learned something today that I think will make *you* buy."

Reva cast him a glance, but said nothing. It was a short walk to reach the King's Herald. The building had been tucked between two others, the many trees coaxed through magic to interweave their branches to create a small canopy over the tavern. The sides of the building were actually part of the trunks of several trees, also altered through magic to grow horizontally to form the walls. Small, irregular openings had been set with glass for windows, and an orange light flickered from inside. Some evergreen bushes flanked the door, and an old wine barrel sat right next to it, a calico cat curled up on the top of the barrel.

"This looks like a nice place," Amalaki remarked.

"It is," Reva agreed, pausing to scratch the cat's ears as she opened the door. The cat purred but didn't move. "It's far enough off the main road that only us locals know about it, so there are no adventurers. Plus, Rogue here," she pointed to the cat, "keeps the riff-raff out."

The inside was just as nice as the outside. Many of the branches had been interlocked together to form the ceiling, and more magic had kept them as healthy and leafy as if it was high summer. Two fireplaces were going, and two large chandeliers with dozens of candles hung from the ceiling. There were several tables in the room, but only a few patrons. Reva stepped up to a large oak bar accented with brass trim and ordered them drinks and food—mulled wine, venison stew with black bread, and a side plate of cheese and sausage. (She was hungry, having missed lunch.)

"Here you go," said the lady behind the bar, handing over two pewter goblets of wine.

"Thank you, Eolia," Reva said. She pointed toward the back of the room. "We'll be in the back."

"I'll bring your food out in a few minutes," Eolia replied, as Reva led Amalaki to the back of the tavern. There was a smaller room there, with its own fireplace and just a couple of tables. Reva picked the one set against the wall and sat down at it.

Amalaki took the other seat and fluttered the note. "I think this is the first time you've ever sent me anything at the Red Keep." He held up the note as if it was some master-piece painting. "Maybe I'll frame this."

"If you want to be that sentimental, go ahead," Reva sighed, as she took a sip of the wine. It was warm, with a heavy taste of cinnamon and clove.

Amalaki folded the note and tucked it into his tunic. He picked up the goblet and took a sip, making an appreciative face. "So, what was so important that you sent me an actual note?"

"I know what Constable Sulwynd is up to."

"Straight to the point, for a change," Amalaki quipped. "But I think you may be trimming a branch that's already felled. I learned some information today that leads me to be-lieve that Sulwynd may not be my target after all. I'm afraid I have been climbing up the wrong tree all along."

"Really? Why the change? You've been pretty sure that he's been up to no good for a month now. Hells, you wouldn't even listen to me when I suggested that you get me the evi-dence to prove it."

"I don't know," Amalaki admitted, shrugging his shoul-ders. "I have my doubts now, is all." He took a drink of the mulled wine. "But I guess I had better hear what you have to tell me, otherwise this date will be wasted."

"It's not a date."

At that moment, Eolia arrived, carrying a large tray with two steaming bowls of stew, half a loaf of black bread, and a plate with a selection of cheeses and sliced meats on it. She carefully arranged the food on the table and inquired about refills for the wine, which both Reva and Amalaki accepted, and then returned to the main room.

"All this food and drink, and you're buying; it seems like a date to me." Amalaki gave her a wink.

"You should have your coins ready to pay after I tell you what *I* learned today."

"Enlighten me, then," Amalaki challenged her, as he dug into the stew.

"It seems that your first instinct about Sulwynd was right all along," Reva began, tearing off some of the bread. "He met with a halpbloed the other night, and they discussed a plan to kidnap Prince Orlean."

Amalaki nearly spit out his stew at the news and started to choke. He coughed, and then drained his goblet of wine. "What? How did you find this out?"

"I have my sources," Reva smiled, as she dipped the bread into the stew. "Of course, I don't know when this will happen, or how many are involved, or exactly how they will accomplish this feat, but I know that *is* the plan." She bit off a bite of the bread, savoring the peppery flavor of the stew. "I'll be sure to tell Eolia that you're paying."

"Is he now?" Eolia asked, as she appeared with a pitcher to pour more mulled wine.

"No, Reva is still going to pay," Amalaki replied, "after she hears me out."

Eolia poured the drinks, and then hovered a moment, until both Reva and Amalaki gave her a pointed look and she walked back to the main room.

"Enlighten me, then," Reva said, echoing his earlier words.

"I think that the plan to kidnap the Prince is a ruse, or at least a plan to draw out malcontents."

"And why is that?" Reva asked, as she stacked cheese

and meat together before taking a bite.

"I was tailing Constable Sulwynd today on his patrol in Bay Grove, and he met with Grand Inquisitor Agera. That's why I have my doubts. If he's working with the Grand Inquisitor on something, then it can't involve any actual threat to the King or the royal family."

"Why would Agera work with a Constable instead of one of you Green Cloaks?" Reva asked. This was unsettling news, because she was pretty sure that she was going to have to tell Amalaki something he would not want to hear, or believe, for that matter.

"We've worked with the constabulary before," Amalaki hedged. Reva knew it was rare that it happened, and never, to her knowledge, with a rank-and-file constable. "Agera is probably using Sulwynd to draw out a potential group of traitors before they can do anything dangerous."

Shit, Reva thought, as she took a drink. She knew Agera better than Amalaki did, and she didn't like the implication of Sulwynd meeting with the Grand Inquisitor. She was going to have to tell Amalaki what she knew.

"I'm about to tell you something that you won't want to believe. Hells, you'd be within your right to haul me off to the Red Keep and throw me into a cell. I'm even sure that Agera would promote you on the spot to Senior Inquisitor." She paused, as his eyes widened. "But it's the truth."

"What would be so bad that I'd do all that?"

Reva took another drink, and then set her goblet down. "Do you remember the serial killer a couple of months ago? The one cutting people in half with the enchanted sword?"

Amalaki nodded. "I do. That was right before Senior Inquisitor Malvaceä was shipped off to—"

Reva gave him a playful smile and leaned forward.

"—I don't know where. Honestly." He held up his hands. "But he was sent away after that case. I don't know why, but I remember that you managed to stop the serial killer."

"Malvaceä was sent away because he lost something important to Agera."

"Lost what?"

"The Fury Blade."

"What?" Amalaki leaned forward, his face filled with incredulity. "But the weapon was recovered and then sent to the wizards at Auros to destroy it. I remember hearing that from some of the others at the Red Keep."

Reva shook her head slowly. "The *fake* Fury Blade was destroyed."

"There was a fake Fury Blade? Then what happened to the real one?"

"I gave the real Fury Blade back to the dark elves that claimed that it belonged to them." Reva poked at the stew, but she had lost some of her appetite.

"Dark elves?" Amalaki's voice rose a bit.

"Hush," Reva chastised him. "See, now you *are* starting to think of hauling me off and throwing away the key."

"I am not," Amalaki huffed, as he sat back in his chair. "But really? Dark elves? Here in Tenyl? You can't be serious."

Reva met his gaze and held it. "Dead serious. I stabbed the Fury Blade, the real one, into their leader." She looked wistfully up to the ceiling. "I wonder how they ever managed to get it out of him?"

"B-but..." Amalaki leaned forward, "how does this involve the Grand Inquisitor? And why would he send Malvaceä away for something that *you* did? How did he even know there *were* two blades?"

"Because the Grand Inquisitor is a fraud," Reva stated. This got her a quizzical look from Amalaki. "He's secretly plotting with the dark elves to overthrow the King."

Amalaki started to laugh. "Oh, come on, you have got to be twisting my branches."

Reva stared at him until he finally settled down.

"By Basvu, you're making that up," he hissed. "I don't know why you would spread such seditious lies, but none of that can be true."

"The truth is the truth, whether we like it or not," Reva said. She picked up a piece of cheese and nibbled at it, but it had no flavor for her now. Amalaki was about to say something else, but she held up her hand.

"Grand Inquisitor Agera is the head of a secret order that used to be based out of Pfeta fey Orung. Their members can trace their heritage back to the dark elves, and they've been plotting for a thousand years to overthrow the kingdom. I don't know how many members there are, but I do know that Malvaceä is a member, as is LCI Betulla. So were Lady Ochroma, the former First Magistrate, and Olea Aucarii. There are others, too." She paused, her mind going to the family tree that she had hidden in her room, the neat lines on the illustrated parchment heading from her family to some dark elf ancestry. *No, that's a lie,* she told herself. *Locera told me it was a lie. And he had no reason to lie to me, right?*

"Are you alright, Reva?" Amalaki asked.

Reva saw that she had grabbed her spoon and had been gripping it so tightly that her knuckles had turned white. She set it back down. "Yes, I'm fine. This secret cabal has many members. I'm pretty sure that Constable Sulwynd is one, which is why he's working with Agera to kidnap the Prince."

"This is too much. How could such a plot be carried out for that long right under our noses? The Sucra would have known. We'd have uncovered any plot to overthrow the King."

"Of course you would," Reva agreed, letting the bitterness she felt at her own dark secret fill her words. "That is, if the head of the Sucra wasn't also the head of this secret cabal. It's a pretty efficient way to keep nosy inquisitors away from things."

Amalaki reached for his drink and took a long pull. "Suppose all of this is true," he started, returning the goblet to the table.

Reva interrupted him. "It is. I was in their little secret clubhouse under Pfeta fey Orung. I saw their family trees, their flags, the portraits. It's all gone now, of course, since Agera had it all removed the same night I stopped Locera." *Not all of it is gone,* she reminded herself.

"That's pretty convenient."

Reva shrugged. "You can believe me or not, it doesn't change the truth."

"So, what do we do about it?"

"Do? We stop Sulwynd. Whatever he's planning in Nul Pfeta with the halpbloed is Agera's idea. I don't know exactly what Agera's plan is, but that doesn't matter. We stop Sulwynd."

"But what about Agera? Let's assume that you're not twisting my branches for some reason, and he is actually plotting to overthrow the King. We have to stop him."

"We?" Reva shook her head. "Uh uh. One, I'm not a Green Cloak; protecting the King is your job. Two, Agera is as slippery as an eel. If you try to do anything to stop him directly, or try to prove that he's not what he claims to be, you'll find yourself dead, or worse."

"What's worse than death?"

"Trust me, you don't want to know."

Amalaki gave her a quizzical look, which she ignored. "Look, you need to forget about Agera. Yes, he's the one at the top, blowing all the branches, but you'll never be able to prove it or to stop him. Not directly. And if you start poking around and looking into things, he will find out, and you will get hurt."

"You sound like you actually care about me."

"I don't, but you're way better than Malvaceä, and I'm just getting you broken in."

"You're breaking me in?"

"The truth hurts sometimes," Reva smiled, and picked up her spoon, some of her appetite returning. The stew had grown cold, but she needed to eat in order to take her mind off of her family tree. "I believe I've given you enough that you're buying."

Amalaki nodded, as he stirred the remains of his stew. "What about Sulwynd?"

"We'll stop him. But we'll do it my way. Your house is compromised; who knows who else in the Red Keep reports to Agera?"

"And yours isn't? Sulwynd works for you."

Reva made a dismissive gesture. "If the Sucra go into Nul Pfeta, all hells will break loose."

"Again, how will having the constabulary take the lead be any different? I'm pretty sure the halpbloeden don't like either one of us."

"You said it, Sulwynd is one of us: a constable in Nul Pfeta Division. They're all bullies and corrupt constables there. The halpbloeden will love to see us taking down one of our own."

Amalaki didn't say anything to that, he just raised one eyebrow.

"Well, they *better* love it."

Chapter 33

The Minister set the mug of hot, mulled cider down on the table and regarded the object that was sitting on the table in front of him. It was a piece of bone, part of a skull, yellow with age and polished smooth from being handled hundreds of times. The bone had been taken from one of the abominations that he had defeated: a particularly vile sorcerer who had fought hard to defend herself, and who had continued to struggle and fight while The Minister had interrogated her in order to learn the name of the demon. She had died during the process, never having given up the demon's name. The Minister was sure that he had been close to discovering the name of the foul creature and fulfilling his quest, and the fact that she had refused to name the demon that had given her access to Qurna's blessing had merely confirmed to him that he needed to redouble his efforts.

The Minister had been working on his detect sorcerer spell at the time, having grown frustrated with his many failures in his attempts to create the spell. It should have been so easy; the detect magic spell was one of the most basic, simplest spells to learn. His detect sorcerer spell was a natural continuation of the magic, yet the spell had been eluding him. But the death of that sorcerer, who had refused to name her demon master, had given him insight. Like begat like; it was a truism of magic that was taught to young wizards, and often forgotten as they went on to study more complex spells. But it was the foundation for why so many spells required material components. Water to control water, a prism for color spray, brimstone for fireball. And a sorcerer to find a sorcerer.

Blood and bone had been some of the first material components, as they were readily at hand and available. Over the millennia, most spells had been refined to the point that simple gestures and words were all that was needed to cast them. Material components had also been refined as well; new items were discovered that could lend their power to the magic more efficiently, but blood and bone still worked. In this case, The Minister knew that the sorcerers' ability to cast magic had been imparted to them by the demon on the most intimate level, into their very blood and bones.

Blood would work, but blood was hard to keep, and it eventually dried out. While he would always be able to get more blood, The Minister knew that the sorcerer that had refused to name her demon master was special. She had been a true believer to the very end, a believer of hate and evil to be sure, but a believer nonetheless. Her connection to the demon was strong, strong enough that she had endured his interrogation, never giving up her master's name. So, The Minister had taken part of her body, cutting out part of her skull to craft the material component that he needed. A few more refinements, an inscribed sigil on the bone, and his spell had finally worked.

The Minister now picked up the bone, running his finger over the smooth surface, feeling the edges that marked the sigil. He looked around the room. It was another pub, the Violet Clover this time, in West Gate Grove, another place that swelled with adventurers, and always an ample hunting ground for his needs. He sat at a table that gave him an unobstructed view of the bar and the rest of the room. It was time to bait his next lure.

The Minister spoke a couple of words, and the room, along with most of the people in it, took on a pale, washed out gray hue. His spell essentially deleted them from his vision, as they were unimportant, and therefore not worthy of any attention. He scanned the room with a practiced, casual gaze. Nothing but grayness filled his sight. He was too patient to feel any sort of disappointment, and he continued to watch the room, getting new glimpses as the people moved around.

Then he spotted it: a flash of color in contrast to the palette of monochrome. The color became blocked as a person moved in between him and the source of the color, but then came back. He saw an arm, shining in bright color as if a beam of sunlight had pierced the ceiling. More of the body appeared, and The Minister now had found a target. Quickly looking around, The Minister saw no other targets in the room, and he did not have the luxury of time, not on his current mission.

A male elf was sitting with a small group of friends. He dressed like a wizard, but The Minister was not fooled. The small party was in a celebratory mood, drinking and laughing. Based on the number of cups, goblets, and steins that littered their table, they had been at it for a while.

The Minister ended his spell and continued to watch the party, plotting how he would act and move to dispatch his target. It might be a long night; he would probably have to follow them to their lodgings. While he needed to act quickly to set his trap for Ansee Carya, he also could not act rashly. A protracted fight, especially one that involved this sorcerer's companions, would attract attention that The Minister did not want. It would also probably attract the constabulary before he was ready.

He continued to watch the party for the next hour. They never left the table, but their server had delivered several more rounds of drinks. The party laughed and cheered as they regaled those around them with tales of their exploits. Clearly, they believed that they were special, The Minister thought, with a contemptuous snort.

Suddenly, Jansure delivered him a blessing for his patience. The Minister watched as the sorcerer stood up, on unsteady legs, and made his way toward the back of the pub by himself, presumably heading for the latrines located outside. The sorcerer left behind his cloak and other personal effects, clearly intent on returning to his revelry after emptying his bladder.

The Minister stood up and followed his target. He had no concern about being observed by anyone in the pub; they would just see an old elf heading out to relieve himself, as many other patrons had done during the night. Certainly, his target was not aware of his presence. The sorcerer stumbled through the crowd, clearly feeling the effects of his libations.

The sorcerer stepped out the pub's back door into the cold night air. A line of four privies stood across a small, muddy yard, with tall walls enclosing the space. The Minister slipped to the left of the door as he watched his target try to open one of the privy doors. A loud yell came from within. The privy was clearly occupied, and the sorcerer mumbled some words of apology before moving to the next one. This one was unoccupied, and the sorcerer stepped in to relieve himself.

The Minister was happy to let his target empty his bladder. He didn't want to have to deal with the stink that would come once he killed the elf and his bladder let go. While he waited, he prepared himself. One of the other privies was also occupied, and the simple application of a piece of wood through the handles on both doors would ensure that those two occupants would not interfere. The Minister turned and cast a spell on the door to the pub, locking it in place so that nobody else could come out that way for at least a couple of minutes.

His hand reached into the folds of his robes, and he pulled out a small silver-gray disc that was etched with a six-pointed star on its surface. The Minister had no idea what kind of magic this abomination of a sorcerer might have, but he certainly didn't want him to escape. The anchor stone would prevent any form of teleportation, and The Minister set it on the ground and activated its magic with the touch of his boot.

The Minister then activated one of the spells imbued by his staff, ensuring that nobody other than himself and his target would hear anything that was about to transpire. Then he waited for the sorcerer to emerge from the privy.

And waited. The Minister began to worry that the occupants of the other privies would try to leave and begin to make noise. He was also concerned that someone from inside would soon discover that the door had been locked. This plan, as impromptu as it was, would work, but if his preparations attracted any attention, that would just create more problems that he would have to deal with. He had just begun to wonder if the drunken fool had fallen into the privy when the door to it opened and the sorcerer stepped out.

The sorcerer was noticeably drunk, staggering a bit as he stepped out of the privy. The wizard snapped his fingers, and a flare burst in front of the sorcerer's head. The bright flash of light lit up the small courtyard, and the sorcerer reeled back from the flash, temporarily blinded. He staggered about, calling out, unaware that his words did not travel beyond the small circle of magic that was created by The Minister's staff.

The Minister started to prepare a spell, the same ray that he had used the previous night on the human sorcerer, but then hesitated. He had time, and he might use this chance to get some valuable intelligence. Why waste the opportunity?

Instead, The Minister pulled out his small crossbow, pulled back the string, and set a poisoned bolt on it. His target was still stumbling about, but not enough to make the shot too difficult. The Minister pulled the trigger and the bolt fired, hitting the sorcerer in the center of his chest. He took only two more steps before he dropped like a rag doll to the ground.

The Minister quickly cast several spells in succession to lift the body with a floating disc and to obscure the area with a thick fog. He picked up the anchor stone, and he pulled out the bolt so it wouldn't fall out later and leave behind a clue. Satisfied, The Minister climbed the fence, aided by another spell, and he led the unconscious sorcerer on the floating disc away from the pub. This would have to be a quick interrogation, but maybe he'd get extra honey on the cake and get the name of the demon. Regardless, his second lure had been secured, and he knew exactly where he would set this one.

Chapter 34

An insistent croaking and fetid breath that smelled of stale crickets awakened Ansee from his sleep. For once, it had been devoid of his usual nightmares, although in his dream he felt as if every person had been staring at him, watching everything he had done. He opened his eyes to see Ember sitting on his chest. She created a warmth that made him want to stay in bed, but she croaked again and pushed her body up and down on his chest, her way of saying, "Get up, you lazy elf! I'm hungry."

Ansee started to pull back the covers, and Ember jumped down and headed over to the bookshelf where he kept the box with the crickets. She looked up at the shelf, then back at him, and then ran back to him as he slowly got out of bed. She butted her head against his ankle.

"Okay, okay, I'm up," Ansee complained, as he stood up. "Be patient."

She gave another insistent croak and ran back over to the bookshelf. Ansee padded across the room, his bare feet on the chilly floor. "You know," he said, "you could at least start a fire in the morning before waking me up, to take the chill off. Not all of us maintain a fire within our bodies, you know."

Ember cocked her head and flicked her tongue out over one eye. Ansee called that her "You must be crazy" look. He pulled the box off of the shelf and pulled down a small key. He had bought this box, crafted from ash and alder and nicely filigreed with openings in the lid, not because it looked nice—it did—but because it had a key. It was supposed to be a jewelry box, but after Ember had managed to bust open the previous box that he used to store her food and eaten all the crickets in a single sitting (and then barfing them up again on the rug) he had used it to better secure her food.

He unlocked the box and tossed out a few crickets. They jumped around the floor and Ember gave chase. Ansee noticed that there were only a couple of crickets left. He would need to stop and buy more. He only fed her a couple of them, since he knew that Ember also managed to hunt the few insects that managed to make their way into his apartment. They never made their way out.

Ansee locked the box, replaced it and the key on the shelf, and then headed to his water closet. His morning business completed, he returned to the living room and got dressed for the day. Ember was still chasing one of the crickets, pouncing on it, and then letting it go so that it would jump away and she could then pounce on it again.

"What do people without pets do to wake them up before the crack of dawn?" Ansee asked her. She ignored him (typical) as she jumped on the cricket, catching it in her mouth this time. "I wonder what it's like to be able to sleep in?" She turned, half of the cricket sticking out of her mouth. She cocked her head and tried to lick her eye with her tongue, but that opened her mouth and allowed the cricket to make its escape. Though injured, it leaped away, with Ember giving Ansee what he could only describe as a stink eye.

"Hey, don't blame me, you were the one that opened your mouth."

Ansee put on his breeches and shirt, and he was getting ready to put on his puttee when there came a loud scream from outside, sounding like it came from right outside the front door of his apartment. Ember heard it and raced across the room to the fireplace, her meal forgotten. "You're certainly a fierce predator." Ansee chastised her as he stood up. "I hope I never have to count on you to save my life."

He walked over to the window that looked out onto the front of the tree, and saw that a small crowd had gathered right outside the front door. There was a lot of commotion, and then he heard the sound of running steps coming up the stairs, heading toward his apartment. Ansee hurried over to the door, pulling it open just as Lanai, one of his neighbors, was about to knock.

"Constable Ansee," Lanai said, panting. He was an older elf, and the exertion of running up the stairs had winded him. "Come quick. A body."

Ansee nodded and headed out of his door, not bothering with his cloak or the rest of his uniform. He pulled the door shut, ran down the stairs, and headed out the front door.

The morning air was cool, with an edge of crispness to it. It was still dark, maybe a half hour before sunrise, but that hadn't kept a crowd from gathering and blocking his view.

"Constabulary, make way," Ansee called, and several people, neighbors and people he knew, made a path for him. Laying on the ground, not five paces from his front door, was a body. It was staked to the road, with iron spikes piercing the hands and wedged between the cobbles of the road. The victim was male this time, and an elf, but like yesterday's victim, this one was nude from the waist up.

Ansee set his face. He knew that being a constable meant having to investigate scenes of damage and rage, examining people who had been seriously injured, or who were, all too often, the victims of grisly murders. He had seen his share of pain and suffering when he had worked in Nul Pfeta, and his two months in Acer Division had been filled with more death than he thought possible, but never in his entire time in the constabulary had he expected to find a murder victim right outside his front door. This felt like an invasion of his own privacy. It felt personal.

He got a tingling sensation on his skin, that feeling that he was being watched, and he ignored it. He *was* being watched; by people who were his neighbors, people who he knew and spoke to all the time, people who trusted him because they knew that he was a constable. They lived their lives a bit easier, knowing that someone was there who would protect them, and give them aid if they needed it. But he could see the look of shock and horror on their faces. This body, this murder, had shattered their sense of security and safety. They were looking to him for guidance, and for assurance.

Lanai had come back outside and stood behind Ansee. He turned to his neighbor and directed, "Lanai, please help me get the crowd back. We need to get some space around the body."

Lanai nodded and grabbed another neighbor. Together, they started to push the crowd back. Ansee tapped a younger elf who had been staring, wide-eyed, at the body. Ansee knew that he worked at the green grocers just down the street. "Tolen," he turned the boy away from the body. "I need you to run and get a constable, find one of the Birches. I think Constable Wynstead will be at the patrol shack at this time of the morning. Tell him that a body has been discovered here. He needs to get Constable Inspector Lunaria here right away. Tell him I'm already here. Got that?"

The young elf nodded and ran off in the direction of the Old Grove patrol shack. Ansee turned back to the body and spoke an incantation, "*Bana sihirli ışığı göster.*" His eyes took on a golden hue as the detect magic spell activated. He looked at the body, already expecting what he would find, and dreading it.

His eyes went wide as he looked at the magical auras. The arcane mark he expected was there, but this time, there was something else. Something personal.

Chapter 35

Reva pushed her way through the crowd that was standing around the scene. She had never understood the fascination that common people had with death and tragedy, the way that they liked to watch on from the sides at a scene of horror. It was a perverse sort of voyeurism that she just couldn't understand.

As she approached, she looked at the large tree that had become apartments for several families. It looked vaguely familiar. She then looked at the murder scene and saw Ansee already hard at work collecting auras, although he was barely dressed.

"You're out of uniform," she remarked, as she walked up to look at the victim, who was staked out nearly identically to their victim from yesterday.

"Yeah, I just ran down the stairs when I found out," Ansee replied.

Then it hit Reva. "This is where your apartment is," she said. Ansee nodded.

Reva stifled a yawn. "I'm getting tired of these early morning crime scenes."

"Out late last night, Inspector?"

"Late? Not really, but Amalaki and I were busy discussing some business."

"You've been spending quite a bit of time with Inquisitor

Amalaki," Ansee commented.

"What's that supposed to mean? I'm not dating him, if that's what you're implying. And even if I was, it wouldn't be any of your damn business!"

"No, I just meant that with the way you acted around Senior Inquisitor Malvaceä, I figured that you despised the Sucra. I didn't think that you liked any of them, but Amalaki seems to be an exception."

Reva scowled to hide her own shame. She had bitten Ansee's head off without thinking. *This is why I need to have a cup of hot cacao before I start my day.* Since she didn't have any of that, she pulled out the tin of Wake. It was getting empty again, but she had enough to get through this crime scene. She brought a pinch up to her nose and inhaled sharply; the Wake hit her like a bucket of cold water thrown into her face. She chose to ignore the look of disapproval coming from Ansee, and he wisely kept his tongue.

"What do you know?" she asked.

"Male elf, killed using an evocation spell. There are other auras this time as well, another evocation, but a different spell. I will have to verify them, but I think they are from a lightning shock spell."

"Your favorite spell," Reva teased, some of the tension going away.

"One time," Ansee rolled his eyes. "I used it one time."

"Yeah, on *me*," she smiled to let him know that it was just leaves in the wind. "What else?"

"The victim has the same arcane mark on his chest."

Reva looked, but she didn't see anything. The victim's chest had what appeared to be burn marks and some bruising, but there was no symbol. "I don't see anything."

"Our killer magically hid it this time."

Reva turned to look at Ansee's home. "Any idea why the body was left here? On your doorstep?"

"Yes," Ansee replied. She turned to look at him with a questioning glance.

Ansee held up a quartz crystal. "Here, you'll need to look

through this. It's not perfect, as the view will be a bit distorted, but I enchanted this so that you can see what our killer left."

Reva took the crystal and held it up to her eye. She was shocked by the amount of color that seemed to radiate from the body. She had a basic idea of what Cas and Ansee would see when they cast their spells, but she had never seen it with her own eyes. It was strangely beautiful, or it would have been, if the prism of auras wasn't coming from a dead body. She could see several bright splotches of orange on his chest, one in his stomach that was brighter than the others, and a faint violet glow coming from his back and the back of his arms and legs. But right in the center of his chest she saw the symbol, the same one from all the other victims, outlined in a brilliant blue aura. Under that, looking as if someone had poked their finger into paint—or blood—and then scrawled on the body was a message: "You and your demon master will be next, Ansee Carya."

"Well, that seems very personal," Reva said.

Ansee gave a snort. "You think? Our murderer wanted me to find this. That's why it's written like it is, using an arcane mark."

Reva pulled the crystal away from her eye. "You seem to have pissed somebody off. And it's not even me, this time. Have you been moonlighting behind my back?"

"Like you've been moonlighting with Inquisitor Amalaki?"

Reva made a crude gesture. "Still, it seems that our previous killer had a friend. One who really doesn't like *you*."

"Or we could be dealing with a secret order of assassins," Ansee added.

"That only target sorcerers, apparently. Seems like you're doubly in trouble, then."

Ansee stood a bit taller. "I fended off a mad serial killer who was wielding a sword of mass destruction using only a dagger, remember? I can take care of myself."

Reva nodded. Ansee was not Cas, but she had seen him

in enough close scrapes and fights in the past couple of months to know that he could handle his own. "That, you probably can," she agreed.

She knelt next to the body to look at it without the aid of Ansee's magic crystal. She could see a small puncture wound just above the victim's left breast. She stood up. "We need to see what we can learn about this mysterious group."

"I looked again yesterday through the records that we have," Ansee said. "Same results as we had on the previous case. Nothing."

"Nothing in the constabulary records, you mean."

Ansee nodded. "I was planning on visiting Auros today to see if they could help."

Reva tucked some hair over her ear. "Maybe. Let me go talk with someone today and see if I can get a lead on this symbol. You finish up here and make sure that we have all the magical evidence sorted."

"I always do," Ansee sighed, sounding more weary than annoyed.

"And make sure you get into uniform. I'd hate to have to dock you a day's pay for a violation of regulations." This time, it was Ansee that gave her the crude gesture.

A noise came from the crowd, and Reva turned to see Thea and the other Alchemists making their way toward them. She turned back to Ansee. "And make sure you have your shield spell prepared, just in case."

Ansee looked her in the eyes. "I always do."

Reva nodded and headed away, pausing to let Thea know about the puncture wound and asking her to perform an alchemical analysis on the victim's blood. Then she weaved her way through the crowd. She was hoping that she could catch Rhoanlan early and see what information he might have about the strange symbol.

She walked quickly through the streets, her boots striking the cobbles with fast, determined steps. As she reached the Grand March, she saw a Green Cloak step away from one of the plinths, a large statue of a long dead king, and fall into step with her.

"You seem to be having a busy morning," Inquisitor Amalaki remarked.

"It usually is."

"Anything you need help with?"

Reva gave him a look out of the corner of her eye. "Is this coming from you, or from the Sucra?"

"From me. The Sucra could care less about a dead body, unless there's a threat to the King."

"Well, unless the King is secretly a sorcerer and has been hiding this fact from everybody, then I think he's safe." Reva went past the line of people who were waiting for the ferry and headed to Embankment Road.

"The victims are all sorcerers?" Amalaki asked.

"Yep. It seems like we are dealing with a group of very specialized assassins. You ever heard of a group like that?"

"No."

"And you'd tell me the truth if you did?" Reva asked. She knew the Sucra rarely told the truth.

"Yes, I would. And I did." There was genuine hurt in his voice. "I don't know any groups like that."

"And will the Sucra be willing to share your extensive collection of magical auras with my Seeker to see if we can find a match?"

Amalaki hesitated, but then said, "No." Reva glared at him as they walked. He quickly added, "I'm sorry, but not without a formal request to Grand Inquisitor Agera. He's the only one who can approve it."

"Yeah, that's what I thought. I guess the sharing of resources only applies when there's something that the Sucra wants." She didn't hide the bitterness in her voice.

"Then I guess that this is the wrong time to tell you that Sulwynd visited Nul Pfeta early this morning."

Reva stopped walking and swore, earning a glance from an old woman walking along the road.

"We need to find out what is happening," Amalaki insisted.

"Damn it, Inquisitor! If you didn't notice, I have a murder investigation that I'm trying to run. Sorcerers are dropping like leaves around the city." She turned and started walking again.

Amalaki hurried to catch up. "The safety of the royal family is at risk. I need your help."

"Need?" Reva gave a bitter laugh. "Are you pulling rank on me?"

"My duty is to the safety of the King and the Kingdom. Your murderer will either be caught or not," Reva gave him a withering glance that made Amalaki flinch, but he went on. "You already said that there's nothing with this murder investigation that concerns the safety of the King."

"That's the most Malvaceä thing you've ever said to me," Reva snapped. She was glad when he flinched again.

They had reached King's Bridge and Reva turned to cross, but Amalaki reached out and grabbed her shoulder. Reva stopped and turned, glaring at his hand. Amalaki removed it from her shoulder, but said, "There is a known threat against the royal family. For the Sucra, for *me*, that takes precedence over everything else."

He lowered his voice and leaned closer. "And after our discussion last night, you know that I can't depend on the Sucra. You said it yourself: my house is compromised."

Damn me and my big mouth, Reva thought.

Amalaki gave her a weak smile. "I need your help. You know the situation, and you're the only one that I can trust right now. We need to know what's happening in Nul Pfeta, and you have the contacts there."

Reva snorted. "Yeah, I wouldn't really call Pfastbinder a contact. He's really more like a nuisance. Or a pet. One that always seems to be underfoot, always wanting something."

"It's more than I have."

Reva hung her head and put a hand to her forehead. *This is not what I wanted. A member of my team is being threatened by a serial killer. I don't have time for this.* She looked up and saw Amalaki watching her, patiently, his hands clasped in front of him. She knew that he was right. She was the only one that could help him. If there was a plan to kidnap the Prince, and if Grand Inquisitor Agera was behind it, then there was practically zero chance that Amalaki, on his own, would be able to stop it. The family tree hidden in her bedroom, and the threat that it posed, came to the forefront of her thoughts. Was there a way to neutralize that threat by helping Amalaki?

"Shit," Reva grumbled. "I guess Rhoanlan can wait."

"What?"

"Never mind," Reva said. She started across the bridge. "Come on, let's go visit a cleric of Banok."

Chapter 36

Pfastbinder folded his arms in a huff, "I still say that it is not only irregular, but also rude. My very presence here has brought you business, Ellanna."

"Hmph," the owner snorted. "You ain't never brought in but one customer, and you spend hours taking up space and driving away what customers I do have. Nobody wants to hear you yammering about your stupid chaotic god." She held out her hand. "Now pay me the Acorn, or you don't get no hot water."

"You are forcing me to find a new business to frequent," Pfastbinder said, with airy confidence.

"Good riddance," she spat. "For a cleric of chaos, you are as regular as clockwork when it comes to bugging me and mooching off my generosity."

Pfastbinder paused to consider that. He had been making a habit of visiting this tea house for a considerable amount of time, but that had been because Ellanna had always allowed him to bring in his own tea and provided him with the hot water. It was an arrangement that benefited him, and his meager income, but he had never stopped to consider Ellanna's side of things.

"What if I gave you something else in exchange?" Pfastbinder asked.

"If it ain't shiny and metallic with the picture of an acorn on it, I ain't interested."

"What about water? I can make it for you."

"Water, I got," Ellanna said. "I get it from the well every morning."

"Ugh," Pfastbinder made a face. "No wonder you have no customers," he said, but then saw her ears redden, and back-pedaled. "Though, of course, I don't mind the well water. It adds a new flavor to the tea every day. But all of that hauling, and having to wait at the well? Especially in the winter? With me, you wouldn't have to do all that."

Ellanna narrowed her eyes. She gestured to take in the nearly empty room of the tea house; only one other person was currently there. "I ain't got no coin to pay you, or any cleric—not even those idiot followers of Telen and their sup-posed vows of poverty. They all want money to make water. And it never lasts, so you've got to pay them every day. It's nothing more than a scam."

Pfastbinder paused, wondering why he had never thought of doing such a scam before, himself. "But that's the beauty of my offer, Ellanna," he gave her a wide smile. "I'll do it for free. I'm here every day, and I can create the water for you. All I ask, in exchange, is that you heat some of it for me. It's an offer that benefits us both!"

Ellanna continued to stare at him, her eyes narrowed as she chewed her lip. "You can do that? Every day?"

"Of course," Pfastbinder replied. "And your water will be the purest in the city, bestowed by Banok himself. Why, just having it will allow you to bring in more customers. You could even charge more because you'd be using pure, clean, water. Not that nasty stuff from the well."

"Every day?" she repeated. "Cuz I know about these supposed magics and blessings and whatnots from the gods. I know it's a racket for the churches, since the water goes away if it ain't used."

"Every day," Pfastbinder assured her. "I would never lie to you."

"Ha!" The bark of a laugh came from behind them,

and Pfastbinder and Ellanna both turned to see Constable Inspector Lunaria and a Green Cloak standing in the doorway. Pfastbinder couldn't see the Green Cloak's face, though his build seemed somehow familiar.

Reva said, "Everything that you say is a lie, a scam, a cheat, or something that will benefit you."

Pfastbinder put a hand to his heart. "You wound me, Inspector. I have never lied to you, just to silly adventurers. And you know that they deserve it."

Reva threaded her way through the tables, followed by the Green Cloak. "Yeah, well, they do deserve it."

Pfastbinder turned back to Ellanna. "Is it a deal, then? Can I have my hot water now?"

Ellanna continued to chew her lip, but then pointed a finger at him. "You deceive me, even once, and I'll do more than kick you out." Her finger turned to take in the Constable Inspector and her silent companion. "I's got witnesses."

"On Banok's word," Pfastbinder said, bowing.

Ellanna nodded, then turned to the Inspector. "Mint-cherry tea and honey?" she asked, and he saw Reva's eyes widen at the remembrance of what she had ordered a month ago. Reva nodded, and Ellanna pointed at the Green Cloak. "And you, Inquisitor?"

"A blackberry tea, if you have it," he said. Ellanna nodded, and went the two steps to her workspace to get their orders.

"For a cleric of the god of chaos, you have a very orderly routine every morning," Reva remarked.

Pfastbinder smiled and spread his arms wide. "It is not order, Inspector, but Banok's own will that I meet at a known time of day to preach his glory to the masses."

The Green Cloak gave a skeptical look around the room along with a snort of derision.

"To what do I owe the pleasure of a meeting with the constabulary and the Sucra? Oh, let me guess," he smiled at Reva, "you've told the fine Inquisitor here all about my skill in stopping the Disciples of Dreen, and he wants me to come work for the Sucra."

"What?" the Inquisitor asked, clearly confused.

He turned to look at the Inquisitor. "Well, I might consider it, but I won't wear one of those horrible green cloaks. It totally doesn't work for me." He picked up the folds of his own, magnificently chaotic cloak and gave it a flourish. "Never mind," Pfastbinder said, dismissing the idea with a wave of his hand. "I've thought it over, and it is my calling to become a constable." He turned to Reva. "So, did you bring my bracers this time?"

"Inquisitor Amalaki is interested in the halpbloed that lives above the bakery," Reva said, nonplussed by his request. "The one you were spying on the other night."

Pfastbinder raised his eyebrows and held up a finger. "And a good job I did, too. Thus, the presence of this illustrious Sucra Inquisitor." He looked at the Inquisitor as Ellanna arrived with the tea and his hot water. "Isn't there a bounty for turning in traitors to the kingdom? My temple was almost burned to the ground the other night, and I could use the Skips to make repairs."

"A bounty?" Amalaki scoffed. "It's your duty as a citizen of Tenyl to report any traitors to the kingdom to the Sucra."

Pfastbinder pulled out a pouch of his own tea, a special blend that was infused with some of the leaves of his sacred canab plant, added some to the cup, and then poured in the hot water, all the while staring at the Inquisitor. "It seems a bit two-faced, since the King doesn't even recognize me as a citizen."

He turned to look at Reva, who was adding a generous portion of honey to her tea, and he held up a hand to his mouth, as if to whisper, but he didn't lower his voice. "I'm not sure if I trust this Green Cloak."

Reva smiled. "Me either. But maybe if he was able to make a donation to your church, you might tell us what you know?"

The Inquisitor had just taken a drink of his own tea and nearly choked on it. "A what?" He glared at Pfastbinder. "I'm not going to pay this crazy halpbloed anything."

"Blessed, not crazy," Pfastbinder corrected, as he snuck some of Reva's honey and stirred it into his tea.

"Sometimes you have to grease the gears," Reva added. "You Sucra might get better results if you used more honey," she tapped the small honey pot, "and less vinegar."

The Inquisitor looked to Reva, then back to Pfastbinder, and then sighed, reached into a pouch, and pulled out a silvery Skip. He set it on the table, and Pfastbinder grabbed it so quickly that the Inquisitor blinked several times.

"You know, I nearly had my temple, my home, the one place in all of Tenyl that is the most holy to Lord Banok, nearly burned to the ground because of what I heard."

He watched Reva stifle a laugh while Inquisitor Amalaki gritted his teeth. Finally, Amalaki pulled out another Skip and set it on the table, but kept his finger pressed down on it. "What do you know?"

"Cedres, my neighbor above the bakery, had another meeting with the good Constable Sulwynd this morning."

"I know that," Amalaki said, with a predatory grin, "I was there following him."

"Ah," Pfastbinder smiled knowingly. "That was *your* shadow lurking in between the bakery and that excuse for a tenement."

Amalaki's eyes went wide, and he pulled his finger off the coin. Pfastbinder snatched it away before the Inquisitor could react. "Banok's sight never fails me, Inquisitor. I am so attuned to the chaos of the world that I can see when the normal order is broken." He gave them both a wide grin.

"Hawkshit," Reva commented, before taking a drink of her tea.

Pfastbinder shrugged, and then rested an arm on the table and leaned close to Inquisitor Amalaki. "What *you* didn't see, my dear Inquisitor, was Cedres making a mark on the bakery wall just above the water barrel. After that, no less than six halpbloed walked by the shop, their eyes drawn to that very spot. It is clearly a signal to meet."

"You saw all that?" Amalaki asked.

Pfastbinder raised both hands, palms to the sky in supplication. "Banok's sight has blessed me to see that which is out of the ordinary." He lowered his arms, and then said, "That, and I had hidden myself under the stairs to see who might be looking for this unexpected signal." He winked at Reva.

Inquisitor Amalaki took a slow drink of his tea, then rubbed his chin. Pfastbinder gave a questioning look to Reva. She merely shrugged and drank her tea.

"They must be planning to meet." He pulled out a third Skip and tossed it towards Pfastbinder, who caught it.

"And the most glorious blessings of Banok on you, oh, great Sucra Inquisitor," he said, as the Skip disappeared into the folds of his cloak to join the other two.

Reva rolled her eyes and said to Amalaki, "Don't encourage him like that. Are you satisfied now? Can I go back to my murder investigation?"

"A murder?" Pfastbinder cooed, rubbing his hands together. "You know that I am always willing to assist you, Inspector."

Reva ignored him and continued to look at the Sucra Inquisitor. "I'm afraid not," Amalaki replied. "We have a lot to plan."

Reva sighed and pulled out a tin from a pocket, flicked it open and lifted a pinch of the red-orange powder to her nose.

"Why, Inspector," Pfastbinder said, surprised. "I have always said that you would make the perfect follower for Lord Banok. I would be happy to have you as part of my congregation."

Reva snapped the tin shut and put it back in her pocket. "I've had enough of gods after dealing with Dreen last month." She turned back to Amalaki. "What's next, Inquisitor?"

Pfastbinder leaned forward, clasping his hands together, "Yes, what's next, Inquisitor?"

Chapter 37

Ansee knocked on the doorframe of First Constable Aescel's office and waited until he heard the First Constable say, "Enter."

Ansee stepped into the office and handed a parchment to the First Constable. "That's our update on the sorcerer killer," he stated. "I figured that you'd want something to refer to in case you needed to speak with the Mayor or LCI."

Aescel looked at the parchment, his eyes squinting a bit to read the fine scrawl that was Ansee's handwriting. He nodded his head as he looked up to Ansee. "Áeorias, Seeker Carya," he responded. "Though I could have used something like this earlier this morning." His words sounded tired, and not filled with any malice.

"The Mayor is still climbing a tree for answers from LCI Betulla, and she chewed off what was left of my ass earlier." He held up the parchment and gave a weary smile, "But thank you for this. It will help hold them both off, the next time they come demanding answers."

Aescel turned to look out the window to the Stable. "Murders like this are not supposed to happen in Old Grove," he said. "You don't know the political pressure that we are under to get this solved."

"I wish we had more progress, sir," Ansee said. "Though I'm hopeful that Constable Inspector Lunaria is making headway on this mysterious symbol left on the bodies."

Aescel looked back at Ansee. "It's the same one that our previous murderer left at the crime scenes?"

Ansee nodded. "We think it's a symbol for an organization, some kind of assassin's guild. Reva said that she was going to get a lead on it, and I was hoping that she'd have been back by now. Maybe we'll have something to go on this afternoon."

"Keep me informed," Aescel commanded, and set the parchment onto an already tall stack of other parchment-work.

Ansee turned to leave, but then stopped and stood there for a moment before Aescel asked, "Something else on your mind, Seeker?"

"Sir, it's clear that I am the target for this killer."

Aescel nodded. "I heard that the murderer left a personal message burned into the latest victim."

Ansee didn't bother to correct the First Constable, as it wasn't that important a distinction. Instead, he said, "If we're to catch this murderer, then maybe I should stand in the middle of the Grand March with a target around my neck."

Aescel narrowed his eyes. "Sarcasm sounds better coming from CI Lunaria, Seeker."

"It wasn't sarcasm, sir. If this killer is after me, let me get out there. Especially if it will keep more innocent sorcerers from dying."

"You do know that the murderer already knows where you live?" Ansee nodded. "He could have killed you last night, but he didn't."

"I know, sir. He's playing with me, trying to scare me. I don't know why he's picked me as his target."

"You did kill his friend," Aescel replied, "and you are a sorcerer."

"Reva said something similar. But there's something else going on here, something that is hiding just inside the bushes. If he was only after me, he could have attacked me last night." Ansee suppressed a shudder, as that thought had been bothering him all morning. This was different than being attacked by Roya Locera. He was being targeted, and Ansee didn't know why. He was sure that there was more to it than him being a sorcerer. Wasn't there?

"I don't think letting you paint a target on your chest is the right idea," Aescel said. "Better for us to find this elf and stop him before he targets anybody else."

"I'm not afraid to face him," Ansee pointed out.

"I know that. But even if it worked out for you before, we can't be having duels with our suspects all the time. Think of how bad an example that will set for CI Lunaria." He smiled as he said the last bit, and Ansee had to smile with him.

"Just tell CI Lunaria, as soon as you see her, that we need to solve this as quickly as you can. I will be able to hold off the Mayor and the LCI for another day, but after that, they will be demanding that I give the case to CI's Pflamtael or Kiliaopii."

Ansee nodded and turned to leave. "And Seeker," Aescel called after him. Ansee stopped in the doorway and turned. "Make sure you're prepared for this elf. I don't want to have to send the Alkies to collect your body, too."

"I am prepared, sir," Ansee said confidently, walked into the Stable, and returned to his table. He saw Norah giving him a strange look, but decided that it was best to ignore her. He didn't need a distraction right now, and everything having to do with Norah in the past month had been a distraction. He didn't understand why she hated him so much, and she had pushed him away each time that he had tried to talk to her about it. He knew she didn't like him because he was a sorcerer, but he couldn't understand why she thought that way. And once Seekers Hedera and Kupferhedge added their pranks into the mix in their misguided attempts to protect Ansee, she had refused to even speak to him.

He looked over toward her table and caught her glancing his way. She quickly went back to her work, and even turned her back towards him. Ansee sighed, knowing that he needed to talk with her, to clear away the leaves, but now was not the time to do that. He needed to focus on finding out who this mysterious assassin was, so that they could stop him.

Ansee went back to his notes comparing the auras from all of the victims, from the original murders to the most recent two. It was clear that they were dealing with two separate wizards, but finding out exactly who was involved was nearly impossible without being able to compare the auras to a known sample. Not for the first time, he wished that the Sucra would share their archives with the constabulary. The Sucra tested each wizard that graduated from Auros Academy, as well as all the other magical schools in the kingdom. They had a collection of reference auras that they could use to compare spells against, in order to be able to identify an individual wizard. Even though each spell left a different kind of aura, individual spells had a unique spectrum that could be seen when viewed through a prism. That's how one could tell a fireball from a lightning bolt. The constabulary had a few reference tomes that could be used to identify a spell by the aura spectrum, but the thing about magic was that each spellcaster could also be identified by unique traces within the aura spectrum. Not only could you tell a fireball from a lightning bolt, but you could also distinguish Wizard A's fireball from the same spell cast by Wizard B. That is, as long as you had a reference aura to refer to. Ansee knew that the constabulary's Seekers could be so much more efficient, so much more effective at their jobs, if they could just access the Sucra's aura reference library, or if they could start collecting their own references. But until now, the Sucra had kept their references to themselves, and the constabulary did not have the funding to build their own.

He sighed, and went back to the task at hand. He was concentrating so hard on his notes that he didn't notice the person standing at his table, at least not until they loudly cleared their throat. Ansee looked up to see Seeker Hedera standing there.

"Do you need something? I'm pretty busy."

"Is it true?" Hedera asked. "Did the murderer leave a

threat to you carved into the victim's chest?"

Ansee sighed. "Yes, it's true, but it wasn't carved in. The murderer used an arcane mark to leave the message."

"So only you would see it?" Hedera shook his head. "By Basvu, how are you not cowering under your table?"

Ansee gave a half smile. "Because I'm not a sniveling coward like you are."

Hedera laughed, but said, "Seriously though, I couldn't work if I was constantly looking over my shoulder. How do you know this maniac isn't watching you all the time? Tracking your movements through the city? He could strike at any moment."

"Don't be so dramatic," Ansee chastised. "I've been attacked before, and by more dangerous people than this psychopath. Plus, I survived an encounter with a deranged cultist and his pet disciples." Ansee cast a look over at Norah, but she was still studiously ignoring him. He looked back at Hedera. "I'm not scared of this elf. I just told Aescel that I'm willing to fight this murderer, to call him out and face him, just so nobody else gets hurt."

Hedera shook his head, "That's the stupidest idea I've ever heard, but since it's coming from you, I shouldn't be surprised." He pulled something out of his pouch. "Well, just in case Aescel decides to send you out to battle this maniac in a duel for the safety of the city, take this." He handed the thing to Ansee.

Ansee held it up. It looked to be a charm bracelet of some kind. It had a rectangular silver plate inscribed with a couple of magical symbols held between thick silver links. The markings appeared to be for protection. "Why are you giving me jewelry? If you wanted to go on a date, you just had to ask." He smirked to hide his irritation. He didn't want to be thought of as somebody who couldn't protect himself.

Hedera smacked Ansee on the back of his head. "Idiot. That's a family heirloom. It belonged to my sister when she was an adventurer. It will allow you to resist any magic this killer might try to use against you."

"Thanks, but no." Ansee shook his head, and held out the bracelet to Hedera. "I don't need any help. Besides, won't your sister need it?"

"She was killed on a delve last year," Hedera said quietly.

Ansee again tried to give the bracelet back. "Uh uh. Apparently, this thing doesn't work very well."

"Stop being such a baby," Hedera said. He grabbed the bracelet, but instead of putting it away, he grabbed Ansee's arm and tried to put the bracelet on, while Ansee tried to pull his arm away. "You're not Reva. I know how some people feel around here," he jerked a thumb over toward Norah's table. Ansee looked that way but saw that Norah had left. "But some of us care if you die or not. Just take it until this murderer is arrested, okay?"

"Okay, okay." Ansee relaxed and let Hedera put the bracelet on. He held it up to look at it. It looked weird over his bracer, but he appreciated the gesture.

"Don't forget to give it back to me," Hedera smiled. "I don't want to have to pull it off your corpse."

"Thanks for the vote of confidence," Ansee replied.

Footsteps approached, and Ansee turned to see Constable Whitlocke appear. "Message for you, Seeker," she stated, handing Ansee a roll of parchment.

"Áeorias," Ansee replied, taking the parchment. Whitlocke nodded and headed back to her desk downstairs.

"Ooo... getting secret messages now?" Hedera teased. "Maybe it's from the killer. He wants to meet you at high noon on the Grand March for a duel."

Ansee opened the message. "It's past noon, idiot. Besides, it's from CI Lunaria."

The message was short, although a bit confusing. He read it through twice, and then said, "Shit."

"What is it?"

Ansee looked up at Hedera and pointed to the message. "Have you ever been to this part of Port Grove?"

Chapter 38

The door to New Port slammed shut behind Norah as she stalked out of the building and across the courtyard. She had gotten sick of watching Hedera cozy up to Ansee, fawning over him like some kind of hero. She couldn't stand listening to them talk about what The Minister had been doing, and Ansee's damned, stupid false bravado had been infuriating. She had almost exploded when he had said that he was willing to face The Minister to protect others. The idiot wanted to become a hero, or a martyr, and she couldn't stand another minute in the Stable. She'd had to leave before she had said or done something that she would have regretted. Not that the pair of them didn't deserve to be pushed off the branch. None of the Seekers had respected her at all after last month. She knew that Hedera and Kupferhedge had been harassing her, playing their petty pranks against her. And that, in itself, was so infuriating to her. Did they not understand the threat Ansee was to them? Did none of them understand that Ansee was not normal, that he was not like the other Seekers? He was a walking abomination, and she wanted him gone.

Gone. Norah walked out of the main gate and turned down the road, her mind a jumble of emotions. Not just gone, dead. Because she knew that Ansee was a dead elf walking. The Minister would make his move eventually, and Ansee would die. That was a given, now. It had been a given from the moment that Norah had spoken to LCI Betulla. She had sealed Ansee's fate that day. That was a good thing. He was a sorcerer, a threat. He didn't belong in the constabulary. He was a danger that was ready to explode in all of their faces.

Then why does the thought of his death make my stomach flip? she asked herself. *I only ever wanted him off the force, out of my life. He saved my life, sure, but he's still evil, even if he pretends to be otherwise. So why do I care if he dies?*

Was it because he had saved her life? Or was it some other reason? There was a connection between her and The Minister now. When Ansee died, that connection was going to come out. She held no illusion that the LCI would protect her; that would never happen. Betulla only cared about herself. And Norah knew that, when Ansee was dead, Reva would do everything to find out who had done it. To find everyone that had been involved. And Norah had been involved. She had told Betulla to do something, and that had caused The Minister to be here. She knew that The Minister was hunting Ansee, and she wasn't doing anything to stop him. How could she, when it was the right path. Wasn't it?

Norah had been walking, unaware of her surroundings, when she noticed that someone had fallen into step next to her. She could feel his presence and knew that it was The Minister even before she glanced over and saw his distinctive blue robes and broad-brimmed hat.

Someone will see me with him! The thought sent a chill up her spine. She couldn't allow that to happen. She turned quickly and headed between two buildings, The Minister following her wordlessly.

Once they were deep in the shadows and hidden from the main road, she turned to The Minister, her finger stabbing at his face. "What do you want?"

The Minister smiled, "Why, to thank you. And to let you know that, by tomorrow, that sorcerous abomination will no longer be a threat to you or the constabulary."

"Good," she said, though her stomach still churned. *It is*

good, isn't it? That's what I wanted, right?

"You seem to be less than pleased by that news," The Minister commented. "You are still fully committed to our cause?" His voice had dropped to a menacing whisper.

"Yes," Norah stammered out, licking her lips. "Of course, I'm committed. But if anybody learns about this, about my involvement, I will lose everything."

"You have nothing to worry about. I will make sure that *Shádpfed* Asclepias knows how useful you have been. He will make sure that the LCI knows of your importance. And *I* know. You will be protected."

"No," Norah spat, nervous. "You don't get it. Betulla isn't the threat. It's Reva that I'm worried about."

"Reva?"

"Constable Inspector Lunaria. She's Ansee's partner. If you kill Ansee—"

"*When* I kill that demon spawn."

Norah swallowed, "Yes, when you kill him. Reva will hunt down anybody involved in his murder. She's tenacious. She burrows in deeper than a hawk tick and she won't stop until she's found who killed Ansee. She will find out that it was you. And she will find out that I was involved."

The Minister glared at her from beneath the broad brim of his hat. "So, CI Lunaria is comfortable working with this abomination?"

"Yes," Norah replied, the word nearly choking in her throat. "She's only ever cared about Ansee's competence. I don't know how long she knew that Ansee was a sorcerer, but she doesn't seem to care about that, only that he's competent at his job. And he's proven that to her, several times."

The Minister gripped his staff firmly. "Áeorias. It seems that my task here is not quite finished, then."

Something seemed to grab hold of Norah's heart and gave it a squeeze. "Wait... you aren't... you can't kill Reva!"

"Can't I?" The Minister gave her a wary glance. "This Reva seems to be under the thrall of the sorcerer and its demon master. These creatures are insidious in how they work, burrowing into a community and befriending people so that they can spread their evil without being checked. Those that willingly work with the sorcerers are just as much a threat as the sorcerers themselves. Have you forgotten this?"

"No... but... I mean, once you have killed Ansee, the threat to Reva will be broken, right? She will no longer be in Ansee's thrall."

"It's possible," The Minister said, but then added, "but I cannot take that chance. The only way to ensure that the demon's influence is completely removed is to purge all of its connections. Plus, there is a practical matter to consider, as well. There can be no investigation if there is nobody alive to investigate."

Norah's mouth had gone dry. *I did this. Me. This is all my fault. I only wanted Ansee to leave the constabulary.*

The Minister grabbed Norah's arm. "Too much is at stake now, and I do not have time to stalk another quarry. The abomination knows that I am coming for him, so I must strike swiftly before he can prepare. Tell me about this Reva. Where can I find her so I can remove that threat as well?"

Norah's stomach continued to twist and tie itself into knots. She hadn't wanted any of this, just to get Ansee out of the way. She hadn't wanted him dead, and she hadn't wanted Reva dead, either. She had gone too far with Ansee, so she couldn't prevent his death, and maybe he did deserve it, but Reva was not a threat. Not after Ansee was gone. The Minister would understand that, after he killed Ansee. She was not going to help him attack Reva.

"N-No..." she said, the words barely above a whisper. "I understand that Ansee must be... handled, but Reva is a friend. She is not in the thrall of the demon. Once Ansee is gone, you will see that. I won't help you hurt her."

The Minister straightened his back, looking at her with disapproval. "Perhaps it is too late for you, as well. You seem to already be under the spell of this sorcerer."

"No. I'm not, I swear. And neither is Reva."

"I cannot take that chance. Tell me about her." He drew

her in close to him, his hand like a vise as he gripped her arm. Norah tried to pull away, but that only caused his grip to become tighter.

The Minister spoke a few words of power and Norah could see the magic building, a glow coming to his eyes. "Tell me about Reva Lunaria," The Minister commanded.

Norah struggled against the magic, putting up defenses, trying to keep The Minister and his command out of her mind, but he continued to press her, his will smothering her as she struggled. "Tell me everything about Reva Lunaria."

She began to scream as the spell forced its way in, breaking down her defenses. The Minister clamped a hand over her mouth to silence her scream, and her defenses failed. She no longer resisted. It was the right thing to do to tell The Minister everything that he wanted to know. Doing so lifted her spirits. Why wouldn't it? He was her friend, a confidant who needed to know everything that she did. She didn't know how long she talked, but once it was all said, all the words spoken, she felt relief, and a sense of accomplishment at having shared her knowledge.

Then the spell ended, the geas lifted, and the reality of what had happened struck Norah like a spear through the heart. She had betrayed a fellow constable! She had betrayed Reva, and all the elation and relief that the spell had provided her turned to ash in her mouth. She leaned back against the wall, shaking slightly, drawing her arms close to her body.

The Minister adjusted his hat and said, "I will overlook your transgression in this matter. You have sinned against Jansure, and I will pray for your absolution from him. But if you continue down this path, I will be forced to remove your taint from Ados, just as I will be removing that of Ansee Carya and Reva Lunaria."

The Minister turned and strode back the way they had come, turning onto the main road. Norah collapsed to the ground and watched him leave with trembling lips.

What have I done?

Chapter 39

Ansee stopped and looked at the intersection, wondering if he had taken a wrong turn. Port Grove was a warren of streets and alleys, all jumbled together in a chaotic mess. It made Nul Pfeta seem like a well thought-out and planned grove. Ansee picked a direction and continued up the narrow road, not because he knew exactly where he was going, but because standing idle for too long in Port Grove invited pickpockets and rogues. Most of them knew better than to attack a constable in broad daylight, but there were always a few who looked forward to meting out their own brand of justice against the constables that constantly dogged them and put them into the dungeons. He kept one hand on the hilt of his dagger as he headed deeper into the thicket of buildings.

He still had no idea why Reva had sent him here. Her message had been short, "I got dragged into something. Go see Rhoanlan the Lombard in Port Grove. Ask him about the symbols from our victims." When Ansee had asked Hedera if he knew where Rhoanlan's shop was, he had been unable to say anything other than that it was in Port Grove. That had earned Hedera a smack on the back of his head. Ansee had asked around in Acer division, but nobody there was of any more help than Hedera had been. Finally, Inspector Thaenwell over in Betula Division had given Ansee directions, and told him to be careful, since Rhoanlan was a notorious fence.

Ansee made another turn, finally recognizing one of the landmarks that Thaenwell had given him. The day was mild, but that only meant that the odor of fish and saltwater, mixed with many other smells that Ansee didn't want to contemplate, was strong. Not for the first time since leaving New Port, he wondered why Reva was sending him to ask a known fence about the symbol. Why would this criminal know anything about it? This was going to be a waste of time, time that could be better spent at Auros Academy or one of the guilds, searching their records. They had better information than Ansee was going to get from this Rhoanlan person.

Still, he trudged on, knowing that Reva would ask him specifically about what Rhoanlan had said. That it was bound to be nothing didn't change that fact. As he dodged around a group of sailors coming out of a rundown pub, he wondered how Reva knew Rhoanlan. He remembered Reva mentioning the name in their search for the Fury Blade, but she hadn't told him at the time that he was a fence. Now he wondered why Reva would trust a criminal like this with any information, or why she would believe anything that he said.

Ansee finally spotted the weathered sign that said "Lombard" with four brass-colored acorns hanging beneath it. He paused outside the door and looked at the shop window. The glass was cracked in many places, and the wooden frame was weathered to a grayish color. The windows were filthy, and it was hard to see into the shop, even though the only thing that he could see was a tall stack of junk that was piled in front of the window. Ansee shrugged and opened the door, which seemed to protest at the effort.

Inside, he nearly sneezed, as the air was redolent with mold and dust. In fact, he could see motes of dust hanging in the air through what little light filtered in through the front window. The entire shop was stuffed to the high branches with a hodge-podge of stuff. Ansee could see books and scrolls stacked on shelves and on top of tall piles of other junk. Parts of armor, shields, and some weapons seemed to be jammed into any free space, as well as cloaks, boots, chests of drawers, and all manner of things that had been seemingly tossed about at random.

At the front of the shop, in the only clear space that Ansee could see, sat a small wooden table. Behind the table sat a large elf with long, mahogany-colored hair worn loose, in a manner that resembled the chaotic piles of junk in the rest of the shop. He wore a light blue vest with polished brass buttons over a cream-colored shirt, both of which seemed to strain as they contained his massive body. He glanced up as Ansee entered the shop, giving him a quick appraisal with eyes the color of acorns ready to be harvested, but he made no other acknowledgement of Ansee's presence.

Another customer stood in front of the table. He wore a patched and torn cloak and soft-soled boots. Ansee could see the scabbard for a short sword sticking out from the folds of the cloak. He had long, wheat-colored hair that was pulled into a loose ponytail. He glanced over his shoulder at Ansee, and then turned back to the large elf, seeming to have forgotten what he had been saying. "Rhoanlan, this is... uh, this... item is of the best quality. You can see that in the design, and the attention to detail."

"Maybe," said Rhoanlan, "But you know I care more about provenance in a piece like this, not the quality. I want to know more about where it came from." Ansee thought he saw the slightest of smiles twist at the edge of Rhoanlan's lips.

"Prove... look, Rhoanlan, I got it—" The elf glanced back over his shoulder at Ansee. "I... I mean, it's been in my family for years. I think my grandad, or his grandad, I can't remember, so many grandads." He gave a nervous laugh and tried to step closer to the table. "But it's worth more than 100 Hawks."

Ansee unconsciously gave a low whistle that seemed to carry through the shop. Hawks—officially called Crowns by the treasury—were pieces of gold, worth about 13 Skips. 100 Hawks was a steep price for any item, certainly for anything here. The seller gave another nervous laugh and shuffled his feet. Rhoanlan seemed nonplussed by everything, and he made a show of pulling out a jeweler's loupe and fixing it to his eye. He picked up the item. Ansee still couldn't see it with the other elf standing in the way, and Rhoanlan made some non-committal hums as he examined it.

"Look," said the seller, "you know I wouldn't try to scam you. It's a good piece, hardly been used, worth at least 125."

Rhoanlan continued to look at the item. "Possibly, but without knowing its source, I'm afraid the best I can do is to offer you 75 Hawks."

The seller gave a gasp and looked back over his shoulder, a snarl on his lips. "That's lower than before," he hissed.

"As I said, provenance is important. How do I know that this isn't just some trinket you found on the street or in some garbage heap? Without knowing, I will have to expend resources to confirm everything. I sell high end artifacts that many people want, but only if they know what they are getting. My customers trust me on my goods."

"But you know me, Rhoanlan. Have I ever failed to… err, you know the quality of my goods. I mean, the stuff I bring you from my family. Can you at least give me the hundred?"

"Can't you tell me anything more? How did your grandfather come by it?"

"He… uh, I… uh, it was always in his family."

"Look, I can give you 90 Hawks, but without knowing more, that's my final offer."

The seller mumbled something and Rhoanlan smiled. "Good. Let me see." He turned in his chair and pulled out a small iron casket from some hidden recess in the pile of junk behind him. Ansee half expected the pile to topple over, but it stayed in place. Rhoanlan put a finger to a spot on the front of the casket. It opened with a CLICK and he pulled out several small bags of coins and set them on the table.

"Always a pleasure to do business with you, Arwin."

Arwin made a shushing noise, and then grabbed the bags and hurriedly put them into a larger pouch that he wore at his side. He turned and headed out of the shop, doing his best to keep his face turned away from Ansee.

Ansee stepped up and could see that a pair of well-crafted boots sat on the table, or they did before Rhoanlan quickly scooped them up and they disappeared into the jumble of junk around his chair. No, not junk, Ansee realized. Rhoanlan had just paid ninety Crowns for those, and even the best-made boots by the best cobbler in town would never sell for more than 10 Skips, possibly more if they were embellished with precious jewels or rare leather. But never for more than a couple of crowns, and certainly not ninety. That meant that the boots were magical. Ansee wondered how many other magical items were stored within the nooks and crannies of this shop.

"I do thank you for waiting, Constable."

"Seeker," Ansee corrected. "Seeker Ansee Carya."

Rhoanlan's eyes widened just a bit. "Ah, Reva's new partner. I have heard quite a bit about you. I shall have to scold her for not introducing us the next time we see a play together."

Ansee wasn't sure what part he should be surprised about; that Reva had talked about him with this person, or that they went to plays together. "Reva and you go to plays together?"

Rhoanlan smiled, his eyes twinkling with mirth. "Of course, Seeker. Though, not many in the past few weeks. What is she doing that is keeping her so busy?"

Ansee still couldn't get his head around the idea that Reva and this elf, a known fence, would be seen in public together. "But, why would Reva go to a play with you? You're a fence."

Rhoanlan's ears reddened, and he poked a long, thin finger at Ansee. "I will forgive you that insult, since Reva has clearly not educated you." His face relaxed and he held up his hands, palms up. "I am nothing more than a humble lombard, buying and selling items from a select clientele. I resent the accusation that I am a thief. You saw how important it is for me to know where my inventory comes from."

Ansee had seen and started putting the pieces together. That seller, Arwin, was most likely a thief, and the boots that he had brought in to sell had not belonged to his grandfather. Maybe to *somebody's* grandfather, but not his own. Rhoanlan had been trying to find out where the thief had gotten the boots, which was probably the best way to stay ahead of any constables that would be coming to look for the stolen goods, and Ansee's presence had prevented that. He had to assume that Reva knew that Rhoanlan was a fence, and the fact that she apparently trusted him enough to go to plays with him, let alone to not arrest him for peddling stolen goods, meant that he should also trust him. Or at least not blatantly call him a thief.

"Yes, I can see how careful you are with the goods that you buy," Ansee agreed. "My mistake."

A thin smile spread across Rhoanlan's lips. "Perhaps Reva is teaching you well, after all. You know, maybe I should have a constable present for all of my transactions. You saved me several Hawks today."

"Well, I'm sure we'd be happy to send a Birch here every day to help you determine the provenance of the goods you buy. We wouldn't want you to accidentally buy something that had been purloined."

Rhoanlan gave a laugh, "I will consider that generous offer but, as you can see, there is barely enough room for me in my humble little shop. I don't know where a Birch might stand all day long. Plus, we wouldn't want to deprive the rest of the good citizens here in Port Grove of the services of the constabulary."

"True, that might please the guilds, and I doubt the First Constables will go for that. I guess you will have to continue to vet your customers yourself."

Rhoanlan folded his hands across his ample chest, intertwining his fingers. "So, how might a humble lombard help the Royal Tenyl Constabulary today?"

"I honestly don't know," Ansee admitted. "Inspector Lunaria said I should visit you about our case."

"Ah, the copycat sorcerer killer," Rhoanlan said.

Ansee couldn't help but be surprised, blinking rapidly. "How....?"

"My dear Seeker," Rhoanlan smiled. "Reva sent you here because I know things. I probably know more about what goes on in this town than anybody else. Did you know that I have helped Reva on every major case that she has worked on? The Tenz River Troll. The Fury Blade. Those nasty Disciples of Dreen last month. Plus, many others. One might say that she owes all of her success to me."

Ansee folded his arms. "I doubt that Reva would say that."

Rhoanlan tilted his head, "You're probably right, but that doesn't alter the truth." He smiled again. "Tell me what you want to know. I may surprise you."

Ansee reached into a pocket that had been sewn into his cloak and pulled out one of the calling cards that was left at the original murder scenes. He handed it to Rhoanlan, who took it with nimble fingers. Rhoanlan looked at the paper, rotating it over in his hands to look at the front and back. He brought it up to his nose and inhaled deeply. He set the jeweler's loupe into his eye and brought the card close to his face, scrutinizing every square hand of its surface. Finally, he set the card down on the table and removed the loupe.

"I'm afraid that I really cannot be of much help to you, Seeker."

Ansee felt a bit of satisfaction at having been proven right. He had known that Rhoanlan wouldn't be able to tell him anything useful. He was also disappointed, since he had just wasted part of his afternoon chasing this down.

"Thank you for trying," he said, reaching down to pick up the card. But Rhoanlan had placed a single finger on the card. He cleared his throat.

Ansee tried to pick up the card, but Rhoanlan pressed

harder with his finger. Ansee stared at him, and Rhoanlan tilted his head and widened his eyes. He looked pointedly at the table. Ansee pulled harder and finally freed the card.

Rhoanlan sighed loudly, and made a big deal of rolling his eyes. "You really *are* new to this, aren't you? Didn't Reva tell you how this worked?"

"How what worked?" Ansee asked. "She said I should have you look at the symbol to see if you knew anything about it. You said you didn't."

"Of course I *said* I didn't. That's just the opening offer."

"Telling me you can't tell me anything is an opening offer?"

"I am just a humble lombard, I buy and *sell* everything," he held out his hands to take in the room, then folded them on the table in front of him, "including information."

Ansee finally understood, and it irritated him. Not that he had missed how this process worked, but that it had to work this way. He was sure that Reva could hand out Skips and Pfen as if they were leaves falling from the trees, but he didn't make that much as a Seeker. It was also wrong from an ethical perspective. He shouldn't have to pay somebody for this information when he needed it as part of a murder investigation.

He and Rhoanlan continued to stare at each other, Rhoanlan tapping a finger on the table. He was perfectly happy to wait Ansee out, or even to let him leave. He knew he had the advantage and the information, and he knew that Ansee needed it. But Ansee was not going to give in to this *thief*, because that's what Rhoanlan was. He was picking Ansee's pockets to give him the information that he wanted. Ansee flipped the card over in his hands, stalling for time. Then, an idea struck him.

"It seems that I have already paid you for this information," he tapped the edge of the card.

"Already paid?" Rhoanlan snorted and made a show of looking at the empty table. "Unless you are giving me invisible coins, I do not see any payment."

"Have you already forgotten your transaction with Arwin? I seem to recall that you saved at least ten Hawks in that transaction, probably a lot more. I believe that is certainly sufficient payment for the information you may have about this." He held up the card. "You have earned more than a fair sum for the information just by my presence in your *humble* shop."

Rhoanlan leaned back and laughed, tapping the side of his nose. "Ah, well played, Seeker. Well played. You remind me very much of Reva's previous partner. Seeker Rubus was also devious and ruthless in her negotiations."

Ansee felt a bit of pride at being compared favorably to Cas. That it was the first time it had happened, and that it had come from this fence was a bit irritating. But he'd take the compliment. Rhoanlan held up his hand, and Ansee gave him the card.

Rhoanlan pointed at the symbol. "This is a unique symbol, rarely seen by anybody not associated with this particular group. They are very secretive, maybe even more so than those pompous idiots over at Pfeta fey Orung."

"So, you know nothing about them?"

Rhoanlan smiled. "Did I say that? This is rarely seen by anybody, but that doesn't mean that I don't know about them." He tapped the side of his nose. "Have you, Seeker Carya, not heard the tales, the rumors whispered in the dark by sorcerers? Certainly you, as a sorcerer yourself," Rhoanlan smiled, as Ansee couldn't help but be surprised that Rhoanlan knew that he was a sorcerer, "have heard the stories, the myths?"

Ansee shook his head.

Rhoanlan cleared his throat, and his voice took on a more dramatic lilt. "In the great depths of magical history, Qurna gave magic to the world, bestowing it to the elves. According to some, there were only seven elves to be blessed with this knowledge, and they became the first wizards. They were called the Pfetashád, and they became the pure bloodlines for magical knowledge. Those that have descended from these pure bloodlines consider all other magic users, all other wizards, to be beneath them. Later, sorcerers came about, able to wield Qurna's gift without all the words, gestures, and *heritage* that the wizards had to follow."

Rhoanlan leaned back, placing his hands on his stomach as he worked into his tale. "Nobody seems to know exactly how the sorcerers came about, or how they got their ability to use magic. Though I'm sure you've heard those rumors?"

Ansee nodded, as he had heard plenty of stories about this. "Sure, we're the illegitimate children created from matings between wizards and all manner of nasty creatures like necromancers, dragons, devils."

"And demons," Rhoanlan said, lifting one finger. "And not just from these creatures throwing their seed around willy-nilly with anyone willing to spread their legs. Some believe," he tapped the card, "that a demon has made a pact with people here on Ados, offering them the power of magic in exchange for their allegiance. This demon claims their souls for the chance to wield magic, and the sorcerer, in turn, agrees to do the demon's bidding here on Ados."

Ansee couldn't help but laugh. He had heard variations on that myth before, and he had never taken it seriously.

Rhoanlan leaned forward in a conspiratorial manner. "Tell me, Seeker, who is your demon master?" He leaned back and laughed.

"This group," Rhoanlan tapped the card, "considers themselves to be part of the pure magical bloodlines. The symbol belongs to the Qurundora—Qurna's Pure—and they are a very nasty group. Not only do they think that people like you," he pointed at Ansee, "get your magic from a pact with a demon, but that you are evil and in league with this demon, waiting only for the right moment to allow the demon to rage across the world. The Qurundora have pledged to find this demon's true name so that they can summon it and trap it, destroying the creature. To do this, the Qurundora hunt sorcerers so that they can be interrogated, in order to find the name of the demon."

Ansee gave a nervous laugh. "This is crazy. How can a

group like this exist? I mean, I've heard a lot of wild theories about how sorcerers get their powers, but this is the craziest. How can they believe that any information they get from interrogation can be true?" Rhoanlan merely shrugged in response.

"How long has the Qurundora been around?"

"That, I do not know," Rhoanlan admitted, "but I would assume for hundreds of years at least. Maybe thousands. They are an old group, and very proud of their heritage."

"Do we know who in Tenyl might be part of this group?"

"Again, I do not know. What I have told you I have pieced together over many years, from small tips and whispers. They do not advertise who they are. But if you are looking for someplace to start, I would suggest looking for the most smug, most arrogant wizards you can find who think that sorcerers are pure evil. Anybody that full of themselves would probably be part of the Qurundora."

Ansee's stomach felt like it had just fallen off a cliff. He had one idea of who might be a member of the Qurundora, and the name that came to mind caused his blood to run cold.

Chapter 40

Reva dug some dirt out from under her fingernails with the tip of her dagger. She watched Inquisitor Amalaki from her place on a bench against the wall as he paced around the small space that Pfastbinder called his temple. "Be careful, or you'll end up making a trench," she said.

Amalaki continued to pace, and Reva turned to look at Senior Constable Ghrellstone, giving him a shrug. Willem smiled and went back to tossing the bangstone that Amalaki had given them into the air, and then catching it. He was teasing Constable Gania with it, pretending to let it drop, and causing the younger constable to flinch every time that he did it.

"Another one," Pfastbinder said, from his chair outside the door. He was sitting by the small fire, his usual evening perch, in order to keep an eye on who had arrived at Cedres' place above the bakery.

"Sulwynd?" asked Amalaki, the tension clear in his voice.

"Did I say that it was Sulwynd?" asked Pfastbinder, rhetorically.

"Settle down, Amalaki," Reva chastised, rubbing the hilt of the dagger between her hands.

"We need Sulwynd," Amalaki stated. He finally stopped his pacing and turned to look at the door. "He's the key.

Without him, we can't bring down these conspirators."

"We know." Reva sighed. "You've only told us a dozen times since we got here." Amalaki went back to pacing. Reva sighed again, and slid her dagger back into its sheath. She pulled out a bangstone of her own and started to roll it between her fingers.

Why am I here? She asked herself. *I should be at New Port, trying to find this assassin.* Not for the first time this afternoon, she wondered how Ansee was doing. She'd hoped that he had gone to see Rhoanlan, and that the lombard had been able to help. He probably had. He always seemed to know everything that went on in Tenyl, and she was mad at herself for not going to see him for the first case. They might have been able to prevent these latest deaths.

She stared at the bangstone, looking at the rough surface and many holes in the volcanic rock. This wait was making her realize just how exhausted she was. Her body was physically tired, screaming at her to relax, to take a break, but she didn't have that luxury. *This is why I need to keep working. If I slow down, I'm going to collapse, and then nothing will get done. Too much depends on me to let that happen.*

She set the bangstone down and pulled out the tin of Wake. She flipped open the lid to expose the reddish-orange powder. She had managed to slip away for a few minutes today to get a refill. She pulled out a pinch, savoring its earthy odor. She brought it to her nose and inhaled some of the powder into each nostril, already feeling energized by the action. She leaned her head back, letting the Wake work its magic. The cobwebs in her mind were blown away, and she felt her heart beating faster.

She opened her eyes and watched Amalaki as he continued to pace. *I should be out there finding an assassin, but I have to be here. But if I wasn't here, then who knows what Amalaki would have done.* It had taken more effort than it should have for her to convince Amalaki that they should keep the rest of the Sucra out of this operation. He was only focused on one objective, stopping Sulwynd, and he only knew of one tool to get the job done: the Sucra. She'd tried to tell him that you didn't use a crossbow to pick a lock, but he'd been too distracted. She'd finally put her foot down and threatened to go back to New Port before he'd finally agreed.

Amalaki stopped pacing. "You all remember what you need to do? We have to make sure we do our parts, otherwise Sulwynd will get away, and that's the last thing we need. You," he pointed at Constable Gania, "Gania, what will you be doing?"

"Relax, Inquisitor," Willem said, still tossing his bangstone. "This is not our first time arresting someone. We know what we need to do."

"I don't know what I'm supposed to do," Pfastbinder added, from outside.

"You stay out of the way," Reva replied. "Otherwise, people will think that you were helping us. I don't think that will win you many converts."

"And letting you stage this little party from my house is better how?"

"Tell them that the Sucra forced you to let them be here. Everyone will believe that," Reva said.

"Except there's only one of him and three of you. Everyone will know that I let you constables push me around."

"I thought you wanted to be a constable," remarked Constable Gania.

"Just for the bracers," Pfastbinder said. "People like a cleric in uniform."

"You know," said Willem, "I'd be happy to bash you in the head to make it look more realistic."

"I see that Nul Pfeta is starting to rub off on you," Pfastbinder said.

"Only when it comes to twisting your branches." Willem blew him a kiss, and Pfastbinder gave a small laugh.

"Another guest," Gania said, pointing out the door. "Not Constable Sulwynd." Reva glanced out and could see someone climbing the steps to Cedres' apartment.

"What if he doesn't show up?" asked Constable Gania.

"I don't know about them," Willem pointed a finger at Amalaki and Reva, "but you and I will go back to the gatehouse and make sure that it hasn't fallen down."

"He'll show up," Amalaki argued. "He called the meeting. He'll be here."

Reva turned to look at the Inquisitor. "Maybe they're just getting together to exchange bread recipes." She rolled the bangstone between her hands, enjoying the feel of the rough texture on her skin.

"You know, I have a really good recipe for a sourdough starter," Pfastbinder claimed, as he poked at the fire. "If you care for it right, a good sourdough will keep for a while. I once had a sourdough that I kept for nearly a year. Of course, that was before I was given the wonderful opportunity by our dear King to move to my current splendid location."

"Give up the desire to bake?" asked Gania.

"I gave up my desire to do anything that involved fun," Pfastbinder remarked.

"Except for picking on stupid adventurers," added Reva.

"Ah," Pfastbinder held up a finger. "Creating chaos among adventurers is part of my daily devotions to Banok. But it *is* fun."

They all fell quiet for a few minutes. Reva was wondering if she might be able to salvage some of this day by getting back to New Port to see what Ansee had managed to get done. Maybe she could head to his apartment and surprise him there to get caught up.

She was about to suggest that they give up, when Pfastbinder said, "He's here," in a creepy sing-song voice.

"Sulwynd?" Amalaki asked, heading to the door.

Reva held him back to make sure that he didn't accidentally get silhouetted in the doorway.

"The good constable himself," Pfastbinder confirmed.

Reva and the others watched as Sulwynd approached the bakery and quickly headed up the stairs, not bothering to look around. He knocked twice on the door. After a moment, it opened, and he slipped into the room.

Reva stood up and pulled out the Wake, quickly lifting another pinch to her nose. Amalaki drew his small crossbow and pulled back the string, setting a bolt on the weapon. Willem and Gania each drew their service swords. Reva replaced the tin and drew her own sword, gripping the bangstone in her other hand.

"Ready?" Amalaki asked.

They all nodded, and then headed out the door.

"Have fun storming the bakery," Pfastbinder chided, "without me."

Amalaki led the way, followed by Reva, and then Willem. Constable Gania brought up the rear. Amalaki took the stairs two at a time and slammed his shoulder into the door as he reached the top. It burst open with almost no resistance and he immediately crouched, keeping the door from slamming back. Reva was right behind him. She could see a small space that was barely lit by a few candles. Several people were standing in a small group, with Constable Sulwynd and another halpbloed standing apart from the others. Reva hurled the small bangstone toward the group of halpbloeden.

It hit the floor and exploded in a burst of bright light and sound. Reva had turned her head to shield her eyes, but her ears still rang from the noise. Since she had known what was happening, she was able to continue into the room, pushing past Amalaki and shoving the door open.

Amalaki stood up from his crouch and took a step to his left to allow Willem to come in. At the same time, he fired his crossbow at Constable Sulwynd. Sulwynd was already moving, so the bolt was slightly off target, but it still struck him in the arm.

Reva locked eyes on Cedres, who was blinking rapidly and shaking his head. He staggered, but seemed to recover quickly from the effects of the bangstone. His eyes widened as he recognized Reva. He kicked a stool in her direction. It clattered to her right, but it had given Cedres a chance to grab a large pouch. He turned and headed to the back of the room, and Reva tried to run after him, but she fell forward, tripped by something. She threw out her arms as she hit the floor, and her sword slipped from her hand. She looked up to see Cedres jumping down through a hole in the floor.

Somebody was clawing at her boot, trying to grab her foot. She heard yells and cries and sounds of fighting that seemed to be coming from all around her, but she needed to go after Cedres. She struggled to pull her foot away, and she twisted around to give a kick when her foot was released. She saw that the halpbloeden that had managed to crawl across the room and grab her foot was now laying unconscious on the floor. Standing above him was Pfastbinder, who was whistling and tossing a mace in the air, catching it after it flipped.

Reva kicked the halpbloed's hand away and struggled to her feet. "I thought I told you to stay out of this!"

"What can I say?" Pfastbinder shrugged. "Cleric of the god of chaos. I'm a leaf on the wind, going wherever I am needed."

Reva picked up her sword and looked around the room. All of the halpbloeden were either down, knocked unconscious, or were on their knees with their hands on their heads, as Constable Gania held his sword in front of them. She saw Amalaki kicking a dagger away from the prostrate form of Constable Sulwynd. He had managed to get several paces before succumbing to the Sucra poison. Still, Cedres had gotten away.

Amalaki gestured to Willem to put the manacles on Sulwynd. "In a moment," Willem said, pulling out a spare set of Nul Pfeta bracers.

"What are those for?" Amalaki asked.

"My idea," Reva said. "If everyone out there," she jerked a thumb toward the door, "sees that we're arresting a constable in this mess it may keep some of the resentment and panic down."

"We'd like to avoid a riot if we can," Willem added, tying on the bracers before pulling out a pair of manacles.

Amalaki nodded and looked at the room. "Let's get any

evidence we can together, and then get this group over to the constabulary gate house. We can keep them there until I can get them moved over to the Red Keep."

Reva sheathed her sword. "Cedres got away. He slipped out a hole in the floor."

Amalaki seemed unconcerned. He was smiling as he searched Sulwynd for evidence. "All that matters is that we got Sulwynd. He's the key to all of this. Besides," he glanced at Reva, "what harm can one halpbloed do, anyway?"

Chapter 41

Ansee knocked on the door and waited a moment. He could hear the muffled cry from Gabii coming from inside, letting Reva and her mom know that someone was at the door. Gabii was better than any door knocker. After a moment, he heard someone say, "Alright, just hush, already. I'm opening the door."

The door opened and Ansee saw Aeollas standing there. "Oh, it's just you, dragon spawn." She smiled, and gestured for him to enter. "Come on in. Reva's not home right now." She headed across her shop to the stairs.

Ansee closed the door and followed Aeollas. "Do you know when she might be back?"

Aeollas shrugged, "Who knows with her?"

"Who knows? Who knows?" called Gabii, who fanned her wings from her perch near the dining table. Ansee saw that it had been set out for two people, and he could smell a soup cooking on the stove.

Aeollas pointed to a seat. "Care to join me? I don't know why I keep bothering with setting a place for Reva. Habit, I guess. She's not eaten a meal with me for nearly a month."

Ansee hesitated. He was hungry, having skipped lunch himself, but he didn't want to impose. Aeollas noticed and insisted, "Sit. I'm tired of eating alone."

Ansee took off his cloak, hung it up on the rack, and then

sat down. Aeollas was ladling out a thick soup into her bowl. "Her father always ate his evening meal at home, no matter what was going on. He insisted on it, to make sure that we remembered what was most important in our lives. And it wasn't work, or school, or the constabulary, or anything else."

"Family," Ansee replied, taking the ladle from Aeollas to begin filling his bowl. It was a thick barley and fish soup with onions, mushrooms, and carrots. He inhaled. "This smells wonderful."

"Flattery will get you everywhere, dragon spawn," she smiled.

"Flattery!" called Gabbi, plucking a shelled nut from her bowl and working it with her beak.

"I know that Reva's been working a lot, but I didn't know that she had been skipping her dinners with you. I remember when we met, she said that it was a family tradition. It doesn't seem like her to miss them."

"If you can stick it out, you will soon learn that this is how my daughter sulks."

"Sulks?"

Aeollas slurped from her spoon. "Uh huh. Ever since that whole thing with the undead at the port, and Aavril's 'betrayal', Reva has been sulking. But Reva doesn't close her petals or burrow into the ground when she sulks. Instead, she deals with it by working herself to death."

Ansee nodded. He'd noticed how Reva had been working almost nonstop since returning from her suspension after the Dreen case. "I guess that also explains the increased Wake use, too."

Aeollas nodded slowly and sighed. "I know that she's been using it more lately, and that she's been more blatant about it, as well. She used to be discreet about it, so much so that I had to snoop around in her things to know when she was taking it. Not this time."

Ansee smiled as he ate his soup. He could picture Reva's mother going through her things. "I'm concerned," he said. "I think it's affecting her mood, even more than normal. She's been irritable a lot lately."

"More than normal? My daughter has never had the sunniest of dispositions."

"Yes. I'm wondering if there's something wrong with the Wake that she's been taking, something that might be causing this change."

Aeollas turned her head and looked at him, "You haven't tried to steal her Wake again, have you?"

Ansee's mouth gaped. When he had first started working with Reva, during the Fury Blade case, she had started taking Wake, and Ansee had noticed a rapid change in her mood. He had taken her Wake from her, and he had tried to get the Alchemists at New Port to test it, but Reva had prevented that. "You knew about that?"

"Of course, Reva tells me everything. She was so mad at you. I'm surprised that she let you stay on as her partner. I know I didn't want anything to do with you after that."

"I thought that was because I had replaced Cas." Ansee said.

"Oh, that helped. Plus, finding out that you were a dragon spawn was another knothole against you."

"So, you're saying I'm lucky to still be Reva's partner."

Aeollas pointed her spoon at Ansee. "You're lucky you're still alive," she said, in a serious voice, but then smiled. "But you did good, and you got Gabii to cooperate, so you're not all bad."

"Cooperate!" Gabii repeated.

"For a dragon spawn," Ansee added.

"Yep," Aeollas smiled.

"Is there anything we can do?" Ansee asked, quickly adding, "about Reva. I'm afraid if she keeps this up, she's going to wear herself out and start making mistakes. That might get her hurt."

Aeollas sighed, and set her spoon in her bowl. "It's hard to say. Reva can be stubborn at the best of times."

"That's an understatement," Ansee agreed.

Aeollas glared at him, as if she was the only one who

could insult her daughter, and said, "She'll stay like this until she can exercise all the demons that are bothering her. And Aavril was a pretty big demon. I've only managed to drag out of her that he lied to her, and for Reva, that's the biggest betrayal that anyone can make."

"I'll keep that in mind."

Aeollas smiled. "The Wake isn't helping matters, either. It's allowing her to string things along, to continue to focus on her job and not get over what Aavril did."

"Is there anything we can do?" Ansee set his own spoon down, and took a drink of water.

"If Gale was here, he might be able to talk some sense into Reva. She'll sometimes listen to her brother. But I've not heard from Gale in," she leaned her head back, "oh, I guess it's been a couple of weeks now."

"Is that unusual?" Ansee knew that Ghalen—Gale to Reva and her mother—was a ranger in the army.

"It depends. He usually writes us at least once a week when he's stationed at the barracks in Tolan. But if his unit is on a patrol, it might be weeks before we hear from him."

"Maybe I could talk to her, then."

Aeollas laughed so loud that Gabii squawked and jumped from her perch, flying over to the railing for the balustrade that overlooked the shop below. "You? No offense, dragon spawn, but that won't do anything but make her even more stubborn than she is, and she's already more stubborn than a dwarf having to give up his gold. She won't listen to you, not after what you did to her the last time."

"I took her Wake for her own good."

"Plus, you shot a lightning bolt at her," Aeollas grinned.

"It wasn't a lightning bolt!"

Aeollas patted his arm. "Whatever, dragon spawn. No, the only person that Reva might listen to at all is Cas. She's the only one who could always talk sense into her."

Ansee suppressed a sigh. Even after two months, he was still being compared to Reva's previous partner. Being told that only Cas could talk some sense into Reva just added oil to the fire.

"I guess I can send Cas a letter and let her know what's going on. Maybe she can pull herself—"

At that moment there was a CRASH of splintered wood and breaking pottery that came from the front door. Ansee and Aeollas both jumped to their feet and looked down to see that the door had been smashed in, the wood now nothing but splinters. In the doorway stood an elf wearing a dark blue robe with silvery lettering sewn into the sleeves and hem. He wore a broad-brimmed hat and, in his hands, he held a staff and a small crossbow. The intruder pointed the staff at Ansee, a large gemstone glinting in the light.

"Ansee Carya, it's time to meet your destiny!"

Chapter 42

Before Ansee could react, the intruder pulled the trigger on the crossbow and a small bolt flew across the room. The bolt flew true, and it would have struck Ansee right in the chest, but at the last instant, a red shimmer appeared; Ansee's shield spell triggered, and the bolt fell harmlessly to the ground. Ansee thanked Qurna that he had continued to cast the shield spell every day. Sometimes habits were a good thing to have.

"Who are you?" Ansee asked, although he already had a good idea of the answer.

"Get out of my home!" shouted Aeollas, brazenly leaning over the railing.

"Get out!" Gabii called, "Get out!" The bird took flight and flew straight at the intruder, who seemed surprised by the parrot diving toward him. He tried to hit Gabii with his staff, but she was too quick and dodged the blow. She grabbed his hat with her talons and tore it from his head.

Ansee jumped over the railing, landing on the floor of the shop in a crouch behind one of Aeollas' displays of pottery. He unsheathed a dagger and darted to his right toward the stairs. Behind him, the room lit up as a fiery beam blazed through the space where Ansee had just been. Several of the pots exploded from the sudden heat, and the wall was scorched and blackened.

Aeollas yelled an obscenity that caused Ansee's ears to burn red as she was coming down the stairs. "You'll regret coming here," she yelled. Ansee saw that she was holding a longsword in her hands. The weapon shook slightly, but there was fire in her eyes.

Reva will kill me if anything happens to her mother, Ansee thought. He stepped around another display and threw the dagger at the wizard. It spun, aimed right at the wizard's head, but then stopped and fell to the ground. A red shimmer of light flashed briefly from the wizard's own shield spell.

"Two can play that game, demon," the wizard taunted, "but you will find that I command the purer magic."

Aeollas had reached the bottom of the stairs, preparing to charge the wizard. Ansee saw the wizard smile. "Those in league with the demon will be destroyed as well," he said. He started to weave a spell, and Gabii flew past his head again, her talons glancing off the shield spell.

Ansee was too far away to interpose himself between the wizard and Aeollas, so he did the next best thing: he yelled, "*Yukarı çık!*" and pointed at Aeollas. A yellow light enveloped her as another beam of fire spewed from the wizard's outstretched hand. She disappeared a mere breath before the ray would have struck her. Instead, it hit the wall and burst into flames, blackening the stairs.

The wizard and Aeollas both cursed Ansee.

"You cannot protect your thralls forever, demon spawn!"

"I didn't need your help, dragon spawn!" Aeollas called from upstairs.

"Will you two make up your minds?" Ansee said, pulling another dagger. "Am I the spawn of a demon or a dragon? I'm getting confused here."

The wizard growled, "When I am ripping the name of your demon master from your bleeding lips, there will be little humor left on your tongue." The wizard lifted his staff and pointed it at Ansee, the crystal in the tip glowing softly.

Ansee felt the magical energy strike at him, felt it trying to tear his shield spell away. He resisted, willing the magic to remain in place, and he could see the bracelet that Hedera had given him glowing with a red light. The energy from the wizard's spell dissipated, and Ansee could tell that his shield spell remained in place. At least for now.

The wizard realized that his spell failed, and he snarled. "All your demonic trickery won't save you. In mere moments, your thrall will be dead and my interrogation can begin."

"You'll have to catch me first," Ansee taunted. He rolled forward and threw a second dagger, its blade glowing red. It struck the wizard, the magical enchantment allowing it to slip through his shield spell, and then arcs of lightning danced across the wizard's leg.

The wizard gave a yelp that was more surprise than pain, as he seemed unaffected by the blast of electricity. *Shit,* Ansee thought. *That spell is usually enough to knock a normal person unconscious.*

"Your feeble magic cannot harm me, demon," the wizard gloated. He took a step towards Ansee, pulling the dagger from his leg and let it fall to the floor. He pulled out a silver-gray disc and dropped it. Ansee noticed the six-pointed star etched on the surface and recognized the anchor stone.

Great, there goes my one way of getting Aeollas and myself out of here.

He could hear Aeollas coming back toward the stairs after his gate had teleported her to Reva's bedroom. She was as stubborn as her daughter. Ansee couldn't let anything happen to her, or to the rest of her shop. The scorching rays had already set small fires that were not yet a serious problem, but the flames were hungrily licking at the wood and sending smoke up into the air. Through the open door, Ansee could hear cries of alarm coming from neighbors, and a shrill whistle coming from somebody on the fire watch.

Ansee's mind raced, trying to find a solution. The wizard easily resisted his shock spell, so he would likely be able to resist a more powerful lightning bolt. That would also do more damage to Aeollas' shop, and Ansee didn't want Reva's mother mad at him for that. His shield spell would end soon, and he didn't know how long his opponent's own shield spell might last. Help would be coming. The alarm being raised outside guaranteed that, but would it arrive in time?

Ansee had already figured out that this wizard was the murderer, the one that had killed the other sorcerers and left their bodies on display in Old Grove. And it was clear that he believed that Ansee got his magic from a demon, the stupid myth Rhoanlan had told him about. He had seen the manic fanaticism that flickered in the wizard's eyes. Ansee wouldn't be able to reason with him, and trying to overpower him would destroy the shop and maybe harm Aeollas.

Ansee's thoughts spun in his head, like leaves caught up in a whirlwind, with no clear solution coming to mind. Then he realized he had taken too long to act. The wizard stretched out his hand and snapped his fingers, and then everything in front of Ansee disappeared in a burst of brilliant light. Ansee blinked, trying to regain his vision, and then felt a sharp pain across his arm. Blood began to well up from the wound, soaking his shirt.

The room spun, and all Ansee could discern was light and shadow as his eyes tried to recover. He heard Aeollas yelling from the top of the stairs, but her words were drowned out by the loud screeches coming from Gabii, who sounded like she was flying right over his head.

"May the flames of Jansure purify this unholy dwelling," the wizard chanted.

Ansee turned to the sound, his vision still filled with blurry shapes, but he was sure that the shape next to him was the wizard. He leaped to interpose himself between the wizard and Aeollas as the wizard's spell was cast. Flame and heat shot from the wizard's hands and enveloped Ansee. His shield absorbed most of the attack, but not all of it, and he felt his skin singe and peel, his clothes burning. The shock of the pain froze Ansee in his tracks, and he saw a blurry movement from the wizard, followed by a sharp pain in his neck, and then the cold embrace of unconsciousness.

Chapter 43

The night was cool, the sky clear, as Reva crossed Victory Bridge and turned south toward her home. Beside her, Pfastbinder continued to hum a nameless tune. "I didn't invite you to tag along with me," she complained.

"No invitation necessary, Inspector. I go where I am needed."

"Needed?"

"Of course. That dashing Inquisitor has taken Sulwynd to the Red Keep. He's probably firing up the brazier of hot coals and oiling the rack as we speak. And my fellow constables are busy dealing with those halpbloed traitors."

"So, why did you come with me?"

"I figured you could use the company. To console you about the one that got away."

"I don't need to be consoled. I'm sure we'll find Cedres hiding in some hole in Nul Pfeta." She turned to look at Pfastbinder. "I think you invited yourself along so that you could avoid the crowd of angry halpbloed that had gathered by your temple."

"They're not angry, they're just agitated from learning that a group of traitors had slithered into their midst."

"Sure, and the fact that they threw mud and rocks at us as we took the prisoners away had nothing to do with it."

"Well, I do live there. Those were my neighbors, and I

didn't want them to get the wrong idea."

"Is that why you threw mud at Constable Gania and called Willem a son of a succubus?"

"All in jest, of course. I'm sure they understand. Besides, I couldn't expose my secret to my neighbors."

"What secret?"

"That I'm a constable. Nobody would ever stop by my temple again if they knew that."

"You *aren't* a constable," Reva countered. "Just a pain in my ass."

Pfastbinder laughed, and they continued down Embankment Road toward Reva's house. She was relieved that Amalaki's mission was over, and that Sulwynd was in the custody of the Sucra. If she was right, and Sulwynd *was* working for Grand Inquisitor Agera, then, at most, he'd be held for a day before being released. But the halpbloeden plot had been stopped, so that was a victory, and it meant that Amalaki might leave her alone and she could get back to doing her job.

"I don't need you to keep me company," Reva stated, as they passed Queen's Bridge.

"Who said I was keeping you company?"

"You did," Reva replied, "just a couple of minutes ago."

"Did I? Maybe I came along so that *you* could keep *me* company."

Reva sighed. She should probably just give up ever trying to understand Pfastbinder's motives or reasons. He seemed to make everything up as he went along, which made sense for a follower of Banok, she supposed. But it still aggravated her to no end.

"Do you smell smoke?" Pfastbinder asked.

"What?"

"Ahead," he pointed, and Reva could make out a crowd gathering and smoke coming from a building. Not just any building. Her home!

"Shit!" Reva broke into a run. The crowd appeared to be disorganized at first, but then she saw that they were forming a bucket line outside her home. As she skidded to a stop, she saw that the front door had been forced open, bashed in. Heat and smoke poured from the opening.

"Mother!" Reva yelled. She looked around, but she didn't see her mother in the crowd. "Mother!"

"She's not here," someone in the crowd commented.

Reva saw Pfastbinder arrive, and she ignored him. She turned and ran into her home.

Inside, smoke billowed up to the ceiling, and the crackle of flames filled the air. Heat, seemingly hotter than her mother's kiln, made a thick wall. A few small fires were already consuming the display tables, but the bulk of the fire was at the stairs and seemed to be greedily consuming the steps one at a time.

A loud, piercing whistle rent the air, and Reva saw movement on the stairs, followed by loud cries of "Help! Help!" that sounded like they were coming from Gabii.

Reva ran to the stairs and saw her mother laying on the steps only a few hands above the creeping fire. Gabii sat by her mother's head, flapping her wings, but not leaving her side. The fire was burning on the bottom third of the stairs, and there was no way to jump over it. Reva hesitated, only long enough to make sure that the stairs were still intact, and then ran through the flames to her mother.

The fire folded around her like a burning cloak. She felt her skin and her hair burning, and the fire seemed to mock her. *This is your fault. You abandoned your mother to this. For what?*

Then she was through the flames, and she leaned down to pick up her mother. Gabii squawked, and Reva could see that several of her feathers were singed. "What in the hells happened?"

As she bent down, she saw a small bolt laying on the stairs. Reva picked it up and slipped it under her bracer, and then she picked up her mother, gently putting Aeollas over her shoulder. She turned to look at the fire, assessing her options, when a wall of water appeared above her and fell from the air. The flames hissed in protest, and steam erupted, but the water continued to flow and cascaded down the stairs like a wild cataract. In moments, the flames were extinguished, and Reva saw Pfastbinder standing at the base of the stairs. He flourished his cloak and gave her a bow that was fit for Pfenestra's stage.

Reva carried her mother down the stairs and out the door, passing her neighbors who were carrying in buckets to put out the remaining fires. Pfastbinder and Gabii followed her out.

Reva laid her mother softly on the ground, and Gabii made a wobbly landing next to her, unusually quiet now. Pfastbinder knelt and started to place his hands over her body.

"I think she's just unconscious," Reva said. She pulled out the bolt and showed it to him.

Pfastbinder's eyes widened, and he mouthed "Sucra" to her.

"I don't know. This is their usual tactic," she waved the bolt, "but burning down the building seems like overkill, even for them."

Pfastbinder nodded, and then stood up and went back to the building. Her mother was breathing slowly, like she was sleeping, but soot and ash covered her clothes and smudged her face. Reva began to stroke her mother's hair, the fire's accusations still ringing in her head. *You let this happen. You could have prevented this if you had just been home. Whatever happened here, this is your fault.*

"Oh, my gods," a voice called out. Reva looked up to see Norah standing in the road, a hand covering her mouth, her eyes wide as she stared at Aeollas. She leaned heavily on her staff, and she looked like she would fall over without its support. "Reva? Is she...?"

"Just unconscious," Reva replied. She knew that Norah lived across the river in Alnua Grove. "What are you doing here?"

Norah stepped forward as Reva's neighbors continued

to mill about, some still carrying buckets from the river, not knowing that most of the fire was already out. Norah knelt next to Aeollas and grabbed her hand. Reva saw tears starting to form in her eyes.

"Norah, why are you here?"

Norah still didn't answer. Before Reva could ask her again, Pfastbinder came back outside. He was carrying a sword and a couple of daggers. "I found these inside," he said. "The sword was on the stairs, about where you found your mother. The daggers were here by the door. This one," he held one up, "has some blood on it."

Reva stared. The sword had belonged to her father, and her mother kept it mounted above the mantle at the top of the stairs. *Why would she take it down?* The daggers looked familiar to her, but she couldn't place them. She only knew that they weren't her mother's.

"I saw another one of those bolts in there, against the back wall," Pfastbinder added. "and maybe another one by the stairs, but it was pretty much destroyed by the fire."

"What in the hells happened here?" Reva asked. "It looks like a Sucra raid, but who was here with Mother to fend them off? And where is everyone now?"

"It wasn't the Green Cloaks," Norah said, her voice almost a whisper.

"What?" Reva and Pfastbinder both asked.

Norah looked up at them, still holding Aoellas' hand, tears streaking her face. "I'm so sorry, Reva. This is all my fault."

"Your fault?" Reva shook her head. None of this was making any sense to her. "How is this your fault?"

"The Minister," Norah began, laying Aeollas' hand back on her stomach. Norah brought her hands up to her chin. "This wasn't supposed to happen. The Minister wasn't supposed to do this."

Pfastbinder gave her a questioning look, and Reva shrugged. "Who's the minister?" she asked.

"I just wanted Ansee gone," Norah continued, not hearing Reva's question. "That's all I wanted. I didn't want this. None of this should have happened. Why couldn't anybody understand? Why couldn't anybody just get him out of the constabulary? That's all that needed to happen, and then The Minister wouldn't have had to do this."

Reva had no idea what Norah was saying, but she was starting to fit the pieces together. "Norah," she grabbed the Seeker's hand. "Who is the minister? What did he do?"

"The Minister, that's what he calls himself," Norah replied, her voice sounding hollow. "He hunts them, to remove the danger." She turned and stared at Reva. "They are a threat. But not Ansee, he's not evil. I know, I checked. I just wanted him gone."

More pieces were falling into place for Reva, and she didn't like the picture that they were starting to form. "Who does The Minister hunt?"

"Sorcerers," Norah responded, as if it was common knowledge. "It's their duty."

"Their duty?" Pfastbinder asked.

Norah nodded. "It is the duty of all Qurundora to hunt the sorcerers." She paused for a moment and looked down at Aeollas. "But only the sorcerers. Not this. Others aren't supposed to get hurt. But The Minister..."

"It's his holy duty," Pfastbinder interrupted. Norah nodded. "Why do you do this? Why sorcerers?"

Norah seemed to shrink away, turning her head. "They are an abomination to Qurna. They stole her magic by selling their souls to a demon. This demon will order them to do its bidding, putting all of us at risk."

Reva found herself gritting her teeth, trying to control the fury that was seething inside her. "This is hawkshit!" she yelled. "Ansee saved your life. He's not under the control of any demon! How can you believe this, Norah?"

Norah gave a half-hearted shrug. "I do believe it. Or I did. I don't know what I believe now. Nobody else was supposed to get hurt." She turned away.

Reva looked up. The fire was out, and most of her neighbors were gone, back to their own homes. Somebody had managed to patch the door enough so that it would close.

"Not... a demon," came a ragged voice. "A dragon spawn."

Reva turned to see her mother straining to sit up. "Mother." She reached over and helped her.

Aeollas turned to Norah, touching her shoulder. "Ansee saved my life, and Gabii's." The parrot gave a squawk of approval. "He protected us from that crazy old wizard."

"The Minister," Pfastbinder supplied.

Aeollas gave a snort. "He was no priest. He said I was to be destroyed, too, that I was in the demon's control. What hawkshit."

Reva couldn't help but laugh. Nobody could control her mother. "Where are they, Mother? Where's Ansee?"

"I don't know. He saved me from a spell. I saw a wall of fire, and Ansee stepped in the way, blocking most of it. Then the wizard shot Ansee, and then me. That's the last thing I remember."

They all stood up, Reva supporting her mother until she pushed Reva away. "I'm fine." She turned to look at their home. "How bad is it?"

"I don't know," Reva replied.

"It's not too bad," Pfastbinder offered. "There's some damage to the stairs, but the rest of the building is fine, although everything probably smells of smoke."

Aeollas turned to Pfastbinder. "Who in the hells are you?"

Reva motioned them both to be quiet. Her home wasn't important right now. "Norah, how could you do this? Ansee's a fellow constable. A friend."

"He wasn't *my* friend."

"He saved your life!" Reva's voice rose. "And he's *my* friend. I am going to save him from this maniac."

"You knew about this?" Aeollas asked Norah. She made a tsk tsk sound. "Cas will be so disappointed in you."

Norah turned to glare at Aeollas, but she didn't flinch.

"You know it's true," Aeollas continued. "Cas didn't want

anything to do with your little cult."

Reva looked at her mother, "What?"

"Oh, come on," Aeollas said to Reva. "Cas told me lots of stuff that she didn't share with you." She turned to look at Norah. "And she tried to get you out of that group. Didn't she? She knew that they were a bunch of bad apples. Anybody who's only concerned with their own purity, whether it's blood or magic or whatever, is the real danger."

Reva stared, wondering where that had come from. She agreed with her mother, but a small part of her wondered if her mother knew about the family tree that was hidden in Reva's room.

Norah turned to leave, and Reva grabbed her shoulder to stop her. "No. You don't get to leave. I need you. I can't stop this Minister on my own."

Norah whirled around, her fists clenched, and tears streaked down her cheeks. Her eyes blazed with anger and defiance, but Reva was sure that the anger was directed inward and not at them. Three sets of eyes returned her look, and Norah wilted under their gaze. Her shoulders slumped, and the fire in her eyes went out. She looked down at the ground. "I will help," she looked up to Aeollas, "for Cas. And for you. I never wanted you to be hurt."

"Where are they?" asked Pfastbinder. "Where would this Minister take Ansee? And why take him?"

"He's taking Ansee to interrogate him, to find out about the demon. That's the only thing that matters to him. To find the name of the demon. Once he's got that, he will kill Ansee." She managed to look embarrassed. "But I don't know where he took him. I don't know where he's staying."

"I have a pretty good idea where he took Ansee," Reva said.

Chapter 44

Ansee blinked his eyes and slowly raised his head, trying to determine where he was. He wasn't at Aeollas' shop, and it took him a moment to clear his vision. Once he could see clearly, he saw bookshelves, a bed, and a fireplace. *My apartment?*

He was in his apartment. That was the good news. The bad news: he was naked and tied to one of his kitchen chairs. His arms were pulled behind the chair and his hands were bound together with rope. His legs were spread and his feet were tied to the legs of the chair. The rug and the rest of his furniture had been shoved out of the main room, and he sat in the center of what appeared to be a magic circle that had been drawn on the floor. *That had better not be drawn in blood,* Ansee thought. He didn't recognize the symbols, but that wasn't a surprise; he struggled with the most basic magical writing, and this looked to be some complex form of the basic magical script. Probably created by the wizard that had...

Ansee jerked his head up, the events at Reva's home now flooding back through the haze of the drug-induced sleep. There had been flames, the shop had been burning, and Aeollas had been... He didn't know what had happened to Reva's mother. He struggled against the straps that were holding him to the chair, which made noise as the chair rocked against the floor. A form moved in his kitchen, and then stepped into the room. The wizard.

He had taken off his cloak and broad-brimmed hat, revealing a blue shirt that glistened in the firelight. Dark color breeches were tucked into black boots. In one hand, he held a goblet—one of Ansee's goblets—and he took a drink from it as he picked up his staff.

"It is useless to struggle, demon thrall," the wizard said. "Those bonds will not break, and you are within a magic circle that will contain your vile and evil magic."

Ansee wanted to respond, to yell at the maniac, to find out what had happened to Aeollas, but he knew that would be pointless. He had learned a few things during their brief fight, enough to know that he wouldn't be able to reason with this elf.

The wizard set the goblet down on the mantle, and then pulled out a wand from a pocket in his breeches. It was a gnarled piece of wood, with many grooves and cracks that crossed its surface. At the handle was set a gemstone of some kind, and the tip was capped with copper. The wizard stood before Ansee, holding the wand in his right hand, the staff in his left. He planted his feet wide, standing just outside the circle, and spread his arms.

"Your end begins, demon spawn," the wizard said. "I am The Minister, and you will tell me what I want to know about your demon master. Answer my questions truthfully, and your end will be swift and painless. Lie, or refuse to answer, and—"

The Minister moved swiftly, lunging into the circle, jabbing the wand at Ansee, who only had the briefest of moments to notice a crackle of blue-white light trace down the wand before the copper tip struck Ansee in the chest. Pain erupted from the spot as electricity danced and arced across his body. Ansee screamed, louder than he needed to, hoping that his neighbors would hear.

"I will bring you pain," The Minister finished, stepping back. He gave a thin smile. "Do not worry about your screams.

I have ensured that your neighbors will not hear us."

Figures. Ansee thought. His eyes watered from the pain, and he hung his head. At the edge of his vision, he saw a form scurry out from under one of the bookshelves and into the fire. *Ember.* He also saw a silver-gray stone sitting just inside the magic circle. *The anchor stone.* His options for getting out of this mess were dropping by the moment.

"Let us see who has control of your tongue, demon spawn. I will start with a simple question. Lie, or hesitate, and I will shock you again. What is your name?"

Ansee didn't hesitate. He wasn't willing to bring about pain over something that this crazed wizard probably already knew. "Ansee Carya."

"How long have you been a Seeker?"

"Five years."

"How old were you when you bargained away your soul to the demon?"

Ansee hesitated, trying to understand the question and decide how to respond. The Minister was swift, and he jabbed the wand into Ansee, this time aiming for his right shoulder. The electricity arced, and the pain seemed to jump from his shoulder to each of his other joints. Ansee screamed, and he tried to kick, but his bonds wouldn't give.

The Minister stepped back. "I told you that refusing to answer would be punished with pain."

Ansee fought through the pain, trying to focus his attention on the elf. "I didn't refuse. You didn't give me a chance to respond."

"You had ample time to respond. You expect me to believe that the most important day in your life, the day the demon granted you the ability to cast magic, isn't something that you can easily recall?"

"I can't recall something that never happened," Ansee answered, regretting the words even as he said them.

The wand sparked and flashed in his vision, and pain erupted, this time from his other shoulder. Ansee jerked and convulsed in the chair, so much that it fell over. That broke contact with the wand, but the pain wouldn't leave his body. The Minister leaned over to stare at him. There was anger in his dark blue eyes. Anger and hatred. It was clear to Ansee that The Minister had no real interest in the questions. They, like the search for this mythical demon, were just a means to an end, causing as much pain as he could, before killing Ansee. That was going to be the outcome, no matter how Ansee answered these stupid questions. The Minister had long ago stopped caring about the reason for his actions. Only the actions themselves, the suffering, injury, and death, gave him any sort of release now, any sort of feeling of having fulfilled his purpose. Ansee was sure that even if The Minister did manage to drag a name from a sorcerer that could summon a demon, he wouldn't know what to do after that. He would be driven to continue to hunt and to kill sorcerers, making up any excuse to justify his actions, because the actions were all that mattered now, not the results. He was dealing with a psychopath, and that realization caused Ansee's blood to run cold.

"How long have you been the demon's thrall?"

"Go to hell!" Ansee spat, bracing for the shock. The wand jabbed his stomach, and he screamed again. The pain was so intense that he nearly blacked out, but The Minister withdrew the wand before that could happen.

Ansee panted, trying to draw breath. He caught movement in the coals of the fire, and he saw Ember poke her head out. He would be dead soon if he didn't do something, and the number of somethings that he could try was essentially one. He met Ember's gaze, and then looked to The Minister's robes that were draped over the back of a chair, the hem pooled on the floor. "Fire, Ember!" he yelled, praying that she would understand.

"What?" The Minister asked, confused by the words. He didn't understand, and he lashed out in the only way that he could, by hitting Ansee with the wand again. It struck Ansee in the leg, and he spasmed as the electricity skittered across his body.

But the pain was worth it, as Ansee saw Ember scurry out of the safety of the coals. She paused by the robes, probably remembering all the times that she had been scolded for setting fire to the rug, or a book, or a pair of pants that Ansee had carelessly left on the floor. She turned to look at Ansee as he writhed in pain, and then turned back to the robes and opened her mouth.

The retching noise was covered up by the sounds of Ansee's screams and, within moments, she had regurgitated her stomach contents onto the robes. The foul concoction immediately burst into flame, and soon the robes were burning.

The Minister withdrew the wand, and he was about to jab it down again when he noticed the fire. He turned to see his robes engulfed in flames, and then caught movement as Ember scuttled forward, running between his legs. He gave a most undignified yelp of surprise, and started to incant a spell, his hand pointing toward Ember.

Ansee struggled to focus his mind, to push the pain away. His body throbbed, and he wanted nothing more than to curl up into a ball and let the pain win. But he managed to form the words, to coalesce his intent and will into casting the spell. "*Cübbeleri üzerine at.*"

Ansee's spell was not as refined as Seeker Hedera's, but it did the trick. The robes were picked up by an unseen force and then tossed toward The Minister. They landed on his head, covering his eyes, and enveloping his back with burning fabric.

Ansee felt Ember nuzzle his hands, and then he felt a slick wetness, like snot or— His hands began to burn as Ember's vomit burst into flame. He ignored the new pain, and he tried to pull his hands apart. The rope gave way, and he was able to bring his hands around, touching the ropes around his ankles. "*Kuma iple,*" he commanded, and the rope binding his legs to the chair was transformed into a coarse sand.

Ansee crawled away from the chair and kicked the anchor stone as hard as he could. He felt a sharp pain in his toes, but the stone flew past the struggling form of The Minster and landed in the fire. Ansee had to hope that it would be far enough. He grabbed Ember and crawled across the room to his front door. She struggled, wanting to get up onto his shoulders, but he held her close.

Behind him, he heard a cry of rage and glanced back to see the wizard toss his burning robes to the ground. Ansee reached the door and grabbed the handle, but it didn't move. Locked. Behind him he could hear The Minister begin to cast a spell. Ansee turned to face The Minister, Ember cradled in his arms. *Let's hope this works.*

Ansee yelled, "*Uzağa!*" as The Minister completed his spell. A fiery beam of energy raced toward Ansee as a yellow light enveloped him and Ember.

Chapter 45

Reva crossed The Grand March at a run, with Norah and Pfastbinder in tow. They had wasted precious time at her house, and The Minister had a head start on what he was planning to do. Reva didn't buy the story that Norah had told her about the Qurundora and the demon that gave sorcerers their magic. That was religious hawkshit, as far as Reva was concerned, and they could believe any tripe that they wanted to, until those beliefs hurt others. The Minister was doing that now. His 'belief' may have been what motivated him in the beginning, but he was acting beyond any sort of faith, any sort of logic, now. An illness had invaded his mind long ago, and the only way that he could cure it was to inflict pain on others.

That he used the guise of faith to hide what he was only made it worse. He was no better than Erroll Saliceä, that deranged crewelf from the *Majestic Tern*, blindly following his faith to justify his own ends. Whether it was turning people into undead Disciples of Dreen, or torturing people to find a demon that didn't exist, they were the same.

"Are you sure The Minister took Ansee back to his apartment?" Norah asked, as they crossed into Old Grove. "He could have taken him anywhere in the city."

"I'm sure," Reva replied. "This whole case has been about Ansee." *No thanks to you*, she didn't add. She needed Norah, and antagonizing her further wouldn't help. "The Minister may think that he's a follower of Qurna—"

"Jansure," Norah corrected.

"Whatever. He thinks that he's being righteous and faithful to his god, but this isn't about any demon, and you know it."

"Are you mocking my faith?"

"I mock any faith that is too short-sighted to not see the facts that are right in front of them. You're a constable. You deal in evidence. In thousands of years, if there really was a demon behind every sorcerer's magic, wouldn't that name have come up? At least once?"

"They lie," Norah offered, though she hesitated. "The demon forces them to lie."

This caused Pfastbinder to laugh. Norah turned to glare at him as they ran down the street. "You dare mock me, too, halpbloed?"

"When it is so deliciously funny? Absolutely. You and your other true believers miss the obvious, and it is a joke that would make Banok proud."

"Killing others over misplaced faith isn't something to take pride in," Reva countered.

"Of course not," Pfastbinder agreed, "but it is still humorous the way they have deluded themselves."

"My faith does not make me delusional," Norah huffed.

"When it causes you to miss the obvious, it does," Pfastbinder said.

"And what is that?"

"That the demon doesn't exist," Reva stated. "It never has. The Minister is so deluded by his faith that he no longer cares if he finds evidence of a demon. He's a psychopath now, getting his pleasure from hurting others. That he does this under the guise of religion doesn't make it right."

"It gives the faithful of every religion a bad name," Pfastbinder added.

Norah stayed quiet but continued to run alongside Reva as they made the last turn to get to Ansee's apartment. Their footsteps echoed off the cobbles and trees, and the shadows urged Reva forward. A sliver of doubt tried to worm its way into her thoughts. *What if The Minister hadn't taken Ansee here? What if he just killed Ansee instead of trying to learn anything from him?*

A yellow flash of light lit up the road ahead of them, followed by an audible POP, and then a figure stood in the road outside of Ansee's apartment. The person took one step, and then collapsed to the ground. Reva recognized that it was Ansee. He was naked, and he held something that squirmed in his hands: a black-skinned lizard with red, flame-like stripes along its side—his pet fire salamander.

Reva slid to a halt and knelt next to him. "Ansee!" Ember hissed at her, squirmed from Ansee's grasp, crawled up onto his shoulder, and stared at the door to the apartment. Ansee's body was bruised, and strange, circular burns scarred him in several places.

Norah lowered her head and muttered something that Reva couldn't hear. Pfastbinder knelt next to Ansee's head and ran a hand over the burns. This caused Ansee to groan in pain, which told Reva that he was alive. "Can you heal him?" she asked.

Pfastbinder was already rummaging in his satchel. "I will try. These wounds look serious. I'm surprised he's even still breathing."

"Reva."

She looked up at Norah, whose eyes were glowing with a soft green light, and saw her pointing to the door. She turned and saw an older elf standing in the doorway. He wore a blue shirt that appeared singed in a couple of spots, and he held up a staff in one hand while he pointed a finger at them.

"I knew you were weak," The Minister spat, glaring at Norah. "You, and the rest of these thralls, will feel my wrath!"

"Drop the staff," Reva commanded. "I am arresting you for murder." She stood up and drew her sword.

Behind her, she heard Norah draw her own service sword. "It doesn't have to end this way."

Reva wasn't sure if Norah was speaking to the wizard or herself.

"You called me here to rid you of this filth, and now you defend it?" He pointed to Ansee, who was looking less like he was at death's doorstep. "Your lack of faith has led to your demise. I will take pleasure in destroying you all!"

"You're outnumbered," Reva said.

"And your magic is nearly spent," Norah added. "I saw what you did at Reva's home. I can see the auras now. You don't have the magic left to face all of us."

"Jansure will ensure that his justice will prevail," The Minister said. He put his hand into his pocket and withdrew a vial of inky liquid. In a swift motion, he flicked off the cork with his thumb and brought the vial to his lips.

Norah yelled, "No!" and thrust her hand out, saying, "*Sihirli füze!*" Four scarlet bolts of energy lanced through the air, but they harmlessly struck the shield spell that protected The Minister. He laughed, and then threw the vial down, shattering it on the cobblestones.

"Shit!" Norah cursed.

"What?" Reva asked. The Minister's body took on a reddish glow, and Reva thought that she could see the air shimmer around his body.

"He just took Maker's Ink," Norah said. Reva heard a gasp come from Pfastbinder.

"So?"

"It gives him renewed access to all of his magic, like he has just prepared his spells for the day. All of them. Every spell that he knows, he can cast, and they all become more powerful. He's not limited by any of the regular magical laws now."

"That sounds bad," Reva said.

The Minister gave a deep-throated laugh. "No mortal power can control me now! Jansure's will be done!" He pointed at Reva and she didn't hesitate, diving away as a dark red ray of light shot from his hand. It missed her by a hand's breadth, but she could still feel the heat. She rolled, and ended up in a crouch.

Norah planted her staff and began to incant a spell, while Pfastbinder touched Ansee's forehead as he said a prayer. Reva jumped to her feet and ran toward The Minister. He turned to her, a red light circling his eyes, and smiled. He made a gesture with his hand, and said, "*Yavaş*."

A blue light came from his hand and struck Reva. Suddenly, it seemed to her that everybody was moving at twice their normal speed. The Minister turned back to the others and spread his hands wide, a jet of flame reaching out to engulf Norah, Pfastbinder, and Ansee. Norah dove away from the flames, but Pfastbinder and Ansee were caught by the blast. Pfastbinder was badly burned, but it looked to Reva that Ansee was unharmed.

She didn't have time to figure out what had happened, and she tried to swing her sword, but The Minister almost casually blocked her attack with his staff. It was like she was fighting through molasses. All of her movements were a struggle. She tried to bring up her sword to block an attack from The Minister, but her arms wouldn't move quickly enough. The staff struck her on the head, and she stumbled backwards, blood dripping down her face, and a ringing headache threatening to split her skull in two.

The Minister continued his assault, firing another ray at Ansee. This one struck him in the chest, and Reva saw both him and Pfastbinder yell as red light surged from the site where the magic had struck Ansee and enveloped Pfastbinder. The attack caused Ansee's salamander to sit up, like it was basking in the fireplace, and Reva saw some of the fiery energy being absorbed into its black and red skin.

The Minister either didn't see what was happening or didn't care. He was laughing maniacally as he pointed toward Norah, and flames shot from his hand again. She continued to evade the attack, and tried to cast a spell in Reva's direction, but The Minister pointed his staff at Norah, the crystal in it glowing briefly, followed by a flare of light and Norah yelling a curse. It seemed to Reva like Norah had been made irrelevant to the fight. Pfastbinder looked like he had been severely burned, though he had a grim look on his face as he continued to say prayers.

Then Reva saw Ansee hold up a hand, blue-white light crackling between his outstretched fingers. Then the lightning bolt exploded through the air and struck The Minister, the electricity arcing across his body. His shirt was burned and shredded by the lightning, and the blast should have dropped him, but he continued to laugh, even though Reva could see the burns on his skin.

Reva now saw Norah move around The Minister, trying to get behind him. Reva struggled, forcing herself to move as fast as she could, putting every ounce of strength into her limbs. It still felt like running through water, but she managed to land a glancing blow against The Minister's side. Her sword must have been deflected by his shield spell, but it still left a long cut that was now bleeding. Plus, it got his attention.

"I guess demon magic's not so bad after all," Reva said, doing her best to taunt The Minister. "When we're done here, I might have to get some of it myself." Even to her own ears, her words sounded slurred and far away.

"After I've killed you, I will have much more work to do in Tenyl to purge this city of the vileness and corruption that has festered here for too long."

His words seemed to come out in one long sentence, apparently another effect of whatever spell she was under. She didn't care. She lifted her sword, threatening a strike to his head and, despite her sluggish movements, he had to take the threatened attack seriously. He did, pointing his hand at her. Another ray lanced from his hand and struck Reva in the chest. Fiery pain erupted from the wound, her armor seemingly doing nothing to protect her. It was as if a red-hot poker had been shoved into her body, and she cried out, but she struggled forward, continuing to threaten The Minister. He brought up his staff and gripped it in both hands, preparing to bash Reva's head in.

Then, two things happened at once. Out of the corner of her eye, Reva spotted Ansee's pet bound over and open its mouth. Blue flame jetted from it and struck The Minister in the legs. At the same moment, a sword tip erupted from The Minister's chest, as Norah had finally circled around behind him and had thrust her weapon through his back.

The Minister's eyes went wide with shock and pain. He jerked his leg away from the flames, though his pants were now on fire. He opened his mouth, but the only thing that came out was frothy blood. In a moment, he had fallen to his knees, with Norah's sword the only thing keeping him upright. She pulled it out, and he fell forward. Reva suddenly found herself able to move at normal speed again.

The fire continued to burn his pants, but The Minister didn't move. Norah looked at the sword in her hand as if it was something vile. She tossed it to the ground and muttered, "I'm sorry. I'm sorry," over and over again. Reva wasn't sure if she was speaking to The Minister or to her and Ansee. Norah then turned and ran into the darkness of the night.

Chapter 46

Willem leaned against the table, and he stifled a yawn as First Constable Pueraria went through the morning routine of making announcements and giving out assignments. Willem was only half-listening, as he was keeping an eye on Constable Gallwynn and his cousin, Lhoren, who had been holding a whispered conversation ever since they'd arrived for their shift this morning. The pair had been glaring in Willem and Kai's direction as well, and they were clearly plotting something, which only went to show how smart they thought they were. Their intentions were as clear as a well-trodden path, and the fact that they couldn't keep their animosity a secret just made it easy for Willem to shake their branches.

The door to the tower opened at that moment, and a cloaked figure stepped into the room. *Right on time,* Willem thought.

The unexpected visitor caused Pueraria to pause, and everyone in the room (except Willem) turned to see who had entered their sanctum. The door closed, and the figure strode across the room. If the haughty stride wasn't a clue, the distinctive dark green cloak told everyone in the room who the person was, or at least what he represented.

The Sucra Novice ignored the stares, and he stopped in front of the First Constable. He held out a rolled parchment to her and said, "Complements of Inquisitor Amalaki and the Sucra."

Pueraria stared at the parchment for a moment like it was poison ivy, but then reluctantly took it. The Novice saluted, hailed the King, and then gave a crisp turn and walked out of the room.

Pueraria stared at the parchment, apparently reading something that had been written on the outside, and then looked up, her eyes immediately turning to Willem, as if blaming him for the disruption and for whatever problems that this message was sure to bring.

She broke the wax seal, unrolled the parchment, and quickly read the message. Shock and surprise flittered across her face, like clouds crossing the sky. She looked up again, at Willem and Kai, but this time there was a slight smile on her lips.

"We have just received a message from the Sucra," she said. "A unit citation from Inquisitor Amalaki for the assistance of Nul Pfeta Division in the capture of several insurrectionists that were plotting an attack against Prince Orlean." She held up a black ribbon that had been included with the parchment. It bore the Nul Pfeta Division pinecone emblem, as well as the words "Meritorious Service to the Crown" and the date, both sewn in gold thread.

There were several gasps from the assembled constables, and a few heads turned to look around, trying to see who might have brought this boon upon their small corner of the city. A unit citation was usually awarded to military units for exemplary service to the King, and it was rare for one to be given to any part of the Constabulary. It wasn't much more than a pat on the back, although it was an official recognition by the King for a job well done.

"And there are special commendations here as well, for Senior Constable Ghrellstone and Constable Gania, for their direct assistance to the Sucra." She held up two other pages that had been written in precise calligraphy and stamped with a small red and black ribbon. "Your assistance was *critical,*" she nearly choked on the word, "to the operation, and the Sucra recognizes your service and presents you with these letters of thanks from the King."

A couple of the constables clapped. It was mostly Rhi, Naresh, and Pfellcreek from the night shift, but Inspector Touradoor and Seeker Sablewood also joined in. Kai walked up to the First Constable. Willem noticed that Lhoren, Gallwynn, and Senior Constable Slywynd did not clap. He wasn't surprised.

"Keep up the good work," Pueraria said to Kai, as he accepted the letters. She was smiling now, as she should be, since Willem and Kai had just elevated her own prestige within the constabulary. "The rest of you should take note of what they've done, so that you can become better constables."

She turned, the morning meeting over, and headed upstairs to her office. A few of the constables came over to offer their congratulations, and Willem let Kai explain what they had done, which, honestly, hadn't been much. But Inquisitor Amalaki had wanted to thank them for their assistance, so Willem and Reva had suggested the unit citation. Willem hadn't wanted to put himself or Kai up on a tree stump, but apparently Amalaki had decided to do that on his own. Willem looked at the letter, and the large, broad strokes of the King's signature, and he wondered how Amalaki had managed to pull off getting the King to sign the letters so early in the morning.

"You think you're better than us, cousin?"

Willem looked up from the letter to see Lhoren, Slywynd, and Gallwynn standing next to him.

"Lhoren," Willem smirked, "a kobold picking the shit out of his arse is better than you."

Lhoren growled and pulled a fist back, but Slywynd put his hand on Lhoren's shoulder. "Rumor has it that you also arrested Sulwynd along with those filthy halpbloeden. That true?"

Willem ignored the question as he carefully rolled up

the King's letter.

"He'd never work with these mongrels. You messed with the wrong elf," Slywynd poked a finger against Willem's chest. "He'll be out of the Red Keep soon enough, and then we'll get you back for this. This is going to cost you. Sulwynd's one of us, and we protect each other."

There were obedient nods from Lhoren and Gallwynn. Willem gave a thin, mirthless smile. "Then I'll be sure to let Inquisitor Amalaki know. I'm sure that he'll want to question you about these insurrectionists and what you know."

"Wha—" stammered Lhoren.

"We ain't no insurrectionists," said Gallwynn.

"Well, then you won't have anything to fear when the Sucra hauls your asses to the Red Keep, then." Willem smiled. As tough as these three thought they were, the mere thought of being questioned by the Green Cloaks was enough to cause Lhoren and Gallwynn to lose all the color from their faces. Slywynd sneered at Willem, and then spat on the floor, missing Willem's boot. He walked off, and the other two followed him.

"I take it they weren't congratulating us," Kai remarked.

"Can't please everyone."

Kai held up his own letter. "This is nice and all, but I can't help but feel that we don't deserve them."

Willem raised an eyebrow. "How come?"

"We didn't finish the job. One of them got away."

"Cedres Vanda." Willem nodded. It had been a surprise to learn that the only witness to the Fury Blade killings had been involved in a plot to kidnap the Prince. "I don't think we need to worry about him. He'll show up again but, after last night, I doubt he'll do anything. Having the Sucra and Constabulary kick down your door is enough to scare anyone back onto the right branch. I'm sure that's the last that Cedres will bother us."

Chapter 47

Grand Inquisitor Agera set down his cup of hot cacao and picked up a slice of cheese, as he opened the morning dispatches from the Red Keep. He was taking his breakfast in his study this morning, the better to attend to important matters while also providing nourishment. He sat at his large desk with his breakfast—a small plate of cheese, slices of apple, and fresh cranberry bread, along with the ubiquitous pot of cacao sitting over a flame—neatly arranged on his left. That left room for him to go through the dispatches and make notes on the right. A fire burned in the fireplace behind him to keep off the morning chill.

The overnight news from the Red Keep was mostly routine, until he got to the letter from Inquisitor Amalaki. Agera had just picked up his cacao when he had started to read the letter, and he had to quickly set the cup down, lest he spill it. His hand was shaking in furious anger as he read the letter, which explained how Amalaki had stopped a group of insurrectionists who were plotting to kidnap Prince Orlean. He pounded his fist on his desk, and then picked up the letter and crumpled it into a tight ball. He stood up abruptly, and then threw the letter into the fireplace. "Damn!"

There was a knock at the door, and Agera turned away from the fireplace. He took a moment to smooth down his robe and steady his nerves. "Enter," he finally said.

A servant stepped in. "Constable Inspector Lunaria is here to see you, sir."

Agera's first reaction was to tell his servant to send her away. He was not in the mood right now to deal with her. Then he remembered that she was the liaison between the Constabulary and the Sucra, and that Inquisitor Amalaki had taken over that role from Senior Inquisitor Malvaceä. He realized that her presence here might have something to do with Amalaki's letter.

"Send her in," Agera said, sitting down. The servant nodded, and then walked out. In a moment, there was a knock, and Constable Inspector Lunaria was ushered into the study.

"Why, Constable Inspector," Agera said, "this is a surprise. To what do I owe the honor?"

Reva scanned his study, looking at the bookshelves that were filled with books, scrolls, and other knick-knacks, the painting of the grotto behind a waterfall on the wall, and then, finally, his desk. She didn't give any reaction as to whether she approved of his décor or not. "I wanted to let you know that we found the murderer who's been killing sorcerers in the city."

Agera had been expecting something about the insurrectionists, and her words left him speechless for a moment. He blinked a few times. "Well, certainly that is good news. But isn't that something you should be telling your superiors and not me?"

"I will," Reva replied, "but I wanted some advice first."

Again, she had surprised him, and Agera had to work hard to not let it show on his face. He had a reputation for always knowing everything that went on in the Kingdom, and reacting to her request wasn't something that he had the luxury of doing. "Of course, Inspector. I am always willing to offer my advice."

"I wonder if I should keep Lord Constable Inspector Betulla's name out of my report or not?"

"Why would the LCI's name be in your report at all?" Despite his feigned aloofness, Agera was genuinely curious where this was going.

"My investigation has revealed that LCI Betulla hired the assassin."

Another surprise. She was certainly full of them this morning. Agera let himself react to this news by raising his eyebrows slightly. "Did she? And you have evidence of this?"

"I don't work for you," Reva sneered. "Of course I have evidence."

Agera ignored the professional jab, but he wondered if Reva was lying to him. She had a reputation of expecting honesty from those around her, but he'd known Reva to bend, and even break, a few rules to get what she wanted. That didn't necessarily mean that she would lie, and he had no reason to suspect that she would lie to him now.

"It seems to me, Inspector, that you are duty bound to include that information in your report, then." He laced his fingers together and rested them on his stomach. "Certainly, this will create a huge scandal, but the constabulary has survived worse."

"Even if that scandal will touch you?" There was a slight twitch of her lips, the faintest of smiles, as she said this.

Agera gave a genuine laugh. "And how would that happen? Nyssa Betulla is her own person. I have no control over what she does."

Reva stared at him, clearly not believing a word that he had just said. He didn't care. She was well aware of his cabal, but he also knew that she had no proof that Betulla was part of the cabal, or that it even existed. Nothing that would be accepted by the wider community. Nothing that would jeopardize the group.

Reva nodded to the stack of dispatches on his desk. "I'm sure you've probably already heard, but Inquisitor Amalaki and I arrested a group of insurrectionists last night."

"And good riddance," Agera added.

"Did Amalaki tell you that one of the conspirators was a constable? Constable Sulwynd."

Agera had to think. He had been so angry at Sulwynd's

incompetence at getting caught, at blowing the mission, that he didn't recall if Amalaki had mentioned him in the letter or not. He probably had. Amalaki was a good Inquisitor, unfortunately.

Reva took his silence to mean that Sulwynd hadn't been mentioned in the letter. "Our evidence is that Constable Sulwynd was in charge of organizing the conspirators, but he wasn't the one giving the orders. I'm sure Amalaki will get the details when he interrogates Sulwynd."

"I still don't see how this involves me," Agera sighed, feigning disinterest.

"Because we already know that you met with Constable Sulwynd in the past few days. And Sulwynd was transferred out of Nul Pfeta in the past week, probably as added cover to allow him to work with the conspirators. What did you meet with Sulwynd about? Did you order Betulla to transfer him?"

Agera leaned forward and pointed at Reva. "Be careful, Inspector. I do not like to be questioned over something that has all the appearance of leaves blowing in the wind."

"It is certainly a tangle of vines," Reva admitted. "And maybe the Mayor and the King will want to untangle it."

"I certainly doubt that. They have more important things to deal with than petty accusations."

"Maybe. But can you take that risk?"

"What are you getting at, Inspector?"

"I am willing to make sure that Betulla's—and your—names are kept out of the reports. Mine *and* Amalaki's."

"And what do you expect in return for this... omission?"

Reva crossed her arms and locked eyes with him. "I want every copy of my family tree from under Pfeta fey Orung given to me."

The fog lifted, and Agera finally knew what Reva was after. "I see. In exchange for you being quiet about some supposed conspiracy between myself and Betulla, you want to keep your family's tainted history secret."

Reva's jaw tightened slightly. "Something like that."

Agera leaned back in his chair. "What makes you think

there are any copies? Or that I have them?"

"Because that would really lower my respect for you. It's hard to apply leverage against somebody if you have nothing to use against them."

"And is that all that you want?"

Reva nodded.

Agera sat there and stared at Reva. She was playing this like some drama at Pfenestra's Playhouse, something that was sure to ooze with intrigue. She was right, he did have a copy of her family tree, and he had been holding on to it in case he ever needed to apply leverage against her. Prior to her father's death, he'd had his own researchers go through the lineage that he had presented to gain access to the cabal. He knew that it had been faked. It was a good fake, but the lineage couldn't be independently verified. It had been the reason that he'd had Malvaceä kill Reva's father. He didn't need a mole in his group. But even though he knew it was a fake, just the mere existence of the lineage would be damning evidence against Reva should it get out. It would be nearly impossible to prove that it was a fake, and certainly not before she suffered from the repercussions of being accused of being a dark elf halpbloed.

He watched Reva slowly begin to tap one foot and unconsciously pull a strand of her hair and wrap it around one finger. She was looking for freedom from his control. Something that Agera knew to be as elusive as the wind. Even without the lineage, he had other ways to manipulate, to control. Giving her the family tree would be a minor inconvenience, and he had other pieces in play. This might also work in his favor, as he was sure that Reva would relax after she got the family tree, secure in thinking that she had outwitted him. That would make her overconfident and open to his moves in the future.

"Very well," he agreed. He picked up a bell from the desk and rang it. In a moment, the door opened. "Go with Juran and wait for me by the front door. I will bring you what you want."

Reva hesitated for a moment, but then left with his servant. When they were gone, Agera stood up and went over to the grotto painting. He pulled it aside, on hidden hinges, and opened the hidden panel behind it. He pulled out the rolled parchment, and then closed the panel and replaced the painting.

He stepped over to the desk and picked up his cup of cacao. It had grown cold, but he slowly drank it, stalling for time. Appearances were important, and he didn't want Reva to suspect where he had hidden her family tree.

After taking a bite of an apple slice, he finally left his study and slowly made his way to the entrance to his villa. Reva was waiting for him, and he saw that she was now biting the strand of hair.

"Here you are, Inspector." He handed her the parchment.

Reva took it, untied the ribbon, and unrolled the document enough to see her family name inscribed at the top. She gave a single nod, and then retied the ribbon.

"You may have your leverage," Agera said, "but secrets can never remain hidden forever."

Reva paused, and then said, "Seems like advice that you should take to heart, as well." She saluted him with the parchment and turned for the door.

Agera watched her leave. He then turned to his servant, standing patiently along the wall. "Get my litter ready. I have business at New Port."

Chapter 48

Grand Inquisitor Agera strode up the stairs of New Port, his steps echoing off the walls. His boots were polished to a high gleam, and the crease in his jodhpurs could have cut wood. His dark green cloak billowed behind him as he headed toward Betulla's office. Her door was shut, and her assistant stood up, bravely placing his body in Agera's path.

"T-The Lord Constable is in a meeting currently, Grand Inquisitor. If you will be gracious enough to—"

Agera turned his gaze on the young elf, who withered before him like a dying rose in the summer heat. The elf wisely stepped aside, and Agera opened the door.

Betulla was sitting at the table by the windows with two other constables. "I said I did not want to be disturbed!" she exclaimed. "Who in the hells—"

Her voice cut off as she saw Agera. He leaned against her desk and folded his arms. He looked pointedly at the door. The two constables were looking back and forth between Betulla and Agera.

"We'll pick this up later," she said. The two constables nodded, picked up their parchments, and then scurried out of the office, shutting the door behind them.

Betulla turned to him. "What in the hells are you doing barging into *my* office?" She started to stand up, but Agera walked over to the table, causing her to sit back down. *He was going to control this conversation, not her.* He leaned on the table, his face looming over her.

"You had Constable Sulwynd transferred out of Nul Pfeta."

"Wh—" she stammered, trying to regain her composure. Betulla sat up in her chair. "Yes, I transferred him. He was a loyal constable under me when I was First Constable. Plus, he's one of *us*. He deserves better than that hell hole."

"And you never once considered that he was there for a reason. *My* reason?"

"What? How would I know what your reasons are? Besides, Sulwynd is one of *my* constables. The last time I checked, I am the LCI, not you." She leaned back in her chair and gave a slow nod. "Something has happened. Are you going to keep me in the undergrowth, or will you share your secret with me this time?"

Agera stood up. "Sulwynd was arrested with a group of halpblood last night by the Sucra for fomenting an insurrection against the King."

"Arrested? You let one of my constables get arrested? One of *us*?"

"Had he stayed in Nul Pfeta, that wouldn't have happened. His arrest is *your* fault, Betulla. *You* decided to make a change without consulting me. And in the process, you *ruined* my plans."

He saw Betulla's face and ears flush crimson. "Maybe if you didn't keep everything a damn secret." She leaned forward, her green eyes piercing into his like a beetle digging into a tree, trying to establish her authority. "We have a shared goal."

"A goal that can only be achieved when we work *together*," Agera said. "But your ill-conceived actions have caused incalculable delay and problems. Problems that I must now fix. You don't need to know what is going on, only that you follow orders."

"Follow orders?" she spat out the words. "I am the

Lord Constable Inspector! I do not take orders from you, on *anything*. And, clearly, your schemes are not so great, if the transfer of a single constable could mess it up."

"What messed it up was your blundering about and playing at being in charge. You are not in charge of anything. You forget your place. You forget that *I* am in charge."

Betulla pursed her lips. "Then maybe it's time for a change in leadership."

Agera wanted to laugh at the idea, but then had a thought. He bowed his head slightly. "Maybe you're right." He saw her eyes widen at the sudden agreement. "I will allow you to petition the Emissary when you explain to her how this operation failed. You can even explain how you will correct the further delays in our plans because of this failure."

"But... the Emissary... I—I wasn't involved. I am not to blame for Sulwynd's failed mission! How can I be when I don't even know what it was?"

"The Emissary will expect answers. And you know how she reacts to failure." Agera saw Betulla's face pale.

Betulla's spluttering slowed as she considered his words. The Emissary had a reputation, spread by Agera, for reacting forcefully to bad news. Certainly, the Emissary did not enjoy hearing about failure and setbacks, no more than any other elf—Underforest or Pfeta—did, but Agera had a way of spinning the truth, both to the Emissary and to his fellow conspirators. He had managed to do that when the Fury Blade had been stolen, allowing most of the blame and punishment to fall on Malvaceä. It was what he deserved for letting the Fury Blade be taken. Agera was sure that he would be able to twist the branches of what happened toward his own clearing this time, as well. It would require another sacrifice, but that was a small price to pay for the greater good.

"Are you willing to take on the mantle of leadership?" he asked Betulla. He didn't know what sort of fantasy of violence played out in her head. He had never disclosed to any of their group what his own punishment had been for the loss of the Fury Blade, but he'd implied the worst. Fear was always a good motivator, especially among the weak. And Betulla was certainly one of those. She confirmed it by shaking her head.

"Then *I* will explain what happened to the Emissary. It is a shame that Sulwynd went against the plan and got himself arrested. He wanted more, and he thought that he could interfere."

Betulla seemed to absorb the lies at the realization that Agera was removing her part in what happened. "He's one of us, he was following your orders. Will you not protect him?"

"Like I'm protecting you right now? No. Sulwynd failed, and the Emissary will expect a fitting punishment. She will want to dispense her own punishment to our group because of this, but I will be able to mitigate what she does if I give her Sulwynd. He will rot in the Red Keep for a time, and then be executed as a traitor. An unfortunate martyr for our cause."

The fire had gone out of Betulla, and she sat back in her chair, her shoulders slumped.

"In the future, you will not take any actions, or make any decisions, that might impact my plans, without my approval."

Betulla nodded, and Agera turned and walked out of her office.

Behind him, he didn't see the cruel smile that formed on Betulla's lips.

Chapter 49

Reva walked across the Acer Division Stable and tossed her cloak onto the back of her chair. She turned to Ansee, who was busy writing on a roll of parchment. "I thought I told you to take the day off."

"I'm fine," Ansee replied, not looking up.

Reva stepped up and put a hand on his shoulder. That made him stop, and he looked first at her hand, and then up at her. "I'm fine," he insisted. "Pfastbinder was kind enough to heal me without too much of a donation to his church."

She smiled. "Well, if you want to take time off after everything..." she let the words trail off.

"Like you've done?"

That comment struck too close, and an ember of anger tried to flare up.

Ansee must have realized that he'd messed up, because he said, "How's your mother? And Gabii?"

"They're fine. No serious injuries that our personal cleric couldn't take care of. For a price, of course."

"Of course."

"But the shop is a mess. It will take some time to repair. And money."

"I can help."

Reva found herself shaking her head. "You don't need to help."

"But I'm responsible. I knew The Minister was targeting me. I should have anticipated that he'd follow me. By going to your home, I put your mother at risk."

"That wasn't your fault. You didn't put my mother at risk, that was someone else."

"Who?"

Before Reva could answer, the door to Aescel's office opened, and the First Constable called out, "I need everyone's attention."

Reva turned to see Aescel standing at the front of the Stable. Next to him stood Norah. Her head was down, her shoulders slumped. Reva noticed that she wasn't wearing her bracers.

"Norah has resigned and turned in her bracers," Aescel said, his voice flat. Stunned silence filled the Stable, and the only sound was the quiet sobs coming from Norah. "I'm sure we all wish Norah the best—"

At this, Norah's tears couldn't be held back anymore, and she hurried out of the Stable and down the stairs. Inspector Pflamtael called after her, and then he hurried from the room as well.

Every constable in the room tried to talk at once, but Aescel quieted everyone down. "Seekers Carya and Hedera will be splitting up her assignments until we can find a replacement. That is all." He walked over to Reva's table as everyone started talking.

"I heard what happened to your mother," he said. "I hope she wasn't hurt too bad in all of this."

"She'll be fine," Reva replied.

"I will want a detailed explanation of what happened," Aescel commanded. "I know some of what happened from Norah, but I will need your side of things before I present all this hawkshit to the LCI."

"You'll have them today," Reva nodded.

Aescel ran a hand across his face. He looked older, and more tired, than Reva had ever seen him. "Tomorrow morning, late, is fine. Make sure your mother is safe. Go home early today, if you can." He looked up to Ansee. "You too, Seeker. It's going to be a shit storm until we can replace Norah, and I will need you rested."

Ansee nodded, and Aescel returned to his office. Reva sat down and pulled out a clean parchment to start her own report on what had happened last night. Before she could dip her quill into the inkwell, a figure in a dark green cloak walked up the stairs and headed toward her.

"When do you want *your* report?" she asked Inquisitor Amalaki.

"I don't need one from you, unless you want to write one."

"Oh, I'll write one. I don't trust you to make sure that you'll get all the facts right."

Amalaki shrugged. "I just wanted to tell you that the Grand Inquisitor has ordered that Constable Sulwynd be tried for treason."

Reva's eyebrows went up at the news, while Ansee said, "Wait, Constable Sulwynd is being tried for treason?"

"I'll tell you about it later," Reva said. She turned to look at Amalaki. "Then we'll need to compare our notes for the report. I told the Grand Inquisitor that certain names would be kept out of it." She could see Ansee's mouth open in surprise out of the corner of her eye.

"You met with Grand Inquisitor Agera?" Amalaki asked. He leaned forward and whispered, "Why? After what you told me."

"And I told you not to head down that path. Only death lies in that direction." She ignored the snort that came from Ansee.

"Well, I hope it was worth it."

"It was," Reva confirmed. "Protecting my family is always worth it."

Amalaki shook his head. "You might be a good constable—"

"The best," Ansee corrected, before Reva had a chance to do so herself.

"But you suck at intrigue."

"Good," Reva smiled. "I told you before that I have no desire to work for the Sucra."

"Fine, then I guess you can meet me at the Red Keep this afternoon so we can compare notes. I'd hate to put in something that wasn't true." He didn't bother to keep the bitterness from his words as he turned and left the Stable.

"Do I need to know what's going on?" Ansee asked.

"No, you don't." Reva sat and tapped her quill on the table. She had done what she did to protect her family. And she'd do it again. After a minute, she tossed her quill down and stood up. "Come on," she told Ansee. "Aescel isn't this soft all that often. Let's go get something to eat."

Ansee looked at the parchment that was filled with his neat, fine script, and then he set his quill down and stood up.

"Are you going to tell me what happened with Sulwynd?"

"Sure. I think it's time you knew what was going on."

Ansee gave her a quizzical look. "And maybe we can discuss your Wake use, too?"

"Don't press your luck."

Epilogue

Cedres Vanda walked up the stairs behind the old woman. Her pace was slow, and he had to force himself to not be impatient. Gone were his shabby and filthy halpbloed clothes. In their place, he wore simple breeches, pale green in color, and a tunic of faded yellow. The clothes were not new, but new enough, and much better than the rags that he'd had before.

As they walked up the stairs, his hand went to the large pouch filled with coins. After fleeing his apartment on the night of the raid two days ago, he'd managed to slip through the darkened streets of Nul Pfeta until he had come to the edge of Salicae Wood. The thick forest served as a natural barrier for Nul Pfeta, and its thick brambles and thorns prevented most halpbloed from venturing in, even to collect firewood or hunt for mushrooms, nuts, or mosses to supplement their food. But the woods were not impenetrable, as smugglers often used them to bring in contraband. Cedres used them that night to flee Nul Pfeta. He'd moved as fast as he could, trying to keep the clink of coins from calling out to the thieves and cutthroats. At one point, he'd slipped and fallen into Cicata Creek, and he had almost lost the pouch. He'd managed to cross the creek and hide in the woods, trying to ward off the night chill with fallen leaves.

The next morning, he had finally opened the pouch to

look at the prize that he'd stolen during the wild melee. In the morning light, he could see the reflection of silver and gold coins; Skips and Hawks flowed through his fingers. He didn't take the time to count his loot, as he was still too close to Nul Pfeta, and he didn't want to attract attention to any smugglers who'd be happy to relieve him of his new wealth.

He had slipped into the city proper, and he headed to the docks, where he could blend in with the workers and travelers. He had purchased the clothes from a fat lombard who had made him feel like Cedres was stealing from him as Cedres had bartered for them. He stayed the next night at an inn in Port Grove, huddled on the bed, as he expected the door to burst open any moment with Green Cloaks. Every noise in the inn had set him on edge, and he had dared not sleep. So, he had watched the door for any intruder, and had counted his wealth. 150 Skips and 24 Hawks sat on the bed in small piles. It was more money than he had seen since his days as a blacksmith, before his life had been turned upside down. He was far from rich, but this was enough money for him to disappear, to become a new elf... yes, a new *elf*. He was an *elf*. And he was going to make sure that people would remember that.

So, he had found a small apartment that was available in North Gate Grove. The elderly elf reached the top landing. "What was your name again?" she asked.

"Aeolus Sorbaria," Cedres lied.

"Well, Mr. Sorbaria, I want to apologize for the mess." She paused by a door and withdrew a key from the pocket of her dress. She opened the door. "I really haven't been in the mood to clean up this place since..."

Her voice trailed off and Cedres stepped into the apartment. It was musty and smelled heavily of dirt and rotting vegetation. He saw an oil lamp on a table, and he managed to get it lit after a few tries with the flint and steel that sat next to it. The lamp gave off a warm yellow glow, and he could see that the apartment was filled with dead plants sitting in colorful pots. They sat on nearly every surface and the windowsills where the curtains had been drawn. He went over and opened the curtains, letting in the sunlight. It did not improve the scene. A thick layer of dust covered the sparse furniture in the room.

"The apartment has been empty for a month, ever since the previous tenant... left."

"Why did she leave?" Cedres asked, trying to be polite.

"She was murdered."

A chill suddenly ran up his spine, and Cedres looked about the room. Had the constables been here? Would they be back?

"Oh, she wasn't killed here," the landlady said, misunderstanding Cedres' nervousness. "She was murdered at her shop. She was a florist." There was a sadness in her voice. "Her parents came and got her personal things, but they didn't want any of this other stuff. It's a shame. All these plants died. I really should have removed them, but I didn't have the heart. It felt wrong for some reason."

Cedres relaxed, figuring that if the constables had been here already, it was unlikely that they would be back. "I don't mind. Maybe I can get something to grow, instead."

"You want the place?" the landlady asked.

"I do."

"I will have to charge you a bit more, since the place is furnished now."

Cedres felt like that was akin to robbery, as the furniture appeared to be cheaply constructed, but he liked the location. He pulled out his coin pouch. "How much?"

"It's five and twenty a month. I need your first month now. Payment on the first of every month."

Cedres did the sum in his head, five Skips and twenty Pfen a month wasn't unreasonable. He dug in his pouch and pulled out a single gold coin. "How about I pay for two months now?" He handed the Hawk to her. To her credit, she inspected the coin to make sure that it was real. "You can keep the difference."

"Fair enough." She put the coin into her pocket and handed over the key. "Pleasure to have you here, Mr. Sorbaria."

Cedres walked her to the door and thanked her. He then shut the door and gave a sigh of relief, as he put the key in the lock and turned it with a satisfied CLICK. Cedres then turned and walked to the window, opening it to begin airing out the apartment. He leaned against the sill and looked out onto the city. From here, he had a nearly unobstructed view of Ilvalé Arena and, in the distance, the red walls of Castle Tenz.

The future was unwritten but, as he stared at the castle, he knew that the King would give him back what belonged to him. He'd give Cedres his life back. His honor back. When Cedres was done, the King would declare to the entire Kingdom that Cedres was a full elf.

A show of force. That is the only thing that the King will understand. Constable Sulwynd's words echoed in Cedres' mind as he watched the castle.

"A show of force it is, then."

Author's Notes

As with any creative undertaking Coy and Geoff could not have completed Reva's latest adventure without help from many other people. First of all, a huge thank you to everybody who has read *Wrath of the Fury Blade* and *Joy of the Widow's Tears* and liked them enough to leave a review or let us know at cons.

Second, a huge thank you to Mike Wagner, who did another fantastic job on the cover for this book. We've worked with Mike before, not only on the previous *Constable Inspector Lunaria Adventure* books, but also on our *Ados: Land of Strife* D&D campaign books and we are always blown away by Mike's skill.

A special shout out to Jennifer and Kristin Vinck, and Jessica Smith, the writing trio that are behind A.E. Lowan and their wonderful Book of Binding series for graciously allowing us to plant their first book, Faerie Rising and a couple of morsels of the plot, as an Easter egg in our humble story.

We plan on continuing to tell Reva's stories as long as you continue to read them. If you enjoyed this tale, we would appreciate it if you would let others know about it as well. Leave us a review on your favorite place on the web where people review books (Amazon, Goodreads, Bookbub, etc.) Getting reviews really helps and is a way that you can spread the word about our books.

We also encourage you to follow us on social media. We maintain an author page on Facebook (**facebook.com/ HabigerKisseeAuthors**) and Geoff is active on Twitter (**twitter.com/TangentGeoff**). Drop by and leave us a comment.

About the Authors

The writing duo of Geoff Habiger and Coy Kissee have been life-long friends since high school in Manhattan, Kansas. (Affectionately known as the Little Apple, which was a much better place to grow up than the Big Apple, in our humble opinion.) We love reading, baseball, cats, role-playing games, comics, and board games (not necessarily in that order and sometimes the cats can be very trying). We've spent many hours together over the years (and it's been many years) basically geeking out and talking about our favorite books, authors, and movies, often discussing what we would do differently to fix a story or make a better script. We eventually stopped discussing other people's work and started developing our own material, first with RPGs and card games, and now we do the same thing with novels.

Coy lives with his wife and one cat in Lenexa, Kansas. Geoff lives with his wife, son, and two cats in Tijeras, New Mexico.

You can stay up on the latest about our writing at our website **www.habigerkissee.com** where we encourage you to check out our blog and to sign up for our newsletter. Subscribers will get behind the scenes details about our mysterious writing process, advanced information about new books and projects, and other cool stuff.